NEW YORK TIMES BESTSELLING AUTHOR

TED DEKKER
WITH **TOSCA LEE**

FORBIDDEN

HODDER &
STOUGHTON

First published in Great Britain in 2011 by Hodder & Stoughton
An Hachette UK company

Copyright © Ted Dekker 2011

A CIP catalogue record for this title is available from the British Library

Trade paperback ISBN 978 1 444 72490 5
ebook ISBN 978 1 444 72493 6

Typeset in Walbaum MT

Printed and bound by Clays Ltd, St Ives plc

Hodder & Stoughton policy is to use papers that are natural, renewable and recyclable products and made from wood grown in sustainable forests. The logging and manufacturing processes are expected to conform to the environmental regulations of the country of origin.

Hodder & Stoughton Ltd
338 Euston Road
London NW1 3BH

www.hodder.co.uk

THE BEGINNING

IN THE YEAR 2005, geneticists discovered the human gene that controlled both innate and learned forms of fear. It was called Strathmin, or Oncoprotein 18. Within fifteen years, genetic influencers for all primary emotions were similarly identified.

Nearly a decade later, in the wake of catastrophic war that destroyed much of civilization, humanity vowed to forsake all that had conspired to destroy it. Out of the ashes rose a new world in which both the advanced technologies and the passionate emotions that led to its ruin were eliminated. A world without hatred, without malice, without sorrow, without anger.

The only emotion genetically allowed to survive was fear. For 480 years, perfect peace has reigned.

Until now...

ROM

CHAPTER ONE

THERE WAS NEVER A BODY.

Not even at a funeral. Mourners sat angled toward one another in the stiff pews to avoid looking directly at the empty casket and the destiny hanging over them all. They all knew that only one of two things happened when the body died, one outcome more likely than the other.

The terrible outcome, of course.

Rom, the twenty-four-year-old son of Elias Sebastian, sat in a back pew by himself. He was a plain man by any measure. Not unattractive, but neither was he truly beautiful by the standards of the Order, which reserved true beauty for royalty.

He'd sung earlier in homage to the dead man's life. It was a humble yet noble job, singing for the dead. Humble because any artist's life was humble—only by the grace of Sirin, who'd written about the educational merits of the arts, did artisans find work at all in a world unmoved by creative gifts. Noble because being near the dead was fearful business for most. But Rom didn't mind. He needed the work, and the dead needed their service.

Finished with his job here, he folded the funeral program lengthwise as he waited for a good moment to slip away. There, on the upper flap, was the name of the deceased: Lucas Tavor. Rom folded it again. There was Tavor's age: sixty-eight. Not so old in this advanced world where one might live to 110 or 120.

He glanced at the man's empty coffin lying atop its metal carriage between the front pillars of the great basilica. It was one of the finer basilicas in the city, in Rom's opinion—not because of its size, as it was far from the largest, but because of the intricate stained glass above its altar.

All basilicas boasted their treasures, but this depiction of Sirin, the martyred father of the Order, was more exquisite than the rest. The numbered, compass-like marks of his halo spread like a fractured sunburst above his head, even on a dull day. It was the universal picture of peace, an inspiring image of the man who had preached freedom from the excesses of modern life and from the snares of emotion.

Sirin's right hand cradled a dove. His left rested on the shoulder of a second man: Megas, holding the bound Book of Orders, canonized under his rule. Every basilica housed the same image, but none as intricate as this.

The priest stood behind the altar, the ordinal rays of Sirin's halo reflecting faintly upon his shoulders. Two clerics flanked him on the dais as he smoothed the pages of the Book of Orders upon its stand.

"Born once, into life, we are blessed."

"We are blessed," echoed the assembly, perhaps fifty in all. Their murmurs rose like specters to the arched vault overhead.

"Let us please the Maker through a life of diligent Order."

"Let us please the Maker." The mouths of the clerics moved with the congregation. Beyond them on the dais, the silver censers that exhaled incense through normal assembly hung empty upon their chains.

"We know the Maker exists by his Order. If we please, let us be born into the afterlife, not into fear, but Bliss everlasting."

Bliss. The eternal absence of fear—or so it was said. Though Rom was less given to fear than most, it took some abstract thinking to imagine being forever untouched by at least some tinge of it.

It was said other emotions existed before the human race evolved, but they, too, were difficult to imagine. These sentiments of a baser age, like excised tumors, never reappeared; humanity finally resisted the black plague that had almost destroyed it.

Rom wasn't sure he even knew the words to describe them all. And those he did know were meaningless to him. That archaic word *passion*, for example. Try as he might to grasp this thing, he could only conjure up thoughts of varying degrees of fear. Or another: *sorrow*. What was sorrow? It was like trying to imagine what his life would be like if he'd never been born.

No matter. Humanity's one surviving emotion granted Order in this life and the possibility of Bliss beyond. Trying to imagine such a future, though, was enough to make his head hurt.

In front of Rom, a curly-haired boy turned around in the pew. Sticking his fingers in his mouth, he stared bug-eyed as Rom continued to fold the paper program. Rom held up the small project so the boy could see the thing taking shape between his fingers.

A eulogist approached the podium, printed page in hand. The heads of those assembled were now fixed on that empty coffin, no longer able to look away.

"Lucas Tavor was sixty eight years old," the man read.

"He fell," a young woman two pews up whispered. The basilica's unrestrained acoustics carried her words to Rom. "Broke his hip. One of his children found him a day after it happened."

It was easy enough to surmise the rest of the story. Society had long embraced the custom of transferring the infirm, the severely injured, and the feeble to an asylum under the auspices of the Authority of Passing. There, humans closer to death than to life might live out the minority of their days, sparing their peers the caustic reminder of death's inevitable pall. Thus, there was never a body at a funeral, because the one for whom the funeral was held often had not yet died.

Not technically, at least.

Rom stood and adjusted the strap of his shoulder bag. Slipping from the pew, he handed the finished paper crane to the boy, who accepted it with wet fingers.

Outside, on the steps of the basilica, the city spread out before him, concrete-gray beneath the ominous clouds of late afternoon. On each of the city's seven hills, the spires and turrets of centuries-old buildings stabbed at the heavens like so many lances piercing a boil.

This was Byzantium, the greatest city on earth, population five hundred thousand, home to three thousand of the world's twenty-five thousand royals, who had come from every continent to serve in her government and state-run businesses. It was the center of the earth, to which all eyes turned in matters politic and religious, social and economic. It was the seat of power to which all earthly dominions had deferred since the end of the Age of Chaos five centuries before, when the world had bowed to the great powers of the Americas and Russia.

Chaos. It had nearly killed them all. But humanity learned from her mistakes, and Null Year had signaled a new beginning for a new world cleansed of destructive passions. Peace had ruled in the 480 years since, and Byzantium was the heart of it all.

The city was more crowded than normal as it prepared to host the inauguration of the world Sovereign—Feyn Cerelia, daughter of the current Sovereign, Vorrin, of the royal Cerelia family. Never before had a future Sovereign been the direct descendant of a ruling Sovereign, and yet the random hand of fate was about to change history. And so Feyn Cerelia's inauguration was considered a particularly auspicious event, one that would swell Byzantium's population to nearly one million for days.

Her image had already graced the banners on streetlamps and city buildings for months. For weeks, train cars had brought construction equipment, barricades, and food from all parts of the world to supply Byzantium for the occasion. The black cars of the Brahmin royals and those in service to them had become a common sight on streets unaccustomed to motorized congestion. There had been no mass production of automobiles since the Age of Chaos, and no roadways beyond the city were intact enough to justify the vehicles' exorbitant cost. Businesses carried out their trade by rail, subway, rickshaw, or private courier. Rom himself had never driven a car.

Rom glanced up the street to the west. In five days, all traffic would be blocked within a one-mile radius of the Grand Basilica near the Citadel. Construction crews had already spent a week erecting the high stands on either side of the Processional Way, which the new Sovereign would travel atop one of the royal stallions. All other attending royals and citizens alike would approach the inauguration in sedate order, on foot.

Beyond the city to the east, the hinterland stretched all the way to the sea. The territory had been reshaped by the fallout of the wars, testament to Chaos. What was once a land of agriculture was now arid and unsuitable for producing the food Byzantium's population lived upon. Erosion had etched new canyons on the barren face of a countryside previously lush and fertile. And so the city relied on the provisions of Greater Europa to the north and her more fertile sisters—Sumeria, to the east; Russe to the northeast; Abyssinia, to the south. These ancient territories, once better known as Europe, the Middle East, Russia, and Africa, provided willingly for Byzantium, the city once called Rome. Their imports were the tithe of Order, a small price to pay to live in peace.

To the south of Byzantium lay the industrial towns that nearly reached the coast, connected only by rail, her roads as broken as the landscape itself.

Only in the last century had the land shown signs of true recovery. Trees grew along scraggly creek beds, and in some places grasses had reclaimed the soil. Today the countryside was sparsely dotted by the estates and stables of royals wishing to escape the confines of the city for a scrubby patch of green. It offered only meager peace, but anything that reduced fear was a welcome respite.

Rom had heard the city was a place of light at one time, of sun by day and city lamps by night, like sparkling gems strewn against a backdrop of velvet. Televisions and computers connected everyone. Planes crisscrossed the sky.

Citizens owned weapons.

Now personal electricity was rationed. Televisions existed in public spaces and for state use only. Many had phones but computers were restricted to state use. Planes, reserved for royal business, were a rare sight in Byzantium's overcast sky. And the only firearms in the world existed in museums.

A streetlight sputtered overhead, and Rom turned his head to the sky. No, not a streetlight, but lightning, striking out toward the Tibron River. Rom snugged his bag close and hurried down the sweeping steps to the street.

By the time he reached the underground, it had begun to rain. He hurried down the concrete stairs into the stale subterranean warmth and was greeted with the electric light of the station, the shuffle of foot traffic, the squealing brakes of an oncoming train.

His route home included a five-minute ride to the central terminus, and then a twenty-minute journey southeast. It was enough time to take out his notebook, lay pen to new lyrics for the funeral he was to sing at next week. But even after he had returned the pen to his pocket, they seemed inadequate, too similar to the song he had sung today.

That was to be expected. If there was one thing that had not evolved since Null Year, it was art. Art and culture. As an artisan, Rom understood that the creativity of both had been squelched by the loss of their emotional muses. Even the subtleties of language had remained relatively unchanged. A small price to pay for Order. But a price, nonetheless.

He exited the underground six blocks from home, making his way past the distracted, worried expressions of those descending into the station. A steady drizzle issued from the lighter gray sky above; to the north, the hard edges of the skyline he had just left were obscured by the veil of a proper downpour.

Foot traffic was thin. Those who were out darted to their destinations beneath umbrellas and newspapers. In the street, the lone dark car of a royal sped by, sending an arc of water toward the curb.

Rom ducked his head, rain already running off the wet spikes of his hair into his eyes, and pulled his jacket more tightly around him. He kept to storefront eaves before turning into a narrow alleyway between the broad brick backs of an old theater and an out-of-use hostel.

Today he had done his work diligently. He had earned his modest living. He had been in assembly three times already this week, but he would go tomorrow, a fourth time, for Avra.

Avra, his friend since childhood, who avoided basilica. Avra, with her quiet gaze and fearful heart. His attendance had been their pact for several years now, and why not? It cost him nothing to go for her, and though it might not be condoned by the priests, it might make a difference to the Maker. It was her only chance, anyway.

He was thinking of her troubled brown eyes when a voice sounded behind him.

"Son of Elias!"

The cry echoed against the lichen-spackled brick, over the patter of the rain. Rom turned and stared through the drizzle. A lean figure lurched through the alley's narrow file, his long, ragged coat flapping wetly behind him. His gaze was locked on Rom.

Son of Elias. Rom hadn't been called that in years. He squinted against the rain. "Do I know you?"

The old man was now so close that Rom could see his grizzled brows and sunken cheeks, the gray hair plastered to his head. Could hear his wheezing breath. The man closed the distance between them with surprising speed and seized Rom by the shoulders. The thin lids of his eyes were peeled wide.

"It's you!" he rasped between panting breaths. Spittle edged the corners of his mouth.

Rom's first thought was that the man had managed to escape the Authority of Passing and was fleeing the escorts of the asylum. He was certainly old enough. And obviously crazed.

But the man knew his father's name. A sliver of fear worked its way beneath Rom's skin. What was with this old fellow?

"It's you," the old man said again. "I never thought to lay eyes on Elias again, but by the Maker, you have the look of him!"

Two men rounded the corner at the end of the alley and sprinted toward them. In the dull splatter of the rain, it almost appeared that they wore the silver and black of the Citadel Guard. Odd. The jurisdiction of the guard was the Citadel itself—on the other side of the city. Perhaps because of the inauguration...

The man tore his gaze away to look over his shoulder. At the sight of the two men, he tightened his grip on Rom's shoulders and spoke in a rush.

"They've found me. And now they'll come after you, too. Listen to me now, boy. Listen well! Your father said you could be trusted."

Rom blinked in the rain. "My father? My father's dead. He died of fever."

"Not from fever! Your father was murdered, boy!"

"What? That can't be true."

The man let go of him and fumbled with his coat, tearing at an inner pocket that didn't seem to match the rest of the garment. It bulged with a square shape the size of two fists put together. He tore it free.

"He was killed. As all the other keepers were killed. For this." He shoved the parcel at Rom. "Take it! There's no one else now. Take it, or your father died for nothing. Learn its secrets. Find the man called the Book. The Book, do you hear me? He's at the Citadel—find him. Show him you have this!"

Displays of fear were not uncommon, but the old man was clearly demented with it. In reaction, the sliver of Rom's own fear wormed its way to Rom's heart.

A third man had appeared at the entrance to the alley. One of the first two shouted back for him to go around. And now Rom could see that they did indeed wear the colors of the elite Citadel Guard. All for an old man?

Rom felt his fingers close around the parcel, damp and still warm from the man's body.

"Swear to me!"

"What—"

"Swear!"

"I swear. I…"

The guardsmen were no more than twenty paces away, running far harder than their aged quarry warranted.

The old man's voice rose to an unexpected roar. "Protect it! It's power and life—life as it was—and grave danger. Run!" The guardsmen were only a dozen steps away. "*Run!*"

The sound of that scream startled Rom so much that he took five or six long strides before he faltered. What was he doing? If the guard were after the man, for whatever reason, he should stop and assist them. He should give them the bundle, let them sort it all out. He pulled up hard and spun back.

They had the old man, sagging in their hold. Something flashed in the rain. The serrated blade of a knife. Not the ceremonial variety Rom was accustomed to seeing in pictures, but a weapon strictly forbidden.

"Run!" the man screamed.

As one guardsman held the flailing old man, the one with the knife ripped the blade across his wrinkled throat. The old man's neck opened with a dark, yawning gush. His last cry devolved into a gurgle as his knees gave way.

And then the gaze of the restraining guardsman locked on Rom. The old man was no longer their quarry.

He was.

Chapter Two

GRIPPING THE parcel, Rom sprinted between the two buildings to the street and took the corner at full speed. The third guardsman was there to cut him off, and neither had time to pull up. They crashed into each other with force that knocked Rom's breath from his lungs and set the world ringing in his ears.

The guardsman went down beneath him with a grunt. The parcel slipped free of Rom's grip and skittered on the pavement.

Rom threw himself past the guardsman's clawing fingers, lunged for the parcel, and rolled to his feet with the thing in his hands. But in the process he lost his bag.

Shouts from the alley—too close.

He should stop, turn back, and give them the package. Clear this up. But the image of that knife and the dark gush of blood catapulted Rom across the street. He barely missed a second collision, this time with an oncoming bicycle.

He veered onto a side street, barely avoiding a young woman carrying a grocery bag. Her arms flew up. He heard her bag crash to the pavement behind him. He sprinted to the first intersection and tore down a street to his right: Entura Street, five blocks from home.

He had just watched a man's life spurt out of his throat. The look in the man's eyes hadn't been madness, but extreme fear. And now that same fear consumed Rom in a way he had never experienced.

Your father was killed.

His mother had never said anything of the sort. Surely she would have known.

At the end of the block he veered left onto a slender cobbled street. It had no streetlamp. He sprinted its empty length, lungs burning.

At the end of the lane was an abandoned print shop, its windows long boarded over, its decorative crenels broken or crumbled away. He knew this place, had poked around it before, even shown it to Avra once, wondering if it would make a second workshop before he gave up the idea as too expensive.

Rom slowed, panting, and looked around. No one present that he could see. He jogged a few paces, searched along the first floor of the building. There—the boards of a ground-floor window, still missing where he had once broken them away to climb inside.

He shoved his way through, grunting as a splintered board ripped the shoulder of his jacket down to the skin. He hesitated just a moment inside as his eyes adjusted to the darkness. The uncanny still of the stale air filled his nostrils.

He staggered past the front room to the larger one in back and fell against the wall just inside the open doorway. He listened for long moments, straining to hear shouts or the prying of window boards. Only his own labored breathing and the skittering of rodents along the far wall broke the silence.

Rom exhaled an uneven breath and slid down onto his rear, ignoring the plaster that dusted his shoulders. Hands trembling, he rubbed the rain from his eyes. But it wasn't all rain. His fingers came away red. Blood was on the dirty muslin of the parcel, too.

He set the parcel down. But the sight of it, the blood-smeared price of a life—more than one, according to the old man—seemed obscene.

What have I done?

He had run in panic and would surely pay a terrible price. But why had the old man run? And why had the guard killed him?

15

He was killed, I tell you! As all the other keepers were killed. For this.

What could be worth the price of a life?

He listened one more moment for any sound of pursuit, then, satisfied that he was alone with the rats, he gripped the package and pushed himself up. Rom stepped toward a patch of gray light between the boards of one of the old windows.

His fingers curled in the damp muslin and pulled it apart with a pop of threads along the seam where it had been sewn to the old man's coat. He got it open. Pulled out a box.

It was a small wooden box, no bigger than the little jewelry box he had once made for his mother. It was dark and damp, as though it perspired on its own. And it was ancient.

The box wasn't locked, but the iron latch refused to budge when he pried at it with a fingernail.

Even as he tried again, he knew he should turn it over to the authorities, unopened, explain everything. But in running he had broken the law. There was no mercy for those who broke the laws of Order. If what the old man said was true, had the same thing happened to his father?

He crouched, set the latch against the stone edge of the windowsill, and pried it open.

A small bundle nestled inside. Something wrapped in a thin piece of—what? Parchment? No, leather. A section of vellum, folded and rolled, surprisingly supple. He lifted the bundle out and set the box aside. Unwrapping the vellum, he eased out the thing rolled inside it.

A glass vial. It was the length of his palm, narrow at the top and swelling to the width of two fingers at the base, sealed with a stainless cap.

He lifted it up to what little light came in through the window. Shook it. Inside, dark, thick, viscous liquid coated the glass.

Now he could see four marker lines on the vial. Five measures.

For this, a man had lost his life?

Power and life…life as it was, the old man had called it.

Grave danger…

That, it had been. As good as a vial of death.

He started to rewrap it but then noticed several faded markings on the vellum. Holding the vial between the fingers of one hand, he stretched the ancient leather open. On one side was a list of what looked to be names—names with dates, each of them struck through. The other was covered with line after line of letters that spelled out nothing he could decipher except for a single, plainly written paragraph wedged into the margin at the top, as though added at a later date. He tilted the vellum toward the dusky light and made out the words:

> *The Order of Keepers has sworn to guard*
> *These contents for the Day of Rebirth*
> *Beware, any who drink—*
> *Blood destroys or grants the power to live*

He read it again. And then once more. But it made no more sense to him the third time than it had the first. *The Order of Keepers?* The only order he knew was the Order itself. And a Day of Rebirth happened every forty years at the new Sovereign's inauguration, as it would in five days.

He had never heard his father speak of anything like this. Had never seen anything like it in his father's possession. Surely the man would have said something? But Rom had been a boy when his father died.

Rom knew only one thing: If what the old man said was true, his father had died for this vial and this message. And if what the message said was true, his father had been a keeper, presumably of this very vial.

Now it was in his possession, and he was as good as dead himself.

Running from authority was a capital offense.

His mother. His mother would know what to do and if there was truth to anything the old man had said.

Rom wrapped the vial in the vellum, set the bundle back into the box, and pushed it back into the muslin casing. And then a horrible thought seized him.

He'd left his bag behind and with it, his wallet and identification. The guard would know who he was soon enough. They would come for him at home. And his mother was home.

His pulse lurched into a new, frenetic pace. He had to talk to her before the guard got there, if only to learn the truth.

He snatched up the box and hurried to the opening in the window. Silence. He crawled outside and glanced down the darkening street.

No one.

Rom tucked the box under his arm, lowered his head, and ran for home.

Chapter Three

T HE CITADEL at the heart of Byzantium contained more power
behind its thirty-foot-high walls than in all the world's continents put together. Within her three square miles lay the marble
and limestone apartments of the Sovereign, the supreme court, the
senate, and the world's highest administrative offices.

The secrets of Chaos roamed her ancient tunnels and haunted
her archives. The whispers of a passion-filled age flitted through
her crypts. The Citadel might be the compass by which the world
navigated, but it was to those who dwelled within it foremost a
house of secrets.

Saric, son of Vorrin, paced inside a small chamber beneath the
center of the great walled capitol. Few of those buzzing about their
business above would ever guess the extent of the sprawling subterranean maze beneath them. And few knew these underground
chambers as intimately as Saric did. Especially this chamber tucked
two floors beneath the assembly hall of the senate.

Here, Megas had drawn together the council that canonized
the Book of Orders. Here, he had given the command to destroy
all works of Chaos: the mechanized weapons of war, the net-
works, the technology, the religion, the art, all the reminders of
a time when unchained passion ruled—and ruined—the hearts
of man.

Here, Sirin, the founder of the Order before Megas, had been assassinated.

Feyn, Saric's half sister, called the room morbid. Until recently, Saric had agreed with her. Seven days recently, to be exact. Now he found the chamber filled with strange energy and with the specters of a history he had only begun to appreciate.

The room hosted a variety of items in similar states of disuse or decay, each of them an illicit survivor of Megas's decree: ancient books, some of them frivolously written for nothing but entertainment and the heightening of emotion, their crumbling pages barely legible; a pewter goblet from a time when basilicas housed worshippers of a different god; a collection of curved knives, one of them with a jewel-crusted sheath from the ancient region of India; several swords and a long spear, the head of which had deteriorated to a metal nub; and an automatic weapon that had long ago ceased to function properly. Saric had never learned its origins.

The hexagonal chamber itself had once been nearly destroyed by fire. Ever since, the blackened stone walls had a propensity for retaining moisture. Anything hung on them tended to molder, including the chamber's focal point: a tapestry of Saric's father, the Sovereign Vorrin, defaced for a decade now by the lichen living upon its threads.

Saric ran a ringed hand over his hair and down to his nape, smoothed the V-shaped patch of hair beneath his lower lip. Like the chamber walls, he was sweating.

"You will tell me again what is happening to me," he said, very quietly.

The alchemist standing near the center of the chamber was not a young man. Corban was one of the High Peers of Alchemy, those advanced members of the alchemists' secretive inner sect.

"I have already explained, my lord."

"Fragments!" Saric said, turning on him. The word ricocheted off the stone. He lowered his voice. "I am not one of your mice to collect pellets when you drop a few in my direction. I want to know *every-thing* that is happening to me. Now." A tremor ran through his bones.

So much had happened in seven days. In the space of so many scant hours, a new world had lifted the hem of her skirts before him. A world of seething pleasures and sweaty rage.

Rage in particular was its own form of pleasure, he had learned, one of a few truly pleasurable releases for the new beast that grasped at the world from the cage of his chest.

Corban inclined his head. "Then I will start at the beginning."

When the alchemist tilted his head, his neck looked exceedingly fragile. He was a slight man, though the long robes of his office disguised the fact well.

"Within a generation of Null Year, our alchemist forefathers began to apply analysis of the human genome to systematically curing the diseases that ail humanity. The cancers, the blindness, the epidemic viruses—"

"Save me the propaganda."

"You ask for answers. You must be patient—"

"You school me on patience?" Sweat snaked down Saric's spine. "I don't have another five hundred years. My sister is preparing her inaugural address at this moment. *I* have days. Which means *you* have minutes."

He willed the tightness around his lungs to relax. Right now, he felt that he could kill a boar with his hands. That he could leap, unharmed, from the turret of the Citadel's watchtower.

That he might tear out his own eyes.

He dragged his sleeve across his forehead, half expecting to see it come away red. His entire body hurt. His entire being burned.

The alchemist folded his hands. "As we learned to correct the inherited mistakes of our DNA, we decoded the emotional ills of humanity as well. You must understand that the limbic system of the brain—a circuit comprising the amygdalae, the hippocampus, and the hypothalamus, among others—"

"Too much!"

Corban blinked. "When we identified the coding of these emotions, we also discovered a way to eliminate them, all but that one required for our survival—"

"Fear. Yes. Yes, I know all about the evils of emotion as preached by Sirin. Tell me what has happened to *me*."

"As you say, Sirin preached against the volatility of emotion and denounced the passions. To that end, Megas offered a solution: a pathogen with the genetic code to alter the DNA of any host. Airborne, highly contagious. They called it Legion."

Legion. The name hung in the room.

"Sirin wanted nothing to do with Legion," Corban said. "Even though his philosophies were already failing, he would not embrace the solution. And so he was removed—not by emotion-crazed zealots, as history teaches, but by Megas."

Saric drew a slow breath. "You are telling me Sirin was assassinated by Megas himself." The whole world believed that Sirin had been assassinated by radicals. It was the inciting event of the world's new Order.

"Yes. And those few who know it guard this secret with their lives."

Saric looked around the chamber with new eyes. "So. In that moment the Order gained both its martyr and its proof against every zeal Sirin condemned."

"Indeed. And Megas had the means to ensure the world's eternal loyalty."

"So it's true, after all, that Sirin was killed by zealots. Just not the ones we thought."

"I suppose so."

"This pathogen, this Legion that stripped humanity of all but fear—you're saying it worked."

"The virus did its work within the space of a few years."

"And so the nonemotional state of the world is not the selective preference of evolution as we have all been taught, but an act of oppression."

Corban hesitated. "*I* would call it an act of liberation."

Saric drew a slow breath. The knowing filled him with strange satisfaction. It also unsettled. He moved to the console and lifted the jewel-crusted knife, thoughtfully dragging his thumb over the twisted prongs of the settings. "You're saying everyone—including me—is infected with a virus."

"No. It's no longer a viral infection. Nearly half our genetic code is derived from viruses. Think of it…as a new volume added to the library of our genetic code."

"So in the face of all our talk of living as evolved humans, you're saying we've selectively *de*volved?"

The alchemist pursed his lips. "I would say we have customized our emotional makeup in the same way that we selected the translucence of the skin that you Brahmin seem to favor, the paleness of your eyes that you consider beautiful."

"By simply turning off the switches to those emotions that no longer serve us."

"In a manner of speaking, yes."

Whatever this virus had done to humanity, the alchemists had found a way to undo it in him. The chaos of emotions had come roiling back into veins and neurons too tepid to house their fire, and Saric wasn't sure if he wanted to kill the alchemists or thank them for it.

Emotion. So long forgotten, even the words for emotions had become nothing but a wisp, a feckless currency without backing. Hope. Envy. Disgust. Love.

Love. The archaic emotion in the Age of Chaos was now simply understood as a duty based on honor and respect, stripped of emotion. But what had it felt like? He tossed the jeweled knife atop the console.

"So that's it. The world has been castrated."

"Despite our vast knowledge, emotion retained her mysteries. The most complex workings of Legion were not completely understood by us."

Saric glanced at him.

"The alchemists continued to study emotion's underpinnings. Through the process, we learned to restore some of the emotions we once turned off with Legion."

"The serum."

"Yes, the atraviridae. We call it Chaos, for obvious reasons."

"The dark virus," Saric said softly.

Corban continued. "And so I came to you seven days ago and the rest you know. You are looking on the world as a new creature. I say *new* because although we have reanimated the emotion centers of your brain, it is not exactly the same as it would be had you been born that way. It is, I like to think, an improvement. Pravus chose well."

Pravus the Elder, foremost among the Peers. He, too, had taken the serum quite a while before ordering Corban to administer it to Saric.

"You are his right-hand man," Saric said. "I wonder why he didn't choose you for this... honor."

Corban's gaze slowly lifted. It was flat but guileless.

Saric said, barely above a whisper, "You would have done it, wouldn't you?"

Corban was silent.

"But you don't have the royal blood that Pravus needs. Ah. Pity."

But Corban could not comprehend pity. Even for himself.

Saric felt a sudden stab of something like loneliness. He wondered where Feyn was, if she had finished writing her inaugural address, and in what posture she sat now, at this moment. He wondered what she had chosen to wear today and what supper her breath smelled of and the directional cant of those ice-cloud eyes.

Corban must have seen the tremble in Saric's hands or the sweat on his brow, because he pressed with a question of his own.

"You are confused about what you're feeling?"

Saric stepped away and took a deep breath. "I have...strange sensations that I don't know how to describe. I can barely contain them. The effort of it is like pain. I crave things I never wanted to possess. The women—"

The man whispered. "Desire, my lord. Lust."

Saric gave a slow nod. "I crave to take things from others. I think of killing someone just to push the life out of their lungs with my hands, especially if they would stop me."

"Anger. Perhaps jealousy."

Anger. Jealousy. They might as well have been the names of colors to the blind.

"Anything else?" the alchemist asked.

"I want things. The robe of my father, which is fine velvet embroidered with gold. But more, I want the office that goes with that robe. I am jealous for it." There, he had said it, given voice to the two-headed asp that struck even now with great pleasure and fury at his insides.

"Ambition, my lord. And clearly, that is the whole point. Pravus would return power to the house of alchemy through you, who is half alchemist by blood."

Indeed, the plan. So Pravus had the same thirsts but needed Saric to quench them.

Ambition. It was the greatest of those serpents within him. It made him feel full, to have them inside him, and very tall. He felt great in this room, as though he filled it merely by standing in it. As though the Citadel could not contain him, as though the world itself would not, perhaps, sate him. Everyone else—everything else—felt minuscule in comparison.

"I wonder, my lord," Corban said, coming closer. "Do you feel anything else? Joy perhaps?"

"Joy?"

"They also called it *satisfaction*. A sense of well-being, according to the record. Fulfillment."

Saric looked at the relics around him. "I feel joy every time a new woman is brought in for me. I feel joy at the sound of her screams."

Corban was studying him with intense scrutiny.

"Has your lab rat satisfied your curiosity, then?"

"You misunderstand my motivation," the older man said. "And I do not believe that what you describe is joy. We have reignited some emotions, but not all. Only those of a darker nature, apparently."

"My appetite for meat has increased. It's what I crave, to the exclusion of all else—"

"That isn't unusual. Meat is the mainstay of the world diet."

For nearly two centuries, the law had restricted citizens' caloric intake, monitored carbohydrates, and eliminated sugar. It was common knowledge that carbohydrates, even those found in vegetables, shortened life. To think, in the age of arcane science there had been diets based on vegetables!

"No. I can't even bear the thought of overcooked food. It repulses me. In fact, the smell of the venison that you ate for supper repulses me."

"You can smell that?"

"I can smell blood anywhere and prefer my meals running with it. And then there is this—" Saric pulled away the sodden neck of his cloak and in three strides loomed over the alchemist.

"Do you see how my veins stand out against my skin?"

In just the last day his jugular had turned nearly black beneath the surface, as though it ran with ink. Saric's skin was already translucent, so much so that he never needed to accentuate the vein along his forearm, as some royals did, with blue cosmetic powder. Indeed, Saric had been pleased at the change and marveled at it. But as he had watched the blue branching of his veins darken, he had wondered with fear and fascination what it meant.

"As far as side effects go, I would think you'd find it pleasing," the alchemist said. "Now, if that is all, my lord—"

"It is *not* all. I want to know what the Chaos serum might do to my wife, Portia. Each of the women I've given it to has died, sometimes before I finished with her."

Corban shook his head. "I strongly urge against it. We've allowed it in the women brought to satisfy your new tastes, knowing they would not survive. But giving it to Portia is inadvisable. We studied your bloodline for months before administering the serum. Clearly, it does not suit all bloodlines, and many of our initial samples did not yield...favorable results. Let me remind you that there are only three who know of your recent conversion, including yourself. It is extremely dangerous to share this secret with anyone."

Saric turned away. So there it was. Was he even now dying as a result of his reanimation?

If he was, he would wrest from this world *every drop* of pleasure and power he could. What did it matter? The very foundation of the Order was a lie.

Besides, he was in Hades already.

A shudder passed up through his spine. It took all his resolve to keep it from overtaking his limbs.

"And yet, Corban, we will have to get a fresh sample of the serum. Because I am most interested in sharing this—these new passions—with my wife."

A sharp rap came from the other side of the door. And then he smelled it: copper and salt.

Blood.

"Come!"

Two guardsmen entered the chamber. One of them, the taller of the two, carried a sack, the mouth of it gathered in his fist.

"My lord."

Saric took the sack from him, hefted it once as though weighing it, and then emptied it with a heave in Corban's direction.

The head of an old man rolled out. It lolled before coming to rest faceup. The eyes were open with an unlikely mixture of fear and amazement.

"That's him?"

"The keeper, yes," the taller one said. The other, who looked far stronger, glanced at Corban.

"He's the last, then."

"The last that we know of. Besides the one you have in the dungeons."

"The vial. Where is the blood?"

The guard hesitated. "The old man found him."

"Found who?"

"The son of Elias. The keeper passed it to him, before we could get it."

"You're saying a dead keeper's son has the blood."

The guardsman nodded.

Saric let out a slow, controlled breath. "You saw this."

"Yes."

The blood was rumored to be superior to the Chaos serum Saric had received. It would return the one who took it to the fully devolved state of chaotic man. A reawakening, to be precise, more complete than the one he was now experiencing. Whether it actually had such properties remained to be seen, but at least one thing now was certain: It existed.

"You know where he will go?"

"Yes, sir. We've had him under surveillance for years, since the death of his father."

"Find him. Get the blood. If I don't have his head by day's end tomorrow, I'll have yours."

Chapter Four

ROM THOUGHT the familiar sight of the narrow lane behind the houses on his block would calm the hammer of his heart. He expected the modest homes on Piera Street, with their cracked paint and old brick, to set right the axis of a world suddenly jarred askew.

They didn't.

The slim houses with their straight sides and asphalt shingles seemed at strange odds to him, even against the mundane sounds of barking dogs and someone replacing the lid on a metal trash bin.

He glanced back twice as he ran down the left side of the drive, then slowed near the outbuilding of the fourth house. The paint on the outbuilding had peeled to a nondescript gray, though the sill of the lone window was new and still almost white.

Rom's workshop, inherited from his father.

His father, a simple artisan like him. Was what the old man said even possible, that his father had been one of these keepers?

Not twenty feet away, he could see the back of the home he shared with his mother. Light shone through the kitchen window, which was cracked open. From inside came the sounds of dinner in progress: a spoon scraping the contents from a pot, that pot being set with a clatter in the sink below the window.

No sign of the Citadel Guard.

The familiar form of his mother, Anna, leaned over the sink. His fear began to abate at the sight of her making dinner as though it were any normal night, but it sailed again at the reality that he had just committed a capital offense.

What would she say when he told her? Would she turn him in? She was obligated by Order to do so, but he didn't think she would—not if she knew they would kill him. To disobey Order was a fearful thing, the courting of Hades. But to aid or introduce death to your own flesh and blood was equally fearful, akin to bringing death on oneself. It was a conflict of fears that the Order couldn't resolve, no matter that assembly services preached obedience regularly.

He glanced down at the muslin-wrapped box in his hand. It felt glued there, stuck tight in the clasp of fingers that had forgotten how to unclench. He had to get control of himself, to think.

Rom rounded the small building, digging in his pocket for his key ring. He found it and quickly unlocked the shop. Flipped the light switch.

No guardsmen waiting to kill him.

He latched the door behind him and gazed at the trappings of his life, oddly irrelevant now in the face of crime: the distressed worktable in the center, the equally weathered workbench along the wall. The lathe, the bins of wood and metal scraps he'd salvaged from other projects and abandoned buildings. The workshop was just as he'd left it that morning, even down to the half-finished cup of coffee on the workbench.

He glanced at the tattered chair in the corner, the one with the permanent dent in the seat cushion. It was where Avra sat when she came to visit after she was done for the day in her father's laundry shop.

Avra. Again, he tried to picture what she would say if she knew what he had done. Because of their association, she would soon fear for herself even more than she already did, which was saying much.

But right now he had his own fears to contend with.

He walked to the worktable, set the box down. One thing he knew: He couldn't run from the Order forever. They would find him and kill him because of a mysterious vial, the importance of which he couldn't begin to grasp.

He wet a rag and wiped blindly at the dried blood on his face, then threw the rag into the trash. He paused, grabbed the rag back out of the trash, bundled the box in it, and pushed it to the bottom of the bin.

After exchanging his dirtied jacket for another one lying across the back of the chair, he headed out of the workshop to the house.

Inside, the glow of a lone electric light illuminated the kitchen. Another lit the small living room toward the front of the house. These were the two small extravagances they afforded themselves, those two lights that would be replaced by candles as soon as dinner was over.

In the kitchen, Anna retrieved two glasses from the cabinet. A secondary school teacher, she had always been considered wise and was often sought out by her students for advice. "If Bliss truly exists in the hereafter," Rom's father had once said, "your mother will be the first to receive it."

And then he had gone on to investigate for himself. That was five years ago.

"How was your day?" Anna said to Rom over her shoulder.

Stew steamed from a bowl at the center of the small kitchen table. But rather than soothe, the smell of it only turned his stomach.

"And take off that old jacket before you sit down. Didn't you at least wear your good one to basilica?"

When he didn't respond, she glanced up, struck by his frozen silence. "Rom? What's the matter with you?" She set down the glasses and came to him. "Are you ill?"

"Something…" He cleared his throat. "Something happened today."

"What do you mean, *something*? And what happened to your head?" She pushed back his bangs and leaned in to examine him.

"I was coming home from basilica and there was an old man waiting for me on the way home. He said he knew Father."

Her brow arched, but she remained her stoic self. It took a lot to awaken Mother's fear, a trait she'd passed on to him. "Many people knew your father," she said, as if to say, *So what?*

The place settings on the table were as clean and vacant as fresh faces. What he wouldn't give for it to be any normal dinner on any normal day.

"I thought he was crazy, but then the Citadel Guard came. They must have been following him—"

"The Citadel Guard?"

"He said Father didn't die of fever, but that he was killed."

"But that's not true."

"He gave me a box—the same one he said Father was killed for. He made me take it. And then the Citadel Guard…"

Her gaze held steady, and she said nothing.

"Mother, they had a knife." A tremor had come into Rom's voice. "I watched them cut his throat, there in the alley. They killed him."

Now she paled, showing the first signs of a fear not even she could suppress.

"You must be mistaken."

"I watched it! I saw his blood spill out."

She hesitated, then said quickly, "His path was his to follow. As was your father's. Neither is any of your concern. None of it. Remember that and this will all pass." She turned back toward the table and then hesitated. "I trust you discussed these things with the guard."

So then, here it was. The mistake that would surely earn him his death.

"No."

Anna froze.

"I ran."

She turned back, her face a white slate.

"I dropped my bag," Rom said. "They know who I am."

For several long seconds, they stared at each other, speaking with their eyes what was now painfully obvious. In this one simple act, Rom had done the unthinkable. He had forever altered not only his life, but hers.

"So they know where you live," his mother said.

"Yes."

He felt powerless to stop the fear slicing through his mind. If such a wise and reasoning person as his mother was afraid for her life upon hearing what he'd done, how much more should he fear for his own?

"You should not have run."

"I know."

The words hung between them.

"Don't fear, Mother. I'm going. When they come, there will be nothing here to cast suspicion on you. They won't hurt you."

"Yes, you should go."

He carried the greatest respect for her. He honored her in the way the Order prescribed. And although her living or dying was really none of his concern, he felt obligated to show his commitment by removing her from suspicion when they came for him. He had no business affecting her journey with his own mistakes. Her request that he leave was her way of saying he must take his own journey—with its consequences—without affecting her own.

"But before I leave, I need to know. Did anyone ever call Father a *keeper*?"

"A keeper? What is that? I've never heard the term."

"Then he hid himself from you as well?"

"Your father's path was his path. Whether he was killed or whether he died—what concern is it really to either of us? Our responsibility right now is to love one another enough to do what is best. To keep Order and ensure our own proper passing. Perhaps to meet in the afterlife."

Love. Truly, Mother and he loved each other, for what was love but the obligation of loyalty?

"I'll get the box and go."

She went very still. "You still have this box."

"Yes."

"You brought it to our home?"

"It's in the workshop."

"You must report it immediately! Give it to them and tell them your having it was a mistake."

"They'll never believe me. The time for that is past. I *ran*, Mother. They chased me for a long time."

She averted her eyes, stepped to a chair, and sat carefully, staring off toward the window.

"I'll leave now," Rom said.

"No." She looked at him. "It's too late. Go get the box. We're both at risk now. We'll take it to the Citadel together."

She pushed up from her chair, looked around her, and then started to untie her apron. "We'll go. We'll take it to the Citadel and clear this up."

She seemed sure of herself. In the face of her confident loyalty to Order, her unquestioning regard for compliance, his fear eased. She was right. It was the right thing to do. It was what he should have done from the beginning.

"I'll get my coat," she said. "Go get the box."

Rom went out the back, not bothering to shut the door behind him. Inside the workshop, he dug the box from the waste bin.

It was the box that had determined his father's fate and would now determine his own. His fingers tingled at the thought and he wondered if he would ever know its meaning. The question was cut short by a scream.

Rom's heart seized. It had come from the direction of the house.

Another scream cut through the night air. His mother's. Raised, muffled voices followed in its wake.

He dropped the box and spun toward the door. What Rom did next did not come from a place of reason or wisdom or even honor.

He simply reacted, without thought, tearing for the house before he knew that his legs were even moving.

He flew up the steps to the back porch, crashed through the open doorway into the kitchen, and then pulled up sharply. There in the entrance to the dining room stood a guardsman with his back to Rom. A knife was in his fist, pointed at the floor.

It was the second time that day he'd seen such a sight, and this time it struck him as even more surreal than the first. These images were not meant to exist. Not in real life, not in front of any decent man's eyes, not in his home.

The guardsman with the blade glanced over his shoulder, saw Rom, and turned to face him.

"There you are." He was a thick-faced man with flat lips and dark eyebrows, holding the knife as if it were a natural extension of his arm. "Bring her out!"

Two other guardsmen, also bearing knives, hauled his mother around the corner, each holding her up by one of her arms. Her dress was red from a trail of blood that flowed from a three-inch gash in her right cheek.

This was his mother, frozen by terror. Gone was her customary cloak of wisdom or any pretence of surety. She was visibly shaking in their grasp.

"Rom…" Her lips, stretched thin, were quivering. Her eyes pleaded as though she were a child.

The door behind Rom opened, and with a quick glance he saw that two more men had entered the house. He was surrounded.

"Please don't let them kill me!" She hung between the guards, her words devolving into terrified sobs.

Rom saw it all in still frames, the inevitability of it all. He was going to die. As was his mother.

Oddly, for the moment at least, Rom felt no fear. He felt nothing at all.

"You feel that, boy?" The thick-faced guard lifted his blade and pressed it to his mother's throat. "You feel the fingers of fear wrapping around your heart?"

Blood seeped over the blade's edge where it bit into the skin of her neck.

"You feel it because you have no doubt that what you see with your own eyes will also happen to you."

Fear found Rom like a fist to the throat.

"I know because we all feel the same," the thick-faced man said. And indeed, there was the glint of fear in his gaze. "We all have our ways of serving the Order. Mine is to help you do the right thing. Where is the package?"

Though his mother begged for her life, he knew he could not affect her journey, especially when surrounded by so many guardsmen. So then it was not his concern and she would surely find Bliss.

His own journey might still lay ahead of him, but he knew these men had no intention of letting him live, box or no box.

"Tell me," the man repeated.

His mother's eyes pleaded. Tears spilled down her cheeks. "Please, please. I don't want to die. Rom!"

He was going to die! Panic crowded his mind. He was going to die and the thought of death, so close, rode him like a monster more powerful and vicious than any he'd known to exist. His body began to tremble.

"You're flaunting Order, boy! No?" The guard calmly sawed into his mother's throat, severing her scream along with her arteries and at least part of her spinal cord. Her body went limp like a thing unplugged.

The other two released her arms.

Rom lost his mind to fear before she hit the floor, while the man who'd killed her still had his back to him. He threw himself forward, crashing into the back of one man who stood in his way. The guardsman fell into one of those who'd held his mother, putting them both off balance.

But Rom wasn't keeping track. He was simply getting out. Over his mother's body, into the living room, through the front door before any of the guards could collect themselves.

Only then did he manage to string together enough reason to form logical thought. To realize that the only thing in the world that interested these men now was the box.

The box was his only leverage.

Rom ducked to his left, around the house toward the workshop. With any luck they would pursue him out the front while he made for the back of the house.

Shouts reached him as he sprinted through the workshop door. Then he was inside and across the room, skidding and nearly going down as he grabbed the box from where he'd dropped it.

He regained his balance and ran out of the workshop. They were coming, rounding on him from the side of the house in the falling darkness. He wheeled left and ran toward the waist-high iron fence between his house and the neighbor's. If there was any route of escape it would be here.

He vaulted the fence, landed with a skitter of stones, and sprinted across the narrow back lot—and the next one after that. When he reached the end of the third lot, he veered toward the lane and sprinted across the old cobbles.

A shout issued from the alley less than twenty paces off. Rom ran through the narrow file between two houses on the other side of the lane, out to the opposite street. Past house lots, past a copse of stunted trees to a path at the edge of a tiny neighborhood park.

The perennial clouds that obscured the sun by day obscured the moon most nights as well. But Rom would have found his way along this path in pitch darkness.

He could think of only one person who might help him make sense of his predicament.

Avra.

It took him ten minutes at a steady jog to reach her neighborhood, where he ducked around the corner of a small outbuilding. Hearing no sound, he ran, bent low along the rear walk of several row houses, to the fifth one. When he'd made his way to the back of the building, he stopped midway at a heavy door with a combination lock and listened for any sign of pursuit.

Nothing.

He entered the code and let himself into the building, but he did not breathe any easier.

Seeing his mother die so violently left him with no doubt as to his own fate. If they would kill her simply to put fear into his heart, they would think nothing of killing him.

He saw it again—the obscene gush of blood, the slumping of Anna's body, the way she had collapsed to the floor.

In the Age of Chaos, before humanity had evolved out of its slavery to emotions, he might have suffered their debilitating effects. He remembered the word *sorrow*, whatever that was, and knew it might have rendered him a lump of useless flesh, in which case he would have been dead by now.

Then again, *fear* had nearly incapacitated him. Now he would have to control that fear if he hoped to survive.

He turned up a short staircase of decaying cement. The landing separated into two doorways. He entered the code into the left one and silently let himself in, wondering momentarily if he would enter another death scene.

The kitchen and living room inside were quiet, dimly lit by a single lamp.

"Avra?" His voice seemed too loud.

He hurried past the kitchen to the hallway that led to the only bedroom on the floor. The door pushed open easily.

"Avra?"

She bolted up from her bed along the adjacent wall. A book fell with a *thump* to the floor.

"Rom!" she breathed. "What are you doing scaring me like that?"

For a moment, he told himself it was all untrue. That it had not happened—the murder of the old man or of his mother. Here in the familiar clutter of Avra's bedroom, unchanged in all the years he had known her, he could almost believe it.

But then he remembered the box in his hand, the ache in his fingers from his death grip around it.

And its death grip on him.

He would find no refuge here. They had found him at home; they would come to this place soon enough.

"I need your help," he said.

She stared back with startled eyes so dark he couldn't tell where the irises ended and the pupils began. At first glance one might mistake her for a girl younger than her twenty-three years. Lithe-framed and small-boned, she embodied youthful fragility, though she was stronger than anyone might guess.

"What are you talking about? What's wrong with you?"

They were running out of time. He looked around, found her shoes, and grabbed them. "We need to go. Quick. Put these on," he said, dropping them before the bed. He blew out the lantern on the desk and then drew the curtain aside. "Hurry!"

"Hurry why? You're scaring me!"

"We have to go."

"What? Why?"

"My mother's dead." His voice was as empty as he felt.

"What?" She blinked.

He glanced at her from the window. "I saw a man killed today and I ran. He was killed for this." Rom held out the bundle in his hand.

"What do you mean, *killed*?"

"Killed. Murdered. We have to go!"

"Go where? You're not making any sense!"

He willed himself to talk around the panic rising up within him with each passing second. "The Citadel Guard killed a man for this.

The man who gave it to me, they slaughtered him. With a knife. And then they came to my house."

"What?"

"They came for this. And they killed my mother."

She stared.

"I need your help. And you need mine. They came for my mother and they'll come for you."

"You think they're going to kill me?" Her voice had risen in pitch.

Outside, a dog barked.

Rom peered back out the window into the darkness behind the building. Two forms passed the glow of a lower-level window. "They're here!"

She sprang to her feet but then stood there, frozen.

"I don't want my journey to end today," he said. "But if I stay here, it will. And if you stay, I think yours will, too. If you're ready for that, I'll leave. But I promise, they'll kill you."

She hesitated only one more moment, her breath coming shallow and quick in the air between them. And then she shoved her feet into her shoes.

"Where are we going?"

This, he had already thought out. She wouldn't like the answer.

"Do you trust me?"

"Yes." She grabbed her cloak and threw it over her shoulders.

He took her hand. Together they ran down the hall. When she turned toward the kitchen, he pulled her the other way.

"No. Quickly. The front."

He blew out the lone lamp in the living room. In the darkness, she unlatched the front door.

They waited. Rom blinked, strained to readjust to the dark.

When the dog began its manic noise again, he whispered: "Now."

As they ran down the steps and out into the night, Rom sent a prayer to the Maker. He asked only one thing: that he not witness a third killing tonight.

Chapter Five

ELECTRIC LIGHT high inside the tunnel flickered through the windows of the underground train. It leapfrogged over the empty seats in stripes. It played through the auburn strands of Avra's hair.

They stood together toward the back, Rom with one arm around the back exit rail, the other around Avra, who could not seem to still her trembling. He knew the reason. Avra, of all people, was not prepared to chance her own death. Though the pall of it had hung over her for years, she was less prepared than any one for the inevitable.

Her hair caught in the day-old stubble against his chin. He closed his eyes, inhaled the soapy scent of it, and tried to imagine that it were any other day. That her breath against his collarbone was not uneven, the small fingers digging into his back were not ice-cold.

The box, that toxic bundle, was pressed between them, hidden inside the folds of Avra's cloak where she'd shoved it upon sighting a compliance officer near the underground entrance.

She shuddered and he tightened his arm around her as the train lurched around a corner.

"I can't believe it. I can't believe it," she whispered. "Are you sure she's dead?"

He thought of the gurgling gash in his mother's neck, the way she had crumpled. The blood—so much blood—soaking into the floorboards. He thought of her terror, and his.

"Yes."

He looked across the train car to its only other passengers: an older woman reading a paper, and a university-aged man who stared out the dark windows at nothing.

Rom wondered if he would ever again have the luxury of idle thought or random dreams. Somehow, he doubted it.

She turned her face into his shoulder. "I don't see how I can help you. Maybe you should just turn yourself in."

"I'm not ready to die."

"But if it's your path—"

"And what if it's yours? Are you ready?"

She fell silent.

"I know I'm risking Bliss by running. I know. But I can't go in. Not yet. I need you to help me think this through. And I can help you stay alive. Because I'm telling you, if they find either of us, we're dead."

"You said it's a vial of blood," she said. "Whose? Why would an old man say that about your father, and why does the guard want it? Why didn't the old man just give it to them?"

"I don't know. Shhh."

Across the car, the young man glanced at them. The woman reading the paper had begun to tear one of her fingernails with her teeth. Rom was sure they hadn't overheard, and that they had fears enough of their own to keep them occupied.

The train came into the station. "We get out here."

She hadn't asked yet where they were going, and he hadn't told her.

They passed through the station toward the gate, their gazes flicking along the platform to the other end where two compliance officers stood in conversation. Ducking low, they hurried past the gate and filed up the stairs to emerge on the street. Lamplight reflected in yellow pools on the pavement. The air was heavy, promising rain.

"We're going to the basilica, aren't we?" she finally said.

He nodded.

"Isn't there anywhere else?"

"Not at this hour. Which is why no one will be there."

Overhead, the sky broke. Rain began to fall in light, smattering drops, and then in the onslaught of a downpour. Together they ran across the street, past the wan lamplight, through the darkness to the looming form of the basilica.

He still had the key from the funeral service earlier today; it was routine for him to pick it up in advance so he could come in early and practice. Sometimes, if he had extra time, he lit the candles upon the small aisle altar for Avra. The clerics would say the candles didn't fulfill her need to attend services in person, and they were surely right. But he had done it now for years in secret because she'd asked him to. Besides his mother, there was no one he honored as much as Avra, for reasons that not even he understood.

They entered through the small wooden side door. Inside, the cavernous space of the basilica echoed with the sound of the groaning hinges. The stained-glass depictions of Sirin and Megas seemed oppressively bleak despite their clear eyes, recast in the last few years in the pale, icy blue coveted by the Brahmin royals.

He relocked the door behind him. The sound of the bolt sent a hollow echo like the closing of a vault through the cavern of the sanctum.

"This way." He led her to a narrow door at the side, opened it, and flicked the switch on the landing. Electric light, sallow as the streetlamps and only half as strong, barely lit the old stairwell. They descended past the first landing and the second, and then into the basement corridor past an old service elevator. He stopped at a storeroom midway down. Any farther and they would end up in the ancient crypt. Avra would not be able to endure that.

For the first time in his life, he wasn't sure he could, either.

The room was long—long enough to have two doors on the hallway—and stored several stacks of folding chairs, spare seven-branched candelabras, boxes of candles. And there was the casket from the funeral earlier today. It lay atop its metal carriage against the far wall.

He turned away, unnerved by it now in the feeble light.

He dug several vanilla-wax tapers out of a box, set them in one of the candelabras, and lit them with one of the candle lighters from the corner. He flipped off the room light so that the coffin lay in darkness.

"Better?"

Avra stood in the circle of the candlelight, looking completely lost. Rom took a chair from a stack, set it down, and opened it for her. But instead she just stood there, holding the box with the blood.

"We can never go back, can we?"

"I don't know." He took the box from her and set it on a small table next to the candelabras, noting that her hands were positioned as if she were still holding it. A moment later, she lowered her arms.

Rom strode to the chair and sat in it himself, got up again, rubbed at his face, sat back down. Looked at the box.

"You're making me more nervous," Avra said.

It was everything he could do to remain calm. "Help me think. I can't think."

"You shouldn't have taken the box."

"I know. But the old man talked about my father. He told me to swear. And then...and then they killed him."

She let out a shaky breath. "Anyone would have run. I would've."

"Run, yes. But taken the box..."

"You shouldn't have taken the box."

"But I did."

"We could leave the city, go to Greater Europa," she said. "To my parents'—"

"No. They'll turn us in."

"We can't stay here! Maybe your mother was right. Maybe we should just go to compliance."

"Are you forgetting everything I say the moment I say it?" He jabbed a finger at the box. "They're *killing* people connected to that thing. They killed my father!"

"You don't know that! Your mother took him to the wellness center herself. He was sick with fever." But she shuddered when she said it. Rom knew Avra would never go willingly to a wellness center.

"She was right," Avra went on. "Your mother was a wise woman. She was..." She trailed off, staring at the box. "What about a priest? You could tell one of the priests. They should know what it is. They could take it."

He hesitated, considering that. "The writing inside the box talked about death. Maybe a priest *would* know what to do."

"Then that's it, we'll take it to a priest. The priest can turn it in."

Rom got up and paced away, shaking his head. "I don't know why, but I think they'd still come after me. They killed my mother and she hadn't even seen it yet! No. They're killing everyone associated with it. Which now includes you."

"But I don't have a clue about this box! I want nothing to do with it!"

"They don't know that."

"Then you shouldn't have come to my house!"

"Even if I hadn't, they'd assume you'd lead them to me. You're not understanding the nature of this thing, Avra! They'll *kill* you because other than my mother, you're the closest to me."

"But I'm not even your family!"

"We're closer than family. No one else may know, but somehow they know."

Indeed, Rom and Avra were like twin lungs, breathing the same breath for more years than he could count, through school and afterward. No one knew the secrets kept between them, though it was clear that secrets existed.

Avra went to the chair and sat down. The hem of her cloak pooled against the old stone floor.

"Maybe you should destroy it."

"I thought about that. But they think I have it. No. I'm a dead man either way."

"Maybe you could go to the royals."

"Like who? Do we have Brahmin friends I'm not aware of?"

She fell silent. After a moment, she said, "The canyonlands. We could run to the desert. They say people live out there. Nomads, living beyond the reach of Order."

"It's a myth."

"Are you so sure? People whisper. There are reports—"

"Even if it's not a myth, who would want to live beyond the Order?"

For the first time he realized that Avra herself already did, in a manner of speaking. Of course she had thought of leaving. And he realized, too, the reason she had not.

She would never go without him.

"Think of it, Rom. No Order…no Honor Code. No citizens reporting one another for the smallest infraction, living every day in fear. It would be living. Just *living*, for as long as possible…"

"Outside the Order? Without a chance to attend assembly at all? We'd be damning ourselves!"

Avra was silent. They both already knew where Avra's eternal destination lay.

She abruptly looked away.

"Avra…"

She bolted up and hurried toward the door, stumbling over the hem of her cloak. It pulled askew, dragging wide the neckline of her tunic beneath, exposing skin that was unnaturally smooth and too light. A scar, one giant raised welt, lashed toward her neck.

He remembered the first time he saw that wound, seven years ago. Raw, the skin already bubbling up and coming off where the lantern oil of a wall sconce had spilled on her and caught fire. She had come to him in shock and shaking, nearly collapsing on her feet. But she had not screamed until he called his father to help them.

The Order did not tolerate physical defects.

Somehow, Rom had known his father would say nothing. He had arrived in silence and shown Rom how to help her dress the burns in wet bandages, helping to hide them from the eyes of her parents and from Anna.

"Is helping Avra wrong?" Rom had asked.

He had never forgotten what his father had said.

"The Order honors life out of fear of death. We are commanded to love life, but what we call love, Rom, is the shadow of something lost. It is loyalty born out of fear. Fear and love, sometimes the two conflict. Helping Avra is its own kind of love. But now, you must keep what I'm telling you to yourself."

He had thought about his father's words many times after that— including the day his mother took him to the wellness center.

He never returned.

Today, Avra ran the family laundry and lived alone, her parents having moved to Greater Europa. She had not stepped foot in a basilica until this moment, fearful of discovery, as though a priest might surmise her terrible secret by the look in her eyes alone.

Her fear extended beyond the basilica to society at large. Though she appeared whole to everyone who saw her, she bore the knowledge that she was unacceptable, alive in this life only as long as she could keep her secret...and even then, living only toward an inevitable end. Order rejected her. And Order was the Maker's hand. There would be no Bliss for her.

It had robbed her of her own betrothal. Marriage, for her, would be impossible. Her own husband would be bound by the Honor

Code to report her the moment he saw her defect. And so she had rejected her own betrothal without explanation to her parents.

He hurried to stop her. "Avra! If you run now they'll find you for sure. Both of us!"

She halted, shaking. He went to her, pulled the edge of her cloak up over her scarred skin, gently covering it. She tugged the fabric close around her neck with pale fingers. By the time he drew her back toward the chair, she had gotten hold of herself.

He had to think. They were losing precious time.

Rom crossed to the box and opened it. There had to be more. What had the vellum said? *Blood destroys or grants the power to live.* It had certainly destroyed. He had witnessed that firsthand, hadn't he? But what did it mean, *to live*?

A rustle sounded from behind him. "That's it?"

"That's it." He lifted out the vial, unwrapped it carefully, and set the ancient glass container down on top of the table. He smoothed the vellum open next to it. "See?"

She came to stand beside him. "What does it say?"

Rom read the verse aloud, straining to see in the dim light.

> *"The Order of Keepers has sworn to guard*
> *These contents for the Day of Rebirth*
> *Beware, any who drink—*
> *Blood destroys or grants the power to live"*

She pressed against his shoulder. "*Day of Rebirth.* What Rebirth? The inauguration?"

"I don't know. It doesn't sound like it."

"*Beware, any who drink*—drink what?"

"*Blood destroys or grants the power to live.* Just looking at this, I'm guessing it means the blood."

"That can't be. You don't drink blood."

"But that's what it says. *Beware, any who drink.*"

"Yes. *Beware*. As in don't. It must be poisonous."

"They wouldn't have killed the old man for owning poison. People buy it all the time to kill rodents."

She poked her finger at the words. "*Blood destroys*. It's poisonous or diseased."

"Then what does it mean, *or grants the power to live?*"

"It's just religious speak."

He laid down the vellum. Avra picked it up, her lips moving as she reread the lines of the only legible paragraph.

Rom lifted the vial, held it to the candlelight. He had recoiled from it the first time. Now he watched the way it clung to the inside of the old glass. The liquid was so dark that it only hinted at the deepest shade of red in the candelabra's meager light.

Drink blood? Unthinkable, yes.

But murder had been unthinkable to him just hours earlier. Life without his mother had been unthinkable. Running from authority. All unthinkable.

And all had become reality.

He tried to turn the metal seal. It didn't budge. He twisted harder.

"What are you doing?"

The seal gave way with a metallic scrape.

"I just want to smell it."

"Don't!"

He twisted and pulled. The vial opened with a swift gasp, as though drawing breath for the first time in centuries.

He sniffed it. Metal and salt. Grave danger and life.

He knew what he was thinking before he logically reasoned it out.

So did Avra. "Rom! Don't!"

He tipped it up to his lips. He took a small sip. Made a face. A stale, metallic taste filled his mouth.

"Well, it's definitely blood."

"You're crazy! Put it back!"

He held the vial up to the candlelight, noted the first measure line of the vial. Enough for five.

"Do you have a better option?"

"Yes! Not drinking poison!"

He shook his head. "I don't think it's poison. But if I'm wrong, leave the vial with my body and go somewhere safe until they find me."

He turned, lifted the bottle to his lips, and threw back one mouthful—enough to take the volume down to the first measure.

Avra watched him, aghast.

He had to force himself to swallow. The stuff was foul. More than stale. Bitter. He wondered for an eerie moment if Avra was right about its being poison after all.

He recapped the vial and waited. Nothing. He turned back to her, held out his hands.

"You're a reckless fool!" Avra said, the color drained from her face.

"Maybe." He set the vial back in the box. "But now we know what—"

A force struck him like a steel beam to the gut. He dropped to one knee, grabbed at the table. Missed.

"Rom!"

Fire burned through his veins. He collapsed on the floor and curled up, clawing at his belly. By the time he began convulsing, he was only vaguely aware of Avra kneeling next to him. His legs kicked out at the stack of chairs. One of them crashed down onto the floor almost on top of them both.

She was right. It was poison.

Fear flooded his world and turned it black.

Chapter Six

THE HEELS of Saric's boots echoed sharply as hammer-falls along the upper corridor that led to the Residence of the Office. The passage was lined by the busts of past Sovereigns and draped by velvet and silk gold-threaded tapestries—gifts upon the occasion of Vorrin's inauguration nearly forty years prior. Saric had never noticed until today just how dusty and threadbare they had become.

Their replacements had already begun to arrive in the Citadel's large receiving yard. Crates of gifts, the favors of nations and the leaders that led them, reminders of the world beyond this one…the token presence of the nations and the one billion souls that populated them.

The vaulted ceilings of the atrium, painted gold centuries before, shone down with false sun, their cracks and peeling testament to the ancient age of this capitol that endured history and looked toward the future at once.

Two of the elite guard openly watched Saric as he approached the outer chamber.

"School your gaze," Saric snapped as he passed, despising the peevish sound of his own voice as he said it. It was the poison—the poison pulsing through his veins. It had tested his resolve to retain a sensible composure since he'd first been filled with it and its dark offspring: passion, ambition, lust, greed.

Anger.

He could hardly sleep for the wars they waged in his mind. He relished and loathed them at once.

But he had no intention of betraying himself.

He curled his fingers to still their trembling. The right cuff of his silk shirt had pulled away from his wrist and he could see clearly the veins beneath, so dark now that they seemed black. They were beautiful, he had decided. Still, he kept the neckline and high collar of his robe carefully fastened so that the edge of it brushed his jaw.

He walked past the desk of the secretary and strode to the double bronze doors beyond. Twelve feet tall, as thick as a wall, they were emblazoned with the symbols of the offices of the seven continental houses. On the right, the alchemists of Russe, the educators of Asiana, the architects of Qin, the environmentalists of Nova Albion. On the left, the bankers of Abyssinia, the priests of Greater Europa, and the artisans of Sumeria. The great compass, symbol of the Sovereign office, was framed in the upper-middle panel. Its graded points were the same as those etched upon Sirin's halo.

Sirin…Megas…Order. But Saric knew that nothing was as it had once seemed. Even the great doors of this office no longer shut him out as they once had. Rather, they beckoned him in.

He laid his hand against the compass, fingers outstretched, and pushed his way inside.

Vorrin stood before the full window, his back to the room. Rowan, the senate leader, stood near him as always. The man was never more than three steps away.

Lapdog.

The heads of both men turned. Saric went to his knee, the long hem of his robe collapsing on the lush Abyssinian rug. His own apartments contained nothing so rich as this floor covering. He must rectify that.

Vorrin did not acknowledge him right away. After several moments, Saric glanced up.

Rowan was studying him too frankly for Saric's tastes.

Finally, Vorrin spoke from across the room, his gaze fixed somewhere outside the window. "Son."

Saric rose and went to join him. It was the first time he had attended to his father in weeks. As Vorrin turned to face him, he was surprised by the image.

Though the Sovereign wore the deep purple mantle of his office, Saric had never seen his father look quite so old. The flesh of his hands, of his neck, and even of his face seemed sunken against the bone. Veins and sinew showed through skin thinned with age. Liver spots dotted the backs of his hands and the sides of his high, shaven cheeks. His gray hair was combed back and gathered at his nape, but it had thinned so much that portions of his scalp showed through.

Though he stood four inches taller than his son at a stately six-foot-seven, he seemed to Saric dried as a husk.

Saric, by contrast, had never been more aware of the vitality in his own veins. He had never felt so strong, so absolutely virile. Next to his father's ghostly gray skin, his own was the color of pale marble—beautiful by every standard.

Saric leaned in and touched his lips to the papery skin of Vorrin's cheek. The act disgusted him. At this close vantage, the faint light through the immense windows only highlighted the translucent fragility of the wrinkles along Vorrin's mouth, the spidery purple veins beneath his eyes.

The man appeared dead.

How had he never noticed his father's frail state? How was it that Vorrin had always seemed as virile as a man thirty years younger, as charismatic as a god to him, until today?

Vorrin regarded him as dispassionately as ever before returning his gaze to the city beyond the window. "I have asked Rowan to issue the court's decision on your request."

"Thank you, Father." Saric's heart accelerated. He turned to face the senate leader. "Well?"

Rowan, in contrast with the Sovereign, never seemed to age. His smooth, dusky skin and small ears, the opacity of his eyes and lean stature, even the way he tied his hair back at his nape, all seemed to lend him the sleekness of a cat.

"We have reviewed your request to fill the senate leader's seat upon the inauguration of your sister and find it unconstitutional. The Order decrees that your sister—ordained by the Order and by birth closest to one of three eligible birth cycles during the reign of our current Sovereign—shall elect her own senate leader from among continental prelates past and present, or the house overseers, past and elect, to serve on her behalf and at her leisure in all matters of Order public, private, political, and religious. As you are neither prelate nor overseer, nor have ever been, you are strictly...ineligible."

Saric's vision clouded, but he maintained his composure and looked away. Pravus had anticipated this. They both had. And yet, hearing it roused his ire.

"And the fact that you were prelate for a mere nine days before your own appointment qualifies you for this post above me, the son of the Sovereign?" he demanded.

Rowan didn't rise to the insult. "I quote the book," he said. "'And so these successions are prescribed, that no man should proclaim himself, and no man should endanger his fellow or himself for the sake of attainment or gain. And so no man need aspire beyond his state, or fear the loss of his place in this world. The Maker has made it as it should be. All is well beneath the Maker.'"

"All is well beneath the Maker," Vorrin said softly. Saric, too, intoned the words, his gaze coming to settle at the hollow of Rowan's throat.

"Thank you, Rowan," Vorrin said. He sounded weary, his voice slightly warbled with age and the decades of demands put upon it. The hourly audiences. The speeches made from the great balcony, the privy meetings in his council chamber. The hearings in the senate.

Too used, so worn. He should have been removed years ago.

Rowan bowed his head, his hands folded before him, backed up three steps, and left by the inconspicuous side door.

Saric said, "Father—"

"It is a fair evening, one of too few," Vorrin said, as though he had not heard. He sounded tired. "Will you walk outside with me, my son?"

Impatience snapped inside Saric like the jaws of a great reptile. But he gave a tight nod and followed his father past the cushioned seats where prelates and heads of geopolitical houses had sat too many times to be counted these last forty years, past the giant desk with its claw feet and stone top, where so many acts of the senate were signed into existence as though by will of the Maker himself.

They walked out onto the balcony that wrapped around the corner of the chamber office. The long, columned portico that led to the senate ran directly below, so that every senator, on his way to the Senate Hall, might pass beneath the blessing of the Sovereign. Megas, it was said, had designed this building for that reason, so that he might look out at them, and they might go into their assembly with the face of their Sovereign foremost in their mind.

Vorrin looked up at the clouds, luminescent where they obscured the moon. "Perhaps when your sister's inauguration is complete, we will stand on a night such as this and talk of small matters. And Feyn will be the one to carry our fears on her shoulders, to take them with her to her bed in the evening, to rise to pace in the middle of the night. And Rowan will either be relieved to walk the porticoes as a senator himself or shall serve as senate leader at her leisure, as he has at mine."

Saric turned to grasp the balcony's railing. Beneath his cloak, his wet shirt clung to the muscles of his back. "It's all well for you, and for Feyn, and even for Rowan. But what of me?"

Vorrin turned his clouded blue eyes on his son. "You? You will reside here, with her, and with me. She will have need of your loyalty then."

"Loyalty. A dog is loyal." He couldn't suppress the tension in his voice. "Tell me: How should my loyalty serve her? What of my intellect, my charisma, my vision—what of them? Should they go to waste in *loyalty* to my sister?"

"Of course not. That is not waste, my son," Vorrin said, oblivious to Saric's churning emotions. "The continents look to this family as they have for forty years and, by the grace of the Maker, will for forty more. You are the face of the passing Sovereign's son, and the new Sovereign's brother. You and your wife, Portia, are examples of Order to all the world. Of the purity and peace of our system. Of every blessing. My son..."

He reached out and touched Saric's cheek.

Saric pulled away from the repulsive, papery touch.

Vorrin looked down at the thin pads of his fingers and rubbed them together. "You are sweating. Are you ill?"

"I am not ill. In fact, I am very, very well. So tell me, old man, where is the justice in power passing from my father to my younger sister, and skipping me altogether?"

Vorrin blinked. "My son, I don't understand."

Saric took a deep breath and pushed down his rage. "Forgive me, I'm tired." He stepped close again and took his father's cold, gray hand in his own. "Only listen to me. There can still be justice in the Order, Father. I beg you, in these last days before your office passes to Feyn, grant this small request to me. I've never asked you for anything. I'll never ask for anything again." The bones of his father's hand felt very thin.

"What are you saying? What is it you ask?" Vorrin tried to draw his hand away, but Saric held it tight, squeezing it.

"I cannot lead the senate. It was wrong of me to ask. I will seek Rowan's forgiveness and praise his judiciary responsibility in this matter. I will go tell him so myself. But you can rightfully step down from power."

"But—why would I do that?" The skin around his neck shook a little when he said it.

"Because I am your son. And you would do it as a gift to me. You have had forty years. Feyn will have forty. Let me have five days. A pittance! Days to taste what my father has shouldered and what my sister will as well, so that I will know the true extent of her burden and her privilege. And so much greater will my *loyalty* be."

"But I…" The old man was too shocked to respond. Too weak to understand.

"The law is clear," Saric continued. "If any Sovereign should step down, his eldest child will finish the term. And I should tell you, Father, that I am concerned by the frailness of your hand, and by the thinness of your skin." He squeezed the old man's hand even tighter, idly wondering if at any moment he might feel one of the bones within it pop.

"I see it, you grow feeble. No one else sees it. They don't want to. They see what they've been told to see: their Sovereign. But I, I see truly."

Saric finally let go. The old man staggered backward.

"What you ask is impossible! Utterly outside the Order. Outside the book."

"Damnation to the book!" Saric exploded.

Vorrin stared at him.

"What I'm saying, Father," Saric said, more levelly, "is that it's my duty to report the feebleness in you. That I can *smell* the decay in your cells. Of your own volition, you must step down. The Honor Code demands you turn yourself—"

A gust passed through the chamber, seeming to pull the air from the balcony where they stood. Inside, the heavy doors had opened.

They turned as one, father and son. And Saric saw then that the newcomer entering the room had drawn the very wind to herself. She had this effect, galvanizing the air so that all things must go to her like a magnet.

His sister, soon to be Sovereign.

Feyn.

She walked to the center of the room. The dark hair falling down her back curled in the breeze of the open balcony as though it were a living thing. Her long hands were folded before her, pale against the deep blue of her robe. Her pale eyes, so very like ice, scanned the room, lighting at last on the balcony's open doors, her father...

And him.

Although she went to her knee, there was no mistaking it: She commanded the room.

Feyn dipped her head. "Father."

Saric did not remember stepping inside.

"Ah, my daughter." Vorrin went to her and laid a hand against her cheek. Feyn took it, seeming not to notice his weakness. She turned it and kissed his palm.

What Saric wouldn't do to have that show of esteem from her. No, to give it to her. His father had it right: The world would call itself blessed to bow before such a creature. Did she have any idea the raw power she wielded? The whole Citadel would be a shrine to her.

Saric drew in a ragged breath, lost to jealousy, yet feeling wholly unworthy at once. His new self felt nonplussed, undone in her presence.

Especially when she turned from her father to him.

"Feyn," he said, his voice too unsteady for his own liking.

She crossed to him. "Brother." She kissed him.

He closed his eyes and endured it before saying, "If you'll excuse me, I have some business I must attend to."

He backed three steps from the dispassionate eyes of his sister before he turned, pushed open the heavy bronze door, and strode quickly out. He stormed from the grand foyer to his personal chambers, heavy with desire, barely able to think straight. The poison slid through his veins like a snake, straining to be fed or be set free.

Breathing hard, outraged by his weakness in the face of his own sister, he crashed into his dining room, lit only by two candelabras, each with half a dozen candles. He had taken only two steps toward his bedchamber when he saw a form on the floor to his right.

Portia. She stared up at the ceiling, panting, eyes bloodshot and wide.

She'd managed to escape the bed restraints he'd used after injecting her with the serum not an hour earlier.

The servants were all gone. No one to hear her cries or see her pain.

Saric walked past the table and looked down at his tortured wife. Her back arched, her breath came in the feral bursts of an animal. She had never looked so beautiful to him, ever.

He lowered himself to one knee, then leaned over and kissed her mouth, tasting the blood where she had bitten her own tongue.

Her turning, if she survived it, would take some time. Several hours at least. Perhaps all night.

Far too long for him to sit idly by.

Chapter Seven

FOR SEVERAL horrifying minutes Avra tried to shake and prod Rom back to consciousness. He had gone still as one dead, but he was still breathing. As long as he did, she could keep herself together.

But he could not die. He must not die. For years now she had dreaded the void that would swallow her when Rom finally married Lydia, to whom he had been promised years ago. But that fear paled beside the prospect of seeing Rom die now.

If he did, the probability of her own death would become a stark and unbearable reality. She was no match for the Citadel Guard that were probably surrounding the basilica even now. She had nowhere to go. And while Rom had been diligent to the Order all his life—until just recently, at least—the very fact that she breathed marked her disobedience and coming condemnation. Though she would never be ready to submit to that fate, she was definitely not ready now.

"Rom!" She shook him again.

He had convulsed before blacking out, but now he lay limp and she wasn't sure which was worse, the convulsions or this terrible stillness. His mouth was open and his breathing was fast and ragged, as though he was captive to a nightmare.

But the true nightmare was hers. This morning, her greatest concern had been completing the massive volume of laundry at her father's business. Tonight she faced Hades.

In the face of such horror, she redoubled her efforts. Jaw fixed with fear, she slapped his cheek.

"Don't you leave me, Rom!" She shook him by the shoulders again, not caring that his head banged on the floor. She had to wake him so that he could throw this poison up and out of his stomach.

"Rom, wake up!"

But no effort had the slightest effect on him. He was beyond her help. And that meant she was beyond his.

Avra got up and began to pace, nibbling the corner of her index finger nail. Trying to think.

She could leave him here and go back home.

No, the guard might already be there, waiting for her return.

She could try to find a better hiding place for them both, away from anyplace associated with either of them, on the outskirts of town, perhaps, or in one of the city drains. But that was an absurd thought. How was she supposed to lug his weight out of this place? And what were they supposed to live on, rats?

Water. She should find some water and pour it on him. Maybe if it was cold enough...But if he wasn't waking at her slapping and shaking him, what good would water do?

The minutes ran into an hour, and Rom still did not budge.

Exhaustion edged into her consciousness, and she slumped to her seat in the corner, but she had no inclination to sleep. She had to keep an ear out for approaching guardsmen. Then again, if the guard did find them in this storeroom, neither she nor Rom would stand a chance of survival. The guard had knives, Rom had said. They'd cut Anna's throat.

And if they had done that to Anna, what might they do to her? She imagined them rushing in, finding her helpless, tearing off her tunic and exposing her scars. Falling on her with their knives.

Cutting her. Carving out that entire imperfection until she begged them to kill her.

She covered her face with her hands.

And Rom would be unconscious through it all. How she wished she were the one sleeping while he stood guard! He had always somehow played her protector. Yet there he lay, lost to whatever visions played behind his closed eyes.

She dropped her hands, gazed at his prone and helpless body. At least he wasn't dead!

The thought took her off guard. He wasn't dead. Not that she had established that he wouldn't die, but after she'd watched him unconscious all this time and he didn't get worse, she now could assume that the blood was not poison after all.

She had no clue what it did, but it apparently wasn't killing him.

She glanced at the vial of blood, then at the door. She should go now, out of this hated basilica, out of this room, away from this madness. They would come for him and she might never see him again, but it would be the right thing to do. If they were satisfied in finding the vial with him, maybe it would even save her life.

Perhaps doing the right thing would also atone in some small way for her absence in basilica all these years. For the defect of her scarring. For her very presence among the living.

And what is death? the priests had asked in the liturgy of the last assembly she ever attended. *Death is the gateway to eternal fear or the path to Bliss.*

But the only order she knew was the rhythm of her life and Rom's calming role in it. She wasn't sure she could exist without Rom. Truly, to turn Rom over to the guards was to invite a new kind of death.

The stalemate drained her to the bone.

She let her head fall back against the wall. Her gaze fell on the open box cradling that fearful vial, and the vellum lying next to it.

CHAPTER EIGHT

SHADOWS AND voyeuristic specters played among the folds of the bed curtains, peering through the fine Abyssinian linen, untouched by the dawn. A torch flickered on the wall nearby. Its shadows writhed all the way to the corner.

All night, demons had chased her, each of them wearing the face of her husband, following her with the eyes of a killer.

Portia, faithful wife of Saric, lay in their bed feeling acutely ill. She turned onto her side and for a moment thought she might vomit.

Her skin was sticky, the sheets still damp with her sweat. They smelled rank to her.

All around her, the chamber appeared as it did every morning. But something was wrong. Something that sent a shaft of fear shooting down her spine.

She jerked up onto her elbow, shoved the sheet off her bare torso, and looked around the room. Beyond the bed, heavy silks lined the great stone walls. The bedchamber was richly appointed in every way—from the cedar wardrobe against the far wall, to the floor-length velvet curtains and soft silk carpet. It was also filthy with the smoke of the torches, with the smell of fire and the remains of an undercooked dinner brought in from the adjacent dining room sometime during the night.

She could smell the meat and blood, acrid in her nostrils.

There was something else filthy in here, too.

Portia glanced to her left. There, at her side, sprawled Saric, the finely threaded sheets pushed away from the muscled panes of his chest. Fresh nail marks scored his shoulder.

Beyond the bed, a woman, whoever she was, lay on the floor with her back to them. Her skin, once no doubt beautifully smooth, was marred now with bruises, black beneath the otherwise pallid skin of her arms and legs.

Saric and his latest concubine. Saric and his of-late voracious appetites.

And she—she had writhed in violent throes of her own, screaming for wholly different reasons. Her face hurt. Her entire body hurt. Her heart pounded against her chest and her mind felt as though it might be on fire.

She reached up and traced the line of a welt against her face. There was blood under her nails.

She slid from the bed. Neither Saric nor the concubine stirred. She moved across the carpet. Somewhere beyond the heavy velvet curtains—no one had troubled to draw them last night—morning had the audacity to approach the window and peer in at the evidence of a life she no longer recognized.

She paused before the great mirror in the corner and surveyed her body—the bruises, the welts, the scratches. Confusion racked her mind, fogged her memories. She wasn't sure what Saric had done to her, but she knew this much: He'd given her something virulent and poisonous, and it was consuming her.

She examined the mottled darkness of a bruise along her thigh, then vaguely remembered running into something after leaping from the bed, screaming for help. Saric had laughed at her.

Portia lifted a finger to her chin, following the line of a scratch that would bear the seam of a scab by evening. A new kind of fear more blistering than any sentiment she'd ever felt flushed her face.

She lashed out at the mirror. The glass yielded to her fist with a shattering crash.

From behind her: "Good morning, dear."

She cried out and spun, startled. Saric slid from the sheets without a glance at the form on the floor. He was lean-hipped and well muscled, built like a bronze statue draped in a loose, black robe. The image of him immediately pulled at her.

Had he ever been so alluring? Strange warmth flooded her belly. Was this, too, the work of the poison?

Blood dripped from her fingers onto the carpet. But the pain from the gashes along her knuckles paled next to the wonder of this new desire that rose up within her.

Saric crossed to her, lifted her wounded hand, and studied it for an instant before bringing her knuckles to his lips.

She tried to jerk her hand away but he would not let it go. He pulled her against him.

"I said, *Good morning*." He kissed her mouth long and hard, smearing her lips with blood.

She was nearly out of breath when she managed to pull away. "I want to know what you did to me!"

"You don't like it?"

"I spent a whole night screaming in pain!"

"That will pass."

"You will tell me what it is."

He pushed her away from him. "Don't be tiresome."

"Tell me!" she railed, reveling in the sound of her raised voice. The woman on the floor stirred and whimpered.

The sound struck her as deeply offensive. Sickening. Portia strode across the room, grabbed the drugged woman by the hair, and dragged her toward Saric.

"Portia," Saric said in warning.

She abruptly released the woman's hair and let her head bang onto the floor. The concubine's nose was covered with crusted blood, and one of her eyes was blackened. The mere sight of her filled Portia with rage.

"How dare you bring another woman into our room!"

"This is unbecoming." Saric settled onto one of the sofas. He lifted one of the leftover goblets and took a sip from it.

The crumpled heap of the woman moaned and grasped at Portia's foot. She kicked the concubine away.

"Tell me what you did to me."

Saric contemplated the goblet. "You, along with all of humanity, have been subject to a pathogen named Legion, which altered your genetic code. It dulled you to all emotions but fear. I have now remedied that."

"What are you talking about?"

"Are you deaf? I've fixed you. Show some appreciation."

"Legion? Remedy?" She stormed across the room. "You know what I think? That you're killing me."

"At least you feel." Saric drew a slow, steely breath. "I couldn't stand another day of watching you waft around like a ghost, though I think I may come to regret that decision."

"Look at me—I'm dying!"

"You'll die a whole woman, at least."

"Where did you get it? Where did it come from?"

"From the alchemists. At Pravus's bidding."

She blinked. "Pravus?"

He set down the goblet. "There's a serum rumored to be even more powerful—a blood remnant from Chaos kept all these centuries by a clandestine group called the Order of Keepers. Soon I will have it, too."

Her head hurt. It throbbed. Her blood pounded in every part of her body—in her ears, in her temples, in her fingers.

"To what end?"

"To possess power, of course. Can you not think of these things for yourself?"

"Power over what?"

A smile nudged his lips. "Over everything."

The same mad desire now coursing through her veins, she realized, had taken her husband's mind as well.

"Everything? Have you lost your mind? Your sister will be the one ruling the world in a short number of days. *You* will bow the knee to *her*."

In one swift movement he stood and struck Portia with enough force to snap her head to the side and send her staggering.

He was shaking, his eyes glassy and fixed. "She will give me charge of the senate by the time she takes the oath."

Portia lifted a hand to her cheek. "The senate? And you suppose that will give you the power you need?"

"No. We'll need an army to do that."

An army? It took her a moment to dredge the meaning of the word from the murk of history. She shuddered. Courting the very notion was treason and cause for a swift execution. The world hadn't seen an army for centuries. It was unfathomable.

"How do you propose to raise an army?"

"Put on some clothes." He plucked up a silk robe and tossed it at her. It wasn't even hers. "Get control of yourself."

She slipped her arms through the wide sleeves of the silk. It smelled like sweat, like everything in this rotting chamber did.

"I'll get control of myself when you remove that filth from here." She glanced across the room to the bed, where the woman, her blond hair a tangled mess, had crawled.

"What do you care about a concubine?" Saric demanded.

She went to him then and pressed up against him. "Get rid of her."

He tilted his head. "What do you suggest?"

She slid behind him. "I suggest you slit her throat," she whispered against his ear, her gaze sliding to the bed. "Feed her to the dogs. To please me."

He turned slowly, took her chin firmly between his thumb and forefinger, and lifted her face, kissing her deeply.

Suddenly he released her, reached for the steak knife on the table, strode across the room to the bed, and unceremoniously grabbed the woman by the hair.

"Take note," he said, eyes on his wife. "That I kill whom I wish, when I wish. And that I do it to please myself." He sliced open the girl's neck.

Portia did not miss the way he watched the woman bleed out on the bed, the way the muscles twitched along his jaw.

The cold shaft of fear surged up her spine again.

But all she said was, "Now you've ruined the sheets."

CHAPTER NINE

ROM'S EYES opened. For a moment he was aware only of the peeling plaster on the ceiling above. He could not place its location, could not remember falling asleep under it, had no idea where he was.

He realized he was breathing hard, that his fingers and face were prickling as though they had just regained circulation. That his head was throbbing.

He blinked, following a crack in the ceiling plaster with an unfocused gaze. Was he drugged?

The events of the night crashed into memory like the falling shards of a broken window.

He wasn't drugged.

He'd ingested the blood.

Other details slammed into place. The old man. His father. Avra.

He sat up—too quickly—and the room tipped around him. His heart crashed against the cage of his ribs, hard enough to make him wonder again if the blood had indeed been a poison. One even now about to burst his arteries.

Something wasn't right. He felt as if he dangled on a narrow precipice between life and death, buoyant and terrified at once. The space was darker than he remembered; only one of the seven candles still burned on the candelabra. Shadows crept from the room's edges, sliding with the flicker of the candle along the coffin against the wall.

Coffin. Basilica. For a moment he wondered if he was dying. If the oddities attacking his mind were the onset of Bliss or something horrific.

He stood, managed to get one foot under himself, then lurched to one side and planted his face in the ground. Pain flashed out from his chin, the impact having jarred his brains.

He pushed himself up to his knees and unsteadily looked around. This was the storeroom he'd escaped to, with its stacks of chairs and candelabras-in-waiting. He was not dead, but painfully alive.

Still, he couldn't pretend something wasn't wrong with his head. Not merely off kilter, but terribly misaligned. He couldn't seem to make complete sense of his surroundings.

It had to be the darkness. The horrid shadows.

Rom staggered to his feet, arms out for balance.

The gloom struck his senses like hot tar. It crowded his nostrils and filled his lungs, forcing him to pull hard for breath. But when he did, he sucked in not air but terror—terror and darkness.

For several seconds, Rom stood with his feet planted and his knees bent, trying to breathe. *Dear Maker, help me. I'm dying, help me!* But his dread only swelled.

He jerked his head around, seeking escape. There, to his left, burned the sole source of light: a candle with a low, flickering flame.

Fire. A feline eye winking on the head of a taper.

He blinked, and the finger of flame crooked and beckoned. His fear immediately abated, tempered by a new sensation that stroked at the back of his mind.

He lowered his arms and breathed more easily, captivated by the sight. Had he ever seen such a wondrous thing? How did that effusive glow work? How could something so small and so devoid of substance banish all that was evil?

Around him the darkness breathed as though alive, and yet before him a single flame no more than half the length of his smallest finger called him to wonder.

Tears filled his eyes. Warmth spread down his arms and back. It was beautiful! He stumbled forward and stopped in front of the candle, unable to tear his gaze away.

"Maker," he whispered, his tongue dry inside his mouth. Emotion choked him. "So beautiful."

From the corner of his eye he saw the shadows coiling behind the coffin. Was that possible? The blood worked its power like a drug.

He returned his gaze to the flame. The world had changed before his eyes, and this tongue of light was a work of magic. Rom drew his finger through its lithe body and marveled at its heat against his skin. How had he ever taken such a thing for granted?

He didn't know how long he stayed like that. By the time he straightened, the candle was hardly more than a pool of wax. In another few minutes, it would swallow the flame whole and darkness would smother him.

He followed the dying glow toward a stack of chairs and the wall, to the ebbing ring of light on the floor...

And the form curled in the corner.

There lay Avra, sleeping on her side. Her tiny body peaceful, rising and falling with each breath. Her head rested on her arm, turned toward him with eyes closed, oblivious to his crazed behavior.

Avra.

He couldn't move. The sight of her lying there overwhelmed him.

She was an angel. An angel in his poison-induced dream. His heart filled with strange sensation. He longed for her. For her to be with him.

Rom moved toward her, stilling his breath, daring not to make a sound. He stood over her, stunned. She was beautiful. He spoke her name softly, afraid to disturb her.

"Avra."

The name brought a quiver to his lips. This was Avra, but not Avra. The poison had stolen the former Avra away and replaced her with another woman.

He sank to one knee and touched a strand of her hair. The two women looked identical, but this one was far more beautiful. No, magical. An angel, a goddess, the wildest figment of his soaring imagination.

Desire lapped at his heart. Not a simple wish to have her, but a craving to envelop her, to absorb her completely. A yearning to serve her, if she would only allow him, because such a creature deserved nothing less. She was magnificent.

He wanted to hold her and to kiss her, but he dared not! His fingers trembled, and the strand of her hair with them. And yet this was no angel, but a woman fashioned of flesh and blood.

Avra.

Something stirred in his mind, rousing itself from a gust into a full-blown gale. A door within him blew wide to a new reality. One in which he adored Avra. It was a worship beyond the currency of loyalty he had once called *love*—the same love he had claimed to have for his mother.

The memory of his mother lying in a pool of her own blood crashed into his mind and he dropped the strand of hair. The force of the sensation that struck him shoved him back on his heels.

His mother was dead?

Rom leaped to his feet, spun toward the door, and tore out of the storage room. One thought alone pushed him up the stairs, three at a time. One fear, one concern, one horrible, debilitating thought.

His mother was dead.

Not until he reached the street did he pull up, and then only because he realized that he'd left Avra.

Avra, whom he worshipped.

He stood under the dim streetlights, lost, torn, but then he reasoned that Avra was asleep and at peace. And he…he had to find out if his mother was truly dead or if there was even the slightest possibility of saving her. He would go and return to Avra before she awoke.

Rom bent over and sprinted into the gray drizzle.

It took him less than thirty minutes to reach his house by way of the underground and a direct route through night-emptied streets. He knew that he ran the risk of being caught, especially if they had posted a guard at his house. But the new emotions churning inside him pushed aside all reason and demanded he throw his own safety to the gutter. He had to see his mother. He had to be sure that there was no way he could save her. Nothing else mattered.

He could not understand the overpowering impulse and the pain that had captured him, but it didn't matter. He was its slave. It was all he could do to hide his tears from the few late-night passengers riding on the underground.

When he arrived, his heart stuttered. The back door to his house gaped ajar in the moonlight.

But that was good, right? If the authorities had completed their work here, they would have buttoned down the house. Sealed it off.

On the other hand, if his mother were alive and able to move around, she would have closed the door. But he already knew the notion of her survival to be the desperate fantasy of a despairing son.

He'd known it as he stood on the train, watching the banks of lights blink by. He'd known with every step that his mission to save what was lost would only crush him. But what was possible or practical had been replaced by a far baser impulse.

Hope.

Glancing around for any sign that the house was being watched, he hurried up to the door. No sound from the inside. The lamp in the kitchen was still lit.

He pushed the door gently open and peered through its widening gap. The kitchen came into view. The entrance to the dining room was empty.

His heart surged. He nudged the door wider and stepped quietly in. Black and white kitchen tiles...

Blood.

There was his mother.

Rom stared at her crumpled form, robbed of life. He saw it all again: the guard slicing her throat, the way her eyes rolled back in her head, her body collapsing.

Staring at her, he relived those brutal moments as if they were happening in front of him again with ruthless precision. Death had always occupied the same space as fear, but now something far uglier than fear uncoiled its serpentine shape from a pit deep inside him, rising through his throat like a dragon, eyes red and fangs bared.

The emotion was so foreign to him that his stomach convulsed at its full acquaintance. He could not move. He could only stand there trembling from head to foot, dry heaving but unable even to bend over to retch.

His first thought was that he'd been cut down with his mother and was even now bleeding to death on the kitchen floor.

His second thought was that a blade had not brought his death. The poison in the vial was killing him.

That dragon that reared its head began to bleed, filling his lungs and throat with suffocating terror.

He stumbled forward under the weight of a pain so great he couldn't bear up. He fell to the ground over her body, dug his fingers into her shoulders and sobbed, haltingly at first, and then with great gasps and groans.

He knew then that he had found his way into Hades. Chaos was swallowing him. He'd ingested the forbidden blood and awakened all that was unholy to devour him. In long, unrelenting groans, Rom mourned his mother's death.

What had he done? *He'd* brought death to her! Her skin was cold and lifeless because of *him*! He'd made a crack in the ground and freed evil. His mother had died, but it was now *he* who felt that death in a way that she, loyal to the Order, never could have.

Her peaceful face filled his mind, so stoic and reserved, so slow to alarm and fright. How many times had she hovered over him when he'd skinned his knees or awoken with tremors in fear of death? She was there in his memory, preparing meals every morning and evening so that he would grow strong. Tucking him into a warm bed at night and chasing his fears away with calm and wise words.

Now she lay in a pool of her own blood. Waves of despair gurgled up from that black pit and washed him with revulsion. The fear he'd felt as a boy under her loving care paled next to the dark pain sucking him down.

He could still taste the acidic curse of the blood he'd ingested, and with each sob he cursed his impulse to place that foul poison to his lips. He would embrace his mother's fate over his own horror now.

For a moment he considered ending his own life. If this plague had once afflicted mankind, then humanity had survived only by eradicating its traces. And now he had reversed that Order and invited a living death to consume him.

What have I done? What madness has tempted me to subvert the truth that held all things in perfect peace?

The last moorings tethering his mind to any semblance of reason fell away. The dragon's jaws snapped wide, thrust its head forward, and roared with rage.

Rom jerked his head up from his mother's body and screamed in a full-throated panic, eyes clenched. But the terror only intensified.

His mind blackened. He surged to his feet and lurched forward. Tripped over his mother's body. Slammed into the table, grabbed a chair to keep himself upright and, snarling, shattered it on the floor.

But none of this registered as more than the desperate flailing of a man in the jaws of death. He was vaguely aware that his cries would be heard by any passerby at this early hour, but he didn't seem to be able to control either his pain or his reaction to it. Death was raking its claws along his bones without regard for such meaningless concerns as orderly quiet.

He gripped his hair with both hands hard enough to bring pain to his scalp, then dropped his head against the wall and wept. It was all pointless. Hopeless. What was done, was done.

And there...His mother's form lay unmoved by his violent protests.

Rom stepped to her, sank to his knees, and lowered his arms around her lifeless body, sobbing.

He wasn't sure how long he clutched her, but in the folds of that anguish he understood something new. There was Chaos in his veins. These awakened emotions could only be the worst of diseases. He had taken the blood and it had somehow reverted him to a state of ghoulish darkness. It was why the Order had gone to such lengths to protect humanity from the vial of blood.

He loved his mother in his new and rending way. He wept, bereft, sure the human heart could not survive such brokenness for long.

But even as he thought about the horror of life in this new hellish prison of sorrow, another thought edged into his mind.

Avra.

He'd left the vial in the same room with Avra. What if, finding him gone, she drank the blood?

The thought propelled him off the floor. He had to get back to Avra! But he couldn't leave his mother like this.

In nightmarish stupor, Rom wiped the blood from his mother's wounds and carried her body to her bed. He placed her under the covers and pulled the tangled strands of hair off her face so that she looked almost herself, asleep as on any night.

What are you doing, Rom? You have to get back!

He ran from her room, saw the mess of blood on the kitchen floor, and considered mopping it up, washing every trace of her death down the drain. Throwing open the windows to purge the stench of blood from their house. For a grisly moment he stood unmoving, trapped by his own pain.

But Avra's face hung in his mind, Avra, tipping the vial of poison to her mouth.

With a grunt of horror, he leaped over the blood, flew through the back door without bothering to secure it, and headed for the station in a brisk walk.

The sky had paled. The neighbors would discover her body and call the Authority of Passing. The thought of her in such a place terrified him, but he could think of no better way to honor her than to let her pass on to Bliss according to the Order that she had served.

It was now his duty to save Avra. Dear, sweet Avra, whom he loved and would die for if only to save her from this unholy death that had found him.

Avra...Avra, whom he loved more than life itself.

Rom broke into a run as fresh tears blurred his sight.

Chapter Ten

WHATEVER THE blood had done to him, Rom did not find a way to hide it before he reboarded the early-morning train. It was the extremes of emotion that plagued him most. He struggled one minute to suppress his terrible grief, then was overcome the next by a desperation to save Avra from anything similar. One moment he gripped his hands into fists in an effort to hold back tears; the next he murmured Avra's name like a prayer as he willed the train to go faster.

But he found new sense to his condition in his longing for Avra. He'd discovered a deep desire to protect her, yes, but now a profound love filled his heart with a warmth that felt less like pain and more like intoxication. Love, until now understood as nothing more than one's duty to remain loyal, now raged with emotion.

If Avra hadn't taken the blood, and he desperately hoped she had not, she would still possess a brain that could reason for him.

By the time he reached the basilica, his thoughts were torn. It was the swelling notions of benevolence and compassion directed at Avra that confused him the most. This wasn't the stuff of pain as much as desire and love. Surely, love. Was it possible that he was simply overreacting to his new state of mind? That he no longer possessed the ability to control such mad sentiments? That his heart was simply too weak to contain opposing emotions? Agony for his mother's death...love for Avra.

Perhaps, like a starving man, he would consume anything, anyone right now. And perhaps he would have wept at the passing of a sparrow.

No. He could not accept that. These feelings were far too real. A fresh onslaught of tears came to his eyes when he rushed down the steps to the storeroom where he'd left her.

He tried the door, found it unlocked, and peered inside.

The first thing he noticed was the light. All of the candles had been relit. There was no sign of the vial—he couldn't remember where he'd left it.

He jerked his eyes to the floor. Avra lay there, curled up, shaking. But no vial. Thank the Maker, no vial.

He quickly stepped in and closed the door. She made no move to indicate she'd heard him.

"Avra, I'm here."

He crossed the room in three strides, fell to his knees beside her, and pulled her into his arms. Her arms wrapped around him and he held her tighter.

"Shh, shh. I'm here."

She was tangled in her cloak and he could feel her shoulders shaking—not with tremors, but with sobs. Her hair fell over his arm, dangling toward the floor as he cradled her against his chest. Her mouth twisted with a soft cry. The sound of it, the sight of it, tore at his heart.

He tried to straighten her cloak, to pull it around her and over her shoulders. He cursed himself for leaving her alone to face her fear.

"Avra, don't cry. I'm here! I'm well. See?"

She had always been afraid, and with reason. But now the thought of her suffering roused in him something new and fierce, something so at home in his heart that he knew it belonged there— had perhaps always been there, waiting, slumbering, silent until now.

"Please don't cry." He drew her hair away from her face with a trembling hand. There was just enough light to see that her cheeks were scratched, that one of her lips had bled, that her eyes were swollen from weeping. How long had she been like this?

"Avra. I'm sorry. I'm so sorry." It was a phrase normally spoken from fear after a mistake, but now he felt something else. He felt regret.

He had never seen her like this, without her spine straight, shored up against whatever fear gripped her.

He laid his cheek against her head. She no longer smelled like soap and the clean-lint scent of the laundry, but like skin and the musk of sweat, like something sweet and heady. He turned his face into her hair, breathed deeply.

Sweet Maker. How had he never noticed it before?

He drew her hands away from her face again, kissed her eyes. He touched her lip where she had bitten it. But there was blood, too, at the corner of her mouth.

A chill crept over the back of his neck.

He glanced around the room.

"Avra? Where's the box?"

Then he saw it on the floor by one of the table's legs. It was open, the vellum inside it. The vial lay on the floor nearby where it had apparently rolled to a stop.

Even from here he could see that it was nearly half empty.

His heart pulled through a hard beat, pushing thick blood through his veins as if they had suddenly collapsed, then opened to accept a rush of new life.

He turned back to Avra, mind awash in horror. But there was no terror in her eyes. She was staring up at him with soft, round eyes, swimming in something he hadn't seen before. The glint of fear was gone, replaced by a need that mirrored his own longing.

Neither spoke. Rom wanted to. He wanted to cry his outrage over the danger she'd put herself in. He wanted to beg her forgiveness and weep with her.

And then he suddenly didn't want to. The urge to correct what was wrong here faded, smothered by a desperation to love this woman.

She began to shake in his arms, but not from fear. Her eyes pulled at him with the same desire he felt, he was sure of it, and this realization thrust him into a place so foreign that he wasn't sure he hadn't been sucked into Bliss itself.

Avra was no longer the young girl he had protected through life, but the woman he needed as he needed air. She was rising, eyes fired. She threw her arms around his neck and kissed his mouth with a fierce passion that inflamed him and made his mind rage with hunger.

Breathing hard, they fed on each other, two starving souls who'd found each other near death before finding the only food that could sustain them.

Avra pushed him back, straddling him as he dropped to the floor. Her fingers clawed through his hair. Her lips smothered his. She was breathing through her nose in short, desperate snatches of air.

His hands roamed the firmness of her back, her small shoulders, the drape of her hair as she pressed him down, devouring him. Ecstasy defied the torment that had ravaged his mind. It was physical, yes, but so much more.

His heart was alive. Screaming with pleasure. Eager to love and be loved, awakened to a dizzying and forbidden world of love and passion.

Avra suddenly jerked back an inch. Her eyes were wide and her breath washed over his mouth. They stared at each other, frozen for a moment.

And then she pushed herself off him, rolled to her knees, and blinked.

"What's happening to us?" Her voice sounded lost.

Rom scrambled to his feet, head spinning. He didn't know. Was this life or was this death? An hour earlier he had sworn death, but if what he felt now was death, then he would take his life without hesitation if only to feel its embrace.

She swallowed. "I didn't mean—"

"Yes, you did."

She kept her eyes on him, making no attempt to further discount her feelings.

Rom settled to his knees beside her. "We both did."

He took her in his arms and held her gently. She hesitated, then pulled her legs to one side and rested her head against his chest.

"Are you all right?"

"I drank the blood, Rom," she said, shaking again. "I heard you leaving and tried to call you but you'd gone. I thought you'd left me."

"Never! Do you hear me? Never." He hugged her and buried his face in her hair. The thought of leaving her horrified him, but he couldn't summon the words to convey his feelings. So he held her close, aware of her warmth. The pain he'd felt at finding his mother dead was no less, but now a desperation for the emotions Avra had awakened flooded him with a gratitude that he could not comprehend.

However the blood worked, he was now sure it could not be something as simple as the gateway to Hades. Something far more profound had happened to them both. They were changed. Fugitives. Poisoned, alive, dying—whatever it was.

But above all, they were together.

"Are we dying?" Avra whispered.

"No. I don't think so. Maybe we're more alive."

He wanted to tell her how he felt, to unravel what was happening to them, but there was a more urgent matter now. He knew that the priests would soon come to prepare for first assembly. They had to gather themselves and find someplace safe to hide.

"We have to go soon."

He took her hand and slid his fingers through hers, marveling at the smallness of them, at the delicacy of her littlest finger.

"Do you feel any pain?" he asked.

"My mind hurts."

"I'm so sorry I wasn't here for you."

"Where did you go?"

He looked at the burning candles. "Home. I had to see my..."

"Your mother." Fresh tears spilled from her eyes. "Oh, Anna—poor Anna! Rom, I'm so sorry!"

She clasped him and they wept together, clinging to each other. The wound would not seem to close, and Rom wondered if it was possible for hearts to actually break apart.

"Look at me," he whispered, after the tears had stopped again.

She turned her head toward him, her lashes still wet. Had she ever been so beautiful?

He lowered his head to hers, touched a kiss to her cheek.

"Rom..."

What we call love, Rom, is the shadow of something lost. How had his father known that?

"I love you, Avra." He stroked her cheek with his thumb. "With love as it once was. The blood has turned us back in time. You feel it as much as I do."

Her eyes searched his, understanding. And then she reached up, wrapped her arms around his neck, and pulled him toward her. He kissed her again, gently this time, but when she fell away she was breathing heavily again, trembling.

"Is this madness?" she whispered.

"No." He kissed her neck, the top of her shoulder.

"Don't."

Her scars.

"I never cared about them before and I don't now. I wouldn't have you without them. I swear if I had the power to heal them, I would only do it to please you. You are whole to me." He kissed her neck again.

A soft *thump* sounded over their heads and Rom jerked his head up. The priests.

"Quick." He scrambled to his feet and pulled her up. He collected the box, rewrapped the vial in the vellum, and then carefully set the bundle inside and latched it closed.

"Are you all right?"

"I don't know." But she was steadier on her feet than he had been.

She fastened her cloak as he blew out the three remaining candles. In the dark, he reached for her hand. Pressed the box into it.

"Can you carry this?"

He heard the rustle of her sliding it into the pocket of her cloak.

They moved toward the door.

"Will you be able to run?"

"Yes."

Rom opened the door enough to peer out and listen. Footsteps echoed down the stairwell farther down the corridor, coming their way. He eased the door back into place and led her across the storeroom to the second door, laid his hand on the knob and turned it.

He waited until the footsteps stopped just outside the first door. As soon as it opened, he whisked Avra out, and they fled down the dark corridor in the opposite direction from the stairwell they had descended the night before.

The sound of their steps changed to an echo as they entered the old crypt tunnel. It was pitch dark and noticeably colder as the smooth floor beneath them transitioned to the unmatched edges of roughly hewn stone. Avra stumbled. His hand tightened on hers.

They kept to the wall, inching past the carved sarcophagi that erratically lined the corridor, the intermittent stone walls that jutted out between chambers.

He had avoided this part of the lower level last night, thinking fear might incapacitate them both. But now, even though he recoiled every time his fingers touched one of these homes of the dead, he found himself driven by something even greater than fear of death.

The desire to live.

More than that, to keep Avra safe.

"Almost there," he whispered. He felt for the rail of the winding staircase, the cold curve of it along the landing. A cool but stagnant draft wafted up from below.

"What's down there?"

"More of the same."

He led her up the staircase, their footsteps seeming to echo too loudly on each step. It seemed impossibly long and high, as though they'd climbed forever before the rail finally flattened out onto a landing illuminated by a sliver of light from beneath a door.

He felt for the handle, but then hesitated.

Avra whispered, "What are you doing?"

For a moment, he was unsure how to share what he was thinking.

"Once we leave..."

She finished the thought for him. "We won't be able to stop running."

"Are you sure you want to do this?"

"I can't live without you."

His heart soared. He kissed her fingers.

"Where will we go?" she asked.

He drew a breath. "Right now the only person I can think of is Neah."

"Neah! She's as Order-bound as they come! She'll report us in an instant!"

"It's her or Triphon." Their two closest friends from university. Rom had already run through all the possibilities. For the last six years, Avra had kept personal company with no one but him, and Rom had systematically ruled out every relation, neighbor, or other artisan he knew.

"There's no one else."

"Neah works in the Citadel. She could help us find this man called the Book, whoever he is."

"You actually mean to try to find him? We'll be caught for sure! No, Rom. We have to leave the city. We have to run."

"We'll eventually get caught. This Book may be the only one alive who knows what's really happened to us. Or how we can fix things. Or if we even can."

"Too dangerous. We all know the Honor Code." Those who infringed on the Order were responsible for reporting not only others, but themselves. Anyone who didn't was at risk of being reported for their failure to report.

In a system ruled by fear, the code rarely failed.

"I don't like it."

"Can you think of an alternative?"

When she didn't answer, he tightened his grip on the door handle and opened it enough to peer out. The altar stood at the opposite corner of the sanctum. Farther down, near the narthex, early arrivals filed in from the main entrance. No guardsmen that he could see.

"Stay close."

He opened the door, stepped out with Avra, and hurried to a side door, which he opened.

A voice near the altar: "Rom?"

They both turned. A priest stood on the dais, censers dangling from each hand. "Rom? There was someone here just a few minutes ago looking for you. I think he might still be here, I'll see if—"

Rom grabbed Avra's hand and bolted into the daylight. The door fell shut with a heavy bang.

"Run!" Avra cried, pulling her hand free.

"This way!" He veered toward the entrance to the underground, a block away.

A truck sped by on the street. On the walk, foot traffic was noticeably heavier than yesterday.

Rom glanced over his shoulder. "Walk, walk!" he breathed. "We don't want to attract attention. Pull your hood up."

Together they joined the human stream flowing into the underground station.

A new banner had gone up over the entrance in the last day, bearing the image of Feyn Cerelia and the date of her inauguration, just four days away now. Rom felt her eyes follow them into the subterranean space.

He had to wonder if they would live to see the event at all.

Chapter Eleven

"IS SHE in there? Do you see her?" Avra whispered.

Rom leaned out from the wall just far enough to look through the window. "Not yet."

They were wedged against the wall between the front door and a small window on the private landing of Neah's second-story apartment. The stair that led to Neah's entrance had been built in the narrow gap between two buildings. From here they could loiter without attracting notice.

A long time ago, the window must have overlooked the greenery of a backyard. At least, that's how Rom imagined it. Now, however, it looked out only on the cracked concrete of the stair and the stone of the neighboring building. Its sheer curtain had been drawn aside to let in whatever eastern light it could.

In the distance, basilica bells sounded the hour: eight o'clock. Across Byzantium, assemblies began and would continue throughout the day. It was rest day, set aside for the purpose of rejuvenation and assembly at the workweek's end. How different those bells sounded today, ominous and more lyrical at once.

Rom sank back against the wall and glanced up at the churning sky. For the first time in his life, the mere sight of it sparked wonder in his heart. Even the bells struck their own chord of awe and hollow longing.

Everything was different.

As the last of the bells subsided, voices sounded from within the apartment—a man's and a woman's. Rom glanced at Avra.

She whispered, "She's not alone?"

Rom peered through the window again, his mouth in a tight line. "I guess not."

"Who would be here at this hour?"

He could see into the corner of Neah's well-appointed living room, her cream-colored chair and reading lamp. He had to lean out farther to see into the main part of the space but didn't want to risk staring straight in, not until they knew who was with her.

The voices rose again in such apparent discord that Rom began to worry less about being noticed. He leaned in a little more.

"What do you see?"

"A man, sitting in one of the living room chairs."

"A man? Since when does Neah have a man—any man—around? She didn't get married, did she?"

"Not that I know of. I didn't even think she was promised."

Inside, Neah paced through her living room. A man seated in one of the overstuffed chairs stood up into Rom's line of sight.

Was that—?

He felt a chuckle rise up from his chest and worked to stifle the sound and the odd levity that had caused it. He hadn't known that emotion was associated with laughter, a social nicety. But the humor he felt was far more than a polite response. It was fueled by a hilarity that made him question again if he might be mad. Hadn't his mother just died? Hadn't his life as he knew it just ceased, possibly forever? And yet—

"You'll never guess who's in there."

Avra stared blankly at him.

"Triphon!"

She blinked. "Triphon?"

"Triphon."

It wasn't merriment that flooded her face, but fear. "He's with the guard! We have to go." She pushed away from the wall, but Rom caught her by the wrist.

"Wait. He's only in training. He isn't part of the guard yet officially."

"What's the difference?" she hissed.

Rom leaned toward the window. Triphon's shirt strained across the broad width of his muscled shoulders as he sat forward in the chair and picked up a distinctive-looking paper from the low coffee table in front of him.

Rom felt his pulse spike. "Hades."

Avra's eyebrows shot up. She pushed around him and looked through the window. "What—oh. Maker."

"I think…" He glanced at her. "Are those papers…?" But they had to be. He had seen the same lettering on his own betrothal, several years prior.

Triphon was proposing a marriage contract.

Neah's muffled voice rose inside.

Avra shrank back. "We should go."

"Go where? We don't have anywhere else."

"Training or not, Triphon's with the Citadel Guard. It's bad enough that Neah will turn us in the minute we tell her, but Triphon might kill us!"

"Do you really think a trainee has any idea about missions having to do with old vials of blood, and chasing and killing ancient keepers of secrets?"

She paused.

"Come on."

"We're just going to interrupt them?"

"Why not? Neah will reject him. This is the business of parents. I don't know what he's thinking."

Not that rejection would mean anything to the dauntless Triphon. If Rom knew little of fear, Triphon knew even less.

It took Rom a belated moment to realize that the voices inside had gone silent. He and Avra glanced at each other just as Neah's front door flew open.

Triphon stepped out on the threshold, all six-foot-six of him—seven, counting the stiff inch of his athletic haircut—filling the doorway. "Who's there?"

"Triphon," Rom said, nodding.

"Hey, Rom."

Neah stepped up behind Triphon and crossed her arms. Her blond hair was pulled back in its characteristic braid. Her beige sweater and pants looked more ready for the office—or assembly—than a day at home.

"Well, if it isn't Rom. And Avra. I hardly recognize you, it's been so long. And don't you look a fright. What are you doing here? Spying on us? Tell me you didn't just attend assembly looking that disheveled."

"Good to see you, Neah," Rom said. "Can we come in?"

Triphon stepped aside.

Rom registered Triphon's nod as he stepped past, more conscious than ever of the fact that he was four inches shorter than Triphon.

Inside, he turned back to see Avra step inside and face the full brunt of Neah's stare.

She turned from Avra to Rom. "So? What are you doing here?"

"Saving you from Triphon's proposal," Rom said.

Triphon closed the door. "Neah was about to accept."

"No, I wasn't!"

"You both look terrible," Triphon said. "Are you ill?"

Rom was suddenly unsure what to say.

"We're in trouble."

"Trouble?"

He began to wonder if Avra was right, and coming here was a bad idea.

"We poisoned ourselves," Avra blurted. "By accident."

"What?" Neah paled. "What do you mean, poisoned yourself *by accident?*"

"We didn't poison ourselves," Rom quickly corrected. He glanced at Avra. "We have this vial that was passed to me. This vial of ancient blood. It apparently has some kind of effect."

"Like a drug?"

"Maybe. Yes. Kind of like that."

"Yes," Avra said.

"Idiots," Neah said.

Rom looked from Triphon to Neah. "We need help."

Neah said, "Let me get this clear: You found some old blood. You took it. It poisoned or drugged you. And you come here, to my apartment? What kind of friends are you?"

"We can't go home," Rom said.

"What do you mean, you *can't go home?*"

Rom weighed how much to say. "There are some people after this blood. Because of its properties, I think. It isn't safe for us to go home."

"Don't be ridiculous," Neah said. "You should have gone to compliance immediately."

"We can't," Avra said.

"What do you mean, you *can't?*"

Triphon followed the verbal volley, one eyebrow cocked.

Neah stared at her. "What aren't you telling us?"

"Listen," Avra said, stepping between them to take Neah by the arm. "The point is, we came across something that we're not sure what to do with, and we're not sure what it's done to us. But we think it's something bad, that it might be poison—"

"It's *not* poison." Rom shot Avra a look, stepping up. "If it were poison, we'd be dead, instead of going through this...these feelings. And I wouldn't feel the way I do about...people...with this...attraction."

That stalled them all. Or Triphon, at least.

"Make sense!" Neah said.

"If these feelings are any indication, then it could very well be poison," Avra said, speaking directly to Rom. Why was she countermanding him?

"Attraction?" Triphon said, glancing between them. "What do you mean?"

"Well, it's this... You know." Rom looked at this bull of a man who had circumvented custom to present a contract for marriage directly to Neah. Why? It wasn't out of desire, because as far as Rom knew no one on earth felt true desire for another human being.

No one but he and Avra now.

Rom searched for a way to sound compelling. He took a step toward the taller man. Triphon was more likely than Neah to be an advocate. "Attraction. Desire. Yearning, wanting to be with someone not out of fear of loss but for the fulfillment of something more. It's a magical thing, and now Avra and I have it."

Triphon frowned. "Is that so?"

"The things you're talking about don't exist," Neah said. "Not anymore. Avra's right, you're both ill. You should go to a wellness center." Neah turned to Triphon. "You should escort them there on your way home."

"We can't," Rom said, taking a breath. "We've gone against Order."

"What do you mean, you've *gone against Order*? Then you need to report yourselves!"

Avra gave him a pointed look as though to say, *See? I told you!*

"About this attraction," Triphon said. "You mean like a sexual urge?"

Rom paused. Sex was an acknowledged and common urge, like the urge to eat or drink. But now as he thought about it, with Avra standing nearby, the very notion of sex seemed vastly different to him. No longer a mere need to procreate or to find release, it seemed like something far deeper.

"Yes," he said, drawing a slow breath. "Like hunger or thirst. But for the companionship of another, not simply to satisfy the body."

"Maybe Neah should try some," Triphon said.

Rom continued before she could object. "But it's more than that. I'm telling you, we've stumbled onto something that has awakened our fundamental emotions." He glanced at Avra, who was watching him intently. "Wonder, beauty, love."

"Impossible," Neah said.

Rom ignored her, eyes still on Avra. "There's anxiety and worry, but we already had the better part of that in fear. If I'm right, we're something *more* than we were before."

"That's absurd," Neah said. "You're talking about something archaic. As far behind us as living in caves."

"No. It's alive. In us."

"That's sacrilege."

He could feel his heart accelerate. "If this new blood rushing through my veins is sacrilege, then something is wrong with our understanding of that word!"

"You're against the Order!" Neah cried, stabbing her finger at Rom. "You need to turn yourselves in. And if you don't, then Triphon and I will!"

Despite the steeliness of Neah's gray gaze, Rom knew her sharpness came from fear. She held a good job in the Citadel arranging itineraries for the royals. She had much to lose in not upholding the Honor Code.

"About this magic potion," Triphon said. "Let's see it."

Rom glanced at Avra's coat. Triphon followed his gaze.

Avra looked between them both, cornered.

Rom nodded.

"I'm not going to take part in this," Neah said. "I won't be implicated by your actions!"

"Then don't look," Triphon said.

Avra handed the box to Rom, who took it to the table and set it down. He opened the clasp and removed the vellum-wrapped vial. Triphon pressed close behind, so that Rom could practically feel the bulk of him peering over his shoulder.

Neah edged closer to Avra, at his side. Now all four of them looked down at this bundle that had cost the old man and both Rom's parents their lives.

The memories mushroomed in his head, and with it a bubbling sorrow that filled Rom's chest. He lowered the vial, unable to hold back the sob that erupted from his throat. But he managed to swallow the second before raw emotion overtook him.

"What's this?" Triphon asked. "You're weeping?"

"He's overcome with fear," Neah said. "He knows this is wrong. Look at him. He's lost his mind."

"Leave him alone," Avra snapped, tears in her eyes. "He's just lost his mother to this thing. He's feeling sorrow, and if you weren't asleep yourselves you'd cry, too!"

"Lost his mother?" Neah said. "She's thrown you out?"

"Sorrow," Triphon said, as though it were a foreign word.

"No, she was killed," Avra said.

The words hung between them.

"That's impossible. Who would do such a thing?"

"The Citadel Guard," Rom said. Now they had condemned themselves for sure.

"That can't be right," Triphon said.

Neah looked ill. "Whatever that is, get it out of my house."

"Listen to me," Rom snapped, turning on both of them. "Ask yourselves why the Citadel Guard would kill an old man and my mother for a single vial of old blood."

Triphon blinked. "Old man?"

Rom held up a hand, keeping the wrapped vial close to his chest. He stepped away from them. "Listen, I'll tell you everything from the beginning. But you have to promise to listen until I'm finished. Hear me out."

New emotions reverberated in his voice. The love of his mother, of Avra, of his lost father, the beauty of life. He told them every-thing, beginning with the old man in the alley, ending with Avra's drinking of the blood in the storeroom of the basilica. Neah's jaw grew more fixed by the moment, but Triphon's eyes drifted again and again to the wrapped bundle in Rom's hand.

"I've never felt so…alive," he said, summing it up the best that he could.

"Let's see it," Triphon said.

Rom walked back to the table, unwrapped the vial, and set it down. He spread the vellum and pointed out the verse at the top. It was the only intelligible writing on a landscape of seemingly ran-dom characters. But Triphon's attention was on the vial. He plucked it from the table, held it up, and squinted at it. "You drank this?"

Rom nodded.

"You, too?" Triphon said to Avra.

"Yes, me, too."

"It was the stupidest thing either of you have ever done," Neah said. She stormed to the table and snatched up the vellum. "This clearly belongs to the Citadel. I'll return it myself if I have to."

"Neah!" Avra cried. "You have no idea what it is and what we've been through. No idea!"

"You're a fool. Do you know what you're risking?"

Neah continued berating Avra, but Rom's attention was on Triphon, who already had his fingers on the metal cap.

Triphon opened the top, sniffed once, then brought the glass rim carefully to his lips and tipped the vial back.

Rom did nothing to stop him.

Neah's face went white. "Triphon!"

Triphon lowered the vial. His single gulp had taken the blood down past the next measure—a fact Rom registered with some alarm. There had been only enough for five, but now fewer than two measures remained.

"Well, I can tell you it tastes terrible," Triphon said, wiping his mouth with the back of his hand and resealing the vial.

"Have you gone mad? Now I'll have to report you as well!"

Triphon shoved the vial back at Rom. "I'm doing my duty as one of the guard."

"What duty? You're in *training.*"

"To see if there's a breath of truth to anything these two—"

He grunted and staggered backward, doubled over as though punched in the stomach—and then fell into an end table, knocking a lamp and a ceramic bowl to the floor with a crash.

Rom bounded forward and tried to catch him before he landed on the ceramic shards, but Triphon managed to recover enough to lurch toward the kitchen.

"Some—water—"

He collapsed under the archway between the two rooms.

For a moment they all stared at him, unmoving.

"You've killed him!" Neah cried.

"No—"

"You've lost your minds and killed Triphon!"

Neah spun and ran for the door, vellum flapping in her hand.

"Rom!" Avra shouted.

With a glance back at Triphon's unmoving form, Rom thrust the vial at Avra and took off after Neah, out the door and down the stairs.

He could hear Avra's feet racing behind him. Neah's escape would be their undoing.

It was daylight. If Neah got out into the apartment complex's communal yard, there would be no way to stop her without witnesses. All the apartments on this side of the building looked out on that same yard. Compliance would be on them in minutes.

He chased her, feet firing down the stairs like pistons. She was nearly three-quarters of the way down, five steps ahead of him, when he launched himself past her to the landing below. He whirled just as she crashed into him.

They tumbled to the ground floor in a tangle. The vellum came free from Neah's hand and flew toward the gate on a stiff breeze.

Avra tore down the stairs and rushed past them both, nearly tripping over Rom's foot as she ran for the vellum. She snatched it up before the wind could blow under the gate and into the yard.

"Get off!" Neah screeched. "Get—"

Rom clamped a hand over her mouth and rolled over so that he could get his feet under him. But she was twisting and flailing so hard that he couldn't, screaming into his hand.

Avra strode back. "You're going to have to knock her out," she said.

"I can't do that!"

Neah kneed him in the groin.

Killing her suddenly became a possibility.

Rom fell on top of her, bearing her to the concrete on *her* back this time. When he had recovered, he jerked her upright. Avra grabbed her by the ankles.

Panting with exertion, they hauled her up the stairs and back into her apartment. Avra closed and locked the door. Triphon's long form remained unmoving in the kitchen entryway.

Neah began to twist and jerk with renewed urgency.

"We'll have to tie her up."

"You realize that you have to give her the blood now."

Rom hadn't thought that far ahead, but he saw her reasoning. It would be the only way to persuade her to help, if only for her self-interest. They certainly couldn't leave her bound in her closet to starve to death.

Neah cried her objections into his hand.

"Hurry."

Avra vanished into the kitchen with the vial of blood in hand.

Rom dragged Neah to the couch and pulled her down, back to him, on top of him. He swung a leg up, tried to capture both of hers, but only managed to trap one. He jerked his hand away just as she tried to bite him.

"Avra!"

"Hold on—"

"A little help?"

Neah screamed.

"And maybe a sock or two—the neighbors are going to hear!" He clamped his hand back down on her mouth.

Avra emerged from the kitchen with a cup and a funnel. She set the cup down on the sofa table and pushed the end of the funnel through his fingers. After a few tries and another scream from Neah, Avra got it into her mouth.

"Tip her head back more. Hurry."

He did, the narrow end of the funnel firmly between two of his fingers. He could feel her biting down on it, trying to push it out with her tongue, but his fingers held it in place. Avra retrieved the measuring cup, filled halfway with a lighter red fluid.

"I mixed it with honey water," Avra said.

She climbed onto the kicking Neah, dropped a knee in the middle of her chest, pinched her nose, and poured a small amount of the fluid into the funnel. Neah choked and sputtered. Avra leaned back a little and waited as some of the fluid spewed back up out of the funnel. The rest disappeared into Neah's mouth. She watched her throat work, and then poured the rest of it in.

Neah coughed, whimpered once, and started to settle. When all the fluid had drained from the funnel, Avra pulled it out.

"I'm sorry, Neah. It'll make sense, I promise."

They waited until Neah stiffened with a cry and finally went still.

"She's out?" Rom asked.

Avra climbed off. "She's out."

A few seconds later they stood over Neah's limp form. She was breathing more rapidly than Triphon on the floor behind them, but within a few seconds, her quick pants began to subside.

"This isn't quite how I thought this would go," Rom admitted.

Neah's braid had come nearly all the way loose. Pale strands of her hair were strewn across her face. Her teeth and the inside of her lips were lined in macabre red.

He'd never thought of Neah—hard-nosed and as Ordered as they came—as pretty before, but in that moment he realized that she was quite beautiful. In the silence of Neah's apartment, he found himself wanting to lift her hand, to turn it over and marvel at the crook of her wrist.

A hand lit on hers, but it wasn't his. Avra stroked the back of Neah's hand, traced the line of the other woman's fingers.

"I feel like my heart's breaking for her. I don't know why. Will she forgive us, do you think, for what we've done?"

"We'll find out, I suppose," he said.

He glanced around her apartment, really seeing it for the first time. It was all perfectly organized, from the placement of the pictures on her walls to the neat stack of books on her coffee table. Every color, every texture in her home spoke of calm. There were no bright tones, no alarming hues, no harsh surfaces. Everything in this apartment had been chosen with one specific purpose: to soothe one who lived rigidly within the confines of Order.

Order and fear.

"Now what?" Avra whispered.

He straightened. The room was draped in uncanny quiet.

"We wait."

He reached out for her hand, led her away from the sleeping Neah, past the sprawling form of Triphon, and into the kitchen.

"What if Neah's right, Rom? That all of this is criminal. How do we know if we're doing the right thing?"

Something from his past clicked into place.

He said, in a low voice, "My father said something to me when I asked him a similar question once."

"What was it?"

"He said that what we call love is the shadow of something lost."

"How could he have known that?"

"Because he was a keeper. What the old man said was true. And what my father said about love is true. I didn't know then, but I know now. I don't know what the right thing is, but I do know that we're closer to the truth than we were before."

He thought if he stared into her dark eyes long enough, he might see through to her thoughts. That he might know them without asking. He was trying to search those depths when she stepped into him, sliding a hand behind his neck.

He wasn't aware of his bending toward her, only that her breath was warm against his mouth. That her lips, when he kissed her, were immeasurably soft.

He wanted to taste her. To inhale her. The thought of kissing her—an act born of tenderness in the storeroom—sprang to full-fledged need. How had he never done this before today, how had it never occurred to him in all those years and days together?

He let go of her hand and slid both arms around her, kissing her deeply. She was sweet and salty and wet. Her small fingers tightened in the hair against his nape.

When she abruptly pulled away, he faltered. He could hear her breathing, heavier and more labored than before.

No, that was him.

"Rom?"

He looked at her mouth, the way her lips, still moist, moved when she said, "Triphon's waking."

CHAPTER TWELVE

"HERE ARE the eyes that have captivated the world," the maidservant Nuala said, setting down black eyeliner. She laid it atop the astronomical chart she had insisted Feyn relinquish at least long enough for her to be made up.

Feyn turned on the stool to look into her vanity mirror. Nuala's round face appeared over her shoulder against the backdrop of silk draperies. "You see, my lady, you are beautiful."

Beauty, Feyn thought idly. Such a strange concept. A matter of desirable features—in this case the light gray eyes and pale skin of royalty. The coveted evidence of humanity's evolution, proof they had become something great.

And she must be greater than them all. Not because she personally wished it, but because in four days she would accept the mantle of sovereignty from the hands of the Sovereign, her father.

In the mirror, Feyn's eyes lifted to Nuala's face. She was too round, too broad across the forehead, too short to be considered beautiful by the masses. But Feyn found her pleasing. The sight of the maid could often quell her anxiety. Was that not beauty? Nuala didn't possess the paleness of eye or the translucent skin of the Brahmin, although like many she highlighted her veins by tracing them with blue powder on her forearms. Did her opaque skin make her less evolved? Less beautiful?

It didn't matter. Nuala was one of the wisest people Feyn knew, and this was the primary reason she'd selected Nuala as her maid-servant years earlier.

Feyn reached up to rub her neck. Nuala gently pushed her hand away and began to knead the muscle for her.

Feyn sighed and closed her eyes.

"I wonder sometimes, Nuala...I was born closest to the seventh hour of the seventh day of the seventh month in all the eligible birth cycles during Father's reign. So I am elect. But if my parents had copulated a day later or a month before, would I even exist? I certainly wouldn't be the next Sovereign."

"The Maker makes no mistakes."

Feyn opened her eyes and looked down at the black liner on her vanity table, at the rouge and powder, the brushes and the hair combs, all the implements of Nuala's craft.

"I am the artist and you are my perfect clay," Nuala liked to say.

Clay. It was more true than the woman knew. *We are all molded into something. I only wonder how much the Maker truly has a hand in any of it.* It was a blasphemous thought, one she'd never dare voice. But the thought had woken her many nights, sending her to stare at the thunderclouds from her balcony.

To even think such things was so unbefitting a future Sovereign that she could confide in no one. And so the solitude, too, had become as familiar to her as the late nights gazing out at the rain.

She must learn to put idle ponderings aside, at least for now. Whether being chosen was the will of the Maker or the error of mankind, it made no difference. She would soon be Sovereign, and that would be her course for the next forty years.

She gave a little laugh. It was mirthless, the vestige of a baser life, a conversational nicety with a soothing sound.

"I'll be sixty-five by the time we sit like this again, before this mirror, and talk of life without the office. Do you realize that,

Nuala? And there will be lines by then—here, beneath my eyes, and here." She touched the corner of her mouth.

"You will be beautiful beyond the age of one hundred, lady. And you'll live to a hundred and thirty."

"Hmmm," Feyn said, sitting back. If her father was any example, Sovereigns aged far faster than their constituents. Feyn sighed and got up.

She wore her customary black leggings and snug-sleeved tunic and would have thrown on a simple overcoat were it not a public day for her—her last until her inauguration. Tomorrow she would leave for Palatia, her family's country estate, to spend the prescribed days of solitude before her inaugural entry into the city. They would be her last private days for forty years.

When Nuala went into the adjacent closet to choose a gown for her mistress, Feyn made her way into the front room of her quarters to pick at the breakfast tray on the table there. The food was cold. She pulled at a few green leaves and left most of the meat on the plate. The kitchen had begun to undercook it of late.

Nuala came into the room carrying a cobalt gown trimmed in silver. The blue was the color of the sky on a bright day, Nuala had proclaimed, the day the tailor had first shown them the bolt of fabric.

"My lady?"

Feyn slid her arm into the sleeves, shrugging the heavy garment onto her shoulders. The business of fastening it took several minutes, with Nuala securing each of the small buttons up the front before coming around to smooth her hands down the back. The bell sleeves revealed the tight undersleeve of the black tunic. Feyn felt no inclination to reveal the smooth skin of her forearms; the coveted translucence of her skin was evident enough in her neck and face.

Nuala sniffed in the direction of the table.

"Undercooked again. I'll say something to the cook. This is your brother's doing. He's decided he can hardly stand cooked meat. I saw a whole rabbit prepared for him just the other day and it bled so much when he cut into it that I wondered if the heart had fully stopped beating."

"Royals do tend to like their meat rare," Feyn said.

"I heard that another dead woman was taken from his chamber this morning."

The revelation sent prickles down the back of Feyn's neck. She didn't know what to make of these recent rumors. But to Nuala, she said, "Death is everywhere. It is with us, and that's simply the fact. I'm sure there's a reasonable explanation."

Nuala shifted her eyes but held her tongue. Feyn couldn't blame the woman. *Everywhere* or not, no one wanted to view the specter of death. Not even one as orderly and wise as Nuala.

A low voice spoke from across the chamber. "What do you care what they carry from my chambers, maid?"

The women turned toward the sound together. Saric stood next to the silk drape that shielded the drafty back stair, dressed in an overcoat so rich it put the curtain to shame.

"Brother," Feyn said as Nuala backed a step away.

Saric had stood behind the drape in silence for several minutes after descending the stair. He'd done so on several occasions these last few days, but this was the first time he'd made his presence known.

He dismissed the ever-present maidservant with a nod and watched her take leave of her mistress. The she-dog would ordinarily be far too common and uninteresting for his tastes, but as of late he wondered what it might be like to take her too-round body.

When she had gone, he returned his gaze to his sister. Had he ever really seen the pale of those eyes until lately? He could smell the heavy scent of her perfume. More than that, he could *smell* the skin of her neck and face and the blue veins running with her life.

Though in this last week he had seen himself more beautiful, more singular in all the world, he felt positively earthen beside Feyn.

He wouldn't have it any different.

Saric stepped forward, eyes on her. "Hello, Feyn."

"Is there something wrong with my door?"

"I'm your brother, not your servant. Can't I come as I please? You never minded when we were younger."

"My half brother," she corrected. "And that was a long time ago."

She walked to the floor chest where she kept her jewelry. She had so much of it, and even more of late. He'd seen the accessories come in with the other gifts, heard the way the servants scuttled around them, fearfully handling the tribute of nations. Yet he knew without looking that she would choose from that considerable treasure the same simple rings she favored every day: a moonstone and a large aquamarine given to her by their father at the announcement of her inauguration nine years ago.

He strode to the small table and examined the remains of her meal, which only disgusted him. "Forgive me." He helped himself to the cup of water on her table, ignoring the meat, which smelled like a corpse. He nudged the tray aside; a stack of charts lay on the table beneath it.

"So many stars, so many figures. How do you keep so much in your head, sister? I'll never understand you mathematicians."

"What's this about a dead woman in your chambers?"

He dropped the cup back on the table, sloshing water onto the stack of charts. "A woman they ran some experiments on. Can I help it if they practically killed her by the time I got to her? I try to content myself with their castoffs but find myself traumatized by morning."

She hesitated as if considering whether to voice her disapproval of his activities again. But she resisted.

"By *they*, I assume you mean the alchemists," she said.

"I do." He drew in a steadying breath and approached her.

"There are proper concubines, Saric. Make use of them."

"Yes, sister. But here now, let me help you. You should wear the favors of your constituents." He opened the doors of the jewelry chest and slid out one of the drawers. It was full of jewels of every kind. He pushed the drawer back in and pulled out another. She stood watching him rather than the chest.

"I mean it, Saric. It isn't fitting."

"Fine." He stirred through the assortment of baubles, each of them valued at several years' worth of any ordinary citizen's wages.

"Once is terrible enough, but twice in the same week? Where do these women come from? Are they ill and dying? How do you stand it—how can Portia?"

He could smell the fear on her. It was as heady as her perfume.

"Yes," he said. "They are ill. Here." He lifted out a pair of large diamond-and-sapphire earrings and held them out to her.

She turned away. "They're garish."

"They're the best stones in the lot, and they still do you no justice." She flicked a glance to him.

Her eyes were like the sun and ice at once. He felt his breathing thicken.

"What is it about you, brother? You look different. Are you sweating? You seem unwell these days."

"I'm not unwell." His gaze fell to her lips. "I am very well. In fact, I'm more full of life than I have ever been." He found himself wanting to touch her cheek and was fascinated by his own restraint. He reached for her hand instead.

This was the hand that had gathered Vorrin's just yesterday, that had held it as she touched her lips to his palm. He turned her hand over, traced her palm with his thumb, briefly considering doing the same. But she was not his Sovereign yet.

"I'm glad to hear it," she said. "At any rate, it can't be good for you—"

"Do you remember when I used to come down in the middle of the night?" He looked into her eyes, and she shifted her gaze away.

"Of course."

"You used to let me lie beside you and tell me there were no such thing as monsters, that the shadows did not move."

"I remember. What do you want, Saric?"

There was no tenderness in her voice. Not even pity. She was capable of neither.

"You saved me from a thousand terrors every one of those nights," he said. "But now perhaps I'll be able to repay you. By helping to quell your fears before you become Sovereign. Or in the very least by giving you a gift that will allow you to mitigate those fears."

She gave a short laugh. She had mastered the sound, even if she knew nothing of the emotion that caused it. "What you speak of isn't possible."

He turned her hand over, stroked a line upon her palm lightly with his finger. "But what if it were? Possible, I mean."

"Saric, I've never known you to be given to dreaming."

"Only of monsters and shadows." He forced a smile, irritated by her response. He released her hand, reached for the earrings in her open drawer, and held them up. "May I?"

She turned so that he could slide the small hook through her earlobe, indulging him with the same forbearance that she indulged Nuala, he thought. Perhaps less.

"Beautiful," he said. "The other?"

She let him affix the second earring. The prong pricked his finger.

"I see great fears on the horizon," he said.

"Then your fears run away with you again, as they did when you were a child."

"And would you champion me again, as you did then?"

"You have Portia for that."

"Yes, I have Portia," he murmured. He stepped back and rubbed dry the bead of blood between his finger and thumb. "Still, you must admit it's an irresistible thought."

"Please, Saric. I'm not one of your concubines to bring you comfort. I'm your sister."

"Half sister," he corrected. "As you pointed out. You know as well as I that I could legally marry you."

"Don't be ridiculous. Sovereigns don't marry."

He was surprised by his sudden urge to strike her as he might strike Portia for speaking in such a tone.

Saric sighed. "So you will be. Sovereign. In four days all the world will bow to you, as will I." He dipped his head.

"Yes, well, I'm not Sovereign yet."

"No, but in my eyes, you've always been Sovereign, Feyn. We both know that. I've always stood by your side."

She hesitated but then nodded. "Yes, you have."

"Which is why I'd like to ask you one small favor." He let it stand.

"I'm not sure I'm in any position to grant favors."

"But you *will* be. And I'll still be your flesh and blood. Surely you can't deny that much."

She studied him. "I don't deny it."

"So you could grant me a favor when you become Sovereign. A trifle that would forever indebt me to you beyond my loyalty, which you know you already have."

"What trifle?" she asked.

So then, here it was.

"Let me serve you as your senate leader."

For a moment she didn't move. Then, a smile. And he thought he might have won her confidence in the matter.

"Wait." He laid a finger against her warm lips. "I will give you something in return."

Still smiling, Feyn brushed his hand away and pulled her hand back. "You will, will you? And what's that?"

"I will show you that the monsters are real."

Her smile faded. It had never held any warmth. He continued before she could speak.

"That there's more to this life." His heart accelerated as he spoke; the words alone sent adrenaline thrumming through his veins.

"Saric—"

"I'll show you that there is far more power to be had than the power any Sovereign has yet seen."

"What are you talking about?"

"I can give you a life overflowing with desire, rich with new sensibility, dear sister."

"Stop this." She stepped away. "I don't know what's happened to you or what you're talking about. But we stopped playing games when we became adults."

He stiffened. "I can assure you, I'm not playing games. On the contrary, I've learned something that you have to know. The question is whether you have the stomach for the truth."

She eyed him, obviously uncertain, disturbed by fear.

"What truth?" she asked.

"That in our so-called evolution, humanity's loss of the baser sentiments wasn't advancement at all, but the casualty of a virus called Legion. It was let loose on the world four hundred and eighty years ago at Null Year by the alchemists. Alchemy—not the Maker—has defined our fate, and it will again."

Saric paced to his left, leading her stare. "You've been taught that we exist in the only Order. But there's another order. There is an anti-Order. There are the vestiges of Chaos living among us today."

"What you're saying is sacrilege!"

"It is. It's also the truth. This very moment the alchemists have in their custody the last surviving member of the Order of Keepers—a man, a historian they call the Book, who carries in his memory every known fact of these keepers. His anti-Order would bring back every emotional vice that led to the zealotry that nearly destroyed humanity."

She blinked. "The keepers."

"Yes."

"You're saying they've lived among us all this time?"

"They have. And if this last one has his way, the world will be thrown back into a second Age of Chaos."

"You say your gift is new sensibility. And yet you speak against Order and for Chaos?"

Saric stepped closer. "There is so much you don't know, sister. I can teach you. Bring me into the senate to stand at your side. We'll be like Rowan and Father. Together. You will never be afraid to be alone, because you will have me. Entrust me with this duty. For the sake of your rule. For the sake of the people."

For an impossibly long moment, she searched his eyes. The beat of his heart struck a single and unfamiliar note.

"Don't be absurd. Even if all of this is true, you know it doesn't work that way. I could never just turn the senate over to you, not without their full support."

"Are you so naive? The law gives you the power to appoint whomever you wish. To do whatever you wish. The senate exists only for the comfort of the people and the symbolic participation of the continental nations. But you and I know the truth. Sign the decree and it would be done."

"For that reason—for the comfort of the people—it must always be done properly. I will uphold my commitment to Order. I won't have it any other way."

Her words cut deeply. It surprised him how much.

"As for this so-called keeper, you can be sure that I'll look into it. From what you're saying, one could assume that you yourself have practiced his dark alchemy. You must stop immediately. If you haven't given it up and reported your every association to it by the time I'm Sovereign, you'll answer for it. To me."

He stood as though struck. And then rage filled him with such force that he wondered if he would lose all restraint.

"You're a fool! I've offered you everything! I've offered you the world as you will never possess it, for one paltry price!"

There. Fear. It flitted before her face, like a shadow over those brilliant eyes.

But the satisfaction of seeing it was gone as quickly as it came. She was denying him. The desire he'd felt at the sight of her fled, leaving him feeling only pathetic.

What was he doing?

He knew. It was the emotion. It held him in thrall. And because of it, she held *him* in thrall. He couldn't afford that. Ever. Struggling before Corban was one thing. But getting carried away by his intense desire for Feyn was too dangerous.

He had said far too much. He dare not leave her harboring suspicion toward him. She must believe he had her best interest at heart.

Saric took a deep breath and dipped his head. "Forgive me, sister. My fear has gotten the better of me."

She didn't respond.

"It seems those monsters you once saved me from chase me still."

"Then I suggest you send them away," Feyn said.

"Please forgive me," he said.

"Of course."

"Thank you. I'll think on what you've said. Meanwhile, please at least search out the truth in these matters."

"Be certain: I will," she said. "I'll have further questions for you in days ahead."

He knew that she would, and on the surface her inquiries might seem to betray his purpose. But at least he had her trust, despite the fact that he had nearly betrayed himself.

Never again. By the time she ferreted out the truth and turned against him, it would be far too late for any of them, including her.

Chapter Thirteen

"THERE'S ANOTHER way, Rom."

Avra sat before Neah's coffee table, where she'd been studying the vellum for the last hour. Next to it lay the newspaper, which Rom had ventured out and retrieved two hours earlier. His own face dominated the front page with the caption *FUGITIVE* in bold letters below it.

"What way?" he asked.

"We could still flee Byzantium."

Rom had been pacing for what seemed hours, unable to sit down. He glanced at Neah, who was curled into a corner of the sofa. She'd come out of her blackout uncharacteristically quiet except for periodic stifled sobs. Her subdued state unnerved Rom, especially in light of Triphon's manic extremes. They had been doing the best they could to ignore his outbursts throughout the day.

A *thump* sounded in the back room. Triphon cried out and started laughing, only to devolve moments later into giant bullish sobs. He had been fighting demons in there for hours.

Rom shook his head. "We've already discussed that. No. We have to get into the Citadel. I have to find this man called the Book, this keeper."

"What if they've killed him, too?"

Rom raked his fingers through his hair.

"I'm sorry, Rom. But we have to consider it."

"I don't know. I don't know. But right now he's all we've got."

He knew what Avra was thinking. In his wild tangents—and he had chased them all throughout the day—he imagined their escape to a place where they might be safely together. A place where the Citadel Guard had no jurisdiction. A part of him longed for that more than any other thing. To be alone with her, to simply live and discover the far reaches of love.

But he needed answers. They both did. And he needed to know about his father; it wasn't just them at issue here.

"You realize the Citadel is the most dangerous place you could possibly go right now," Avra said.

"It's for the truth."

"How much truth do we need?"

"It isn't just us. What about the responsibility we have now? What about the rest of the world? Do we just hide this from them?"

"We don't owe the world anything!" She looked away. A moment later she said, "You're right. I know it. I just wish there was another way. There have to be others who have experienced this or at least know about it. Somewhere. Anywhere else but the Citadel."

"That's why I need to ask the Book."

He sat down beside Avra. Neah had gone near catatonic; he wasn't sure if she was even conscious. Here was another reason they couldn't simply flee: Triphon and Neah were only now emerging from the throes of their conversion.

He picked up the newspaper.

Rom Sebastian is dangerous and a fugitive. Do not harbor him, do not assist him. If seen, notify your local compliance office immediately. Obey the Honor Code.

The fact that they hadn't listed Avra as missing or with him had at first seemed like a good sign. Now he wasn't sure. Surely the guard knew by now she was gone, but they'd kept that knowledge to themselves. And that worried him.

He stared at the picture: his identification photo from the Office of the Census. His likeness smiled slightly, politely, but what had he known about smiling? What had he understood of life, of anything but going to basilica to sing when he was summoned, of returning to the comforts of the workshop and his mother's house? The philosophical talks that he and his mother had shared around the large hurricane lamp on the living room table...

Had been only a shell.

Avra joined him in staring at his image. "Even then you had a way about you that made me believe there could be meaning in everything. You were right."

"My mother called it naïveté." Grief swept over him.

"Rom, think of it. She died without regret, without sadness, without even anger at her attackers. And now she's in Bliss."

Rom was quiet for a moment before he said, "She died without love. And so did my father."

Worse yet, his father had somehow known it.

And for that, Rom felt crushing sadness. For that, he wondered if he could ever forgive his father's killers. For that alone, he had to know exactly what he had found in this vial, and what it meant to this life, to this world.

He had been so accepting of Order. He had taken it all at face value. He had not been naive. He had been a fool.

Rom tossed the paper aside.

A thud sounded from the direction of Neah's bedroom.

Triphon came bursting out into the living room, executed a flying side kick, and crashed into the wall. Rom had tried to engage him earlier, but the man had gone off in a rant. He'd taken more than one portion of the blood and seemed to be suffering all the effects.

Or was Triphon just coming fully into his own?

Rom hoped his reason would catch up with his emotions soon. For all he knew the guard were on the stair outside Neah's apartment now.

Neah broke her silence from the sofa. "You're destroying my apartment." Her eyes were red-rimmed and swollen, and she began to poke at a patch of darkening bruises on her upper arm.

She faced Rom. "So what happens now that you've dragged me into this mess? Not that it matters. We're going to get hauled off. You hear me? They're going to come for us!"

It was the most she had said all at once in hours.

"No," Rom said, standing. "We have to get into the Citadel." He turned toward Triphon, shadowboxing against the wall. "Triphon, are you with us?"

Triphon stopped and stared at his hands. "This is incredible. I would fight to the death for any of you right now. You know that?"

"What you feel is a drug," Neah snapped.

"Are you listening?" Rom demanded. "We have to get into the Citadel!"

"I'm here," Triphon announced with a raised fist. "We need to get into the Citadel? *I'll* get us into the Citadel."

"Such an idiot," Neah said.

"Tell me you aren't glad to finally feel something besides fear." Rom said. "Tell me that you aren't the least bit glad to feel anything but that thing that drives you to create your perfect world here, with your soothing cushions and your soft colors. Tell me that you aren't glad."

Earlier that morning, Triphon had knocked over a bowl of glass balls in the foyer. Neah had gathered the larger pieces and then dropped them all to lift the largest one toward the window. The light had fallen on her face, and she'd turned the glass over with infinite wonder in her eyes. Rom had thought she was beautiful earlier, but she was positively radiant then.

"My mother gave these to me," she'd said before her face crumpled.

116

Now he said to her: "Or are you still too afraid?"

Avra touched his hand. "Rom."

Neah was looking at him with the same impetuousness that she had always worn, but then the expression slipped away like an ill-fitting mask that would not stay on. It took a moment for him to realize that he had wounded her with his words. So easily?

"I'm sorry, Neah."

She looked away.

"I'm sorry," he said again.

"You were talking about the Citadel," Triphon said.

"Right. We have to get the vellum to the keeper," Rom said. "He might be the only one who can tell us what all this writing means. We have to learn more if we hope to survive. The whole world is against us right now."

"Finally, a note of truth," Neah said. "The world is against us. What if you get into the Citadel, which, by the way, is near impossible, and it turns out this keeper of yours is dead as Avra said? Do you really think they care about an old man? You'll only be taken captive yourself. You know what I think? That you'll be dead before tomorrow!"

"Neah!" Avra cried.

"It's all right," Rom said. He probably deserved it.

"Think about it! But no, you can't. All these feelings interfere. I can hardly think...while..." Neah's chin quivered.

"They have to keep the keeper alive," Avra said. "What he knows is too important."

Triphon picked the newspaper off the floor and studied the front page for a long moment.

"Dung hills," he said quietly.

They were all silent; Triphon had said it eloquently enough.

He dropped the paper on the coffee table. Outside, the bells had begun to toll for evening assembly. Triphon said, "I can get us into the Citadel. I'm in the guard."

"You're in *training*," Neah said.

"Is *anything* ever good enough for you?" Triphon snapped.

Neah blinked.

"Damnation." Triphon hauled in a breath. After a minute, he said, "I can get into the barracks. And from there, I just need to know where to go. Neah?"

She looked away.

"Never mind. I'll ask around. There are only so many places they can keep a guy like that."

"All right," Rom said, "Triphon will get me in—"

Neah said quietly, "There is only one place they'd keep him."

He glanced at her.

"In the old dungeons. There's a rumor about a labyrinth of corridors and chambers beneath the Citadel. And that they keep prisoners down there." When the severity was gone from her face, she looked years younger. Her gaze flicked toward Triphon, but Triphon was pacing again.

"No one knows for sure?" Rom said.

"No. And no one asks. We have jobs to protect. Do you know how easy it is for one person to say that you're insubordinate, just because they're afraid something you did might reflect poorly on them?"

"So the keeper has to be in the dungeons somewhere," Triphon said.

"If he's a real person and if he's still alive . . . that's where he'd be."

Triphon walked to a high transom window along the living room wall and peered out. Only Rom saw the way Neah's gaze followed him.

"They say the dungeons are in the control of Saric," she said.

"Saric?" Rom said.

"Feyn's brother."

"Feyn, as in . . . *Feyn*?"

"The Sovereign-to-be," Neah said.

"Saric," Triphon muttered and turned from the window.

"Any idea where the dungeons are located?" Rom added.

"You're really serious about this?" Neah said quietly.

"If you're right and I'm going to die by tomorrow, then I want to know what it was for."

The room fell silent.

"Maybe there is a way I could get us in," Neah finally said. "But it won't be easy."

Rom's pulse surged. "How?"

"I don't know yet. But the whole city knows your face now. You can't possibly go."

"I'll go," Triphon said. "I can get as far as the barracks without a problem."

"No, it has to be me," Rom said. "I was the one the old man told to find the keeper." He wouldn't entrust the vellum to anyone. But even more, he had to find out about his father.

"Don't be thick!" Triphon said. "I'm the trained fighter here. If trouble comes, I'm the only one who stands a chance."

"Which is why you have to stay here and protect Avra. They have to know by now that she's with me. And you need to get Neah out if anything happens to me."

Rom turned back to Neah. "How would you get me in?"

She chewed her lip. "The three other people in my office are all women. Maybe you could go as a woman."

"Well that rules me out," Triphon said.

"Let me see what I have." Neah went into the bedroom to find Rom something to wear.

"I don't like it," Avra whispered, stepping to his side.

He stroked her hair. It was soft and fine, waving in auburn tendrils against his fingers.

"It's not going to get any safer. If anything, they won't expect such a bold move."

Neah appeared with two dresses over her arm. "They're the ones with the most room in the shoulders."

"There is no way I'm going to pass for a woman in one of those!" Rom ran a hand over his face. His head hurt.

"Wait. I might have something else." Neah tossed the dresses over a chair and hurried to the closet. She pulled out several long robes on hangers.

"Some of the priests come to the Citadel to conduct private assembly. The Citadel keeps their robes for them. I have them laundered."

"I thought royals were supposed to attend basilica with the public, that that was why there was no basilica within the Citadel itself—"

"One of the Brahmin is afraid of public spaces and refuses to leave the Citadel gates. Another has a near-paralyzing fear of catching a common virus and ending up at the asylum. They bring the priests to the Citadel and have them change into their robes there, so that no one knows they're breaching Order."

Rom took one of the robes from Neah, pulled it over his shoulders, and fastened it at his neck and chest. "Is there a back way out of here?"

"The bedroom window. There's an escape stair on that side of the building."

Rom glanced at Triphon. "If there's any sign of trouble, you and Avra leave. Go north, out of the city."

"Easier said than done. It's harsh land."

"You're a trained guard, as you like to point out. Aren't you all trained to ride horses?"

"For ceremony, but—"

"Promise me."

"If there's a way, I'll find it."

"Rom." Avra was watching him. "Can I speak to you for a moment?"

She drew him aside into the small kitchen and faced him, ashen.

"I don't like this." Her whisper was shallow.

"Triphon won't let anything happen."

"It's not me I'm worried about."

He took both of her hands, lifted them, kissed the knuckles of one, then the other. "I'll be all right," he said, against the backs of her fingers. He pulled her closer and wrapped his arms around her. "I promise I'll be safe."

"I don't think I can live without you. My heart would break."

He gave a soft laugh, eager to calm her. "Your heart's stronger than you know."

"Rom?"

"Yes."

"Tell me you love me. With the new kind of love."

"I love you." The words were a sigh and a prayer. Words wild and sacred at once. "With the new kind of love. More than either of us could know."

Outside, the bells tolled the end of evening assembly and the close of rest day. Avra straightened the neck of his robe, then pulled his hood up over his head. She stood on her tiptoes and touched her lips to his.

"Come back to me."

"I will."

He let her go and then followed Neah out her bedroom window into the night.

Chapter Fourteen

FEYN MADE her way into the Senate Hall. The chamber was vacant, the cushioned seats of the senate and the high platform of the senate leader occupied by nothing but ghosts. It was no secret that the doorway on the side of the platform led belowground to tunnels that eventually reached the dungeons a hundred yards to the west. But the passage was sealed under lock and key and was used only by a few alchemists—Saric among them.

On the surface, she had acquiesced to Saric. But his logic was strange, filled with turns uncharacteristic of him. And there was something not quite right about him, not least of which was his talk of a so-called keeper in the dungeons.

She had taken the only other key she knew of: Father's. No Citadel lock could bar a Sovereign.

Or, in this case, a Sovereign-to-be.

A lone torch burned above the senate dais. Its flame was constantly fed by a supply of gas—the flame of the Order, never extinguished. She reached the door and let herself through.

It was a good twenty steps down into a bell-shaped atrium. She kept left along a passage that led to a small hexagonal chamber rumored to be the room in which Sirin himself had been martyred. The interior of the room was black, the walls adorned by ancient weapons and ruined tapestries. It had an eerie warmth, this room, as if it had never forgotten the fire that nearly destroyed it, or perhaps it had been recently occupied by a number of bodies, sweating as Saric had been in her chamber.

No, she was imagining things. She had simply never understood Saric's affinity for these lower levels with their reek of Chaos and torch smoke. That was all.

She approached a heavy door, fit the key into the lock, and opened the sealed passageway, closing it again behind her. The tunnel beyond was wide enough for only one person to pass. Electric wires ran along the wall, the fixtures they fueled illuminating the tunnel in disconnected patches of wan light. In some places, the top of the tunnel dipped so low that she had to stoop not to scrape her head against the stone crudely carved out of the rock millennia ago.

It was no wonder she hadn't descended this way in so long: She feared being this far beneath the surface, where it seemed the weight of all the earth would crush her. She had felt the same as a girl but forgotten it until this minute.

It seemed a long way before the tunnel broadened into a wider corridor and abruptly dead-ended at a bronze door set deep into the bedrock. A single electric torch was set in a bracket along one wall, casting shadows like ghouls crawling on the crudely carved ceiling. Two guards sat on either side of the door in lazy conversation. They stood abruptly at the sight of her, and then straighter yet upon recognizing her face.

"Let me pass."

"Lady." One of the guards bowed and moved to unbolt the door for her.

The space inside was surprisingly large. After the claustrophobic corridors, she could *feel* its size. The room, which was practically a warehouse, was lit along the walls by electric lights in iron grids.

She could make out several square shapes like giant cages—at least ten of them on either side of a makeshift aisle. Beyond them the sprawling works of an open laboratory appeared abandoned in rest-day repose, their stainless surfaces and surgical lamps at odds with the ancient walls.

A groan sounded, perhaps twenty feet ahead, startling her, not just with its proximity, but its raw quality.

"What is this place?" she demanded, turning back to the guard.

"The dungeons, my lady."

She looked out at the laboratory equipment, frowning.

"Where in this dungeon is kept the one called the keeper?"

"At the end," the guard said, "through a passage to the left, in the old dungeon proper."

Feyn stared ahead without need for light. Her eyes were more than the product of a world's obligation to evolutionary vanity. She had the ability to see farther and more sharply than others, even on the dimmest days.

Truly the product of alchemy, as they all were to some extent.

A moan—a distinctly female sound—issued from somewhere down the line of cages. A trilling laugh, musical and dark, ended in a choking sound like a sob.

What were these women doing here? Were they sick?

And then she remembered Saric's concubines.

She drew up her hood and walked swiftly past several steel worktables, one of them covered with a dirty sheet. It was draped over a thin form. A body.

Now she could see that this dungeon was in fact also one great lab.

A lab complete with human subjects.

Feyn hurried past the cages to the passage at the end. She turned into it, eager to leave the room and its cages behind. A tunnel opened up before her, where, at the end, a single torch cast light on an ancient cell refitted with modern steel bars.

As she approached, she could make out a hunched form inside, someone seated on a small cot and bent forward so that his beard seemed to drag against his knees. His sibilant words drifted in the darkness.

Was he praying?

She moved to within an arm's breadth of the bars, the soft leather of her shoes silent against the stones. He was old. His white hair, unkempt, formed an unruly halo around his head. Indeed, he appeared to be praying, but the words he murmured were none that she recognized.

"…the keepers for the Day of Rebirth. Keep the keepers for the Day of Rebirth. Bring the blood and keep it safe…"

She took hold of one of the cell bars. "Excuse me."

The man's head snapped up. She stared at his old eyes, round with fear. He shuffled to the front of the cage. She did not pull back.

"What are you doing out of your cage?" he asked in a phlegmy whisper.

"I don't have one." Her gaze roamed the wrinkles of his face, the furrows above his brows, the clawed grooves around his eyes. How old could he possibly be?

"Are you sure?"

She nodded.

"Why haven't I seen you here?"

"I'm not an alchemist." She found herself speaking balder truth than she had planned.

"Then what are you?"

"I am Feyn."

"Ah." His face registered something she could not identify. Was he mad then? "The mathematician. The Sovereign-to-be. Born October twenty-fourth, nearly twenty-five years ago. Surely not that Feyn."

"Yes. That one."

"Dear me! Have I missed the Day of Rebirth?"

So strange, so very strange.

"No. It's four days away."

"Ah, lady," the man said, reaching toward her hand with both of his. "May I?"

She let him take her hand, and oddly, she was not afraid of him. "If it eases your fear."

"It does! Because I'm dead, you know?"

"You don't look dead to me. And if I can help it, I'll keep you alive. Unless, of course, you deserve death."

"Don't we all?"

"No," she said.

"You might be surprised."

He seemed lucid enough and yet he spoke so cryptically.

"Are you the one they call the Book? The keeper?" She felt young just then, almost child-like. Of course. Compared with him she was practically a child.

"Can a book be a man?" he said.

"I don't know. You tell me."

"I carry the truth—it is in me. And so, yes, they call me the Book."

She felt her brow wrinkle. "I don't understand. Are you a little mad?"

"The whole world is mad, lady. Tell me, are you?"

"No. I don't think so."

"Ah, you don't *think*," he said, tapping his temple. "But what if what you think is wrong? What if you're ill and don't know it? Or a fool and think yourself wise?"

She'd never heard anyone quite like this old man before. What was it about his inflections, his laughter? He had mastered the mannerism as well as she, except that his timing was so odd and dotted with erratic exclamations. He truly did seem a little mad.

But not unpleasant.

He dropped her hand and leaned forward, grasping the bars of his cell to peer more closely at her. "Tell me something, Feyn who would be Sovereign. If you were to learn something that was true, though it went against all you knew, would you follow it?"

All she knew? Perhaps she had been naive about this place, but she could not believe that all she knew was built upon an untruth.

"I . . . I suppose so."

"Ah. Because there might lie madness for sure—to know the whole world had been led astray, and worse, with the greatest intention, and for the greatest good."

"Perhaps," she said. "But that's a ridiculous question at any rate." Unfathomable.

"Is it?"

"Of course. Now it's my turn to ask you a question. Who are the keepers?"

"Ah, lady, I would be breaking an oath in telling you that. And yet, you seem to carry a light in your eyes. You have a loyal heart. Still, how can I trust one who, though Sovereign, is not to be Sovereign?"

What was he saying?

"Please. Speak plainly."

"I am the keeper. The last, I fear."

"Why would you say I'm not to be Sovereign?"

"Did I say that? If so, I shouldn't have. I've taken an oath."

"Answer me most carefully," she said. "My brother spoke to me of an anti-Order. Is this what you are?"

"The only anti-Order, lady, is the Order itself. As for me, I am proudly out of Order." He grinned.

Clearly, he was mad. But she had to know more.

"He spoke also of life. Strange new life. Brought by alchemy."

"That alchemy brings only death. Then again, the dead rest in peace. And peace reigns on earth, doesn't it, dear Sovereign-to-be or -not-to-be? Life, on the other hand, comes from the blood and is full of terrible danger."

"What blood?"

"The blood. Do you have it?"

"I don't know what you're speaking about."

"No, of course you don't. If you had it, you would know what blood."

It was foolishness, utter foolishness, trying to speak to the insane. Nothing he said made sense. Everything he said was inverted. Truth to untruth, untruth to truth.

But she had found him, this Book that Saric had spoken of. What did that mean, then?

The man leaned close to the bars, eyes round and pleading. "You could set me free, lady. You have that power! I beg you, have mercy on an old man."

"I dare not free you, and if you have any wit, don't say you saw me."

The man blinked and pulled back, put off. "Then the least you can do is help us find the blood."

"Is that what my brother took, the reason he has these bizarre new ways?"

"Your brother?"

"Saric."

The man went perfectly still. "His ways are death."

A sound near the entrance, the scraping of the bolt. Feyn's heart jolted in her chest.

"Quickly," the old man whispered, grabbing the bars and leaning into them. "Find the blood, find the boy. Save them both, save us all!"

"What?" She glanced over her shoulder down the passage and then back at him. Boot heels clipped against the floor. Somewhere between the rows of cages, the occupants of which had started now to moan and rail more loudly, someone turned on a light in one of the lab areas.

"Find the blood! Save the dead!"

Sounds from the other end of the chamber reached her: something heavy being thrown down on a table, and then the distinct *thwack* of a hammer. No, not a hammer—a cleaver. The sounds of butchering. Excited calls issued from the row of cages.

Feeding time?

She had to get out now, before she was forced to speak to anyone. She had to think.

As though reading her mind, the old man said: "Along the back wall, there—it's where *he* comes down."

She assumed he meant Saric and nodded brusquely.

"I won't let them kill you, Keeper," she said, and turned hastily.

"It's too late for that," he said.

"We will see."

But she knew even then, as she hurried from the subterranean levels, that the ancient man who called himself the Book was probably right.

Chapter Fifteen

SARIC SAT on his horse and looked past the twisted scrub trees in the valley below him. The leafless pines reached up like so many claws, gnarled hands from the grave of Chaos.

Beyond the valley, Byzantium's ancient hills were indistinguishable in the darkness, her spires and towers specters of a way of life that no longer applied to this new day.

This new night.

The sky was one churning, effusive sea, reflecting the pallid light of streetlamps, the glow of homes where families huddled around their candles and lanterns.

Saric had nearly forgotten how he used to escape the Citadel to ride on fair evenings. The darkness had seemed less fearful, somehow, than the shadows in his chamber. The wind, on quieter nights, had even soothed him. But tonight he found the darkness not so much soothing as intoxicating, the air itself charged with strange and electric potential.

He closed his eyes and inhaled deeply.

The stallion shifted, pawed at the ground. Saric owned several horses within the Citadel stables, as was customary for royals, but he favored this one in particular for its dark coat, unusual height, and sheer power.

Was it possible that even before his transformation, he had valued power?

The horse, always a little wild, was more nervous around him than usual, a testament to its equine intelligence. Horses were well attuned to the moods of their masters.

The sole guard who accompanied him sat on his horse thirty paces away, under a tree. They'd reached the rise outside of Pravus's country estate minutes ago after an hour's ride. It was the third time Saric had come here but the first time at his own insistence.

He could feel the impending shift of power like a storm marching in from the desert.

The clip of a hoof on a rock reached him from over his right shoulder. A hooded figure astride a pale stallion came to a stop beside him.

For several moments, the two looked out at the city in silence. Overhead, the clouds scurried to the northeast. A storm was indeed coming.

"Your father rejected you." The voice was low and gritty and did not need to be raised above the capricious wind.

"Yes. I anticipated as much." He had no idea how the master alchemist could know it, however.

"And Feyn as well." It rankled, the implication in those simple words.

"She'll soon regret her decision."

"She is beyond seduction."

"*I* am beyond seduction."

The brief silence that followed was unsettling. If he wanted to, Saric reminded himself, he could haul the other man from his horse and kill him with his bare hands. He was stronger by far. But there was a latent strength about the presence beside him that came not from any physical dominance but from a deep-seated power beyond any earthly throne, greater than any Sovereign's crown.

Below them, more than five hundred thousand souls huddled beneath their Maker, whispering to heaven, seeding the clouds with their prayers to him. Fools.

"She will be Sovereign in four days. Our time is running short," Pravus said.

Saric's jaw tightened. "Our time's been short since the beginning. You animated me a mere eight days ago and yet somehow you expect me to seize power swiftly and with only my bare hands."

"Are you saying you can't?"

"On the contrary, I'm the only person who *can*. We both know that you, who took the serum long ago, would not have done it otherwise. No. I am the key to your plans. And now I hold the keeper. Your path to power runs through me."

They were bold words to speak to one such as Pravus. Dangerous words.

When the alchemist spoke his voice was softer, yet it crackled with the absolute assurance of one who had forgotten what it was to fear.

"It's a mistake to think you are singular, my friend. The world will be ruled by a vast army of others just like you."

The army. Thoughts of it both galvanized Saric and sent his heart pounding with anticipation.

"That army won't be raised unless I'm in power," Saric said.

"Then I suggest you do what we've discussed," Pravus said. "As I said, our time is short."

Pravus still had not looked at him. "There is one more thing," Pravus said.

"What is that?"

"Your wife."

Saric's skin prickled.

"Giving the serum to her was a mistake."

Heat crept along Saric's neck. Bringing Portia to her dark senses had been, at the time, a concession to his new appetites. A flex of his power for the simple pleasure of it. But now he felt schooled by the derision in the alchemist's gravelly voice. He clamped down on his anger.

"Portia is my business," he said tightly.

"On the contrary. You can't afford these kinds of mistakes."

"I'll deal with her."

"I already have."

"Have what?"

"Taken her."

Saric turned to look directly at him.

The face within the hood was pale, the eyes nearly white. But it was his skin, raised in lumps on his face, that disturbed Saric the most. That always disturbed him.

Would he himself come to look like that?

"She will be dead by morning."

Saric's fingers clenched into fists. The thought of Pravus having Portia, or even killing her, did not disturb him. She might indeed become a capricious liability.

What bothered him was that Pravus had seen the need to interfere.

He would be more careful. He would not leave these choices to fall into the hands of anyone else. He would never be blindsided again.

Not even by Pravus.

Saric lifted his gaze past the city to the black horizon beyond.

"Next time, you will leave it to my hands."

Pravus pulled on the reins and turned his mount. "There won't be a next time. You know what you must do."

Then Pravus was gone, the sound of his mount swallowed by the darkness. Alone, Saric waited several moments for the pounding of his heart to subside. He did know *precisely* what he must do.

Tomorrow, before the evening assembly bells tolled, the whole world would change.

FEYN

Chapter Sixteen

ROM KEPT his head down on the subway, his face obscured by the hood of the priest's cloak. Neah had insisted they delay their entry to the Citadel until well after midnight, when there would be considerably less security. She showed her badge at the smaller, less ornate gate used by employees and registered Rom as Remko Isser, a priest. "An emergency request," she explained to the guard.

"Apparently these kinds of requests aren't uncommon?" Rom muttered as they made their way at a fast clip toward the administrative building.

"No," Neah said.

Rom glanced at the stone gardens that lined the walkways of several offices, a museum, and a visitors center. The buildings were sizable, but they all seemed to merely crouch at the feet of the palatial building lit at regular intervals by lanterns. Even from this distance, he could see the forms of the statues that stood along the upper perimeter like otherworldly sentries with deep, hollow eye sockets.

"Stop gawking."

"I've never been in the Citadel before."

"Maybe you haven't, but Cleric Remko has. So stop it."

Two guards stood at a post halfway to the palace. He kept his gaze averted, his head bowed beneath the cowl, but his heart stalled as he wondered if they might be the same guards who had come into his home and killed his mother. Those faces would haunt his dreams forever.

He marveled at the way Neah strode past them without a glance. She entered through a side door, led him down a hall and into a small side office occupied by four desks. Even here the building seemed to bear the secrets of times before Null Year, the weight of the centuries saturating the walls.

"This is where you work?" He had always been under the assumption that Neah held an elevated position in the Citadel. But now he saw that she was one among four in a space the size of his old bedroom, populated by scratched desks and chairs that were probably older than he was.

"That's my desk, the one in the corner," she said, closing the door without meeting his gaze.

"It...looks very nice."

"No, it doesn't." She crossed the room to a small coat closet, pulled open the door, and gestured him in.

"What?"

"I have to go find out where they're holding your keeper, and sometimes the cleaning crew comes late. They don't bother with the closets, so you should wait in here. We can't risk them recognizing you."

Rom stepped inside, where there was just enough room for him to stand between several large boxes.

"Hurry."

"I will," she said, encasing him in darkness. He heard the outer office door close, the sound of her key in the lock.

She'd locked him in the office? Panic rose in his chest. He told himself he would have done the same. That he was safer in here than out there.

The minutes, measured only by the sound of his own breathing, crept too slowly. When had he ever been this impatient? When had images of every possible disaster ever plagued him as they did now? At last, unable to wait another moment, he opened the closet door. Darkness.

Rom made his way in the direction of the office door, banged his knee on a desk, cursed in a whisper. A key sounded in the door. He didn't have time to find the closet, so he crouched behind the desk.

The door opened, and the light flicked on. A form strode past him toward the closet, but stopped short before its open door.

A whisper: "Rom?"

Neah.

He stood.

"What are you doing?" she demanded.

"What took you so long?"

"It's not like the instructions to find the keeper are engraved on the walls," she snapped.

"You found him?"

"No. But I found out the way to the dungeons. I even got a key." She held it up.

Relief washed over him. "How did you get it?"

"I said I needed to get a priest down to the lower level as a matter of Order. Come on."

They left the building through a different door, away from the palace. The way was far less well lit, the paths narrower. They passed through a lower garden and approached the mouth of an old grotto. It was situated between two landscaped beds of stunted trees and lichen-covered statues, some so broken that they seemed not so much ancient as amputated. A torch glowed somewhere farther within, giving the entire cavern the feel of one faintly glowing maw.

It smelled like rain and gutter water. Even in the absence of the chill breeze, the temperature seemed to have dropped.

"How far?" His voice echoed.

"Straight in and down through here—this is the main entrance."

"If this is the main entrance, I'd hate to see the back one," he muttered.

They reached the lone torch sputtering in its iron bracket against the wall. Beyond it, Rom could make out the heavy iron bars of an expansive double gate. A huge lock requiring a key far larger than the one in Neah's hand hung on the front of it.

"Hades." He meant it. The place looked like the entrance to the underworld itself.

Neah went to the outer edge of the gate, and now Rom saw a smaller door cut into the stone. She worked the key in the lock for several seconds before finally getting the latch to turn.

"I should have taken one of the torches," she said.

"There's another farther ahead. See? Come on."

Now that they were here, at the entrance to the Citadel's darkest corridors, his heart surged. With fear, yes, but also with anticipation.

They hurried down a long stairway cut into the stone so long ago that the steps themselves drooped where so many feet had worn them down. The stair ended some forty feet beneath ground level at the mouth of a broad tunnel.

Except for the torches every twenty or so yards apart, he could have easily believed no one had been here in a hundred years. "I can't imagine anyone comes this way."

"The guard I asked said that this is the supply entrance."

Sixty yards and two more stair drops farther, the corridor ended at a heavy iron door. A guard standing to the side moved in front of it at their approach.

Rom lowered his head so that the cowl obscured his face.

"I've got a priest here on business," Neah said, flashing him her badge.

"I didn't receive any orders about a priest," the guard said. "Come back in the morning with papers."

Panic rose in Rom's chest. Morning was a wealth of hours away.

They would never get this close during daylight, not with his picture plastered on the front of every newspaper in Byzantium.

"Then you can be the one to explain why the priest didn't get here in time," Neah snapped. "Midnight, they said—we're already late as it is. Maybe too late."

"Too late for what?"

"I don't know. All I know is that he was summoned. Something about an old man."

"Old man?"

"Isn't this where the old man's kept, the one they call the keeper? You don't even know what I'm talking about, do you? And you're questioning me? Fine. It's your job on the line, not mine."

The guard chewed his lip. "I'll get the paperwork. You go on." He pulled the ring of keys from his belt and unlocked the door, which opened more smoothly than Rom would have guessed by looking at it.

The moment they stepped through, Rom could feel a slight movement of air that had not been present in the tunnel on the way down. The space in front of them wasn't only cavernous, but modernly regulated. Ahead of them, low electric light illuminated rows of stainless-steel and glass lab equipment. The entire place was part laboratory, part warehouse, with two rows of what appeared to be storage containers forming a dark aisle down the middle.

"Where is he?" Neah demanded, but her voice had lost a fraction of its edge.

"At the end through the tunnel," the guard said. He closed the door, leaving them alone in the dim light.

Somewhere from the main room, a voice sang. A bit of melody, broken off, followed by a trilling laugh.

Neah grabbed his arm. Her hand was cold.

"Let's go." Rom took her hand and led her along the back wall of the chamber toward the corridor indicated by the guard. Its rock walls were illuminated by a low torch, its glow glinting off the steel bars of a cell.

"That must be it," Neah said, her face pale even in the darkness.

"It must be," he murmured, heart pounding.

"I'll stay here and keep watch. Rom?"

His attention was fixed on the last cell. "Yeah?"

"Hurry."

A faint wheezing issued from inside the cell as Rom approached. He moved up to the barred door. It was too dark to see inside.

"Hello?"

The wheezing stopped. Silence.

"Hello?"

"I don't need a priest," a voice rasped.

Rom pulled back his hood. "I'm not a priest."

"Then why are you dressed like one? Trying to trick an old man? You think I'm a fool?"

"I'm more interested in tricking the guards."

Silence.

"Are you the keeper?" Rom asked.

"Am I?"

Rom moved closer to the cell bars. "You're the one they call the Book?"

"Am I?"

"Please! I didn't come here for fun. If you only knew what was at stake."

The grizzled face of an old man appeared at the bars. Torchlight darkened the furrows of his face. His unkempt hair was dingy gray. The old man's eyes widened. He shoved himself against the cell bars and stared at Rom.

"Elias?"

For a moment Rom couldn't speak. "Then it's true! You knew my father! Elias Sebastian was my father."

"Son of Elias?'" the man said.

"Yes!"

"He said you could be trusted."

"Who?"

"Your father."

The sound of those words momentarily overwhelmed Rom, and tears flooded his eyes. Tears of grief—all these years, and he had never known the truth. Tears of relief—that he did now.

"But what's this in your eyes? What have you done?" the keeper asked, voice suddenly more urgent than before. "Boy, what have you done?"

"I drank some blood," he blurted.

Even with the grime upon it in the dark, the man's face went white. He moved his mouth to speak, but nothing came out.

"I drank the blood and now I feel the world on fire and I'm here for answers."

"Maker!" the man squawked. Then again, in a raspy whisper, "Dear Maker."

"I don't know if it's the Maker. I only know that I need help."

"Then it's here. It's time. Do you know what you've done?"

The old man reached a gnarled hand through the bars and touched his cheek. "Flesh and blood," the keeper said. "Life. Mortality. By the Maker, it's true." He withdrew his hand. "Tell me what happened. Everything! Quickly."

The old man seemed to have shed his crazed disposition as if he'd shrugged out of a cloak.

"An old man found me. He said he knew my father. And now by your own reaction, I know it's true. He gave me the vial wrapped in vellum and told me to find you."

"What happened to him? Where is he?"

Rom shook his head. "They killed him. I saw it."

The man dropped his hand. He withdrew from the door, out of the torchlight. Rom pressed closer to it.

"Sir, please. I need answers!"

From inside the room, he could smell the rancid stench of old food, of urine, of the man himself. Now, his eyes adjusted, Rom could see him faintly in the corner, hear his piteous moan. But then he was back on the other side of the barred door, having seemingly thrown himself against it.

"Your father came to live in the city, as none of us has for a very long time. We have kept in hiding for centuries. He came to live as an informant because we knew the time was coming. He could tell you nothing, you understand? It would have endangered your life. And your mother's."

"They killed her, too. Yesterday."

The old man hesitated. "I'm sorry for it, boy. These are only the first deaths of many."

"What do you mean, *the time was coming*?"

"The time. The time, boy. That we have waited for! And now I am the last. But there is you. Are there five of you?"

"Five?"

"There was enough blood for five."

"Yes. No. There are only four. And only half a portion left."

"Only four? Are you well trained? Learned? You're the son of Elias. You must be."

"I...Not necessarily, no. Well, one of us is a fighter of sorts. In training with the Citadel Guard."

"Four hundred and eighty years. Forty generations, as per the twelve-year cycles of Rebirth. That's how long we've waited for this moment. Do you know what this is?"

"That's why I came!"

"Because you know?"

"No, because I *don't* know. Because the old man insisted I come. Because I don't know what to do!"

"You truly don't, do you? And yet you now know more than I."

"What?"

"What does it feel like?"

"To not know?"

"To *feel*, boy! To be the first man in nearly five centuries to have true emotions. To feel more than the fear that even now courses through my own veins. How does it feel?"

Rom opened his mouth, but how could he explain the rush of emotions he'd felt? The sadness, the love, the hope, the desire?

So he just said, "Terrible. And great. All at once."

"It's the remnant. The remnant that was before all this Order madness. There was a day when man truly lived. And now the remnant lives again. In you. In these other three. Who are they? Never mind." He waved a hand. "So many times I wondered if I would live to see it—if anyone would." He reached out through the bars with both hands, took Rom's hand, and clasped it tightly.

A tear slid down the front of the old man's face, making a clean track on his dusty skin.

"Forgive me, Maker, for doubting," the man whispered softly. "Do not count it against me on that day." He seemed to have fallen into prayer, forgetting Rom despite the fact that he clasped his hand.

"But how is this?" Rom said. "You're crying. You feel more than fear? Then you've drunk the blood yourself?"

Had his father?

The man shook his head. "No. No. The keepers don't know the blood firsthand. We knew it was never for us. We've kept its knowledge and remembered its ways. We've practiced and lived—and behave—as though we have it, in a foreshadowing of our hope to come. Hope. You see. I use that word though I have never made hope's acquaintance. But we've spoken and lived as though that day had come, in anticipation of it. And someday...someday..."

"But you must feel something. Other than fear, that is."

The old man thought about it and shook his head. "No. No, I don't think I do. We keepers spend much of our lives imagining feelings beyond fear, and so in a way I suppose we do, if only the way one might see his reflection in a cloudy mirror."

Rom shook his head. It was amazing. He had never seen anything like it. Like the deaf, mimicking words they could not hear, with more precision, even, than those who did. If anything, the keeper seemed to overdisplay emotion without firsthand knowledge of it.

"You called it a remnant," Rom said. "A remnant of what?"

The man lifted his head. "Of pure blood."

"What blood?"

"They call it the Age of Chaos, when all humans were truly human. They lied, and now the world knows no better. It's life! The real blood will bring life."

"How?"

The old man released Rom's hand and gripped the bars with white knuckles. "What is your name? Tell me."

"Rom."

"Rom, son of Elias. Then you must know, Rom, that there is a boy. You are tasked. You and these others."

"I don't understand. What boy? Tasked with what?"

Neah came several steps into the corridor. "Rom!"

The man's eyes darted her way, then back. "You have to find the boy. We tried but failed. They've taken us all. None of the candidates has fit, but he's out there, he has to be!"

"Hurry!" Neah rasped. "I hear someone!"

Rom turned back to the man and yanked out the vellum. He quickly unwrapped it. "What about these writings, here on the vellum—"

The man's eyes had gone to the vial, and Rom wasn't sure whether to let him hold it or keep it out of his reach. "Do you know what it says?"

"You have less than one full dose left?"

"That—that was an accident. What about the code?"

"Twenty-one," the keeper said. "Vertical."

"What?"

"Remember that. It's in Latin."

"Latin? How does that help?"

The old man stared at him, blinking. "You need a mathematician."

"What?"

"There's a woman named Feyn," the keeper said.

"Feyn? As in…Feyn, the Sovereign?"

"She'll riddle the vellum for you."

"What? That's impossible! Why can't you? Just tell me—"

"She's trained to be loyal to the truth. If you can win her confidence, she will help."

"What do you mean, *win her confidence*? You're talking about the next Sovereign! Why would she help me? She's the head of the Order! No, no, you have to tell us what we've done and what it means and what will happen to us!"

"Don't you understand? This isn't about you! And yet you are the one who must usher in the moment or all will be lost. All I've lived for, and every keeper before me. All that your father lived for. All that Alban died for. That was his name, the man who gave you that. You must usher it in, or we'll all live in this death!" Spittle flew from his mouth.

"Rom!" Neah again.

"Rom, son of Elias, do you know what you've inherited?"

Neah was running toward him. "They're coming!"

"They're coming," the man said, eyes darting in her direction again.

"But I need more answers!"

"The vellum. Nothing is more important than this! You'll bring life, if you succeed. Go, son of Elias!"

"Rom!" Neah grabbed his hand and tugged. "Run!"

Together they ran, chased by the keeper's last words: "Find the boy, Rom, son of Elias! Find him!"

CHAPTER SEVENTEEN

NEAH TUGGED Rom into a room that appeared to be a lab, keeping to the back wall as two guards ran into the tunnel they had just exited. A door at the far side flew open and two more guards burst into the giant chamber.

"That way!" Rom urged as soon as the guards had passed, veering for the shaft of torchlight that shone through the open door. Neah had no clue where that passage might lead, but exiting the way they'd entered would surely be a mistake.

"That way!" a female voice shrieked. "That way!"

Neah's skin crawled at the sound of the voice, the off-kilter cries behind them. Another voice took up the cry, and another, until they were all shrieking, "That way!"

Rom and Neah burst into a corridor lit by a single torch. Rom grabbed it. "Come on!"

Tears obscured Neah's vision, sent the fiery light of the torch in Rom's hand into fractured orange splinters. Her willingness to help Rom had turned into a nightmare. Waiting for Rom, she'd ventured a short way into the lab and seen it all: women, caged like animals, mad and raving. Bodies, laid out for experiments...

The dead, horrifically laid open. If she and Rom were caught, would she end up there?

They came to a large chamber. Rom held the torch up, illuminating stacks of books and myriad documents all crammed onto shelves built into sliding partition walls.

"The archive," she gasped, wanting to weep her relief. "We're in the archive. There should be a way up from here."

They found the small door on the near wall unlocked, its metal handle shiny and smooth from use. It led out to a landing at the foot of a narrow set of stairs, which they took two at a time before crashing into a door at the top. Rom twisted the knob.

"Locked," he panted.

Neah fell against it, wanting to beat it down.

"The key. The key, Neah!"

She remembered it now, fumbled to get it out of her pocket, and dropped it.

"Hurry!"

She fell to her knees and groped beneath the light of Rom's torch with shaking hands, found it. The sounds of pursuit issued up from the chamber.

She stood, thrust the key home, wrenched it hard, shoved the door wide, and burst through. Rom grabbed the key and slammed the door closed behind them.

"Lock it!" she ordered. He did so, quickly. "They might have a key of their own!"

"We're not waiting to find out," Rom said.

Together they ran through a great hall filled with richly appointed chairs, including a throne of sorts overlooking the round mosaic on the floor in the center of them all.

Neah glanced up at the vaulted ceiling. They had come up in the Senate Hall.

"Follow me," she whispered, running past Rom.

They ran out a small side entrance, past a set of heavy doors into a smaller chamber where the senators donned their robes for session.

Relief swept over Neah. She knew the back ways from here. They could be out of the Citadel in less than a minute.

"Come on!"

Rom grabbed her arm and pulled her up short.

"Neah—"

"We have to go!"

"No."

She slapped his hand away. "What do you mean, *no*?"

"We have to find Feyn."

She stared. Surely, she hadn't heard right.

"*What?* Don't be crazy! We have to get out of here now!" She wanted to hit him, to shake him.

"The keeper told me I have to find her."

"That man down there? He was insane!" The image of the body on the worktable burned in her mind.

Rom shook his head. "No. He wasn't. He knew my father. It's all real. And it isn't about us anymore."

"It isn't about Feyn, either. We'll be dead if we don't get out now!"

"She's a mathematician."

"What difference does that make?"

"The old man—"

"I don't care what the old man told you. If we don't survive the night, none of this will matter!"

Footsteps echoed through the empty Senate Hall beyond the door. Rom pulled her into the shadows as the guards ran past the antechamber, through the senate's great arched entry, and out into the main arcade.

"You go," he whispered when they had passed. "Tell Avra what happened. If I'm not back by dawn, leave the city with the others."

"Rom, please!" She couldn't tell him she was afraid to leave by herself, to get on that underground train, to confront a world that she wasn't sure had any true refuge in it. She felt herself on the verge of a breakdown. "You're just an artisan. Nobody! What can you do? For all we know, Feyn's not even here. All Sovereigns go to the country during the last days before their inauguration. She'll go to Palatia."

"You didn't hear what the keeper had to say. Neah, they've given their lives for this."

"It's not your problem!"

She couldn't believe this. She had agreed to help him learn more so that he could get them out of this predicament. That was all!

"It *is* my problem. You didn't hear him, or you'd understand. I'll explain it all later. Just please, tell me where I can find her. That's all I'm asking."

He really meant to stay. She could tell from the look in his eyes there was no way she'd get him to leave. After staring at him for an incredulous moment, she went to a door and yanked it open. It was the only way she could think of to help him, and even then she doubted he could survive.

"Hide in this robe closet and wait until everyone's gone. Across the arcade at the end of the corridor is a service elevator. Take it all the way to the top. Some of the Citadel artists keep studios there, in the attic space. Once you get past them, you'll be in the attic over the residences. Feyn's residence is the last one."

"The last? But I'll be in the attic?"

"Above her residence at the end."

"How do I find her?"

"If she's still here, I'm guessing she'll be sleeping in her room."

"But I'll be in the attic!" he said.

"Well you can't very well walk in through her door now, can you? You'll have to figure it out from there. And for the record I think you've lost your mind."

He looked off into the darkness.

"If you get caught, there's nothing I can do," she said.

"Give me your cloak."

"What for?"

"Just give it to me. Please." He reached out for it.

"It's raining out—"

"I'm going to need it more than you will."

She pulled off her cloak and shoved it at him. He took it and stepped in among the robes.

"Tell Avra I'll be back at first light."

She wanted to slap him, to tell him that he was a fool.

To also tell him that he was brave, braver than she would ever be. That Avra might even be lucky.

But mostly, that he was an imbecile.

She turned and stepped out of the closet. "You don't have all night. This place will be filled with people in five hours."

Neah closed the door before he could say anything, smoothed her cardigan, and walked through the antechamber doors into the Senate Hall.

No sign of the guards. She was going to make it.

"Who goes?"

She spun to the voice and saw that two guards had entered through the main doors.

"Who goes?" the guard repeated.

"I go," she snapped. "On royal business for Lucius. And what are you doing in the senate chambers so late? It's off limits!" She'd never been questioned when citing her overseer, but now her heart was beating so frenetically she thought she might faint in front of them.

The guards walked forward, scanning the chamber, unaffected by her scolding. "Have you seen two people run this way? Two, both in robes."

"I've seen only two guards and now I'm thinking I should report you."

The first guard pushed past her and stepped through the door into the antechamber. The second caught the door and went after him.

They were going to find Rom. For a moment she considered

making an attempt to distract them further. But the thought fled when she heard the faint squeal of the closet door inside.

The closet where Rom was hiding.

Without a second thought, Neah spun on her heel and ran. There was nothing she could do now. If she stayed they would only take her, too, and she'd be down in the dungeons with its terrors.

She ran all the way to the side gate before slowing enough to calm her breathing.

She flashed her badge at the main gate, trying to gauge how far she had to get before she could run again, before she could get home and warn the others. They had Rom. It didn't matter that he had the blood. They would torture him into talking, surely. They would spread him out on one of those metal tables and cut him open until he screamed all he knew.

And then the Citadel Guard would come for the rest of them.

Chapter Eighteen

H E LEFT the priest's robe inside the closet and slipped out of the antechamber just before the guards closed in from the other set of doors. Without the robe to identify him as the intruder, Rom made his way unnoticed to the service elevator and up to the attic as Neah had instructed.

The studios in the attic were divided by the upper level's unfinished wood framing, and he could pass easily from one to the next. Paintings and sculpture were littered everywhere, a veritable wealth of art. It was all fine stuff, proficient to the point of mathematical perfection, no doubt created by the best artisans the Citadel could afford.

It was the artwork in the third studio that quickened his heart.

These were not new works. In fact, they appeared ancient, in which case they should have been destroyed at Null Year. But here they remained, in various stages of repair and restoration. He shifted Neah's cloak in his hands and touched one of them, marveling at the texture of the paint, at the faces twisted in torture and in ecstasy peering out from the canvas. If these were from the Age of Chaos, they were forbidden. And yet here they were in the Citadel itself.

He had to force himself to leave them, to hurry through the last studio, where he grabbed a sculptor's hammer and chisel from a table next to an ancient bust.

At the end, Neah had said. He stepped past the area of finished floor onto an ancient beam and eased down its length into the shadows beyond the lights of the last studio. All the way to the gable wall fifty paces on.

If what Neah said was right, Feyn's residence was directly beneath him. Now the question was simply one of where to gain entrance. And how.

The ceiling beneath the wood framing was plaster, so breaking through wouldn't be a problem. But doing so without being discovered would be nearly impossible. Anyone sleeping directly below would undoubtedly wake at the first pound of his hammer. By the time he finally broke through, a dozen guards would be settled in to welcome him.

His mind skipped back to Neah. To Avra, waiting for him. He was probably a fool not to have escaped while he could. Standing there on that wooden beam, thinking through his options, Rom was sure of it.

It wasn't too late to join Neah. He could retrace his steps and probably flee the Citadel without getting caught. He could run, as he had before, and take Avra out of Byzantium, beyond the city the way she had wanted him to from the beginning. With Triphon's help, they might all survive.

He had no delusions about his chances here. He would likely get caught, might even end up in the dungeons he'd just left.

If they let him live.

The keeper's voice rang out in his mind. *Find the boy, Rom, son of Elias!*

It took him ten minutes to decide which area of the ceiling was the right size and location for a closet. He found one framed eight paces to a side, large enough for anyone else's bedroom, but the smallest space he could see without pipes rising out of it, which would have indicated a bathroom instead.

The ventilation was poor. Sweat streamed down his chest as he stood at the corner of the space and prayed that it was a closet.

Balancing on adjacent beams, he raised the hammer. This was it, then. He'd fled Hades these last two days. The time had come to throw himself headlong into the fire.

With a single swing of the hammer, the ancient plaster cracked and a ten-inch section fell away. Rom caught his breath and waited for the material to rain through to the floor below, for a subsequent scream and the appearance of outraged faces.

Darkness. Nothing. But they could be coming. He had to get through, fast, and hide.

He set the hammer aside, content to keep the chisel in his pocket for now, braced one foot on the adjacent rafter, and drove his other heel through the plaster. A big chunk broke away.

All was still silent and dark beneath. He grabbed Neah's cloak from the floorboards, swung down on the rafter, dangled through the hole in the ceiling, and dropped.

Onto a soft rug. He glanced up. The jagged hole he had just come through was outlined by the faint light beyond.

Rom scanned the area and found himself facing a long row of velvet and silk robes. The scent of sandalwood and some kind of perfume lingered everywhere. An entire wall was filled with myriad shelves of leather boots and brocade slippers.

This could be the wardrobe of only one person on earth.

He found the door, poked his head out into a hallway, and slipped out, grateful for the faint light emanating from another room down the hall.

The apartment beyond was huge. Hangings on the walls hovered like specters as he moved past a small dressing table out into the expansive bedroom.

The drapes were open to a gray sky, allowing enough light in for him to see the lay of the room. A sitting area near the window. A wide bed. A form was lying there, alone. And asleep.

Rom crossed quickly toward the bed, wondering what exactly he was supposed to say.

Hi. My name's Rom.

It was a decision he never had to make; his foot caught against the edge of a rug and he stumbled forward into the mattress.

The form in bed jerked up with a gasp. "Who's that?"

"Sorry—"

Sorry?

The woman, whom he could only assume was Feyn herself, cried out and scooted away from him.

Rom lunged for her, forcing her back into the pillows. His palm found her mouth and cut short the sound of her scream.

"Please! Don't scream. I won't hurt you, I swear!"

She struggled under him, kicking and twisting in a frantic attempt to be free of him.

It occurred to him then that she was probably trained in the ceremonial art of fighting at least and would likely throw him from the bed if he didn't find a way past her fear.

"Shhh, shhh. Forgive me, lady. Please. I need your help, I won't hurt you. I just need your help."

She nearly wrenched free except that her nightdress seemed to be caught under his weight beneath the heavy blankets.

"I'm not here to hurt you. Please, you have to believe me. I was told to find you, told by an old man in the dungeons here. Please!"

That stopped her. She lay breathing hard through her nose, eyes wide, searching his face in the darkness.

Rom went on between labored breaths: "He said you'd be able to give me answers. I've risked everything to come here. They've killed my mother, my father, and an old man to suppress what I now know. Please don't scream—I need your help."

He realized the keeper had been right. He *would* risk everything. His life was over. He could never go back. But that life had been a half life. Somehow, he had always known it. And now that he understood the difference, he would devote all that remained of this life to seeing his mission—whatever this five-hundred-year-old secret was—through. Whatever it took.

TED DEKKER AND TOSCA LEE

Even if he had to knock the future Sovereign out to keep her quiet.

Perhaps she sensed that in him, because she quieted.

"Do you believe me?" he said. Silence. "If you won't scream I'll let go. I don't want to hurt you, but I will if I have to." She remained very still.

"You won't scream?"

A slight shake of her head.

He slowly moved his hand. She started to scream.

Rom clamped down hard over her mouth. "You said you wouldn't scream!"

She jerked and he knew that he would have to resort to the chisel in his pocket. It took him a moment to get it free.

"I have a blade!" He lifted the chisel in his fist. "I don't want to cut you, but you're forcing me! Please, be quiet!"

Her breathing, ragged and erratic, filled the room. There was a very real chance he was going to Hades.

"I'll free your mouth, but you have to remain calm. Not a word. I just want to ask you some questions. That's it. And only because the keeper told me I had to find you, do you understand?"

Finally, she nodded.

"I'm going to let go again. But don't think I won't hurt you if I have to. What I have to talk to you about is critical."

Again she nodded.

Slowly, he removed his hand, ready to smother her mouth at the first sign she'd played him. Her eyes flitted to the chisel in his hand, then back to his eyes. Calm seemed to settle over her.

"This is madness," she said. "You'll be dead within the hour. Do you know who I am?" She sounded young, perhaps his own age. That surprised him.

"It's why I'm here! And I'm committed to seeing this through, you need to know that."

"You're the fugitive who's been in the newspaper," she said. "If you think this kind of approach will get any cooperation from me, you're a fool."

Heat spread over Rom's face as the truth of her statement sank home. The guards were still searching for him. As soon as Feyn realized that he wasn't a trained fighter and that he didn't really have the resolve to hurt her—certainly not with a chisel—she would scream again.

He set the chisel on the coverlet and fumbled to pull the vellum from his pocket.

"See this?" he said, trying to shake it open, to hold it up before her. "I need to know what this means. This is what I'm here for. The old man said you could read it. It's important—not just to me, but to the world. You'll see. Tell me what it means and I promise I'll leave."

She barely glanced at it.

"That old man is mad. And you're as mad as he is if you think I'm going to help you."

Rom realized he couldn't risk trying to persuade her here, where his mission could so easily come to an abrupt end.

He had to get her out.

"When you hear me out, you'll retract those words." He shoved the vellum into his pocket, grabbed the chisel.

When he moved, the gray light fell full on her face and eyes. Maker. He'd assumed the posters and pictures of her were manipulated images—based on a real person, yes, but icons, nonetheless.

But she was an icon come to life. Even disheveled, Feyn seemed more than human. And yet, she had felt fully human in his arms.

Human, and warm. That surprised him, too. He'd never been so close to a Brahmin before. He would have stared, fixated by her, too aware of his lowly station, except for her next words.

"My guards are going to kill you. How did you get in here anyway?"

"Your guards? They're dead. I killed them."

She didn't need to say anything for him to know she didn't believe him.

He clamped his hand back over her mouth, wrapped his other arm around her waist, and pulled her, twisting in his grip, off the bed.

"Stop!" he growled. "I don't want to hurt you. Stop this!"

She did not stop. And so he dragged her, struggling—he'd had no idea she was so tall—to the closet. "Where's the light?"

She wasn't going to tell him, was she?

"Listen," he said near her ear. "I'll knock you out if I have to. I'll do what I must to get your help."

Her eyes glanced at the wall. Rom felt behind a bank of scarves and found the switch hiding behind it. He flipped the light on, grabbed a black scarf, and forced most of it into her mouth.

He had to keep his mind off the fact that he was kidnapping the Sovereign. That she was beautiful, that her presence tugged such an unexpected response from him.

Why should this surprise him? He was still grappling with the newly awakened feast of his emotions after a lifetime of being starved. She might have been any woman; he would have responded like a starving man confronted with a banquet table. It was nothing more.

"We're leaving."

Her eyes widened.

"And you'll help me, or I'll take you out of here unconscious," he said, as much for his own benefit as hers. "I mean it!"

Working quickly, he pulled off another scarf and used it to tie her wrists behind her back.

He grabbed a simple white dress, the plainest he could find, and tossed it at her. "Put this on."

The gown fell to her feet. She looked at him as though he was an idiot and for a moment he realized he was; she couldn't dress with her hands bound.

"If you try to run, I swear I'll hurt you. You have to ask yourself what kind of man would resort to kidnapping. I might be crazy. With four days—three now—until your inauguration, it would be a mistake to take any chances."

He freed her hands and stood near the door so she couldn't make a run for it. "Now get dressed. Hurry."

She looked at him with an impenetrable expression and he turned away, just enough to let her shed the nightgown and don the simple shift, but not enough to let her completely out of his peripheral vision. No matter how much he might deserve it, he couldn't afford a swift blow to the head.

When she had dressed, he retied her hands with the scarf.

He looked at the long shelf of boots along the wall. "That's a lot of shoes. Where does your maid keep the polish?"

She looked toward a lower shelf. He found a container of black polish there and several cloths. With one hand, he wiped copious amounts of polish on her.

"Sorry. I can't have you looking like royalty."

She said something unintelligible behind the wadded scarf in her mouth. He ignored her and finished dirtying her dress.

"I may not be schooled like you, but don't take me for a fool," he said. "If nothing else, my imagination is better than yours. And you're going to find that I'm living a life you can't even dream about, Sovereign or not. Step into these shoes." He held out a pair— the plainest he could find.

She made no attempt to follow his request.

"Then don't. What's it to me if you cut your feet out there?"

She stepped into the shoes.

He wrapped a dirtied white shawl around her head, leaving only her eyes showing. But that was no good—her eyes were unmistakable—so he covered her entire face. Rather than object, she remained quiet and still.

She was a brave woman, he had to give her that much.

Rom took up her nightdress and tore it into strips for his own use. Was he overlooking anything?

Nothing other than his sanity.

He placed Neah's cloak over her shoulders.

Time to go. The faster he got out of the Citadel, the higher his chances for survival.

"Listen to me." He faced Feyn. "This is very simple. You're a diseased serving-woman. If you've been down to the dungeons I just came from, you know what I'm talking about. And I'm a worker here, hauling you out before you infect everyone. The guards won't recognize you, and any attempt you make to struggle will only confirm your illness."

He paused, only moderately satisfied with his strategy. But it was the best he had.

"Now we can go back up the hole in this closet, which could get ugly, or we can take a back door out of here, which would be much easier. I'm going to free your mouth for a moment. Don't bother thinking a scream will be heard from in here. Just tell me if there's a back way out."

She stood still. He eased the scarf from her mouth. "Which way?"

"This is—"

Rom shoved the scarf back into her mouth. "That doesn't sound like an answer to me. Let's try one more time."

She remained quiet for a moment and then obliged him. "There's a staircase behind the silk curtains. Where are you taking me?"

"What's the fastest way out of the Citadel?"

She hesitated and then said, "The service entrance."

He replaced the gag. "If we run into any guards in general and you scream, they'll only take you for deranged and know just how diseased you are."

The guards' fear of disease would keep them off. For the first time since entering the Citadel, he felt a growing sense of confidence.

Rom wrapped a wide strip of her nightgown around his own face, covering his mouth in a makeshift mask against her "disease."

"Let's go," he said. Keeping a tight grip on her elbow, he led the Sovereign-to-be from her room, then along several passageways occupied by guards who were only too eager to let them pass, and eventually out the side gate.

Those few riding the underground at this hour cast nervous glances in Feyn's direction.

"Wellness center," he explained. "Contagious." They all exited the train car at the next stop.

Feyn had only struggled once, at the Citadel gate, and as Rom had predicted her scene only hastened their escape.

They rode north, to the farthest station point outside the city. Only when they were far beyond the station, on the deserted road to the royal stables, did he unwind the shawl from her face and take the damp handkerchief from her mouth.

"Are you mad? You smuggle me out as a diseased whore?"

"I didn't say whore."

"Does it matter?"

The scent of fresh hay and manure drifted through the air. They were approaching the complex of the royal stables, which was so large that the sheer number of workers it employed merited its own stop on the north train.

"And now what—we're going to saddle a horse and go for a predawn ride?"

He didn't really know how this was going to work, so he said nothing as he steered her toward a stable next to what looked like an indoor arena.

The stables were dark except for a single light at the end of each one. Staying near the light—he would need to see what he was doing—he moved toward the first stall.

"Your amulet is Sumerian," she said. "They said you were an artisan."

"I don't see any guards. Are there any posted here?"

"The stables don't usually need them. Most people are afraid of horses."

Now that she said it, he wondered if he would be. He had always thought it would be calming to ride a horse. But now that he was confronted with the prospect, he wasn't so sure.

"You're serious about this," Feyn said.

"I am."

He led her to a stall. A nearly white thoroughbred came to meet them.

Rom unlatched the stall door but made her go in first.

"Do you even know how to saddle a horse?"

"No." He picked up the saddle on the stand outside and turned back to confront the haughty Sovereign and the great mass of horse inside.

"You're going to ruin her. Untie me. I'll do it."

"Just tell me what to do."

"Do you think I'm going to run off like this?"

"You could knock me out and ride bareback out of here."

The thought of her riding bareback on the animal was wildly alluring.

"Put down that saddle and get the pad off the wall."

He took one look at her and put it down before going to fetch the pad and a saddlebag with a couple of canteens strapped to the side.

He followed her directions in placing first the pad and then the saddle on the horse.

"The girth."

He cinched the girth, knotting the end of it.

"Get the bridle."

All this time he had watched her with no small measure of respect and wariness. He hadn't ruled out her clocking him and running. Even as she slipped the bridle over the horse's head and got the bit in place—all with her wrists tied in front of her—he wasn't sure that she wouldn't ride out of here without him one way or another. It was why, when it was time, he mounted first and then reached down and hoisted her up in front of him.

Only then did he untie her hands so she could sit properly and guide the animal.

The horse shifted beneath them, and he grabbed her tightly. If he fell, she was coming with him.

"Take us north," he said, "into the wastelands."

Chapter Nineteen

DESPITE HER exhaustion, Avra couldn't sleep. Not with the ghosts dashing through her mind, mocking and sending her spinning off axis no matter how she tried to reassure herself.

Rom should be back by now, Avra. Rom is dead, Avra. They've cut him in two and left him to bleed out on the side of the road, Avra.

She flung off the covers and went out from Neah's bedroom to the living room, where Triphon was snoring, gape-mouthed on the sofa. He'd been in the same position for nearly three hours and she wouldn't have minded slapping the contentment off his face, if only to have some company in her misery.

"Triphon." She sat down on the edge of the coffee table and shook him by the shoulder. "Triphon!"

He jolted up. "Someone coming?"

"Don't you think they should be back by now?"

He fell back against the sofa's stuffed arm, one leg dangling off the front edge of the seat cushions. "Not necessarily. Have you ever been to the Citadel?"

She shuddered. "No."

"It's pretty big. Depending on where they went and how long it takes them to find what they're looking for, it could be a while. Especially if they're staying out of sight."

Triphon swung both feet to the floor. The sight of him had always been soothing and familiar to her—a poor way of saying, before she knew fondness existed, that she was fond of him.

Now she knew she also trusted him.

He scrubbed at his short hair. "What time is it, anyway?"

Avra stood and paced, hands on hips. "Almost three in the morning."

Triphon got up. He went into the kitchen to look at the wall clock, then came back.

"Two forty. You're right. They should be here."

She stopped pacing. "Maybe we should head toward the underground station to see if they're coming?"

Triphon returned to the sofa but did not sit. "That won't do anything. The last train leaves the Citadel at three o'clock. It's almost an hour commute to the station from here. So if we don't see them in—what, an hour and a half?—they didn't get out in time."

"Didn't get out? You mean they were caught?"

"They might've had to hide for a while. Neah would know to get out of there before people start coming in. The trains don't start again until five in the morning."

"I'm worried," she said.

"They'll be fine."

"We still have time to catch the last train if we hurry. You have clearance—we could get in, go after them."

"What, go to the Citadel?"

"I have a horrible feeling. What if they need us?"

Triphon nodded. "I would, but we gave our word to Rom—"

"That was before they disappeared!"

"We don't know they disappeared."

"I can't lose him, Triphon." She felt a tear run down her right cheek. "I know you understand that. I can't lose Rom."

"I know," he said softly, looking away. "I know how it feels." He grabbed his jacket. "All right."

A key sounded in the door and they both froze.

The door flew open. Neah rushed into the apartment. She was shaking. Ashen.

Avra glanced at the empty doorway behind her. "Where's Rom?"

"What happened?" Triphon said, looking out the door before closing it.

Neah's face was drawn. "They've got him."

Avra faltered. "Who has him?"

"What happened?" Triphon demanded again.

"You just left him?"

"No, I didn't just leave him!" Neah clasped her head.

"What happened?"

"We came out of the dungeons, ready to leave, but Rom said he had to stay."

"*What?*"

"He said he had to stay because the keeper, that crazy old man in the dungeon, told him he had to find Feyn."

"Feyn?" Triphon hesitated. "As in...*Feyn?*"

"What? *Why?*"

Neah shook her head. "I don't know! He said he couldn't leave without finding her. But the guards were coming. They were coming and he was hiding and they found him." She paced past them and back, wringing her hands. "He's probably in the dungeon by now. That horrible place!"

"We have to go," Avra said. "Now, before the underground shuts down for the night."

"No. You can't just walk in there! The guards are on alert. I barely got out. They're looking for me."

"But not me," Triphon said.

"Right." Avra said. "They're not looking for Triphon. Triphon and I can go."

"What good would that do? Even if you got in, you don't know where to find him."

"You can tell us," Avra said.

"Neah's right," Triphon said. "If they're on alert, you wouldn't pass. I, on the other hand, could. I'll get him."

"No," Neah said again.

"Why not?"

Neah met his gaze, seemingly unable to speak.

Avra tried to think, biting at the thumbnail she had already worn down to nothing.

"I could take a hostage," Triphon said.

"No, no." Avra shook her head, glanced at Neah. She had gone silent.

"If Rom does end up in the dungeons, who's in charge of them?"

"Saric," Neah said faintly.

An idea—a crazy idea—took root in Avra's mind.

"I have a plan."

"Are you deaf?" Neah said. "Have you heard nothing I've said? I'm not going back!"

"You won't have to. Triphon and I will go." Avra turned toward Triphon. "Are you with me?"

He grinned. "To the end."

Chapter Twenty

SARIC PAUSED before his chamber's long mirror. It was new, a replacement for the one shattered by Portia.

Portia, who was now...absent.

Outside his chamber, the residence buzzed with activity. Feyn herself, he imagined, had already left for the countryside, not to return until her inaugural entrance into the city—a journey that would begin at the country estate, near the stables, and end on the steps of the Grand Basilica. Until then, she would spend the next three days in solitude.

Three days. So much would change.

He smoothed the sleeves of the robe. Tilted his head and studied the line of his jaw, now perfectly smooth, a translucent veneer over the dark veins that branched like the limbs of an inky tree. This was the face the world would soon come to fear.

It was time.

It took him less than five minutes to reach his father's quarters. This time, he noted, the secretary rose to meet him.

"My lord."

"Are the arrangements as I requested?"

"Yes, my lord. The Sovereign is waiting for you." She gestured him toward the great bronze doors.

"Alone."

"Alone, as you requested."

"There's so little opportunity to share a private meal with my father alone, you understand."

"Yes, but there will be many opportunities with the Sovereign your sister." The secretary's smile was polite, but he found the expression unattractive.

"It will never be quite the same as with Father, will it?" He gave a smile of his own and pushed wide the great bronze door.

Inside, the receiving chamber was filled with the smell of venison and wilted greens, all set upon a simply appointed table.

Vorrin was behind the great desk nearby, writing. Saric went to one knee.

"Saric. Good morning." Vorrin gestured for him to rise. "Give me a moment."

"Take your time, Father. I imagine there's much demanding your attention these last days."

He waved off the servant turning up the gilt teacups on the table. "You may go. I'll serve my father this morning."

"If you would, please take these out to Camille." Vorrin stood and gave the documents to the servant, who left, closing the heavy double doors behind him. Having prepared the tea, Saric went to embrace his father.

He accepted his father's kiss, suppressing the urge to recoil from the crepe-like skin of his cheek, the thin line of his lips.

Vorrin glanced toward the window. "It would be an auspicious end, I think, to see the sun once before the conclusion of my reign."

Saric poured his father some tea, then forked venison and greens onto his plate. "Are we really going to talk about the weather?" He walked around the small table and sat down.

"You're right. Time enough to reflect on these things after." Vorrin bowed his head and Saric paused, hands in his lap.

"Maker guide us in all we do. We are blessed to have Order."

"We are blessed," Saric murmured before reaching to fill his own plate.

They ate for a full minute in silence before Vorrin set down his fork. "Now that it's ending, I confess, I find myself filled with some strange anxiety. But I'm comforted that Feyn will soon take my place."

"Do you suppose that Megas, at the end of his reign, looked back on all that he had accomplished and considered it good?"

"Megas, more than any of us, accomplished great things."

"And yet some say that he had Sirin killed. Have you ever heard that?"

Vorrin stirred his tea. "Yes," he said at last. "It is an old, blasphemous rumor. One of many. Whatever the truth, the Maker has seen fit to grant us Order out of it. That is what matters."

"Is it?" Saric set his fork down and stared across the table at the aged thing that had once been his father. "Is it all that matters, really? You say that, but I have to ask, what *was* so bad about Chaos?"

"Please. Such questions you ask." He set down his spoon. "You've lived so long under the prosperity of Order that you cannot know— none of us can—the horrors of Chaos. The violence of it. The dark ends of hate and jealousy and ambition."

"Are they all so dark?"

"Yes," Vorrin said, lifting his teacup. He took a small sip. "Or have you forgotten the events prior to Sirin—the detonation of the weapons? Millions of lives were lost. Farmlands ruined. Many people starved. Where there is hunger and death, there is terrible unrest. All that makes us human, all of our higher pursuits, become lost to baser ways. Men become like animals. It was Sirin who preached Order out of darkness. But it was Megas who had the vision to give Sirin's Order universal life."

Saric's gaze followed his father's cup as it settled back on the saucer. "You respect Megas, yes? Even if he had Sirin killed."

"There was a time when this rumor troubled me greatly. But sometimes imperfect tools lead us toward perfect ends."

Saric resisted the urge to smile. "Look around you, Father. Do you really see perfection?"

Vorrin glanced up, fork in hand. He set it down, ran his tongue over his lips, and sucked at a tooth.

"Of course it's not perfect. You and I know that. But the people need a way to temper their fear of death. They need their icons, their support rails to hold on to as they walk unsteadily through this life. We need them, too. Order isn't perfect, but it's surely greater than we are."

"Is it? To what end?" Saric said. "Bliss? What do you know of Bliss?"

"I know only what you know: That it is the absence of fear. And I know that the rules of Order mark the path that avoids fear. The Maker does not require the rules of us; *we require the rules of the Maker.* We are the ones who need them, not he. That is the greatest secret. You've never understood this the way Feyn does. But in time, you will. That is my prayer for you."

The old man coughed. He dabbed at his lips, looked down at his napkin as though surprised at the saliva there.

Saric slid back from the table and stood. "Do you know what I think, Father? That I do understand. I understand that this is all so much *rot*. That you've bought into the greatest illusion of all. We're not *more* human because of Order. We're less. The very Maker we bow to has stripped us of passion!"

A muscle beneath the wrinkled skin of his father's eye had begun to tic, like the first mechanical hiccup of a malfunctioning machine.

"Megas was great for his passions, you old fool. For his willingness to take up a weapon and make his convictions a reality. But in doing so he stripped us of the same thing that made him great. And what are we now? We're rats." He dropped his napkin onto his plate. "But no longer, Father. I will not abide in this rat hole."

"What—what are you talking about?" Vorrin said, his last word coming out with a wheeze. He tried to push back from the table as well, but his hands trembled. His strength had left him. "Dear Maker…"

Saric slowly approached him, watching the failure of his body with dispassion. "You refused me the senate, Father. And so I shall take it my own way."

Vorrin pulled at the neck of his robe, gasping for breath. "You don't know what you're doing. You'll throw the world back to Chaos!"

Saric jerked his father's robe, sending the Sovereign sprawling to the floor. "More than that, dear Father, I'll rule that chaos with an army that will make you gasp from your grave."

Vorrin curled and then arched against the floor, mouth open, jaw working, sucking air. Not unlike a fish, Saric thought.

"Your heart is stopping," Saric said, tilting his head to study him. It was just as Corban said. "A small gift of alchemy. A little something that will leave no trace, I've been assured."

"I beg you…I beg you, my son—" Vorrin gasped, his thin lips turning blue.

Saric crouched next to him, peered into his ashen face. "It's so beneath you to beg for your life."

The Sovereign's lips moved, but this time no sound came out. Instead, the breath wheezed from between them as the light slowly faded from his old gray eyes.

The room was silent.

Saric stood and embraced the fear and anguish that now flooded his mind. He'd prepared for this moment, but he hadn't expected his emotions to be so natural, so visceral.

He let out a cry and lurched toward the door. Threw himself against it, pushed it open.

"Help!"

The cry came out as a guttural roar, propelling the secretary to her feet. "Get the doctor! The Sovereign's stopped breathing!"

She went white.

"Now!" he shouted.

He spun and hurried back to his father's side. It would only take a minute; the Sovereign's physician, however rarely needed, lived in an adjacent apartment just as the head of the senate did.

When the sound of pounding feet reached him, Saric sank to his knees beside the lifeless ruler. "This was your fault," he said softly into the lifeless old ear. "You were always a fool."

Saric straightened and pushed against Vorrin's chest. "Breathe, Father!" he shouted. A wheeze slid through the dead Sovereign's lips. Saric pounded his father's ribs with a fist.

Rowan came bursting into the room.

"Help me!" Saric shouted.

In a flurry of robes the senate leader dropped to his knees on the other side of the Sovereign. He tilted up Vorrin's head, listening for breath, but there was none to hear.

Others had pushed through the heavy doors. Some of them held their hands against their mouths, stifling their cries; some wailed fearful prayers.

Some simply stared at the body jerking on the floor as the senate leader pounded upon Vorrin's chest.

"The physician is here—out of the way!"

Saric spun back just as the woman who'd seen to his father's health for the last decade—a middle-aged woman named Sarai—burst through the knot of onlookers. She dropped to her knees and felt his throat, listened near his mouth, and then stacked her hands upon his chest and began a rapid series of compressions. The body of the Sovereign spasmed like a puppet to the audible crunch of bone.

Rowan turned away as though he might be sick.

After several moments, the doctor stopped. Sweat beaded on her temple and nose.

"He's dead?" someone cried from the door.

"Out!" Rowan roared. "Get out!"

"It can't be." Saric let anguish fill his throat. He fell back on his heels and stared at the dead body. "My father's dead?"

That silence was answer enough. Those at the door did not leave but stood transfixed by the sight.

Saric let out a low moan. He staggered to his feet, gripped his robe with both hands, and ripped it wide.

"Father!"

Rowan, trembling and pale, stood to follow the old custom. His long fingers dug into the front of his great black robe. The heavy velvet tore open.

"Maker have mercy on us."

Saric sank back down to his knees. He wrapped his arms around the old man's carcass, so thin beneath the myriad layers of his embroidered robe. "Father, Father..."

You see how low I will stoop now, Father? To belittle myself like this in such a pathetic fashion? How I cradle your body when others shrink from it?

He felt his body shaking, but it was from his own rage and disgust, not the fear the others thought they saw.

"Father..."

They tried to draw Saric up by the shoulders. "My lord..."

It was Rowan. He pulled at Saric with trembling hands.

Saric dug his fingers into the withered limbs of his father and clung more tightly.

"My lord! It's death. You must let go."

Saric turned on the man. "Leave me! Leave us!"

The senate leader looked about him, obviously disoriented by the unprecedented nature of this event. Which of them had ever witnessed the death of a Sovereign? Even the physician had backed away, white-faced.

"Sire, you must know." Rowan's tremulous voice filled the chamber. "I cite the Order: *If one Sovereign shall die before the end of his term, his eldest, should he have progeny, shall rule in his place until the end of that term."*

The senate leader was shaking. Saric could see it now in the tremor of his torn robes where they gaped like wounds against his bare, smooth chest.

"Sire…"

Saric flung his hand out. "Leave me!"

"But you must—"

"My Sovereign lies dead and you cite old laws?"

"The Sovereign lives," Rowan said. The senate leader's face was a mask of terror. Saric saw it clearly—the man's slow swallow, the working of his throat, the tight draw of his brows.

"He is Saric, eldest son of Vorrin." He dipped his head.

"Do not speak this to me," Saric said, this time with dangerous quiet.

Rowan's eyes darted back and forth between Saric and the form of Vorrin. He was fearful, yes, but resolved to follow Order. Doggedly determined. As ever.

As Saric knew he would be.

"Sire, I cite the Order."

Saric stood. "No. Call for my sister." He turned toward the door. "Call my sister, Feyn!"

"It is the law!" Rowan said, and sank to one knee.

Behind him the doctor hesitated, and then quickly followed suit. One by one, those standing in the doorway, the Citadel Guard in the middle of the room, Camille the secretary, all went down to their knees.

"Get up. All of you, get up!" Saric snapped. "I'm not fit to *advise* this man, much less sit on the throne."

No one rose.

"Forgive me," Rowan said. "I never realized until now your great loyalty to your father." There was something new in his eyes, Saric thought. A newfound deference that had not been there before. "We all fear and mourn this loss. But now you must come before the senate. Please. You cannot leave the world without a Sovereign."

"You would have me as Sovereign for three days when Feyn has been groomed for this, has prepared years for it, and is poised, even now, in preparation for this very office? In this one thing the Maker has been merciful. Seek my sister."

"She cannot assume rule yet. Order forbids it."

"There is Order, but there is also practicality and reason. If you won't move to inaugurate Feyn early, then at least choose someone with experience. Miran, Sovereign before Father, is alive and well. Let him serve."

Rowan stood and closed the space between them. He touched Saric's sleeve and spoke in a low voice. "Sire, I beg you. Everyone will be fearful enough that they've lost a Sovereign. We cannot deviate from Order. In such a difficult time especially, you must follow protocol."

Saric pushed back and snapped at those gathered on their knees by the door. "Get out! All of you, out. Have you no respect for the dead?"

They hurried out, leaving only Saric, Rowan, and the physician to contend with the dead body.

When they had gone, Rowan started to speak, but Saric silenced him with a gesture.

"I won't serve a law that's a disservice to humanity," he said. "This law, however inspired by the Order, is not in favor of the people."

"Nevertheless, it's the law!"

Saric looked at the form of his father sprawled upon the floor, and then tore his gaze away. He covered his face in his hands and breathed deeply. At last, he dropped his hands: "Then grant me this. Put me before the senate. Let me make my argument there, not here over my father's still-warm body."

"As head of the senate, I can assure you—"

"I insist. Before the senate or not at all."

Rowan bowed his head. "As you wish. I'll assemble the senate. It will take a few hours. In the meantime—"

"In the meantime the world will have no Sovereign. So I suggest you hurry."

Chapter Twenty-one

SEVEN MILES north of Byzantium, Rom stepped into a broken-down shack with a crooked roof. The boards of its three standing sides were worn to a deathly gray, but a carpet of emerald grass and a sea of red anemones covered the ground. He'd never seen anything so lush, so green or wild in his life. In Byzantium, parks were artificial and stunted approximations of nature. Never had he seen the artful spread of the Maker as he saw it now, where it reclaimed nearly five centuries of barrenness in glorious patches such as this.

Beauty did not help him at the moment, however.

Rom had tied Feyn's hands to an old post, then tied her ankles together for good measure. Now he pulled free the strip of muslin that had kept her quiet all night. He hadn't relished the idea of gagging her for so long, but he couldn't risk her screams being heard by a stray convoy.

She spit out some lint and stared at him. For half a minute, neither spoke.

"Is this really necessary?" Feyn motioned at her ties with her chin.

"Yes."

"We're in the middle of nowhere. You think I'm going to run away?"

"If I let you go, what's to keep you from braining me with a rock and riding out of here?"

He probably shouldn't have offered that.

Her eyes shone like arctic mirrors in the morning light. "You've abducted a future Sovereign. You must realize the consequence."

She rested her head against the post, jaw fixed, eyes steady, her hair a dark tangle about her. It had lashed him in the face like a thousand tiny whips through the course of the last few hours, and he was glad to have it out of his eyes.

Maker, what was he doing?

She was right. He was going to die. Hades had already prepared his special chamber of torment.

Rom glanced up at the sun filtering in through the old boards, the sky open along the eastern side of the old shack as though they sat in a theater. They had ridden beyond the gray stratus clouds that normally surrounded the city. Although the sky was full of feathery wisps, morning light filtered into every corner of the old structure.

He tilted his face heavenward and inhaled.

"What are you doing?"

"The sun. Do you feel it? Isn't it amazing?"

She glanced up. "I suppose it's soothing."

He turned toward her. "Don't you see? Don't you feel it?"

"Yes, I feel it. It's warm."

"No. Not just that…" He felt a pang of sadness. She was so beautiful—was it possible for her to be so unmoved? Yet he would have been the same two days ago.

He sat back on his heels in the grass next to her. It would be so easy for him to become rapt in these surroundings, the sheer light of it, the greenery of the scrub grass, the speckle of the red flowers. This was Bliss if he had ever dreamed of it.

But even this would soon mean nothing if she didn't help him. Time was not his friend.

"Can't you see how beautiful this is to me? How full of life it is? I am?"

"I can see how mad you are," she said flatly. Her skin seemed more opaque in his shadow. The faint lines beneath it were like the veining of fine marble.

"Please, listen to me. I was like you—"

"You were never like me. I'm quite sure."

"I *was* like you. I felt, I knew, only fear. And when the keeper, the one I've been trying to tell you about—"

"The one in the dungeon."

"No, not him. A different one. The one who gave me the vial two days ago." He withdrew the vellum from his pocket, keeping the vial firmly tucked away as he had in her chamber. "You see all of the writing on here? I can't decipher it." He unfolded it and showed her. "But the old man in the dungeon said that you could."

She glanced at the vellum and then back up at him.

"The old man in the dungeon. He's the reason we're here. He's the one who said I shouldn't leave the Citadel without showing this to you. That you could make sense of this."

"And you've done all of this because a madman gave you something to drink, and something that you can't read, and another madman told you to come to me to make sense of it."

He hesitated. "Yes."

"Then you're as mad as they are."

Was it possible to make her understand? He searched around him. "The flowers, the sun. Don't they move you? Don't you want to sing?" He hummed a few notes. "I'm a singer, you know? The thought of it now . . ." He swallowed past the lump in his throat.

Feyn was watching her stallion nip up the heads off several anemones with a clump of grass.

"You're going to be Sovereign. How do you feel about that?"

She refused to answer.

"You accept it, don't you? Maybe you feel anxious. A little fearful. But you'll do it because that's what you're supposed to do."

She glanced at him. "I'm not going to think you're a mystic for guessing that. Anyone in my position would feel the same."

"But are you hopeful that your reign might usher in great things? Do you feel compelled to be a better Sovereign than any before you—better even than Megas or Vorrin?"

"Why would I want that?"

"Because you want to improve the world! Because of your legacy."

"Legacy is ordained by the Maker. Improvement is unnecessary. There is only loyalty to what is right, and the world is already right."

He lowered his head and picked at the grass, at a loss as to how to make her understand. His were just words without currency.

"I'm thirsty," she said.

He glanced up. "Like thirst. Hope, and ambition, desire. They're all like thirst. You think about how good that water will taste. You *want* it. You work for it, and it becomes your driving goal."

"If you're mad."

"No, not if you're mad, if you *feel* something. Anything!"

"Why do you pursue this idiocy? When my men find you they'll send you to the dungeon. You know you'll *die* for this."

"My lady," he said softly. "People have already died for this. The old man who gave this to me was killed by your Citadel Guard. The same guard that killed my mother. Both, right in front of my eyes."

"Nonsense. Violence is of the past."

He leaned in on his knees until he was close to her face. "Do I look like I'm lying to you? Do I look like a crazy person when I say that I watched as she bled all over the floor she used to clean every week for as long as I could remember?"

"I think you might believe that," she said. "And I agree that there are some odd things happening, which I plan to investigate. But I also think you're deluded."

He understood then that trying to convince her of what he had seen would be fruitless. She either couldn't—or simply wouldn't—believe him. He had to take a different tack.

He fell back on his seat and awkwardly hugged his knees. "What I'm trying to do isn't about solving some puzzle. It isn't even, ultimately, about getting your help. It's about…knowing. The rest of the world deserves to know. It's about feeling as you've never felt before. Do you feel love, my lady? Ever?"

"Of course," she said.

But he knew the answer. She didn't. She couldn't.

She was beautiful in the way that ice was beautiful, in the way of marble, or stone.

She tilted her head. "Why do you keep pursuing these vestiges of Chaos? Even if all you say is true, what's to be gained from pursuing them? There's a reason these things have fallen away. Don't you see? You've been deceived. You're being led astray. That's the nature of Chaos—it was a disease that held the mind in shackles. It was the insidious nature of forbidden things that made Chaos so destructive. And for that, millions died. Please, for your own good, consider the logic. Whatever caused you to turn away, renounce it. Return to the truth. I'm telling you—commanding you, as your Sovereign-to-be: Set these things aside."

There was a time when he would have listened to her. Even now, her words pricked conflict within him. He wondered, if only for a split instant, if he should give more credence to what she was saying. Her dogma was as familiar to him as his mother's house, as basilica, as the Order itself.

But he knew it was false. She was the one, along with millions of others, who had been deceived.

"I can't," he whispered.

She shifted her gaze away.

"You won't help me, will you?"

"Nothing can help you if you won't leave these ways," she said.

Win her confidence, the keeper had said. But how?

"I need...I need to think," he said, standing. He looked down at the vellum on the grass in front of her, but then thought better of leaving it with her, so he folded it up and shoved it back into his pocket next to the vial.

"Where are you going?" she said.

Rom retrieved the canteen from the horse's saddlebag. "I'm going to go see if there's any fresh water."

"We can't drink the water out here. My stallion can barely drink it, and even so, he might be sick for a week."

But an idea had taken root.

"I'll be right back."

Rom walked around to the rear of the old structure, glancing back. He could see her through the cracks in the slats, craning to see him.

He walked toward the copse of low trees on the knoll, unscrewing the cap to the canteen. The water wasn't cold, but at least it was reasonably fresh.

It should have been obvious to him from the beginning: There was only one way to help someone really see.

He peered into the canteen's narrow mouth. Gauged the amount of water left in it. And then pulled the vial from his pocket.

By the time he came back to the shack, she had shifted her position against the post. She leaned against it, eyes closed. Her skin was flushed, he thought—she seemed a little pink. Was the sun burning her?

He set the canteen down and stepped up to her as her eyes fluttered open. The blue veins of her skin seemed darker beneath her eyes. She looked tired.

"Would you like me to move you out of the sun?"

She nodded.

He untied her from the post and carried her farther inside, setting her in the shade.

"There's no stream but I found a small puddle. It's a bit stale, but I haven't keeled over. Seems safe enough."

"It's all we have?"

"Better to drink stale water than die of thirst." He picked up the canteen, unscrewed the top, and put it between her tied hands, so she could help herself.

Her first drink was only a swallow. "Ugh." But she tipped it back and drank again.

"I had some—the rest is yours."

She paused, made a face, then finished it off. When she handed it back her mouth was red.

He quietly screwed the cap back on.

Rom waited no more than ten seconds before Feyn gasped. Soon the Sovereign of the world to be was about to see the world as it was.

Chapter Twenty-two

COME HERE, Rom, son of Elias." Feyn's hands reached toward his face. "I want to look into your eyes."

In the space of a single hour her reality had been redefined in a way that still made Rom's head spin.

He leaned toward her on the grassy knoll as she laid one hand against his jaw, the other on his cheek.

"What are you looking for?" he said, beneath her gaze.

"I can almost see what you're thinking. I hear my own thoughts as I never have before. There's something in your eyes I've never seen in the eyes of anyone else. Last night I thought it was madness. But it's far too beautiful." She bit her lower lip. A moment later a tear spilled down her cheek.

He didn't dare interrupt her metamorphosis—there was far too much at stake. He certainly wouldn't tell her not to cry. To say it was to tell her not to feel. Impossible.

He had marveled at this transformation in her, relived moments of his own conversion in the basilica two nights ago. It had been fascinating and humbling. Amazing and horrifying. Horrifying, because he had watched the great abyss from which she had come in so short a time—a far greater distance than any of the others.

Her stoic world of Order had been shattered.

No wonder her heart had nearly burst upon breaking the surface.

187

No wonder she had reeled beneath the sky, laughed at the sun, wept at birdsong on the knoll.

She had long ago thrown off her cloak without care for the dirtied dress she wore beneath, kicking away her leather shoes to feel the caress of the emerald grass on her toes.

He was entranced by it. By her.

"What is it, my lady?"

"Feyn," she said.

He arched an eyebrow.

"Never call me *lady* again. I forbid it." She broke into a heartrending smile. "My name is Feyn."

"I know." He couldn't help a smile of his own. The whole world knew her name. But they did not know her and would never have recognized the woman before him. She had been beautiful before. She was vibrant now.

"I want to hear you say it."

"Feyn," he said. He had been less insistent with her since giving her the last of the vial, his need for answers replaced for the moment by his fascination with her desire to consume everything around her. The red flowers. The marvelous warmth of her stallion, whom she wept over, laying her cheek against his head.

And Rom himself.

"Feyn," he said again. So close to her, he could see the separation of her irises, the ring of white that encased that uncanny glacial blue-gray.

Her lower lip, appearing so chiseled in every street banner and inaugural sign, was so plush that he hardly recognized the mouth of the Sovereign on the woman before him. He hardly recognized her at all, except for her eyes.

"What are you looking for in my eyes?" she said softly. "Tell me, do you see me, really? Do you see behind these eyes?"

He gazed into them, saw the riot of clarity and confusion at once.

"I see you. The real you."

She wiped the tears from her cheek with the back of her hand.

"Do you realize you're the first person—ever? The first person capable of really seeing me?"

She laughed, sprang to her feet, and ran a few steps away. Gone was the austere Sovereign. It was impossible to reconcile one with the other.

"Rom! Let's go."

"Go where?"

She ran back and dropped to her knees, beside him. Her hair fell into his face. "Let's *go*. To my estate. We can take all that we need. Horses, food. We'll shun the train and ride north, to all the old cities. We'll enter in triumph, in love. They'll throw open their doors to us, and we'll walk the old streets by night. No! We'll travel by plane. We'll see the entire world. I want to see it all again, through your eyes. I'll show it to you. And we'll solve this riddle of yours, of ours.

"But for now, let's go. I want to leave, tonight. I never want to set foot in Byzantium again."

"What about your inauguration? The Order?" he said quietly, brushing her hair from his eyes. He didn't want to force the issue. He wished, more than anything, for her to have this moment—this day. But there wasn't time.

She hesitated.

"The Order. Order... I don't know. How does it all work together? We'll figure it out. We'll go away and one day we'll return, having solved it. You and I will tell history a new story. It will be our gift to the world. And we will do it together. The whole *world* will see as we do."

Rom didn't say anything.

"Of course that's ridiculous. Of course," she murmured, rising and stepping away.

He stood and walked up behind her, lifted her hand. "I understand. I do." He did. The wildness was there, and there was something in him that wanted to say yes, that they should go and leave the concrete world of Order behind forever.

He had a vellum that made no sense and the cryptic words of an old man to guide him. Feyn wasn't the only one reeling in this new life.

But there was something else guiding him. He'd told the others to leave the city if he didn't return by dawn. It was late into the morning. Surely they had gone. He had to get back. Find them, find Avra.

Avra, whom he had always worshipped without knowing it. Avra, whom he would always love.

Time is short.

Feyn turned her face toward the sky and twined her fingers through his.

"But just think of such a life. Think of it." She closed her eyes and inhaled. "I smell the anemones like I never have. I smell the air, the rain to the south. I feel it all."

She let go of his hand, spread her arms wide, and fell backward. He moved to catch her and she laughed.

Despite his growing sense of urgency, he laughed, too. "You could have hurt yourself!"

"I knew you would catch me."

He lifted her and she came up breathless, her hair splayed about her shoulders. Her lips parted, her gaze was heavy as it shifted to his mouth.

"I've been so protected all my life. The life of a future Sovereign is so shielded from the world that we don't even marry. It never seemed like a hardship before. Rom."

"Hmm…"

"There's nothing I want more right now than for you to kiss me."

"You'd kiss a lowly artist?"

"I would love to." She wrapped her arms around him, tilted her head, and pressed her lips to his. For a moment he shut out every unanswered question, lost in the warmth of her embrace.

He lowered his head and let his forehead rest against hers.

"Feyn."

He straightened and saw that she was still in the first flush of new life. Reason was an unwelcome presence. But they had no time.

"Feyn, the others I told you about who have taken this same blood are waiting. And there's probably worldwide panic over your disappearance. Please help us. Not for me. Don't do it for me. You know now what this is—please forgive me for tricking you. But it was the only way I knew—"

"I forgive you. How can I hold it against you? I forgive you." She caught herself. "No. I don't forgive you. You should have done it sooner! If I think about it too much, I think I'll regret every year, every day and hour I've lived until this moment. They've been wasted!"

He smiled. "I'll take that as an approval."

She looked at the sky. "You're right, you know. I would never have helped you. I would have had you hunted down as a rebel. I would have had you thrown in the dungeon."

Her gaze fell on a nearby patch of flowers. "But I don't want to talk about this. I've always thought of humanity. Of Order. Of everything other than myself. But right now, I don't want to think of a life other than this one."

"Our time is running short."

"You're a poet." Her gaze dropped to his amulet and rose to his face again. "Speak me a verse."

"Then you'll look at this vellum?"

She shrugged. "If I like your verse."

He glanced heavenward as though seeking inspiration.

> *We rode together through the night*
> *Chasing love, chasing light.*
> *All has changed for you and I…*
> *Let us live before we die.*

You're a queen and what am I?
But let us live before we die.

He wasn't sure if she would smile or weep.

"It's our story," he said.

She abruptly turned away and started down the knoll.

"Feyn?" He ran after her. "What is it?"

"We have to go back. It's the last thing I want to do, but you're right, the world is in our hands. Yours more than mine, I think, strange as that sounds. We must go to my father. The world's going to change. I'll see to it."

She turned back, and he saw her fresh tears.

His heart soared and broke at once. He wrapped his arms around her, and she rested her cheek against his shoulder.

He held her for a full minute in silence, the breeze brushing past them. In the distance, her stallion nickered. There was rain on the horizon, he could smell it. The clouds had begun to churn.

"Show me the vellum," she said.

It lay on a patch of hard ground between them, held down on all four corners by stones.

"This is the only part we could read," Rom said, pointing to the verse at the top. Feyn scanned it quietly.

"The power to live," she said with wonder. "They were right, too, weren't they? Sweet Bliss. They were right."

"But this part—all of this..." He gestured at the faded characters that covered the rest of the page, as evenly spaced as soldiers in formation, none of them forming words or even grouped like words. "None of this makes sense. This is what I went to the keeper in the dungeons for." Rom glanced at her. "Do you know what it is?"

"A Caesar Cipher," she said, not looking up. "Did he give you a key?"

Rom had never heard of such a thing.

"He told me to remember a number. Twenty-one. Vertical. Does that help?"

Her gaze flicked this way and that. Her fine brows furrowed. She rested her finger on the letters then slowly drew it down.

"Are you sure? That's all?"

"Latin! He said it was Latin. Please tell me you know Latin."

"Of course I know Latin. It's the written language of the alchemists."

For some reason, a chill passed up his spine. She, too, hesitated, as though struck by a thought.

"What is it?" he asked.

"I'm not sure. Something my brother said to me. I'm not thinking very well. They cloud the senses, these feelings, don't they?"

As Neah had complained. Neah. She had to be sick with fear by now, thinking he had been captured.

"I need something to write with," Foyn said. "And on. Something, paper, cloth...anything."

He dug in his pocket, pulled out the empty vial and his pen. Feyn grabbed the hem of her dress and ripped it open across her knees.

"What are you doing?"

She tore the section in a wide band all the way around to the back seam, yanked it free. "Can't ride in this anyway," she murmured.

She smoothed the white fabric on the ground next to the vellum, took the pen from him, and began to write, methodically deciphering each character onto the fabric. She worked quickly, one finger on the vellum moving a character at a time, keeping her place. When she had five rows of lettering, she paused, frowning.

Rom's heart had begun to accelerate. "What does it say?"

She ran her finger along the first line of characters. She whispered, "Maker..."

"What does it say?"

"This...this is some kind of account." She scanned ahead again with an incredulous breath.

"What does it say? Please!"

She backed up to the beginning again. "It says, *First year, third, second*...I'm assuming this is a date."

"What does it mean?"

"Listen." And she translated aloud:

I write this now so that you who read will know what really happened. No doubt the history books will put it differently, if they include it at all.

Feyn glanced up at him.

"This is someone's journal?" he asked.

Feyn scanned ahead, shook her head, then backed up and translated:

I am Talus Gurov. My name means nothing to you. What you need to know is that I served my country as a scientist in the years leading up to the Zealot War, when extremists detonated weapons in seven of the world's great capitals, obliterating the governments of Asia and crippling parts of the Americas. The world erupted in a global war. I thought then that we had reached the end of civilization. It was spoken by Sirin that this was the Age of Chaos and his gift to the world was the new Order.

But I tell you the truth, that Order is the beginning of Chaos...

Rom's heart stopped. Then pounded on. "What does that mean?"

"I...I don't know."

"Feyn."

She bent over the vellum and worked with increased urgency.

Chapter Twenty-three

THE GREAT torch blazed above the senate dais. Though it cast light well past the ringed rows of hallowed seats, it gave off no real heat, this flame lit by many flames gathered from all corners of the world.

All but two of the one hundred senators had filed in through the great arch in the last hour, the last hour of three, just as Rowan had promised.

They had come robed in anxious decorum, taking their distinguished seats in the hall's tiered semicircle, which surrounded a dais that projected into the middle of the room. In front of the dais, a lesser circle on the floor marked the place where the senators could stand and be heard.

Anxiety had given way to alarm at the sight of the guard, twenty strong, who shut fast the chamber doors as soon as all were seated. The posture of the robed senate body had gone silent in the space of an instant.

When Rowan stood and delivered the terrible news, the hall filled with the cacophony of fear.

"My peers in this senate, I dread to report that Vorrin Cerelia, the Sovereign of our world, is dead."

It was into the coils of this fear, reaching up to the vaulted ceiling of the hall like smoke, that Saric delivered his subsequent argument.

He made his speech from the dais. He made it with eloquence and boldness to white-eyed, nervous glances that flicked with collective unrest.

Now he drew them into his conclusion.

"So it is with great respect, unwavering devotion to the Order, and dread—not for myself, but for the world—that I tell you today I will not become figurehead of a system that did not elect me, nor assume a fate not appointed to me by the Maker at my birth. To do so would constitute sacrilege. The Maker, after all, makes no mistakes. It is for these reasons that I must refuse. I beg you, find another to serve you for the next three days."

Saric dipped his head and withdrew from the podium.

The distress came first as a rustle, the shifting of ninety-eight bodies uncomfortable upon their velvet seats, and then as a whisper, shared between two and then fifty, until the hiss became an outcry.

Rowan's gavel sounded. Twice, three times, hard upon the podium where the senate leader had gone to stand.

"Silence! Silence!"

A wizened, graying man stood from his seat on the floor.

"Senator Dio of Europa would speak." The man was one of the senate's most tenured figures. A member of the old guard, he might have been the right arm of Megas himself—he certainly looked old enough for it. He had served nearly fifty years as a prelate before his appointment to the senate, and there was no man here, Rowan included, who knew the Book of Orders as thoroughly or who had studied it as deeply as he.

Rowan nodded and stepped back.

The senator rose and came to stand in the round below the dais. He moved with surprising ease, given his age. The sleeve of his robes revealed thick forearms gnarled by ropy blue veins beneath his pallid skin.

"My lord Saric," he said. His voice was thick and slightly hoarse, as though he spoke from the back of his throat. "I should be addressing you as *sire*, but as you say, the mantle is one that must be assumed willingly and purposefully. But have you forgotten that it must also be assumed obediently? Let us remember the great design of the Order, the infallibility of law. You say that there is a flaw in the system. You say that it is not logical, that the Sovereign's eldest should not succeed him when another, experienced Sovereign still lives. Or that your sister, groomed to the office, should succeed you if Sovereign Miran cannot or will not.

"But you must remember that four hundred and eighty years of Order make a case of their own. The Maker has created Order and created it infallible. For that reason, it serves as the foundation of the law. How do we best serve the law? By willful—and purposeful—obedience. Our fears, our experience, even our logic are subject to obedience. And upon this premise, I must speak for the body when I recommend you without hesitation to the office. Let the world have her Sovereign."

Voices raised in concurrence to the backdrop of concurring applause. Saric glanced at Rowan, who gestured him back to the podium. The old senator stayed on the floor. Though Rowan held leadership of the senate, this senator, Dio, held no small amount of power himself. A good thing to keep in mind.

Saric bowed his head and clasped his hands in respect.

"Senator Dio. I cannot prevail against your experience. But I must take exception with your logic. You say that following Order is an act of obedience. But obedience is not done mindlessly. To be human is to think. Feyn, as my father before her, has prepared for this role for years—since the announcement of her appointment. The world looks to her inauguration with great comfort. She is known to them. Her image is seen on every street corner around the world. The day of her inauguration will be one of celebration. Families will go to their beds in serenity knowing they are in the hands of one familiar to them who has prepared the better part of her life for the role. Would you grant me that much?"

The old man dipped his head. "I will."

"I, on the other hand—what does the world know of me? What comfort will the world find in me or in the news that Vorrin is dead? Fear will reign. That creature will be loosed on the world. We combat fear with logic and Order. My ascension to the office might fulfill one, but not the other. And where is the peace in that? Today, logic must prevail over fear for the sake of Order. The law must be set aside."

Cries from the senate floor. A few robed senators—one of them a younger man, another a woman with white hair—rose swiftly to their feet. Senator Dio spoke, finger raised to the air, but was drowned out by the cries of those around him. Rowan's gavel crashed down again and again on the podium.

Saric raised his hand for calm. The room gradually fell silent.

"Senators, yes, it is only for a few days. You are right. The world, even if it is overrun by fear for a few days, may surely be put to rights by the auspices of Feyn's rule. I myself have great peace and belief in her upcoming tenure. But let me remind you that it was this body that, only two days ago, rejected my request to serve as senate leader."

Murmurs from the senators.

"How can you reject me in this lower office and yet recommend me to the highest one? Both in the name of Order? Yes, yes, I understand, the laws are clear. And yet the logic is flawed!"

For a moment there was nothing but the gentle crackling of the senate torch.

Then the arguments started again, and Saric retreated to his seat on the dais. He gave them time, listened to the cacophony, which was like so much melody, really, with a cadence of its own.

Above them, he could just make out the paintings on the vaults of the ceiling. They were nearly obscured by time and the faint smoke of the eternal senate flame. Someone had told him once that it was a vision of the Maker reaching down to man, that painting. A vision of Chaos obscured by the smoke of Order. He thought, looking at it, that he could just barely make out the line of a hand. But to his eye it wasn't the hand of the Maker at all, but of a man, reaching for the heavens.

"Order! Order!" Rowan's gavel cracked. The room quieted.

"Sire, I implore you…"

Saric stopped Rowan with a lifted palm. He stood and approached the podium again. His power was already palpable.

He took a deep breath. "I see that my decision has already cast great fear upon this body. And observing this here, among us, I am disquieted for the world."

The senate leaned forward. And Saric relished the taste of triumph.

"My lord Saric," Senator Dio said. "What would you propose?"

Here it was then.

"Senator Dio, my father lies dead. You are right. This body needs the comfort of its Sovereign. Let us agree to a compromise."

He waited. He could practically hear the machine-like movement of their eyes shifting from him, to Rowan, to Senator Dio.

"I will agree to serve as your Sovereign on one condition. The law of Order is given by the Maker. But the law is not the Maker; it is not perfect. It is in constant state of betterment and refinement. Your role here is proof of that. Refine this law. Fix the flaw in it. Let this situation, should it happen in years or centuries to come, never lead to this impasse again. Give comfort to the people and to those confronted with filling the office.

"Let the law be changed. Let it now read that should a seated Sovereign die before his or her tenure is fulfilled, then the former Sovereign should step into office once more. Let us have and give the world the reassurance of their experience."

Quiet.

"If you could see your way to this," Saric announced, "then I will do your bidding in this matter and assume office. I give you my word."

A tussle at one of the doors interrupted them. A guardsman there was trying to block the way in for someone Saric now recognized as Camille, his father's secretary. She was insistent, her voice raised, though the guard would not let her by.

She broke past them and then stopped short when the body of senators turned to her.

Something was not right here. She would never barge in. Unless...

"My lord, Feyn has been taken!" Her voice was high-pitched and unsteady. "She never showed up at her estate. There's been a breach in her room. She's gone."

Chaos erupted on the floor as Saric's blood turned to ice.

Chapter Twenty-four

"THE AMERICAS. Is that Asiana?" Rom said, pacing next to Feyn, who was propped up on her elbows in the grass, further deciphering the vellum. He watched as an army of characters aligned itself beneath her pen in neat rank and file, in rightful order for the first time in centuries.

"No, the Americas are Nova Albion," she murmured. "They were once two separate continents. A major city in each was destroyed in the Zealot War. In Megas's geographic restructuring, they were combined into one, along with the hinterlands to the north. As for Asiana, it barely emerged from Chaos. It was a great continent known as Asia that once housed the world's most populated cities. Hard to imagine—it's such a scattered region now."

She paused and glanced sidelong at him. Her brow smoothed from its frown.

"What is it?"

"You, Rom. It's so strange to me that yesterday I didn't know you at all. And today . . ." She smiled and in that instant looked like a girl. She dropped her head, her finger still on the vellum, the pen still in her other hand, but she made a soft and marveling sound.

"I, who would gain the world . . . would lose it in an instant to have this. All over again. Only this. Well . . ." The pale gray gaze slid to him, as if to say, *Well, maybe a little more.*

"You're saying you're glad I kidnapped you?"

"Yes. No. I'm saying more. That I'm thankful to the Maker for it." Her gaze fell to his mouth. "Remind me to tell you something when we're done with this."

"I will," he said. She nodded slightly, as though to herself, and returned to the vellum.

Rom looked away. Somewhere beyond them a bird sang. It was like a dream. There was little about his life that he recognized from even two days ago. He'd lived a simple, predictable existence, one of basilica, his workshop, his home. He sang for his supper—literally—and completed odd workman's jobs when he could find them.

Today he was beyond the city for the first time in his life with the future Sovereign, whom he had kidnapped after learning about a secret blood. A blood that had awakened in him feelings long lost to the rest of humanity. A blood he had given to the Sovereign-to-be, a woman who emanated a gravity all her own.

In the space of hours the world had become more dangerous, more beautiful, and more vast than he could have dreamed possible.

Stay focused. Decipher the vellum. It was all that mattered. That, and getting back. His stomach knotted, and he wondered again where the others had gone.

Feyn pushed up, having finished transcribing a large section onto the fabric.

"Rom, listen." She pointed to the character with which she had left off, slid her finger forward on the grid, and began to read again:

In the wake of that war and its terrible aftermath, every man questioned his place in the world and the meaning of his life. Despotism and depravity plumbed new lows. Hope seemed like an ancient relic. We turned from religion, blamed it for the war. Anarchy spread.

Until the day a European philosopher named Sirin began to spread his message of universal Order beneath the Maker. Hu-

*manity, he taught, must master emotion or be doomed to repeat
her failures. And so he disparaged ambition, hatred, and greed
and taught others to do the same.*

*In a matter of years, Sirin became the most powerful figure
on earth. Under his new Order, the world disarmed. All common
human needs—medicine, the production and distribution of
food, power—were socialized. Peace returned to the world. But I
fear that much of Sirin's teaching will now be lost or recast, his
Order distorted for the great evil that has come upon us.*

Feyn stopped reading.

"Great evil?" Rom glanced at Feyn. She stared off into the grass
in front of her but seemed to see nothing of the earth before her.

"I don't think I could give up these feelings for anything. Not
knowing what I know now," she murmured.

All he could say was, "I know."

She looked back down at the writing. "I'm reluctant to keep reading," she whispered. But a moment later, she did:

*Sirin's philosophies began to lose their luster within the space of
a generation. Infighting reemerged. Humanity was on a course
to repeat its history. We all sensed it.*

*Science was greatly esteemed, and I was among seven ge-
neticists who oversaw a secret quest to unravel the genetic roots
of emotion. The project was stationed in a vast level-three bio-
hazard laboratory in the Russian wastelands. In particular, I
developed computer models that allowed us to better understand
our research. New funds poured into our projects. None of us
knew who our benefactors were, only that we could suddenly afford to hire scientists of such high caliber that we soon became
an elite core of intellectuals. Our achievements were too great to
list here, but we found ourselves so far at the vanguard of new
advancements that we smugly called our inner circle...*

Feyn stopped.

"What?" Rom said. "What does it say?"

She whispered the word:

Alchemists.

A chill passed along Rom's arms on the warm day.

Feyn touched the vellum. "Are we sure this isn't a forgery?"

"I'm sure."

She began to decipher more.

Rom paced, fighting the urge to watch over her shoulder. He'd done that once already and she'd shooed him off, promising she wouldn't read for herself until the words were sufficiently translated, and that she would read them aloud.

Finally, when Feyn had finished a large portion, he could hold back no longer.

"What does it say?"

"I'm almost finished."

After risking so much to know what was on this ancient vellum, he could hardly just stand by. So he went to the top of the knoll and watched the clouds gather over the city.

He felt the empty vial in his pocket. The blood was gone, the last of it given to Feyn. The blood was connected, somehow, to an undiscovered, unnamed boy.

And the key to the boy was surely in the vellum.

Feyn was still on her knees bent over the vellum when Rom returned.

"That's it," she said, rocking back. "It's done."

She followed her finger along the line, recapturing where she had left off.

Once the DNA responsible for controlling specific functions of the limbic system—the emotions—was pinpointed, we discov-

ered the first viable means to reprogram that DNA by means of a retrovirus.

It was I, Talus Gurov, who identified the components that make us superior to animals, that define our very humanity. I confess the irony of my pride in the matter. I wanted, like Higgs with his God particle, to be the one recognized for pinpointing this genetic material that makes us truly human.

Rom let out a slow breath. Feyn was staring again, this time at the rows of characters. "This…this can't be real." She was shaking her head. "How can it be?"

"We have to know," he said.

She stood, eyes wide with wonder. "What a strange day. I'll remember it forever."

He gazed at the intensity, the earnestness, the innocence in the eyes of this most powerful person on earth.

"I will too."

"If it weren't for the blood, I'd say we were mad. That it's no wonder these secrets were guarded so closely. Have we gone insane?"

"I don't think so. On the other hand, only a madman would kidnap the Sovereign."

She laughed, and the sound was like water running over pebbles in a brook. Its own music.

"Mad or not, everything is different," Rom said. Was it only a day ago that he and Avra had left the basilica together, running for the subway beneath one of the banners bearing the image of this very woman?

"Read the rest," he said.

Feyn sat down before the fabric, found her place again, and read:

I shared my findings. And then I gathered my research, my notes, my samples, and gave them all up to my supervisor, a man whom I trusted. His name was Megas.

"Megas!" Rom breathed.

"Wait. Listen."

A month later, a stunned world learned that Sirin, its philoso-pher hero, had been assassinated. By zealots, haters of his peace-ful message. The public outcry and the sympathetic recommit-ment to his statutes was instant and worldwide.

It was then that I learned that my research had been used to create a virus called Legion. Highly contagious, it stripped away all emotion but one: fear. Shortly before Sirin's death, Me-gas proposed use of the virus as a way to make Sirin's ideology permanent. By secretly infecting the world, he could excise emo-tion and ensure peace. Only fear would remain, as a means to maintain obedience to the Order.

But Sirin refused, and for that, he was assassinated. Let me state it here: Sirin was not killed by religious zealots, but by Me-gas—a name I believe the world will soon know.

As of today, Legion has been loosed and there is no way to stop it. The course of human history has been forever altered. What was once human will be no longer. I fear that if I stay, I will be killed or soon infected.

I must flee...

Rom was staring, first at the vellum, then at Feyn's translation, and then at Feyn herself. She shook her head faintly. "This can't be."

But a moment later she read on:

March 15, 001:

Two weeks have passed since my last entry. It is worse by far than I could have imagined. Legion is ruthless.

I am in the desert. I have four things: a roof over my head, a generator, a link to the computers I used in my laboratory, and my samples. You must realize: the world is being fed a lie without even knowing it. Legion infects without notice, at first contact.

Humanity is dying. The fact is clear to me: Though blood flows through their veins, those infected by Legion are no longer human but a fear-filled race of dead.

"Dead?" Rom said into their ensuing silence. He could not move. "He's claiming that the world is actually dead?"

She lifted her eyes. "I don't feel dead."

Was it possible? He looked at his hands. But they were the hands of the living, weren't they?

"You don't feel dead because you *feel*. The blood brought us back from the dead," he said, embracing the idea. "That's it, don't you see? We were dead and now this blood has brought us back to life!"

"Dead…" Sweat beaded Feyn's brow. "The whole world, dead? And it's been that way…"

"For four hundred and eighty years," Rom finished.

"You're saying that there are only five living people on this planet."

"I'm not saying it—the vellum says it."

"And that I would be…a dead Sovereign…ruling a dead Order." Feyn turned back to the deciphered account.

This is my doing! It is my burden to right it if I can. I work without ceasing. I sleep and eat only to aid my research. I may have the means to return a few to humanity's true soul, but only a few, and only for a time. I have a sample of purest blood of unknown origin marked only "TH," which proved resistant to the strain. It cannot cure Legion—humanity reverts to death, which has become its natural state. But it may return those who drink it to their full humanity at least for a limited time.

Rom blinked.

Only for a time?

"Keep going," he said, less steadily. She read again:

April 20, 002:

It is a year now since the spread of Legion. Within another it will have reached every corner of the globe. Within this generation, true humanity will be no more. And though my work is not finished, my death is inevitable. So I write this that I might know what my purpose is, even when I no longer feel horror.

Megas has asserted himself as the world's only leader and has formalized a version of the Order that even Sirin would count as blasphemy. He is nothing less than a dictator ruling a race void of the ambition to overturn him.

I see no hope, yet I press on in my search for the means to reverse the effects of Legion on the human race.

August 8, 002:

I have had to move twice for fear of coming into contact with Legion. They know that someone has breached their firewalls, and I fear that my access to their computers may be compromised or terminated soon. But I have finally constructed a model that offers what may be humanity's only hope.

Sometime at or near the new year 471 the human genome will return to its original, undefiled state in the same bloodline of the sample first used to create Legion.

Mine.

Bloodlines should converge to produce a child, a male, probably in the area of Africa, now called Abyssinia. Within his blood will be the means to overthrow Legion on the genetic level. Assuming he survives the war within his body, which may cripple him in his infancy.

In this child is our hope. It is he who will remember his humanity, who will have in him the capacity for compassion and love. And it is therefore he who must free us from Order, the very structures of which go up like a prison around the human heart. This boy will be humanity's only hope.

"The boy," Rom said.

Feyn hesitated as though remembering something, but before he could ask, she hurried on:

It is now for this boy and the hope he brings that I work feverishly. When I am certain of my calculations, I will disengage from my laboratory computers. I have managed thus far to elude capture. What's more, I have found two others whom I believe to be trustworthy. I will establish an Order of Keepers and together we will vow to guard this blood and keep these secrets for the day that boy comes. I will teach them to remember what it was to know more than fear, so that our minds will remember even after our bodies have forgotten.

Though we will surely die under the curse that is Legion, we wait in hope, having abandoned the Order in anticipation of that day.

Until then, I have preserved blood enough for five to live for a while. Only five. And only for a few years. Let the blood ignite the five who must find the boy and bring an end to this death. You who find this, you who drink, you are that remnant. Drink and know that all I have written is true.

Find the boy. Bring him to power so that the world might be saved, I beg you.

"*Find the boy*," Feyn repeated softly, to herself. "The keeper said that."

"To you?"

"Yes. He was reciting the vellum."

Rom's heart beat like a cudgel in his chest. "That's it? There's no more?"

Feyn focused on the vellum. "Only one line, four months later."

"What?" Rom said. "What does it say?"

She stopped, visibly faltered, and a moment later read:

Three days ago, I, Talus Gurov, died.

CHAPTER TWENTY-FIVE

CHAOS GRIPPED the Senate Hall, threatening to pull Order into the abyss once again.

Saric stood, reeling. Feyn was missing. Feyn, who was to be central to everything.

For several minutes, no one seemed to know what to do. Even the guard on duty were looking around for direction.

Rowan's gavel came down with a crash, again and again.

"Order! We *will* have Order! This news is not confirmed. I've heard no reports of this."

But that changed when the captain of the Citadel Guard himself burst in through a side door, motioned Rowan over, and spoke urgently into his ear. The senate leader questioned him and hurried back to the podium.

They came to order without encouragement this time, to a man and woman.

"My friends, last night as we slept, an imposter entered the Citadel and kidnapped our lady, Feyn Cerelia, from her bedroom. It seems we are without a Sovereign, present or to come."

There was no outcry, no more argument. Only dreadful silence.

And outrage, at least on Saric's part.

"In light of this," Rowan said, "we must now acknowledge the wisdom of the new law proposed by Saric. We must move now. The world cannot be left without a leader."

On the floor, Senator Dio lifted his hand. Saric stood off to Rowan's side, mouth dry. He had to find Corban.

"This senator would speak."

"Speak, Senator Dio."

"I move that we amend the law as proposed."

Murmurs now issued throughout the chamber, floating up to roost in the ceiling's high vaults.

He heard the motion's second as though from a distance.

The gavel. "And so will read the law." Rowan's voice rang out in the senate. "*Should a Sovereign die before the tenure is fulfilled, the former Sovereign will step into office once more. It is hereby agreed and ratified to be signed into law by the new Sovereign as his first act of office.*

"My lord," Rowan said, near his shoulder, startling him. "Your request is fulfilled. Please come stand at the edge of the dais." He held in his hand a Book of Orders.

Saric moved woodenly to the edge of the dais. He held up his hand to the assembled senate. It was the posture of blessing the masses. His other came to rest on the book in Rowan's hand.

"I, Saric, son of Vorrin," Rowan said.

Saric repeated the words, but all the while he felt ill.

What if she was dead? Or died in the days to come? This was the work of the keepers, carrying on beyond the grave, using as their instrument this Rom Sebastian.

"...will carry out the office of Sovereign to the best of my abilities, to uphold Order with my life..."

"...to uphold Order with my life..."

It was to be the pinnacle of his life.

But all he could think about was Feyn.

"...under the Maker. Maker, help and bless me, and bring Bliss to the world."

"...under the Maker. Maker, help and bless me..."

"And bring Bliss to the world."

"And bring Bliss to the world."

The senators, all of them standing for the oath, began to kneel. Beside him on the dais, Rowan went to one knee.

"Sire," Rowan said when Saric gazed at him, "you are now Sovereign of the world."

Inside Vorrin's chambers—no, *his* chambers, now emptied of Vorrin's body—Saric stormed toward the windows. He stared out.

"I want to be alone."

"Sire," Rowan said. "If you require—"

"I don't. And if I do, I'll call for you." It occurred to him that Rowan was his senate leader now; Saric might depose him with a word. It was a fact he might have liked to savor. But now that was lost.

Rowan turned for the door, but before he had pulled it open, Saric said, "Please ask Camille to send for Corban the alchemist immediately."

When the taller man had gone, Saric stood in his father's apartments, staring out at the maze of the Citadel with her walkways and her rock gardens, her ancient palaces and museums and her modern administrative buildings, much as he had seen his father do on so many occasions.

One of the heavy bronze doors opened behind him. Saric turned to see Corban walk sedately into the chamber and, almost as an afterthought, drop to one knee.

"Get up. Feyn's missing."

"I've heard," the alchemist said, rising.

"Do you realize what this means?" Saric lowered his chin and leveled a gaze at the alchemist. Corban never changed. He never aged. Though he had no emotion, he seemed to have other uncanny gifts.

"The law is passed?" Corban asked.

"Of course it's passed. But it's now worthless!"

"How can you say that?" Corban asked. "Feyn will succeed you in three days, and the office will pass to the previous Sovereign, you, when she dies."

"What if she's already dead, now, before she's seated?"

"Then rule will pass to the next eligible candidate upon the inauguration. And you will kill them once they are seated."

True. Then he would have his throne either way. And yet, it rankled.

"The outlaw, this artisan. He's the one who took her. It has to be."

"Rom Sebastian."

"Yes." Rage clouded Saric's mind. "But why? What would he gain by kidnapping her?"

"Clearly, leverage. He may have just become the most powerful person in the world. It's not so foolish."

"You will find him and my sister. You'll assure me that she is alive. But you will kill him, and this time you will not fail. I want to see my *beloved* sister safe. I want, as her devoted brother, to see her come to power. It is my duty. I will not be defied. Do you understand?"

The bronze door opened. Both men's heads turned.

"Does no one beg entrance? I won't have people coming in and out of here at will!"

Camille stood white-faced, having never fully recovered from this morning.

"Forgive me, sire. There is a woman here demanding to speak to you."

"Of course," he said drily. "The whole world would demand to speak to its Sovereign."

"She insists that you'd harm me if you knew she'd departed without audience."

"Send her away."

"She says to tell you that she's brought you information about the keepers."

Saric stilled.

Interesting.

Corban, standing between Saric and Camille, tensed.

"Who is she?" he said.

"She came in with one of the apprentice guards. She says her name is Avra."

Chapter Twenty-six

FOR NEARLY an hour they had paced the knoll—Rom, raking at his hair as he speculated how this information might change the world, Feyn lifting the swath of fabric on which she'd translated the vellum, scanning it again and again.

"*The first viable means to reprogram that DNA by means of a retrovirus.* He claims that the limbic system is the seat of humanity, but he must be speaking metaphorically. Surely."

"Reread that part about the virus," Rom said.

"*Humanity is dying. The fact is clear to me: Though blood flows through their veins, those infected by Legion are no longer human but a fear-filled race of dead.*" Feyn set the translation to her side. "I still can't fully grasp it."

"But we aren't dead," Rom said, "you and I."

"And when we were, did we have any clue we were?"

"Can a dead person know they're dead? I don't think so." He shook his head. "But I know one thing: Everything I've been told about the blood so far has turned out to be true."

He watched Feyn as she gazed skyward, then closed her eyes. Standing there like that in her skirt with its tattered hem, she might be a peasant, a nomadic urchin basking in the country air. She inhaled deeply. Her ribs expanded against the bodice of the dress as though to draw as much life into her lungs as she could.

She opened her eyes and leveled her gaze at him. "But you and I are alive now in ways the rest of the world is not."

Feyn came to him then and took his hands. "I'm so grateful."

She laid a kiss against his knuckles. He thought she would laugh, but she didn't. Perhaps it was the mind-bending significance of the keeper's account, but she was already less giddy than before. A hint of the ordered ice that had held her eyes so steady before she'd ingested the blood laced them again, he thought. Or was it only his imagination, fearing the consequence of her not drinking a full portion?

"This vellum...it can never come into the hands of the public," she said, letting go of his fingers. "Not yet. Not now. We have to protect it and keep it." Her voice trailed off, as though interrupted by another thought. He could almost see the play of ideas across her face, the thought captured in the glance of her eyes. Something was there, niggling at her, bothering her

"Feyn..."

"We'll find a way to solve this riddle—all of it." Again, the look of distraction, and then she seemed to shake off the thought, as though by sheer act of will. She reached for him, slid her hands around his neck. "Remember I said I wanted to tell you something?"

"Yes?"

"Come to my estate with me. Stay with me until my inauguration. We'll rest, we'll talk, and we'll eat. I want to eat with you." She laughed then. "Come back and I'll send for instruments. You can make your music. Lie down with me and get up with me, and when the day of my inauguration comes, ride into the city with me. I want you at my side. Sovereigns don't marry, but I could change that. My father has seven concubines he's kept by him for thirty years. He might as well be married. I'll be the world's Sovereign, and we will be each other's."

She tilted her head. The sun was in her face and playing through the nearly blue highlights of her hair. Tiny virgin creases marked the corners of her eyes, and he realized that today had been the first time that genuine expression had reached them.

He opened his mouth to speak, but she laid her finger against his lips.

"Don't say it. You're right, I have to return. We'll bring your friends to the Citadel. We'll release the old keeper. But most important, Rom, we'll be together. Because this is what I wanted to tell you. I love you. I *feel* it. In all its chaotic glory, in all its scandal, against everything I've ever stood for. I love you."

She held his gaze, refusing to let him escape.

"Do you hear me? I love you, Rom Sebastian. And whatever this is—this old vellum, this account and secret knowledge, we'll get to the bottom of it. Together. And my reign will be a reign of love. We'll bring truth, beauty, and love to the world!"

Tears welled in his eyes. He wasn't sure if they were summoned by the thought of bruising the joy in her voice, or by the thought of a reign of love that might come at her hands. The world needed Feyn. Her. And in that way he needed her, too.

In a world without Avra he would lift Feyn onto her stallion right now so they could begin that very journey together. But that was not this world.

"Aren't you in love?" Feyn smiled, but her eyes were filling with confusion. "I can't imagine life without you. Not now. I'll never forget this day. I will never forget waking to the sight of you, the cast of your eyes. I've never seen anything so beautiful. Ever! We will—we must—find a way to bring this to the world. Don't you see? This is what I want every woman and man to feel under my rule."

"Yes. I'm in love," he said quietly, lifting his gaze.

The first flush of her smile vanished.

"Then let's go. Rom, please. I'm asking you." She leaned closer to kiss him, but he brought his fingers to her chin and stopped her.

"Feyn, listen to me . . ."

"What is it?"

"I *am* in love. But with someone else."

The illumination in her eyes faded.

"What do you mean? With who?"

"Her name is Avra."

Even saying her name sparked warmth—and worry—in him.

"Her name is Avra and she's as much a nobody in your world as I was yesterday. I've known her my whole life, and I think a part of me was always waiting to love her—"

"Avra?" She pushed back from him, spun away. Her hands went to her head. "There's nothing left, no love for me?" She turned back. "This Avra was with you when you came through the pain and the sickness of your change?"

"Yes, but—"

"Then maybe it's only a matter of who's present when it happens. Maybe—who's to say that if I had been with you, you wouldn't be declaring your love right now for me? How do you know you don't, or can't, love us both? Surely you can love more than one person."

"I...I don't know...I..." Hades, was it possible?

"What is this to us?" Feyn grabbed his hand and kissed his fingers again. "You'll bring her. And I will love her. This is no obstacle to the Brahmin. It will be perfectly acceptable."

"Feyn. I don't know if she..." His voice trailed. "Avra isn't Brahmin. Neither am I."

"You're an artisan. Don't you know what your name means, Rom?"

"No."

"It means 'highness,' and at any rate, you may not be Brahmin, but I am. I'll be Sovereign. I'll make it happen. We'll be together."

Her mention triggered another thought. The account on the vellum had said that the effect of the blood wasn't permanent, even in its full portion. How long did they have to even know the meaning of love, let alone to chase its far reaches? Months? Days?

"For all we know our ability to love is fleeting," he said. "What if it's gone in a week? Or a month? The vellum said it would be temporary."

"Then...we would love out of loyalty, from fear and duty, as we do now."

"That isn't love. That was never love. Love requires emotion, not simply duty or a contract practiced by dead people. I know that now. It's a living thing. Supported by loyalty, but without emotion it's empty! As dead as we were...and will be again." He felt something inside him recoil at the very thought.

"I love you, Rom." It was an offering. A wish. The cry of a living heart heard by his own.

"And I love you, Feyn." He kissed her pale cheek. "But I also love Avra. We aren't Brahmin. It's not our way." What could he say? Conflicting thoughts spun through his mind.

For a few moments, she held his gaze. Then she released his hand and turned away. "If the feelings of love fade, will the pain of it, too?"

"Pain? How can you say that—love is life itself."

"Then life must be filled with pain."

His own heart felt fractured.

"You see?" she demanded. "This is why they called it Chaos. With the bliss comes such pain. The suffering of loss, the desire for what one cannot have, the ambition to have more...all of it filled with so much pain!"

"But it's also life!" Rom said.

"If so, then I can see why death might be preferred by some. At least in death there is peace."

Her boldness surprised him. Surely she wasn't reverting to death already. A chill spread down his back.

"Feyn, there's something else. I didn't have a full portion of blood to give you. The effects might be more fleeting with you than with the others."

"So then it's true. Humanity reverts to death, which has become its natural state. This fairy tale was real for a day. A beautiful morning of intoxication." She glanced at him with a sad smile. "A part of me wishes now I had never lived it."

"It's not a fairy tale."

"Of course it isn't. Because what do we have? A story. About life. About death. It has no happy ending."

"The boy, Feyn. There's the boy," he said. "That's why we're here."

She gave a short laugh. "How would it be possible for some boy to assume power? A cripple no less?"

"What if he's a royal? In line for the throne?" He glanced down at the translated account on the ground. Feyn had scrawled a note on the edge of the cloth: *Boy. Royal. Nine years old.*

She shook her head as though she had already been through this in her own mind. "I know every royal child who qualified for sovereignty. The list is short. And besides, cripples no longer exist. The royals would never have allowed such a child to live. Brahmin aren't supposed to be born with defects."

"But everything so far has been true! The account of the blood, the virus, the…" Rom stopped.

"What is it?" she asked.

An image flashed through his memory. He strode quickly back to where the original vellum lay and grabbed it, scattering the stones that had held it flat. They'd pored over the first keeper's ancient account on the front. But there was more, wasn't there? A few hand-written notations on the back.

"Rom?" Feyn came over.

"What about this?" He flipped the vellum over. The notations in the upper left-hand corner were faded from handling. Names. Dates. Times. Thirteen of them.

She seized the document from his hands.

"What's this?"

"Later notations."

"Why didn't you tell me about this before?"

"I forgot. I completely forgot. They're just dates and names. For all I knew, they were other keepers or trustworthy sources."

She scanned the list. "These…These are all sevenths, like I was. I know all of these. See, there is my name: *F. Cerelia*."

"Sevenths?"

"Brahmins born closest to the date of the cycle of Rebirth—the seventh hour of the seventh day of the seventh month every twelve years. The last eligible cycle during Vorrin's reign for the choosing of a Sovereign to succeed him began nine years ago. See, here's a seventh from that cycle. A candidate, basically, for my office, except that I was born closer to the mark in the cycle prior. And as you can see, there's no Abyssinian b…" She stopped. Her brow furrowed.

"What?" Rom said.

"Something…Nuala, my maid. Years ago she told me about a boy, a royal boy born with a crooked leg, though I dismissed it as a fearful wives' tale." She shook her head. "In either case, he was immediately killed."

"Why isn't he on this list?"

"As I said, the Brahmin aren't supposed to be born with defects. It's a terrible embarrassment. His name would have been removed from the primary birth record so that the knowledge of his birth would be buried with his body."

"If he had lived, how old would he be?"

She hesitated. "Nine."

They looked at each other.

A boy. A royal. Nine years old.

Rom stared at her. "What if he's not dead?"

Feyn was silent.

Chapter Twenty-seven

A VRA, IS IT?" Saric's gaze dropped down over her where she knelt. "My lord."

Only minutes ago she had been informed she must kneel, that Saric was now Sovereign in his father's place. And though it had shaken her utterly, the tremor in her hands now was not from fear— at least, not fear of what might happen to her.

Only that she might fail.

They'd denied Triphon entrance, but there was nothing for him to do now. It was up to her, and Rom was all that mattered.

There were two men in the chamber, one of them more finely dressed than the other. It was the first time she had ever laid eyes on Saric, son of Vorrin. Dark and brooding, the man circling in front of her who had told her to rise looked nothing like his sister.

She had unfastened her cloak. It lay open down the front, revealing one of Neah's finest dresses. Still, she felt plain compared with the dark splendor of this place, of the Sovereign himself.

"You say you come with information of some sort," Saric said. He left his mouth slightly open, running the tip of his tongue against his teeth as he regarded her.

"I do. About the keepers. I have their secrets."

Saric flicked a glance toward the other man, who stood silently by. His eyes were sharp in his skull.

"And what secrets are these?"

"I haven't come to offer them for free," she said.

"Ah, of course." He inclined his head. "And what payment are you looking for?"

"I'll share them in exchange for a man in your keeping."

"Why would you think I have anyone in keeping?"

"I know you do."

"Then please inform me—which man is this?"

"Rom Sebastian. He was captured here last evening."

Saric tapped his lower lip. "Rom Sebastian. He's…an artisan, I believe."

Avra's heart had been a slow hammer against her ribs. Now she felt the strike of it as though it were a pickax. "Yes."

"Let's say that I have this man. What's he to you? Obviously you've risked a lot to come here."

Her hands were cold.

"Does it matter? His freedom's the only thing I ask in exchange for information. The keepers, I believe, are a group of interest to you."

"And I have the last of them in my dungeons now. I'm not sure that you really can offer me anything more. I'm sorry you've wasted your time."

She had to work to draw breath against the invisible band constricting her lungs.

"The man you killed in the alleyway," she said quickly. "I can tell you what was in the parcel he was carrying. All of it."

The Sovereign paused.

"I already know he carried the blood." He turned and scrutinized her, his gaze resting on the simple amulet at her throat. "This artisan, Rom. He's your brother?"

"No."

"Your husband?"

She faltered. "No."

"What fear motivates this request, then?"

"Not fear."

"Then what?" he demanded. "Why would you offer me these great secrets—whatever they are? For what?"

"Love," she whispered.

Saric's pulse surged.

Love. The mystery. Adrenaline flooded his veins.

She was obviously common. Her pearl earrings were probably the most valuable thing she owned, if they were even hers. Her skin was too opaque, but still, she wasn't homely. Her small nose and the lips that naturally pouted held a certain appeal. She was at least as fair as most of his concubines.

But most intriguing of all, she had just spoken of an emotion that she had no business feeling.

Unless...

He glanced at Corban, who studied her from where he stood. "What do you make of this?" Saric said, jerking his head in her direction.

"We know love existed in Chaos," the alchemist said with some skepticism. "A heady emotion that moved people to reckless acts. In the time of Chaos, it was considered the highest emotion, though it was the least stable."

Saric glanced from the alchemist to the girl. "Continue."

"Its effect was a favorite topic of Chaos Age writers and song-makers," Corban said. "We believe it actually changed the brain chemistry of those who experienced it."

Saric had changed his chemistry in order to feel. What was this feeling that changed the brain?

He could hear the girl's swift breathing, could smell her skin— the perspiration on it. He felt his blood pressure rise. There was something different about her. She was smaller than he might favor, possessing only a simple beauty, and yet...

She loved.

She had to have taken the blood. If the rumors were true, it meant that this creature was more alive than any woman he'd encountered. Perhaps even more than he was, rendering him an imposter by comparison.

"Why haven't I experienced this?" he asked.

Corban faltered. "As I explained, the serum only brings out certain emotions."

"You call love unstable, and yet she looks…" He was having some difficulty describing her. "Stable."

Corban was silent.

Betraying the uncertainty nipping at Saric's mind would be a mistake. A sudden and overwhelming desire to experience this girl filled his veins. To taste her, to couple with this woman of the blood.

"Clearly, you're afraid," he said. "And still, here you are." Saric shifted his eyes from her, oddly unnerved by her steady gaze. "To be willing to go to such lengths for a man…It makes no sense. Unless of course"—he looked at her again—"you drank the keeper's blood."

Her eyes moved swiftly between him and Corban.

He let his gaze fall to her hands. Her short nails and unadorned, delicate fingers—how small and bird-like they seemed. And yet in this moment, she was perhaps the most potent woman in his world. Could she possibly know that?

"Yes," she said. Her voice was soft, one for whispering words in the dark. "I drank it. Rom and I both. We drank it, and it has given us power. Together we have discovered things that you will never see or feel."

He watched the movement of her cloak falling from her narrow shoulders, the way it swayed against her hips. The way her dress was tied at her neck, the fall of her dark hair. Utterly beautiful and yet totally unremarkable. Yet he would be hard-pressed to find Feyn as fascinating as this girl in this moment.

Feyn.

He resented the anxiety the mere thought of her name brought him. It was so close to the fear he had known all his life. Surely this Rom of hers had taken Feyn. But the woman before him would wager her own life because she believed Rom was in his dungeons.

What would it be like to take this woman; to feed on her life, to overwhelm her with his own? If he was so drawn to her blood, she was surely as desperate for him. He had seen the look of desire in the eyes of more women than any other man on this earth. Did she not have the same look in her eyes now? Newly awakened, she could not easily dismiss her own need to be desired.

He held her gaze. Invited it. "Rom received the blood from the old man in the alley," he said. "I was told there was enough for five. I'm guessing that Neah took it as well."

A flash in her eyes.

"Do you think we didn't learn who let your boy into the Citadel the night my sister disappeared?"

She said nothing.

"And the fourth...this guard you came with?"

"I found him outside the Citadel, going in for training, and convinced him to escort me in," she said.

"So there are two portions left." He glanced past her at Corban. "Tell me, Corban, why can't we simply use her blood?"

"It would be like taking the blood of someone on medication and expecting it to heal a sickness," the man said. "It wouldn't be sufficient. You will need the original blood."

"You see?" Avra said. "I have the blood you're looking for. Give me Rom, and I'll give you what you want."

"The blood, yes of course. Your boy didn't have it on him when we took him." He wondered if she could read his lies, being a creature now so like him. "But there's more here than blood that interests me."

She did not blink, did not falter, did not show a hint of dismay at his obvious insinuation. For a few moments, she returned his gaze in kind, either considering his suggestion or suppressing her own eagerness to accept it.

The tension between them thickened Saric's pulse.

"Clearly," she said. "But I would need my boy back."

Something was wrong. Avra had come here ready to use any means necessary to gain Rom's freedom. She'd known from the outset that her decisions were motivated by the newfound emotions coursing through her veins. Like a drug, they pushed her into behavior lacking in logic—or any regard for her personal safety.

She would save Rom or die trying. This she knew.

But she hadn't known how that emotion would influence her in the company of another man capable of desiring her. Particularly a man as powerful as Saric. She'd counted on being unnerved by him. She had been, and more. She was drawn to him.

She hated the way he looked at her. The way his gaze raked over her. The dark blood beneath his thin skin, the smoothness of his hair. But she also found it powerfully alluring.

She, the small girl who'd hidden from the Order for so many years, was now holding sway over one of the most powerful Brahmins in the world. Saric wanted her, she could see it in his eyes. She hadn't even lifted her hand and he couldn't tear his gaze away from her.

What would it feel like to have his arms around her? To hear him whisper of his affection?

The moment the thought came to her, she shoved it away.

"You shall have your boy back," Saric replied. "As soon as I have what I want." His gaze drifted down her body. "But first, tell me something about the keepers."

"I've told you—"

"You've told me you have their secrets. And it appears you've ingested one of them. But I need more."

"More?"

A knowing smile twisted his lips. "More."

"I can tell you about their ways."

"But you see, I know about the keepers' ways. Probably more than you do. We've tracked them for centuries, since their formation. We killed the last of them just days ago, not counting this Book fellow in my dungeon. So that won't do."

If she let herself think too much, fear would overtake her. She couldn't afford that.

She moved closer, pushing aside her dread. "Life runs rampant in my veins. Right now. It's vibrant. It hums. I feel *everything*."

He said nothing. She imagined it was because he'd been caught in her spell.

"Have you ever been with a woman who's consumed life and love?"

He closed the distance between them, ran his thumb along her cheek. "Tell me where to find them."

His words rang in her mind like a bell. Find *them*? He just said he had killed all the keepers.

"Find who?" she asked.

His fingers toyed with the tie that drew her dress tight around her neck. He pulled it loose and slid the edge of her dress aside.

Not until he bared her shoulder did Avra remember her burns. His gaze twitched, and then he stood transfixed by her scarred skin.

For an unbearable breath, Saric remained frozen. His eyes lifted to hers. His face transformed into a mask of rage. His hand flashed up without warning as he slapped her with an open palm.

She reeled, gasping.

She'd been played.

Saric didn't have Rom, did he? He was looking for *them*, and one of *them* was Rom.

"I don't have your pathetic man," Saric snapped. "He kidnapped my sister, the Sovereign-to-be."

"You lied," she gasped. It was all that came to her frantic mind. Shame flooded her, scalding and hot.

"You're deformed," he snapped. "Is your whole body like that?"

"No."

He eyed her as if trying to decide whether his thirst for her had dried up. He turned on his heel and strode away.

"Put the word out to every radio, every paper, every outpost and city within a hundred miles. Let it say this: *Rom. Return what you've taken within twenty-four hours or Avra dies.*"

Corban nodded. "And what about her?"

"Have her sent to my private chamber."

Chapter Twenty-eight

THEY HAD no more water. They had no food. But as she and Rom rode toward the closest outpost in the settling darkness, fatigue, thirst, and hunger were the last things on Feyn's mind.

Rom was sitting behind her, his arms around her. She leaned back against his chest and closed her eyes. She could imagine, almost, that it was another day in another world. That this torn dress was the only one she owned. That she was no ruler-to-be, but the richest gypsy in the world, with scrub grass and anemones for her carpet and stars as her evening jewels.

Almost.

There was Byzantium, waiting for her. A dead capital for a dead world. She shuddered. Rom's arms tightened around her.

And then there was the fact that the two thoughts together should have made her weep.

But they didn't.

She had first felt her emotions start to wane three hours ago, when she and Rom decided they must return. She would not go to her estate, but return to the city, they decided. She had been prepared to release the keeper called the Book and to help shelter him and Rom's friends outside the city, where they would be safe for the time being. Safe, but away from her. There had been such great hope in his eyes as she had said it, and though she had thought it beautiful just a few hours earlier, she was no longer able to re-create that sentiment.

Something was changing. Was she really willing to risk so much by releasing the keeper and bringing forth this boy, assuming such a boy even existed and could be found?

"Rom?"

His cheek brushed against hers as the horse moved beneath them.

"I'm losing this," she said. "It's leaving me."

He said nothing. What could he say? He turned one of the hands around her upward and she laid her own against it, clasping his tightly.

"Does this mean I'm dying?"

"If what we read is accurate, we're both destined to die again. It's only a matter of time. The difference is that we know it."

"I wonder what I'll think about love, having known it." She turned, as much as she could, and he clasped her against him. "Promise me. Never let me forget what it was like."

"Which part?" he whispered.

"All of it. Love. Joy. Hope. Sadness. Don't let me forget what it was to be alive, even if it was only for a day. Promise me."

He didn't respond immediately. "You're afraid you'll forget?"

She faced the horizon. Afraid. Soon it would be all she was capable of feeling. "It's leaving me, but I don't want the memory to leave me, too. I don't want to forget. Is that too much to ask?"

"Of course not. I promise." His hand tightened around hers.

She knew he said it to make her feel better. But the more the afternoon waned, the less she needed his assurances. She wasn't quite as sure why it was important to remember.

Which only alarmed her—if less than before.

I am dying.

She closed her eyes and thought of the warmth of him behind her. The sun on her face, fainter now, through the clouds. Her skin was no doubt still flushed from more sun than it had seen in years. She thought of the anemones like drops of blood on the knoll.

Blood. Blood. So much talk of blood.

All of it felt so distant now. Had she really danced with Rom through the grass in the rapture of the day? Had she kissed his lips and lost herself in their wonder?

When she was seventeen, an alchemist had treated her for a broken bone after a fall from her horse. To help with the pain, he'd given her medicine, and it had filled her head with a numbness that washed away the ache.

She felt that same vagueness now. Numb, after a distant dream.

The outpost they'd been riding toward came into sight, lamplight shining from its lone window. Soon Rom would leave the city, perhaps never to return.

"This boy," she said. "What if he really is alive?"

"I don't know. I don't know what happens then. The keeper said to find him—"

She gave a short, mirthless laugh.

"What is it?" he asked.

"The keeper said to find him, and the vellum said he must come to power. You do realize that's impossible, don't you?"

"What do you mean?"

"I was born within seconds of the seventh hour. It is almost statistically impossible that the boy, if he existed, would be born closer to the mark than I. In which case he would be, at best, next in line."

Rom tilted his head, considering her words.

"*If* he really was born and *if* he's still alive and close enough to the mark to be next in line...it would still be impossible for him to come to power."

"Why?"

"Because I would need to die before my upcoming inauguration. Only then would rule pass to the next in line. But once I become Sovereign, succession will be recalculated according to the cycles of

Rebirth within my reign. And only the new set of candidates will be eligible to succeed me. So I would need to physically die——"

"Don't say that."

"I'm differentiating. Because I'm already dying in one sense."

"You're not dying."

But I am. I feel life slipping away. And then I can feel it a little less...

"As Sovereign, you could change the law."

She knew, though, what Rom did not: The senate would never allow it. But all she said was, "Maybe." Then: "I can understand the appeal of Sirin's Order better now than before, I think. With the burden of emotion, logic suffers."

"So say the dead," Rom said.

"Now you're mocking me?"

"Of course not. You've known life."

"Nevertheless, I'm dying, Rom. I took less of the blood than you did and it's already leaving me. I no longer feel either the joy or the sorrow of this morning. Think of it, a whole world of the unwitting dead. Lost to love. Lost to beauty. Like walking corpses. But now it hardly even seems sad to me."

She drew one of the ragged scarves down over her head as they neared the outpost. The world need not know—must not know—that their future Sovereign was missing. No doubt her father and brother had done their best to shield the world from news of her absence. It would not do to have the masses in a heightened state of fear.

The outpost was a small building offering only simple supplies: dry goods, water, some medicines.

Feyn realized she had no means of paying for anything as a commoner. "I don't have any money," she said. It was a strangely delightful thought that caused her to smile, even if she did not laugh as she might have earlier.

"Luckily, I've got a banknote." He grinned.

In front of the outpost was a channel pumped with safe, treated water. The stallion dropped its head and drank thirstily.

"Can I trust you not to go anywhere?" Rom said after he dismounted.

"Yes. You can."

It took him less than five minutes to find what he needed.

She was gazing in the direction of the city's storm clouds—always circling like gray vultures—when he came running back out of the outpost. His face was ashen.

"What? What is it?" The old familiar fingers of fear reached into her mind. She felt it—welcomed it, nearly.

He held up a paper. It was a public notice, drawn up with the seal of the Citadel. It would have gone out to every government office, outpost, and transport station in the area for immediate posting.

Her skin prickled at the message:

This notice goes out to that one who has fled the Citadel Guard, the outlaw Rom Sebastian. Return what you've taken within twenty-four hours. Avra's life depends upon it.

No picture. Nothing but those words so stark on the page.

"Saric," she whispered.

"Your brother? He's got Avra? We have to go!" He reached for the saddle.

"Go and do what?"

He tore at his hair, paced away and back. In a way she pitied him for all of his angst, for this strange love that had ravaged both of their minds in the fields.

He looked at her with frantic eyes. "I don't know. But I have to go," he said, making to remount behind her.

"No, Rom." She swung down.

"What are you doing?"

Yes, what was she doing? She was dying, she knew that now, and in a strange way she could not help but welcome that death. For all Rom's refusal to speak plainly about the implications of the keeper's words, she could not ignore them. The only way for any such boy to come to power would be for her to die before she became Sovereign.

In the throes of life, she would have leaped from a cliff for love. Now that passion felt like a vague and distant thing. Surely this idea of a boy—romantic as it seemed—was a fantastic notion as well.

And yet she had no desire to see any harm come to Rom. None at all.

"He'll kill you. You took me. That was treason. You can't return."

"Feyn…" The look on his face was purest anguish.

He loves her.

"Take the horse," she said.

"What about—"

"I know my brother. He wants you, but more than that, he wants me back safely. I'll get Avra."

His eyes were filled with uncertainty. She understood. Earlier today, he could never have trusted her with his own life.

"How do I know?" he asked.

"You doubt me already?"

"Please tell me that you still believe all of this," he said.

"All of what?"

"You see?" He motioned at her with an accusing hand. "You're losing it! Not only your emotions, but the reason that goes with it! This isn't just about feeling. Emotion brings with it a new kind of thinking. You no longer believe?"

Something about his fear rang true.

"In what?" she asked, scrambling for reason.

"In the boy!"

"I don't know. He may exist. If so, you may be the one to find him."

"I mean that he's destined to be Sovereign!" Rom blurted.

"Based on an ancient vellum? It defies everything, Rom." Her sudden doubt surprised even her, and she immediately restated the matter so as not to alarm him. "I'm not saying I don't believe that the virus somehow altered humanity, Rom. Clearly something changed in me when I took the blood. But I can't say that I believe you will find this boy. Or that I am meant to die so that he can take his rightful place."

"No one said you would die."

"How else would he succeed my father?"

To this he said nothing.

Feyn looked away. "It doesn't matter. What does is that you and I shared something I won't forget. For that I will help you and your friends. I will save Avra for you. I will see that the keeper is safe."

"And what if I do find the boy?"

She shrugged. "Then fate will take its course."

He stared at her, brow wrinkled. There was more playing across his face, a veritable riot of emotion. Desperation. Fear. Frustration.

"Rom? I promise you. I'll help Avra."

"And then what? What am I supposed to do?"

"Stay away. They'll be looking for you and I can't immediately put an end to that. Get out of the city. Find a hiding place."

"I'm meant to find the boy! I can't just hide in fear."

"Then go find the boy!" she said. "But you must understand that my brother won't easily forget what you've done. The city will be a dangerous place for you."

He threw his arms wide. "Find him where? Feyn!"

She'd considered the question of the boy as they rode, and each mile had only solidified her certainty that he could not exist. Really, what was the vellum but legend and myth? Wishful thinking...false hope? The blood was more likely an intoxicant than true life. Religion had once been full of such claims. Perhaps it was what had gotten under her brother's skin.

And yet just an hour ago she'd half believed in it, herself.

"The family who had the deformed infant...," she said. "I think you might be able to find them."

"How? Where?"

"Not the boy, mind you. But I could direct you to the family my servant spoke of. Go on your quest, just stay clear of the city."

He paced, one hand in his hair. "And Avra?"

"I'll be sure that she knows you're alive."

"Tell her to wait for me. She'll know where."

"Of course." He did not appear fully convinced. "I won't betray you, Rom. I owe you that much."

"For what? What have I done but kidnap you? You'll soon forget all of this."

She reached for his face and offered him a gentle smile. "For showing me love, however fleeting, however distant it may seem."

Why did saying that fill her with such misgiving?

He took her hand in both of his. "Then don't forget. Please, I'm begging you. What we shared was real."

"How could I?"

But they both knew how. And that it was she who now spoke the words to comfort.

By the time she had directed him and given her stallion one last kiss on the neck, fear was all that remained behind, settling over her like a gray cloud.

So this is what it is to die.

She could still see the sadness in Rom's eyes as clearly as if he had voiced it.

A beautiful day. A day for another life.

"Thank you, Rom, son of Elias. We'll soon meet again."

He turned in the saddle. "Remember, tell Avra I'm alive and well. Tell her to wait for me."

"I will. Now go." She slapped the hindquarter of the horse.

She watched him gallop east, wondering if she would ever see him again. It was amazing how quickly her thoughts had shifted. The green hills and their bright flowers seemed so far away.

Feyn turned her gaze to Byzantium where the world awaited its Sovereign. Her name was Feyn and she would rule as none had yet ruled, with wisdom and kindness as commanded by the Order.

And what if Rom does find this boy, Feyn?

A slight shiver ran down her back. But Rom would find no boy, because there neither was nor would be another Sovereign.

Chapter Twenty-nine

DAWN HAD the audacity to bring not his sister or the interloper Rom Sebastian, but feeble, useless light.

Two days until inauguration.

Saric stalked before the great window of the Sovereign's office, raking back his unbound hair. At his command, word of Vorrin's death had never gone out. But of course, Pravus knew. Somehow, he always knew. And he had paid Saric a visit a few dark hours ago.

The unspoken threat of his coming to the Citadel had disturbed Saric deeply. But not as deeply as seeing him here in person.

"You assured me a smooth succession," the hooded alchemist had said. His quiet, more than his implied threat, had set Saric on edge.

"And so it will be."

"It won't be if we have to contend with Feyn's death first. And so quickly on the heels of Vorrin's. The senate has full right to demand an investigation."

"Have I failed already that you come to rebuke me?"

He had not slept or bathed since Pravus's visit.

Now he stared out at the impassive face of the capital and wondered if he really might watch his reign crumble like so much sand under a wave.

The message had come, as he had known it would: an urgent note from Rom, the pathetic lover of the scarred Avra.

240

Feyn for Avra. Send her out and Feyn will be yours.

That was it.

What was he to do, hand her over with no guarantee that he would get Feyn at all? What did they take him for?

And yet what choice did he have?

He had thrown out the messenger and raged the length of the office, called for Corban and then made him wait outside. Corban's presence only exacerbated Saric's own frustration and his awareness, sharper than ever, that he was alone in feeling it.

He sent for Rom's whore, but once the servant who fetched her left them alone as he demanded, he found he could barely look at her.

Her hair was mussed and her cloak was gone. Her eyes were red and swollen. There were chafe marks above and below the ties that still held her wrists. They had bound her to his bedpost, no doubt. The vile scars against her collarbone were visible in the pale light through the window, but worse yet, they seemed to dance in the serpentine light of the lanterns in their tall stands. What was he thinking, having sent her to his chamber? He could never have wanted her.

"Well. Your man fought for you."

"Of course he did," she whispered.

He could not abide the absolute conviction in her voice. He crossed to her and hauled her up by her hair.

"Really? And is it also love that if I don't receive my sister, he'll have condemned you to your death? That you'll die because of him?" Spittle flew in her face, but her eyes were fixed brazenly on him. That there was no fear in them was the gravest insult of all.

Hades, she believed in this Rom. She would defend him at the expense of her life.

A single backhand sent her flying into the desk and onto the floor.

"Dog! Is that the great secret of the keepers, this enslavement to your master?" He strode to his desk and snatched the knife kept there for opening the wax seals on documents. He grabbed her by the wrists, sliced through her ties, and let her fall back onto the floor.

"You disgust me. You spent the night alone because I couldn't *bring* myself to take you. But if I don't get back my sister, the next time I see you, I'll take my pleasure with you. I'll do what should have been done the day you incurred that defect. I'll cut off that twisted skin and put you down like an animal."

He shouted for the guards, who came and lifted her to her feet. She struggled to pull her arms free of them, her hair wild, an angry welt already darkening her cheek.

"Take her to the gate. Set her free. Leave me, all of you."

When they had gone he threw the knife into the corner. He could do nothing but wait. Nothing.

Feyn waited in hiding, obscure in her torn dress, until she saw a dark-haired girl released at the gate. She waited until the messenger she'd sent caught up to Avra and handed her the note with the cryptic words that read only: *Rom is alive and well. Wait for him.*

Avra was a pretty girl, beautiful in her own way. Rom would do well to keep her.

Satisfied, Feyn entered the Citadel and headed toward the Residence of the Office. She pushed wide the great bronze doors and strode into her father's quarters.

But the figure that turned from the window wasn't her father, as she'd expected. It was Saric. And the man near the desk wasn't Rowan, but the alchemist Corban.

Saric's eyes widened. "Sister!"

His hair was in disarray. Dark shadows nested like bruises under his eyes even as they took in her disheveled state.

"What's this? What are these rags? Have you been mistreated?"

"I'm fine. A disguise to smuggle me out of the Citadel."

FORBIDDEN

Her brother crossed to her quickly. "Thank the Maker. I assure you, the guards who were on duty have been punished and released from their positions. You have no idea the sleepless night I've had, how I feared for your life!"

Indeed, she had never seen him in such a state.

"Put aside your fear, brother. I'm alive and well."

His fingers were trembling. "When I think what this could have cost us…Did you know that I had one of the outlaws here? I released her on your account. I had no choice."

"What matters is that I am safe. Thank you."

"Come. You must let me send for some food. Corban?"

The alchemist opened the door and called for a servant.

Feyn wanted to ask where Father was—she needed his counsel now more than she ever had. But Saric cut her thoughts short.

"I'm most curious to know what sort of madman, what kind of dangerous lunatic, captures the Sovereign to be."

Feyn glanced away.

Rom.

His name should have incited a flush within her. The memory of kisses, of all that was beautiful beyond the concrete structure of this world. Sadness, at the least.

She felt nothing except a quick stab of fear for his safety. But she would not betray even this.

"As you say, brother, he's a lunatic, doing what seemed right to his mad mind. Where is—"

"Where did he take you?"

"He's fled beyond the city." She dropped into the chair he held for her, only then realizing how weary she was.

"Did he tell you about this blood that he carries from the keepers?"

"Blood?" She glanced at him.

"The blood he took from the keepers. Did you see it?"

"I don't know what you're talking about," she said.

243

"Did you see something like a document? Something very old. It might not have been with the blood."

The vellum. How was it possible that Saric knew about it?

"Brother, I was in fear for my life, kidnapped by a madman. Besides, do you really think he'd share his secrets with me?"

"Of course. You're right." He regarded her for a moment longer, then strode toward her father's desk. "I'll have them hunted down and killed. It will become my only concern in these few remaining days as Sovereign, even if it means I forgo sleep as I did last night."

"Sovereign? What are you talking about?"

Saric didn't respond. He didn't even turn.

Feyn pushed herself up from the chair. "Where's Father?"

"Father is dead," he said, flatly.

Fear filled her like water rushing into a cistern after a storm. "What?"

Saric turned, slowly, to face her. "He died yesterday, very suddenly. It was a terrible shock. You can't imagine. There I was, eating with him..." His gaze drifted away, as though his attention had wandered back into his own thoughts.

"Father is dead? And *you* are Sovereign?"

"As the law requires. Only until you can take the throne, naturally."

"You have no training! You're unqualified! A person can't become Sovereign without years of preparation. This is insanity!"

"Yes, well, that's what I said..." He paused. "Is that how you think of me? As nothing but an unqualified little brother?"

"Don't be ridiculous! What have you ever done other than please yourself? What was the senate thinking?"

A chill iced his voice. "They were thinking of adhering to the law, to the Order that you yourself are sworn to uphold." Something about his eyes—they flashed.

He was seething.

Anger. Rage. A day earlier she wouldn't have recognized it. How could he feel this jealousy and anger? Was it possible he, too, had taken the blood?

"Given the circumstances, they should have amended the law to allow someone with experience, like Miran, to step in."

"Trust me, I tried," he bit off. "But the senate will do as they see fit. Perhaps if Father had made me head of the senate, we wouldn't be in this mess. What are we but figureheads, to do their bidding? Even you."

From the corner of her eye, she saw the alchemist Corban's nervous glance. The way he stood there, watching, saying nothing. Did nothing seem amiss to him? And where was Rowan?

"Don't look for Rowan. He was the first to usher me to the Sovereign's chair."

"The law is made to support Order, Saric, not one man's ambition for power."

"Ambition? And what would you know of ambition, sister?"

"That it is forbidden. And yet, somehow, it lives in your eyes."

He was regarding her strangely. "Something is different about you."

"I've just learned news of my father's death!" She paced out into the middle of the room, turning to face the alchemist. "And who is this, your senate leader now? You. Will you say nothing to him, Corban?" A dread unease bit at her, a growing gnawing in her stomach.

"It is the law, lady."

"The law isn't everything. The senate has grown shortsighted. Of all people. Rom was right, even their boy would do better to replace me than any of you! Destiny isn't something to be tinkered with!"

"Boy?" Saric said. He had gone rigid. "What boy?"

She'd said too much. Whatever her fears, she did not want her brother, now Sovereign with far too much power, to broaden his hunt for Rom.

She dismissed the notion with a flick of her wrist and turned away. "Nothing but a rumor. I was only making a point."

"What rumor?" Saric stepped toward her. "The next seventh is a girl your own age."

She looked over at him. His curiosity in the matter was striking. Unnerving. Two thoughts clashed in her mind. The first was that she was right. He was full of ambition. In fact, he had been reaching for this power for days, weeks—longer perhaps.

The second was that such an ambition could only come with that same poison that had set her off her feet.

Saric's face darkened. "As your Sovereign, I *order* you to tell me about this boy."

"There *is* no boy!"

"Tell me!" he shouted.

She stared him down. "You've taken the blood, haven't you?"

He blinked.

"Blood, sister?" he said into the sudden silence.

"The blood you spoke of to me, just days ago in my chamber. But how?"

His features turned to ice. "You know what I think? I think you're lying to me. I think you went with that artisan willingly and now conspire to undo what's been done by law." He pressed in closer. "My own *sister*, who will be my successor to the throne, stands in *defiance* of me?"

There was blackness in his eyes she had never seen in him before.

She took a quick, backward step. "I'm only concerned for you."

"You will tell me everything," he snarled. "Everything or I swear I'll rip it out of you!"

Another step back, driven by the fear that Saric would not stop with words.

"Saric, please. What has gotten—"

His hand flashed and struck her face. Feyn stumbled into the secretary. Her pocket caught on the desk's corner and ripped open. She lost her footing and fell to the floor.

There would be no more pretense. No more pandering. He had already quenched the fire Feyn once ignited in him. He had been a schoolboy, looking up to her as the rest of the world.

Now Saric knew better.

Feyn brought a trembling hand to her cheek, eyes wide. "How *dare* you strike me?"

"How dare you mock your Sovereign?"

"I'm your sister!"

She clambered to her feet, hand pressed to her face. A tattered piece of cloth fell from her torn pocket and settled softly to the floor. It was covered in ink.

Her eyes darted down, and by that single look of fright, Saric knew that she hadn't intended on him seeing that cloth.

Her gaze lifted to meet his. She slowly lowered her hand.

"You're hiding something from me, sister."

"And you are acting like a child, brother."

Her voice was strong again. *Here* was the woman who so easily quickened his pulse. It was a pity she had to die. She would have made such a perfect companion.

Saric stepped forward and lifted the cloth with its scribbled lines in Feyn's own handwriting.

"It's only the legend of these keepers," Feyn said. "Their fantasies of overthrowing Order in opposition to me."

The vellum! This had to be from the vellum itself. And yet she'd denied the existence of any such vellum.

"I didn't want to bother you with quibbles over my right to power, but now you have it," she said. "You see how foolish you are? You strike me to the floor when you should be ushering me into authority!"

Saric barely heard her. His eyes were on the writing in his hand.

Sometime at or near the new year 471…Bloodlines should converge to produce a child. A male…

In this child is our hope. It is he who will remember his humanity, and he who must abolish the Order, the very structures of which go up like a prison around the human heart. It is he who must be brought to power to save the world.

He quickly scanned the translation. A notation had been scribbled in the bottom corner:

Boy. Royal. Nine years old.

His pulse spiked. Another line, at the end of the account:

Find the boy. Bring him to power.

A sharp ring resonated through his skull. So then, there was a boy. He lifted his eyes. Saw that Feyn was staring at him disapprovingly. But then she would—he'd just lost control of himself. And right when it was crucial that Feyn not see him as a threat to her power.

"You see no challenge to your office in this?" he demanded.

"If I did, I would have shown it to you immediately. But I was with this deranged artisan. If he intended me any harm, would I be standing here alive? He raved about this impossible legend, but when it became clear to him that I had nothing to offer, he released me and fled, likely to the nomads."

"So you see no basis for the existence of this boy, even though this notation"—he indicated the words at the bottom—"is in your own hand."

"Please. He forced me to transcribe the words from another document. I did what was required to placate him. But now your behavior has me fearing for my life. In my own office!"

Saric drew a calming breath and gathered his thoughts. He had to recover any ground he'd lost with her.

"Forgive me. You can't imagine what it's been like since your abduction. Please...I lost myself. You are the rightful Sovereign, of course. I would never suggest otherwise. But Father rejected my request to head the senate, and now you treat me like a child. I can't bear the thought of your dismissal."

She watched him for a few moments, then offered him a thin smile of consolation. "You surprise me, brother. I honestly didn't think you had the backbone for leadership. Perhaps I've underestimated you."

Her words surrounded him like a tender embrace. It was the most beautiful thing she'd ever said to him, even though he wasn't sure she fully believed the words herself. What he wouldn't give to rule with Feyn! And for her affection, he might give up any hope of power.

But that was impossible. Without the serum, Feyn wasn't capable of such ambition, no matter how alluring the fantasy.

The account she'd transcribed, on the other hand, was not a fantasy. Without the benefit of the blood, Feyn might not understand the threat presented by the vellum's translation, but he had no doubt that the keeper's secret could destroy them all.

Saric cleared his throat. "Perhaps we've underestimated each other. To be clear, you see no threat from this artisan or the keeper's legend whatsoever?"

"No. As I said, his mind was lost. Driven by fear and forbidden sentiment. The poison they take drives them mad. The same blood that I suspect you of taking, brother."

There it was. To deny it would only erode her trust in him.

"Yes. You are too astute. I took it as a way to understand the threat they pose to the Order."

"And your conclusion?"

He frowned. "As you say. Poison. It lingers in my mind still. But you've seen that."

"Yes."

His mind spun with a sudden thought: *And I would give it to you as well. I will kill you after you take your throne, but not before your blood rages with the same passions as mine.*

If he could not have her love, he would at least have her desire, even her rage.

He set the cloth on the desk with an unsteady hand. "You're probably right about these keepers, but we can't allow even the smallest threat to go unnoticed."

"I'm sure you're right. I should have shown you, forgive me."

"We're days from the inauguration," he said. "We can't risk another attempt on your life. You must remain in your quarters under full guard until we usher you out for the world to greet their new Sovereign."

"You're putting me under house arrest?"

"No. I'm assuring your safety. As acting Sovereign, it is my duty. It's customary for the incoming ruler to be sequestered before the ceremony. What is a country estate compared with the Citadel palace? Anything less would be beneath you."

She stepped up to him, fully recovered now, her gaze lingering on his eyes before dropping down to his chest. She reached out and brushed a bit of lint off his shoulder.

"I have, haven't I?" she said.

"Have what?"

"Underestimated you."

Saric felt himself flush. He both relished and despised this power she held over his heart.

"Perhaps Father was wrong as well," she said. "The senate might do well with new leadership. It will be my first decree, brother. You will assume leadership of the senate on the first day of my rule."

Saric wasn't sure what to make of her offer. On the one hand it was a moot point. Ironic in the least. On the other, it would give him more time to facilitate his own desire. In either case, the fact that Feyn was reaching out to him flooded him with a surprising satisfaction.

"I...I don't know what to say."

"Say nothing." She lifted her hand for him.

He took it gently in his own, dipped his head, and touched his lips to her knuckles. And then on whim, he turned her hand over and laid a kiss against her palm. "It is my honor to serve you, my sister...my Sovereign."

"So be it." She smiled with her chill politeness. "But if you ever hit me again, I will have you executed."

"Yes." Saric returned her smile. And in that moment he knew that he would indeed delay her death long enough to satisfy his desire for her. "Of course. Forgive me. On my life, never again."

She turned and strode toward the door. Had there ever been a more regal creature?

"Oh, and Saric..." Feyn turned. "Have the old keeper sent to my chambers. I would have a word with him."

The keeper?

"Not to fear," she said. "I won't let him slit my throat. But I want to know for myself this enemy that poses such a threat to our Order."

It would do no harm. She'd been exposed to the vellum and had emerged sound enough. If any threat to his ascendancy remained, it would come from the blood in Rom's possession. Or from this boy the vellum spoke of. The boy of the altered blood.

"Of course," he said.

Feyn nodded once more and left.

Silence lingered in her wake like a strange and cloying perfume.

"Corban."

"Sire."

He seized the cloth from the desk, handed the translation to Corban, and paced as he read it.

When the alchemist's eyes finally lifted, Saric snatched the cloth from his hands.

"They said the next seventh was a woman from the same birth cycle as Feyn. Twenty-one years old. And that the one after her was a man in his early thirties. Nothing about a boy. Tell me this is lunacy."

"I know nothing about a boy."

"And if there was such a thing? If the next seventh in line is a young boy?"

Corban folded his hands. "He may be inaugurated at age nine but must appoint a regent to rule on his behalf until he is of age—eighteen. If he dies before being seated at age eighteen, his regent would succeed him until the next seventh becomes eligible. If the child is not seated, the passage of power to the former Sovereign, according to your new law, would not apply."

"And I would not become Sovereign."

"That is correct."

"And if both the boy *and* the regent died?"

"Rule would still pass to the next eligible candidate."

"Then if this boy should by some way exist and should become Sovereign instead of Feyn, I am lost."

"Assuming that—"

"Yes, assuming!"

"But surely, no boy exists. And if he does, Feyn stands in his way."

There it was. The new law applied only to seated Sovereigns of age. No one had anticipated the existence—if he truly existed—of a Sovereign who had not reached his majority. Saric's new law would not apply.

He lifted his fist, closed cage-like around the fabric. "And what about this drivel about the blood's power waning after so many years? Is this in keeping with your models? *I've heard nothing about this!*"

Corban took a deep breath. "It would be in keeping with one of our models, yes. But there are no records of——"

"Why wasn't I told?" Saric raged.

"We didn't think it pertinent. As I said, such a boy doesn't exist."

Saric was shaking and found he could not control the tremors of rage in his arms, the fear that there might be even a whisper of truth in the vellum's ancient lines.

"You will issue this decree, by Sovereign order. All children nine years old of royal blood are to be killed immediately."

The alchemist faltered. "Sire——"

"All of them!"

The alchemist, paler than a moment ago, bowed his head. "I'll see to it."

"As for my sister…" Saric glared at the closed doors. "Post four guards at her door. She is not to set foot beyond it without my express permission."

JONATHAN

Chapter Thirty

ROM'S STALLION had outrun all but the edge of the storm blowing north from the city. He and the great horse spent the better part of the night in an abandoned lean-to several miles east as rain beat down on the roof and lightning cracked open the sky. There they made their uneasy peace. The animal chewed grass at the edge of the shelter's tin roof; Rom gnawed on a piece of dried meat he'd picked up at another outpost. He'd refilled his canteen and drank thirstily, parched and exhausted from two days with little water and even less sleep.

Feyn had assured him she would set Avra free, and he believed her, but his worry refused to settle. He had little choice but to trust her despite her fading conviction. With or without the blood in her veins to guide her passions, she was noble to the bone and would surely see no value in Avra's harm.

If she had an enemy, it was her own brother, Saric, or even the boy, he told himself. Not Avra.

A few hours before dawn, he slept for a little while. He woke to the sound of the stallion's nickering and lifted his head to find that the rain had stopped. Faint light illuminated the eastern sky when Rom mounted the horse and set off.

Northeast of Byzantium, he followed an old road that veered through the eastern hills. He was surprised at the lushness of the

terrain, reclaimed from the old wasteland. For a while he even followed a line of new trees near a winding stream.

An hour later, he found the old road Feyn had told him to look
for just beyond the ruins of a small town. Scrub grass had taken
over so much of the crumbling path that anyone giving it a quick
glance might not have noticed it. The road should lead him to a parcel owned by a distant royal. Lila, she had said, if she recalled the
name correctly.

Now, with the midmorning sun at his back, he looked down at
the estate in question. It was a small country home built from stones
that looked like they might have been brought from the ruined
town. It was surrounded by enough trees, including a few bright
green cypresses, that anyone standing on the road might miss it altogether.

Rom guided his horse down the slope and tied it off to a tree near
the estate's front gate. But when he let himself through and banged
on the weathered door of the house itself, he realized he had no idea
what he meant to say.

The girl who came to the door was simply dressed. "Sir?" She
seemed startled to see him. Her gaze flickered past him to the stallion.

"I'm here alone," he said. "I'm looking for a woman by the name
of Lila. Is she here?"

The maid's gaze was wary. She was a fair girl, pretty in the
way the countryside was pretty, probably no more than nineteen or
twenty. "And who are you?"

"I've come from the Citadel, on business. Tell your mistress
that."

Her gaze flicked again in the direction of the stallion, then she
vanished into the house.

A moment later the girl returned and ushered him in.

"Please, sir, follow me." She led him through the wood-floored
hall to the square courtyard in the middle of the house.

"Thank you, Miss—"

"Bianca," she said, then disappeared through a side door.

The courtyard's creator had taken the best of the countryside— the flowers, shrubs, a single stunted evergreen—and set them in artful disarray on either side of a path that led through the middle. The garden was small, but its natural appeal, even under the cloudy sky, put the austere stone of the Citadel to shame.

A woman in her thirties entered the courtyard, her long hair gathered into a pale braid. Her dress was so similar to the servant's that Rom thought she might be one as well, but then he noted the translucence of her skin.

Brahmin. Royalty.

Even so, she was as similar to Feyn as a sparrow was to a hawk.

"My girl says you've come from the Citadel. I am Lila. How can I help you, Mr. . . . ?"

"Elias." He dare not use his real name, not after it had been in the papers. Apparently she didn't recognize him. Perhaps those in the country lived beyond the reach of the city for good reason.

"Mr. Elias. What is this business you come for?"

"I've come at the request of Feyn Cerelia."

The woman stiffened only slightly, but Rom could not miss that telltale show of concern.

"What would the future Sovereign want with us?"

"She sent me here to find a boy. A royal boy."

The woman blinked, then shook her head. "Boy? What boy?"

"I don't know which boy. Only that—"

"There's no boy here, Mr. Elias. I'm sorry you've come all this way."

"Please," he said, unable to keep the tinge of desperation from his voice. "You have no idea how important he is. If you've hidden news of his death—"

"There's no boy, I'm sorry. Now, if you'll—"

"My lady. I know. I know there was a boy. And I must know if he is still alive."

"Please, sir, you put a fright in me! I can't make it any plainer. There's no boy—not for many years now. The child who lived here was taken to a wellness center. Please! It is not right to speak of it!"

"How many years ago?"

She faltered. "Nine. Nine years ago."

His heart stuttered. "A wellness center you said. What for?"

She hesitated, eyes pleading. "You intend to make me talk about it? I lost my husband that same year as well. Please. Tell your mistress that I don't know what she wants with us. We're the humblest of royals, and loyal to Order."

"I'm very sorry. But I must know!"

"We're very simple, as you can see from our modest ways. Please tell your mistress that we are loyal subjects! That we pray to the Maker for her. But please, leave us now before you throw my small household into more fear. Please!"

He looked over her shoulder through the arched entry through which she'd emerged. The thought of turning and leaving here without a clue to the boy's whereabouts was more than he was willing to consider.

"She won't like my returning without word. She sent me here because she believes the boy lives in secret. But more than that, she believes there's a threat to this boy's life. That he must be protected at all costs."

The woman took a step back, now fully in the grip of fear. Rom threw away his last caution.

"If I go back now and tell her that there's no boy, your life will open to investigation. Your house will be stripped. Every detail of your life will be searched and scrutinized. The records will be opened."

Lila stared.

"Feyn is so set on protecting this boy that she's vowed to find him, and you'd better pray that she does. Because I'm telling you she's not the only one looking for him."

"I told you, sir, there is no boy," she whispered.

"I see. Then I'll have to report that I haven't found him." He turned to go. "You can expect another visit from a full contingent of the Citadel Guard in the next few hours."

Rom could feel her eyes on his back as he strode toward the door, though he had no intention of leaving without the truth. He laid his hand on the door handle, about to turn back. He would force it from her if he must. He had already abducted the Sovereign—what was this to that? Suddenly she cried out.

"Wait! Oh, Maker, help me... Wait!" Her voice broke.

He turned back. "Yes?"

She was trembling; her eyes glistened in the midmorning light. His heart broke for her, a mother impossibly trapped not by love, but by fear. A mother as dead as the rest of the world.

Her face twisted. "Please, promise that what you say is true."

He clasped his hands together as if in prayer. "If you believe in the Maker, if you believe that Feyn is good, then believe me when I tell you I haven't come to harm the boy. On the contrary, I believe that he may be the most valuable child in all the world. Please. Protecting him is my only purpose."

"Most valuable? What do you mean?"

Did she know? Could she?

"You must let me see him."

She faltered.

"I know he's here now. You've all but told me that much. I may be the only hope you have to save your boy. Please, I must see him."

It was one of the longest moments of his life, standing there as her gaze flickered to his amulet and then to his hands, to his eyes, and back.

Finally, she said, "Follow me."

She led him into the house, out the back door, and down a path to a large yard lined in cypress trees. They had been carefully cultivated and planted so that, even misshapen as some of them were, they formed a natural barrier, a kind of enclosed garden. At the end of the path, in an area shielded by the low boughs of a gnarled tree, sat a bench. From his vantage point near the house, Rom had been unable to see it at all. But now he noticed that a woman was sitting on one end of it, head tilted, watching—not him or Lila, but a boy sitting cross-legged under the shade of the tree with his back to them.

Rom stopped. For a moment he could scarcely breathe. The boy was small for his age, Rom could see that even now. The child's attention was fixed on something in his hands. His hair was dark and unremarkable. His skin...

Rom's heart faltered. The boy's skin was dark. Olive-toned. Not the pale skin of the Brahmin. Was he then not a royal?

He was dressed in a simple tunic and long slacks made from the same light-colored fabric. His feet were bare.

Lila spoke softly next to Rom. "He's been sickly since he was born. Some kind of rare congenital disease. He came out slightly deformed."

"He's nine years old?"

"Yes. His name is Jonathan."

So he was a cripple. That part was true to Talus's prediction. But where was the fair skin of the royals?

She was staring at him, fearfully gauging his expression. "Maybe I shouldn't have brought you here. Perhaps this was a mistake."

Rom blinked. "No. Please. I was only wondering...How did you keep him away from the wellness center?"

"His father and I didn't like the city. Its constant storms threw me into fits of anxiety. And so we chose to live here in the hinterlands. But then Talus fell riding his horse—"

Rom started. "I'm sorry." He looked at her. "Talus?"

"His father's name was Talus. It's an old name of his line."

"I've heard of it," he said, mind reeling. "You said he fell riding."

"Yes. It was soon after I became pregnant, and when his arm

didn't heal properly, we took him to the wellness center. He never returned."

It was a story similar to many people's.

To his own father's.

"I couldn't bear to go back. When Jonathan was born, I saw that there was something wrong and...Do you have children?"

"No." He shook his head.

"Then you can't know the fear, the *horrible* fear. They could have blamed us for bringing him into this world. I've told you about Jonathan, showed him to you. I've risked everything. You could very well report me under auspices of the Honor Code!"

Rom took her hands. "I don't have children, but you'll have to trust that I understand your fear." He thought of Avra, shivering the night they had laid wet bandages over her shoulder. "The boy—there was no record of his birth?"

"There was, but it shows that he was disposed of. We reported his death and then gave them the frail body of a common boy just recently buried in a nearby town. They hardly looked at the body—just took it away. It was awful. We live in constant fear."

Feyn had insisted that the primary birth record of any cripple would have been changed, but the fact that she'd specified primary must mean there was another. If they could prove that he was still alive—and keep him out of the wellness center—the record would be valid.

"And the nurse?"

"I swore her to secrecy, afraid for years that she might report it. I think she would have except for the gentle way that Jonathan had with her."

Rom nodded, unable to look away from the boy. "You said he was born nine years ago."

"Yes."

"When, exactly?"

"The year 471. The seventh month...the seventh day."

"What hour?" Now he glanced at her.

"Minutes from the seventh hour," she whispered, a tremor in her voice.

His heart stilled. Everything was real. It was all real.

"This child is royal as they come, second only in line to Feyn herself," she said. "Except for his deformity, of course. The fact that he was born a crippled seventh is a great affront to Order. When you said you were here from Feyn, I feared the worst."

Just then, the boy turned his head and looked at them. His eyes were not the typical gray of the Brahmin, but a simple brown. There was a serenity about him, a sweetness, that defied Rom's notions of royalty and cripples both. Something plain and beautiful.

On impulse he asked, "Does your boy laugh?"

Lila turned wide eyes to him. "Often. I don't understand it. He's a peculiar boy, given to less fear. I've never known what ails him."

"May I talk to him?"

The woman hesitated.

"I promise you before the Maker," Rom said. "I've come to protect him."

"I've told you everything," she said. "What choice do I have but to trust you? Our lives are in your hands."

He walked down to the bench. The nurse glanced up at Lila, caught her nod, and left the boy for her mistress's side.

Rom slowly sat down on the edge of the bench before Jonathan. This special boy, who still sat cross-legged, studied him with equal interest.

"My name is Rom."

"Hello, Rom." The boy said it as though they were friends. And then Jonathan looked down at his lap. He was cradling something in his hands.

A bird. Alive and perfectly at peace.

Rom had never seen a bird so close before, let alone touched one. But the creature seemed at ease in the boy's small hands.

"Do you want to touch it?" Jonathan asked.

Rom cleared his throat. "Sure."

He knelt down on one knee and stroked the bird's feathery head with his finger and no small amount of wonder. He glanced up at the mother and the nurse, saw no objection from either, and settled onto the ground cross-legged, facing the boy, who accepted his company without a hint of awkwardness.

Rom picked up a fallen leaf, yellowed but not yet brittle, and began to fold it.

"The only bird I've ever held is one I've made," he said. "I make them sometimes, like this." His attention was less on his own fingers than on the boy, who watched as Rom folded the leaf into the shape of a kite, then back along the edges to form wings. The long end formed a narrow neck. Then the crane's head.

"You see?" He lifted the leaf bird up to the air and then set it down between them.

"Hmm," the boy said in a voice so fragile it seemed the very wind might break it. "That's a nice bird."

Jonathan stood, limped over to one of the bushes, and set his own bird on a branch. He was indeed crippled, but the limp didn't seem to bother him. He returned, sat back down, and lifted Rom's small offering.

"May I have this?"

"I made it for you," Rom said.

His eyes brightened with delight. "Thank you."

Rom's heart nearly broke at the sight of the boy's smile. There was a magic about him that he'd never seen or felt before in any other person.

Or was he simply—and unfairly—transposing Talus Gurov's hope onto this child because of the sheer miracle of his existence?

"There's something else," Rom said, reaching into his back pocket. He pulled out the vellum and unfolded it. "I found this a couple of days ago. It's very old." He laid it out on his knee. "It's is how I knew to find you."

Jonathan stared at the vellum for a few moments, then lifted his eyes. "You were looking for me?"

"Yes."

"Why?"

"Well…" What could he say? Even if the keepers were right and Jonathan *was* the long-awaited child whose blood held the only hope for humanity, the boy couldn't possibly know that, could he? By all accounts he was only a nine-year-old boy who got on well with birds and was full of life without knowing it.

"Because I think you might be a very special boy," Rom said.

Jonathan grinned. "That's a nice thing to say."

Or did Jonathan know more than he was letting on?

"Jonathan, do you ever feel differently than other people? Do things like…I don't know…do sorrow or joy mean anything to you?"

Something like surprise lit the boy's eyes.

Surprise? Not fear.

"You know about those feelings?"

He knew! Surely because he had felt it himself!

"Yes. I drank some ancient blood and it changed me. If I'm right…If the vellum is right, the world is dead. Everyone! But I was brought back to life by the blood." He said it in a rush, desperate to be out with it all. Too much too quickly, he thought. But now he was fully committed. "The keepers say that a nine-year-old boy's blood will bring life back to the world. And Jonathan, I think that boy might be you."

He waited for a reaction. A nod. A knowing look. The boy only stared at him as though waiting to see if he'd say more.

He told himself to remember that Jonathan was only a child. And yet he wasn't reacting with as much surprise Rom might have guessed. Or with as much confusion, for that matter.

"Do you know anything about this?" Rom pressed. "About sorrow?"

"So you think it's true?" the boy asked.

"I've felt it!" He gripped his own forearm. "It's here, in my blood. I *know* it's true."

"I mean about the boy. Do you believe the world is dead and that a boy can bring it back to life?"

"It must be. You tell me, is it?"

Jonathan looked over at the bushes where he'd released the bird. A slight tremor stirred his frail fingers. "I have dreams," the boy said.

"Dreams?"

His eyes were back on Rom. "Are you saying they're true?"

"What dreams?" Rom could hardly contain his excitement.

"I dream every night. That the world is dead and I'm the only one alive. About people called keepers who protect me. About a war."

"A war?"

The vellum claimed the boy must be brought to power but said nothing about a war.

"About people dying," Jonathan said. He blinked and looked away again, but Rom could not miss the subtle lines of fear on his face. Tears glassed the boy's eyes.

Rom laid his hand on Jonathan's arm. When he spoke, his voice was barely more than a whisper. "You're the boy, Jonathan." The bird in the bush fluttered away. He didn't know what else to say. He could scarcely think, much less speak.

"I shouldn't talk about it," the boy said. "The dreams make me cry."

"But what if you're alive, like I am—maybe *more* than I am? What if you're very special—or even the rightful Sovereign?"

Jonathan's eyes darted over his shoulder to where his mother stood. "They're just dreams. I'm a cripple. I'm not even supposed to be alive. Feyn will be the Sovereign."

He knew about Feyn? But of course, the whole world knew about Feyn.

"Yes, Feyn is the rightful Sovereign," Rom said, "but you're more than just a cripple. The vellum *predicted* you would be crippled! That you must be. So you see? It *must* be true. All of it!"

Who was he trying to convince? The boy, or himself? Because in that moment, Jonathan looked nothing like a hoped-for Sovereign-to-be.

But he was here. He was alive. Everything the keeper had said, everything the vellum had said, was accurate.

"What are you feeling?" Rom asked. "You're feeling things that your mother can't feel, aren't you? It's because you're alive even though you haven't taken the same blood I took, which can only mean that your blood is alive and your dreams are real. That your mind is somehow different from ours and you can see things no one else can see. It's true, Jonathan. It's all true. I'm here to tell you that and ... to protect you."

He hadn't known that last part for certain until he spoke it. But now he knew with no lack of certainty that it, too, was true.

Any other nine-year-old hearing these impossible things might think it a game. But there was an earnestness about Jonathan that betrayed him.

He knew. He'd surely suspected all along that his dreams were real. Maybe he'd even been preparing himself for this moment without even knowing it.

"You have to believe me, Jonathan. You are very, very important to the world."

Jonathan stared at the ground. What thoughts lived behind those brown eyes? What was it, to be so unusual, and alone? To know the world had never accepted—would never accept—you? That it would go to lengths to end you if the secret of your existence became known?

To be a boy without a mother who could return his love, or weep, or laugh? Or do anything but be afraid each time that you did?

Rom found himself fighting back tears. What had it been like, the nine years of this boy's existence?

"Do you want to tell me more about the dreams?"

The boy took a deep breath, swallowed, and settled. "If you're right, maybe I shouldn't say anything more about my dreams."

"Why not?"

"Because I don't understand them."

"Maybe I can help you understand them."

"I don't think you can."

"That's all right." After a minute, Rom said, "Can you at least tell me what I'm supposed to do?"

"I don't know. But I think you'll know. Maybe you should listen to your dreams."

"I don't have those kinds of dreams."

Jonathan looked up at him, clearly troubled. "How could I be Sovereign? Feyn is Sovereign-to-be."

"Yes, that's true. Unless..."

He didn't want to speak the obvious. The thought of Feyn's death struck him as a terrible offense. Suggesting it to a nine-year-old boy seemed profane. But if this world's hope of life rested on Jonathan's shoulders and only Feyn stood in his way, maybe he was not the one meant to die. Maybe she was.

No, that surely could not be.

"I think you're supposed to tell me what I should do," Rom said, standing. He paced in front of the boy, running his fingers through his hair. "I was lucky to find you, and now that I have, I'm at a complete loss. But I don't have much time."

"I'm just a boy," he whispered.

"I know."

Rom sighed, looked around, tried to decide what to do. But Jonathan's next words snapped him back.

"In my dream, there were four others."

"What?" Rom's heart skipped a beat.

"They drank the blood."

"You know about the others?"

"I dreamed about them. Are they real?"

"Yes!"

"You found me."

"Yes."

"I saw all of that."

"In your dreams?"

"Yes."

"You saw *me*? Who I was?"

"Not you, just a man. But now I know it's you. And that's how I know that you'll know what to do when the time comes. If the dreams are true, and I have to do what I have to do, then you have to do what you have to do."

There was now no question in Rom's mind that he was staring at a boy who against all logic would one day rule this world.

The boy would become humanity's only hope, and his life had been entrusted to Rom.

The weight of the last three days crashed down on him. He knew that what he'd told the boy's mother was true: He would protect this boy, even at the cost of his own life.

"But you should know, some die," the boy said softly.

"The world is already dead, Jonathan."

The boy's eyes were twin pools of sorrow. "Sometimes death is the only way."

Rom eased himself back down, cross-legged across from the boy. "You believe me, then?"

The boy's finger stroked the head of the leaf-bird. "You found me."

"I found you," Rom said.

"Will you stay with me for a little while?" Jonathan said. "Will you show me how to make a bird from a leaf?"

In that moment, Jonathan seemed like only a boy again.

"I would spend the rest of my life showing you how to make birds if that's what you wanted," Rom said.

Chapter Thirty-One

"WHY DO they call you the Book?"

Feyn's question hung in the air. The man staring out the tall window of her receiving room remained as still as he had been since the guards ushered him in.

Her apartment was the epitome of Order. The bed was made and the hole in her closet ceiling had been repaired. The faint smell of fresh paint still lingered in the air. In the foyer, a bouquet of rare and wildly expensive flowers, forced to bloom and stripped of thorns, jutted from a rare crystal vase. The card beneath them read only, *Your servant—Saric.*

She had sent Nuala away with assurances that she was fine, that she needed time to herself to work, to rest, and to meditate, all in the name of easing her anxiety over her coming inauguration. It was partially true.

But the other truth was that she needed time to think, and to learn more from this keeper.

Her meeting with Saric had played through her mind a hundred times since her return to the security of her chamber. She'd immediately summoned Rowan, head of the senate, and learned the full details of her father's death and her brother's subsequent rise to power. His relief in seeing her safe had fueled his detailed explanation of events, through which she had finally come to understand the political logic behind Saric's temporary rise to the office of Sovereign.

And then there was the related but separate conclusion she'd come to the moment her brother had struck her.

Saric intended to kill her.

She'd learned from Rowan that Saric had ordered the immediate execution of all nine-year-old male royals, an order that Rowan had stalled only at great risk to himself. "He's got the notion of a threat to your sovereignty," Rowan had said.

"You see why the senate was foolish to bring him into power."

"Perhaps, but what were we to do? Your kidnapping threw the senate into a panic, so we fulfilled the letter of the law."

She'd eased Rowan's fears and assured him that he'd done well to delay Saric's order. She did not tell him that her brother was motivated by more than fear, blaming the command on only "inexperience and folly."

Regardless, she was now sure: Saric was driven by dark passions. He would not rest until he'd wrested Sovereignty from her—permanently. With passage of the new law, he would be next in line for the office the moment she died after assuming rule. And she had no delusions that she would indeed die by Saric's hand, if not the day of her inauguration, then the next, or the day after. At any given moment, her life would be forfeit, a container broken open to spill out the power that Saric craved for himself.

And so she'd played into his twisted affections for her, offering him hope where there was none, going so far as to say that he would head her senate once she took office.

But that would never be.

Her brother would never rule because he would die before she did. At the very least he would reside in his own dungeons for treason. It would be her first official act as Sovereign, before he had any time to destroy her. Only the fact that he was the current Sovereign precluded her from making any move now. She had no official power over him or the senate. Saric, on the other hand, did.

And so she must be clever.

She'd said nothing of this to Rowan. But he would know soon enough. She would see to it.

Meanwhile, the keeper who had spoken to her of secrets just days ago now stood silent as a pillar.

"Why won't you speak to me? I've read the vellum and know your history. Didn't you hear me? The man you sent to find me found me."

She'd chased the words of that vellum through her memory. They were little more than the strange beliefs of an ancient sect that sought hope where there was none to be found. Talus Gurov, like her own brother, hounded the forbidden intoxicants of Chaos. As Sovereign, it would be her duty to eradicate for good all traces of that former age.

This is what her mind told her.

But her memory lingered on the image of Rom, trying to summon the way he had affected her. Trying to touch, again, her own heart.

But if it existed within her, she could neither find nor feel it. There was only the fear—fear for the blood's dangerous aftermath and how it might affect her subjects, their future...her own.

There remained the matter of Rom, an innocent trapped by the musings of heresy. He deserved nothing more heavy-handed than gentle correction. This was the true aim and beauty of Order. As Sovereign she was determined not to squash those who erred, but to correct them. Order was its own illumination. It was neither natural nor comfortable for anyone to wish to be outside it.

And what if there is truth to the vellum, Feyn?

But there could not be. The mere thought was ludicrous. They were all dead? Preposterous.

What if there is a boy?

A hollow pit of uncertainty gaped in her mind.

"Rom has gone to look for the boy," she said. "But there is no boy, is there? No, but you wouldn't know that. Your mind is captured by this fantasy."

The keeper slowly turned to face her, eyeing her as if it were he who ruled this world. He had been spilling over with mad ramblings of boys and blood and secrets, but now he was like another person. Distant, as though she were not the same woman who had gone to the dungeon in search of him before. Still, he said nothing.

"Even if a cripple did somehow survive," she said, "the world would never accept him. We are only days from Rebirth."

"The Day of Rebirth," the old man quietly said at last.

"Ah, he speaks," she said. "I had begun to wonder if you were the same manic man I met in the dungeon."

"You do realize there hasn't been a real Rebirth yet."

"So say insurgent heretics."

"That we are all dead," he continued. "That at this very moment you and I stand here, hardly more than breathing corpses."

So the vellum had said.

She unfolded her arms and walked to a small table that held a silver pot of hot tea. "And here I was worried you'd gone mad."

"Oh, I'm quite mad, I assure you. I have been for a while. Try carrying the truth that the world is dead around with you for nearly a century. To be one of the last of your kind. Too much to say, so much to talk about. Only yourself to talk to. It'll make you mad."

She poured the steaming liquid into a porcelain cup. Its twin sat on the small table nearest the keeper, already tepid and untouched. "And yet you believe that I am the one who is mad," she said. "That in reality you are among the few sane still living."

"No, not living."

She took a sip without tasting it, and then abruptly set the cup down.

"Peace has reigned for hundreds of years. The Age of Chaos was filled with so much war and pain. Why would you even dream of returning to such a state?"

"Only corpses rest in peace."

"Then leave us dead! Let the living crave what I already have. The world is at peace!"

"A corpse may rest in peace, but make no mistake, it has no life. No true humanity. No true love or joy, not even true peace, any more than a rock has peace."

"And no anguish or ambition or greed or all of the pain that comes with your kind of love."

His brow arched. "She speaks of the forbidden so eloquently. You surprise me."

Because I have tasted your kind of love, old man, and I have felt its pain.

"Forbidden, yes," she said. "But its history proves that it's not so eloquent."

The keeper stared at her for a moment. "You ask me why I am called the Book." He stepped slowly away from the window, combing gnarled fingers through his white beard. "The questions skitter through the brain like rodents. Who is the boy? Who is this man? Where is the Maker? And the grandest of all: Who is truly mad...and who is dead?"

She crossed her arms. "Tell me about the keepers. About Talus, this first keeper. How has your order kept these secrets for so long? The boy, if he exists—what exactly is he supposed to do? The vellum said he must come to power. What power? As Sovereign?"

"What you are really asking is what's to become of you."

"I know what's to become of me. I want to know what *you* think should become of me."

"I'm sorry, but I can't tell you."

She gave a sharp laugh. "Why?"

"I've taken a vow of silence."

"Then you don't have to worry, do you?" she said. "If I'm dead, I will be as silent as the grave."

"Here we are, two corpses, talking. What use is there in that?"

"Then you don't claim to have this supposed life of yours?"

He paused. "Not yet. Soon."

She studied him. Despite his riddles, this old man had a strange way of easing her fears. He spoke of death, but his eyes flashed with knowledge of something wholly *other*.

"I see the glint in your eyes, and it isn't from the light. You're no idiot and yet you speak in riddles. You sound like an alchemist."

He turned back to the window. "Perhaps because I am," he said.

"An alchemist?"

He folded his hands behind him. "I am a keeper. A protector and warrior of the truth. But the keepers were alchemists first and foremost. What I know of alchemy would confound your brother's finest peers. That said, make no mistake: I can swing a sword with the best. Now that he's dead, I will admit that Alban, the keeper your brother killed only days ago, was a better fighter than I. Well, some days."

"Alchemist or not, you're a throwback to the Age of Chaos. Everything that stood against Order!"

"Yes!" he thundered, twisting back with a clenched fist. "In my day I could have taken out ten of those guards out front! And get it straight: Chaos *is* life! As much as Order is death."

"Blasphemy!"

"Truth!"

"Believe me, if there is truth, I would be the first to embrace it," she said. "But there is none here."

The keeper stared at her. A slight smile toyed with the corner of his mouth. "That's why I chose you, dear Feyn, Sovereign-to-be or not. That's why I told Rom to seek *you* out. You have the unwavering and impeccable character of a true Sovereign. You know nothing but loyalty and allegiance to what you believe is the truth.

You're a *slave* to it. All your life you have been trained to bow only to the truth."

"To the Order."

"Yes, to your Order. But what if I am right?"

"You could never prove it."

"And if the boy exists?"

"Even if he does, how could you bring him to power? What do you propose to do, kill me?"

"As I said, I've sworn an oath of silence."

"Then *break* your oath!"

He stepped forward, eyes bright. "There's one way only for me to bring you into confidence."

"What way?"

He stopped in front of her, his gaze searching her own. Now she could see clearly: His were not the eyes of a lunatic.

"Renounce all you know," he said with stale breath. "Relinquish your right to all that you hold sacred. To Order. To all you have been taught to fear."

"That's heresy."

"Heresy," he mimicked. "Because to do so is to gain Hades itself?"

"Yes."

"There's your fear talking. What you don't know is that you're already in Hades!"

His words seemed to sink to the pit of her stomach. Had she risked her eternity in drinking the blood, in knowing its wild throes? "Perhaps the blood takes one to Hades," she said quietly. "Perhaps it ruins the soul."

"Ruins the soul?" He gave a gruff and mirthless laugh. He had mastered the mimic as well as she. "If you drank it, you'd know better."

"I drank it, and I don't!"

He blinked. "You—you took it?"

"I drank the poison, if that's what you mean."

"How can that be? There's too much fear in you!"

"It seems that I drank less than the allotted portion. The effects wore off."

His face had gone white. "You took the final portion?" he rasped. "What was it like? You've tasted life? Hope? Love? Surely you felt these things!"

"Love?" she said faintly. If she tried, she could remember the way she'd cupped Rom's face, the way she dashed up the knoll...in the same way that she remembered what she ate for breakfast. But it no longer stirred her heart.

He grabbed her by her shoulders and gave her a shake. "Love, woman! Did you feel it?"

"Take your hands off me!"

He released her and stepped back. "Forgive me, but you must tell me. I've waited my whole life to feel what you have felt."

"I can't," she said, stepping away from him.

"I've protected the truth my whole life; I have sworn my life to what you've come by so cheaply—and *you* dictate terms to *me*?"

Feyn turned back. "I'll tell you everything that happened to me, but only in exchange for this fairy tale of how you plan to bring the boy to power." And then she added, "Assuming such a boy even exists."

That quieted him.

"Was it the blood that made you so crafty, or were you like this before?" he asked.

She shrugged. "I'm to be Sovereign."

"Then tell me this: In that moment that you were alive, did you realize that you'd been dead all your life?"

"I was intoxicated! It broke my sense of Order."

"Because your Order is *not* life!"

"So you've said. The vellum claims the boy must destroy Order—"

"No, Talus prophesied that the boy would *free* us from the Order." The keeper grabbed his beard and dismissed her with a flip of his hand. "But why am I telling you this? I can't."

"And yet you must."

"So that you can kill the boy?"

"What? Of course not. It's against Order to murder. On that, I give you my oath as Sovereign. But what's this? We might as well be talking about a mythical creature."

He searched her face. "You've tasted life. There must be a spark of life left in you. It can't have left you completely. And so a part of you knows. *Knows* why we've gone to such lengths. You deny it because you are dutiful and because you will be Sovereign and because you fear for your eternity, and for a thousand other reasons, but somewhere within you, you know. What I wouldn't give for one ounce of that blood," he said, murmuring now, seemingly to himself.

A part of her wanted him to be right. But he was wrong. She didn't know.

"You see an old man gone mad, reeking in his own rags," he said. "But I would seize a sword and fight to my last breath—spill every drop of my worthless blood—to defend the truth. And so would you, dear Feyn. Because when you know what we know, what I know even in my own dead state, there's no going back. There is nothing else. Whatever it takes, we live for this truth, this hope—even if we can't feel it."

"You're rambling, old man."

"You know it, girl. I know you do," he said, shaking his head.

"I'm telling you, I don't."

"She knows it," he said, murmuring again. "If I can be a keeper, then by the Maker, so can she." He glanced up. "And so you will have your deal."

"My deal?"

"Yes. I will tell you more than I've ever told a single soul, dead or alive, because by drinking the blood you surely became one of us even if you didn't know it."

"Tell me what?"

His eyes bore into hers.

"Tell me what it was like to drink the blood. Then I will tell you precisely how the boy will come to power."

Chapter Thirty-two

THE DOOR to Neah's apartment hung open. It swung on its hinges with the wind as though pulled by an invisible diaphragm.

Rom stood rooted to the floor, breathing a prayer. Twilight had brought out a chorus of crickets, but no other sound came from inside the house.

He'd spent most of an hour with the boy, there in the countryside, basking in mystery, believing Avra was safe. But now as he stepped into the living room, his heart froze.

The apartment had been ransacked. Neah's glass vases were broken on the floor. Chairs lay askew. Cushions torn open. Stuffing everywhere. So much for Neah's soothing and fearless world.

"Avra?"

Nothing.

He ran to the kitchen, crushing shards of china underfoot. Open packages of meat and wilted vegetables covered the floor.

Panic. "Avra!"

Every room told the same story, of the search for one thing.

The blood.

Where were Triphon and Neah? And what about Avra? He couldn't be sure that Feyn had been able to free her. For all he knew, they were all being held captive.

"Avra!"

Then he saw it. There, scratched right into the surface of the counter, where he had kissed Avra last:

R—
  The place you hid.
  —A

He blew out a breath. *She got out. They must have all gotten out.*

He helped himself to a knife from the kitchen, tucking it into the waist of his trousers.

The closet in the back room hung open in similar disarray, coats and cloaks spilled onto the floor. Another priest's robe hung among several articles of Neah's personal clothing. He grabbed it, rolled it into a bundle under his arm, and then left, racing down the outside stairway. At the bottom, a neighbor unlocking her front door turned to stare at him as he rushed by.

He wondered how many others saw him through their windows, were even now hurrying to report him.

He ran.

Rom unfurled the robe as he descended into the underground station, pulled the cowl up over his head. Midday traffic was thicker than usual just two days before inauguration, but no one paid attention to the priest who purchased the single pass and rode with his head bowed in pious prayer.

All the way out to the southeast edge of the city, he thought of Avra, of Feyn.

Of the boy.

He knew without a doubt that he would give his life for Jonathan if required. Many keepers already had. For the first time, he could think of his mother's death with a measure of comfort, knowing that her death had been for something. For everything, really.

And now? Avra waited for him, and Feyn was somewhere in the Citadel.

Out on the street, it was all he could do to walk sedately. But as soon as he turned down the old cobbled street, he quickened his pace and then broke into a full-out run. Down to the end of the lane, to the old print shop with the boarded-up windows.

The splintered board that had ripped his jacket was gone, pulled away by stronger hands. A gaping hole yawned in its place. He glanced around and, seeing no one, ducked through the opening into darkness.

"Avra?"

Dripping water echoed from an unseen leaking pipe.

"Triphon?"

He saw, from the periphery of his vision, the small form rushing him from the side before he heard her. Avra flew into his arms with a sob. Relief hot as lifeblood itself flooded him. Only then did he realize he was shaking.

He buried his face in Avra's hair. Breathed deeply. *Thank you. Thank you.* He was only vaguely aware of Triphon standing nearby, of Neah off to his side. He had never felt such gratitude in his life. And then he pulled Avra away to look at her and his heart stuttered. Her face was marked by a dark, angry bruise.

"What happened?"

She pressed back in against him. "Don't let go."

He wrapped his arms around her slight frame. "Who did this? Did Saric do that? Triphon! I told you to keep her safe!"

"It was my idea." Avra said. "I wanted to go."

"I'll kill him."

"It's nothing!" Avra said. "You're safe. I'm alive."

She was right. But it did little to quell the rage.

"Tell me this is all he did to you."

"It is," she said. "He did it knowing he had to let me go. Feyn exchanged herself for me."

So it had worked. Feyn had gotten back.

And Rom had found the boy.

Rom let out an uneven breath. "Never again. You can't ever do anything so stupid again!"

"She saved you, man," Triphon said. "She risked her neck for you!"

"And you, Triphon. I swear if you ever let one hair on her body come to harm——"

"You'll what? Beat me down? With what—your pen?"

"Try me."

"Stop it!" Avra said. "What's this, Rom? Not even a kiss for me?"

He kissed her, hard, desperate for the warmth of her, the taste of her, the feel of her lips against his own. "I love you," he whispered into her hair. "I love you. You hear me? I'll love you forever."

Avra wrapped her arms around him and buried her face in his neck.

"I thought they took you," Neah said, moving toward them, her arms wrapped around herself, her eyes seeming too large in her head. "I thought they had you."

"They didn't. And I got to Feyn. But I couldn't get word to you in time. I had to get her out of the Citadel."

"You—you got to her?" she said faintly. "What happened?"

He told them everything. Barging into Feyn's room, escaping the Citadel, the ride through the night. The blood he had given Feyn. Her decoding of the vellum and Talus's account...that the world was dead.

"Dead?" Triphon blinked. "Dead how?"

"Where there's no capacity to feel and love, where the soul of humanity itself has been stripped from the genetic code, there's no life," Rom said.

Triphon fell back against the wall. "Dung hills. The whole world? A world of walking...corpses?"

"Pretty much."

"And us?" Neah asked.

FORBIDDEN

"The blood brought us back. For now. It isn't permanent."

Neah glanced at Triphon, but then stared at Rom, as though just now understanding him. "What did you say? It isn't? How long do we have?"

"I don't know. A year? Ten? Months?"

"That long?"

"What do you mean, *that long*? It's life!"

"How can it be life if it wears off?" she demanded. "For all you know what we've felt is only the beginning of it. For all you know we could become monsters in a week! Don't you feel the pain?"

Rom hadn't considered the possibility. But surely, the vellum would have pointed this out. Or the keeper.

Then again, the boy's dreams disturbed him. What if he saw a future very different from the one predicted in the vellum? Wars, he had said. He had dreamed of war. Talus was an alchemist, not a prophet. His predictions had come from advanced scientific calculations and mathematics in a time when machines could model more than the mind could.

So the future was still uncertain.

"We have to go with what we know. And what we know right now is that we're alive," he said.

"What about Feyn?" Avra asked softly. "She didn't have a full portion."

"She's reverted already. But we now have an ally."

"That's a pretty powerful ally," Triphon said.

"And the boy?" Avra said.

"I found him. Out east, on an estate beyond the hamlet of Susin. There's a road that leads to a small home. He's there with his nurse and Lila, his mother."

"You're sure it's him?"

"It's him."

"How do you know?" Triphon said.

"If you met him...you'd know."

285

"He knew about the vellum?"

Rom gave him a curt nod. "But he knows more than that, too. From his dreams. He knows about us."

"His dreams? How's that work?" Triphon said.

"I don't know, but until I showed him the vellum he thought his dreams were just dreams. But I think somehow he knew. Maker, he's only nine! I can't imagine what that's like."

"And what does he know from his dreams?"

"Only what I've told you. He wouldn't say more. But he's a cripple, just like the vellum predicted."

"I don't get it," Triphon said. "How's a cripple supposed to do...all that he's supposed to do?"

"Somehow. I don't know." How would anyone, for that matter?

"Maybe it's a mistake."

"It's not a mistake. Because he's also alive."

"Like us? How can that be?" Avra said.

"He was born with the blood."

Avra was shivering. When he looked at her she glanced away.

"What is it?"

"There's something not right with him."

"He's the one, I'm telling you! I was there."

"Not the boy," she said.

"Then who?" But he knew.

"Saric." Avra turned her dark gaze toward him. "The boy isn't the only one alive with some other blood."

"He's alive?"

"Not like us. Not like it seems the boy is. More like a monster." She wouldn't say more.

Saric, filled with emotion?

The thought sent a chill through Rom, and for the first time he wondered if Feyn was in danger. Surely Saric had plans of his own.

Neah lowered her arms, eyes on the obscured window. "We should go and make our peace with him before he kills us all."

"Don't be crazy!" Rom said. "It's up to us to see the boy into power, not make peace with his enemy."

"How can one crippled boy be an answer to anything?" she demanded.

Rom wasn't sure he'd heard right. "Haven't you been listening? This boy has the power to right all that's wrong."

"We have to stop Saric," Triphon said. "We have to kill him."

"No. Feyn has to be the one to fix this. She needs to know that I found the boy."

"How do you know you can trust her? For all we know she's told Saric everything," Triphon said.

It was true, Saric could force Feyn to talk, surely. And Feyn knew the boy's identity.

And Feyn hadn't been the same person when they said good-bye. But she'd kept her word about Avra.

Sometimes death is the only way. The boy's words had plagued Rom for hours as he rode home.

"They can't both be Sovereign," Triphon said.

There it was.

Triphon squinted. "Right?"

Rom shook his head. "Jonathan is next in line. Feyn would have to bring him to power after becoming Sovereign, but I don't know how. She'd have to actually believe he should be Sovereign first. Unless..."

"Unless what?"

He hesitated for the space of a heartbeat. "According to the law, if Feyn died before taking office, the next in line would take power. That would be Jonathan."

"Surely, you're not suggesting—"

"All I'm saying is that if Feyn died before her inauguration, the boy would be the rightful ruler. Feyn said so herself." Whether he could actually come to power at his age would be another matter.

"Hades, man, listen to what you're saying!" Triphon said.

"She saved us both," Avra said.

Neah was silent.

"All I'm saying is that Feyn needs to know about the boy." Rom looked up at Triphon. "And that's why you need to get to the boy and protect him at all costs. Take Avra and Neah."

Triphon hesitated only a moment. "Consider it done."

"What about you?" Avra demanded.

His eyes were still on Triphon. "I don't have to tell you that everything's lost if the boy dies."

"I swear on my life, he won't lose a hair on his head."

Rom turned to Avra. "I'm going back to the Citadel—"

"What? No! Everyone's looking for you! Send Triphon."

Rom shook his head. "I can get in. And Feyn will see me. I need to tell her about the boy."

But there was another reason why he had to go, wasn't there? Maker forgive him for even thinking it.

Avra moved closer. "Then I'll come with you—"

"No. Saric's too dangerous. I'm not letting you anywhere near him."

"What about you? When I thought Saric had you—do you have any idea what that was like for me?"

A knot gathered in his throat. He took her hand, lifted it to his lips. "I can't live without you, Avra. But this vellum found me, I didn't choose it. No, I have to go."

He didn't tell her the rest of what was on his mind. He couldn't.

Her expression twisted.

"Listen to me, Avra. I love you! I swear I'll always love you. Go to the boy. See him for yourself. Keep him safe. I'll be right behind you."

She averted her eyes.

"Avra, please."

"Promise me one thing." She looked at him again. He could barely bear the full brunt of those eyes. "Promise—"

"I promise."

"You don't even know what I was going to ask."

"It doesn't matter. I promise."

"Promise me by this time tomorrow I'll be in your arms."

"I promise."

But they both knew that promises were the stuff of fantasy. It was all Rom could do to keep the sudden surge of sorrow that rose in him from spilling over.

Chapter Thirty-three

HOWEVER ANXIOUS the others were to forge ahead, it would do Rom no good to arrive at the Citadel before morning. Avra convinced him to stay and sleep a few hours. Nothing could have suited Neah better.

The clouds broke that night. Moonlight filtered through the boarded windows, pooled on the dirty floor, and turned it beautiful. But the light evaporated like a dream.

Neah wept. Quietly, and alone.

It took her half an hour to gather herself. There lay Triphon, whose snores had helped ensure that she not fall asleep. Avra was curled up in Rom's arms within her cloak.

Neah picked up her pack, slipped it out the window, and crawled out after it. The night air was cool. Clouds overhead. No more moonlight.

All night long they had talked of the boy, of the vellum, of life, of the beauty of emotion, and Neah had let them.

But all the while, she had wanted to scream. How could emotion be trusted when it came to such far-reaching consequences of the soul? In matters of eternity, the Maker?

It couldn't.

Born once into life we are blessed.

She had never wanted this precarious existence outside the law, outside Order. There were things of this world that could be appreciated and respected without love.

Where did love ultimately lead but to fear? Fear of loss. Of death. Of pain.

Let us please the Maker through a life of diligent Order.

There was a comfort in her former life—even if Rom claimed it had been death—that did not exist in this new one. Fear was a familiar ally. By it she had abided by the strictures of Order. For that, she had been promised Bliss.

There was a reason Sirin's halo bore measure-marks: so that each man could be judged by his works. There was a reason why his nimbus resembled a compass: so that each man might know the way. That was Order. No confusing feelings that tugged at the heart, that blurred the edges of simplicity or morality.

And no pain. Not like this.

And if we please, let us be born into the afterlife…

Only in Order was there a promise of something greater. Something too much to know here and now. But to be lived for, sacrificed for. Earned through obedience.

…into Bliss everlasting.

What she must now do she would do for them all, so that none of them would die, which was the course that Rom had set them on. His meeting with this boy, Jonathan, had robbed him of his senses. There would be no stopping him.

It was now up to her, for their sakes as well as her own.

It took her two hours to get to the Citadel. Nearly thirty more minutes to talk her way in. And now that she knelt before him, she did not see the beast that had brutalized Avra. Not at all.

Here was the gateway, the promise, Order's dark messenger.

Kneeling on the carpet of Saric's antechamber, Neah felt she could have kissed it. She would have prostrated herself if she could.

They had put her in handcuffs, but it didn't matter. This was the first peace she had known in days.

"Rise."

It didn't matter that her slacks were dirty, that her hair was unkempt.

She got to her feet.

"Speak."

His skin was so translucent that she could see his veins reaching like a clawed hand up his neck and across his cheek. The change in him since she had passed him on a chance encounter in a corridor only a week ago was drastic.

"Avert your eyes."

She looked at the floor. "Sire—my name is Neah."

"I know who you are. What do you want?"

Emotion choked her off and she silently cursed it. She could only stand there before him, aware of her own pathetic trembling.

Be strong, Neah. For all of our sakes.

"Take her away."

"Please! I know where they are," she said. "All of them. Including the boy."

The room went quiet.

"Leave us." Saric's order to the guard was of a different tone this time.

The door bumped closed, and they were alone.

"You were saying."

"I know everything," she said but offered nothing more.

"And in exchange?"

"I want my former life. And absolution."

"Death?"

She thought about that.

"If what I have is life, than I gladly forfeit it."

"And yet you drank the blood," he said. "You can feel."

"I can feel pain. Longing. Suffering. I know fear. I have known that much and have lived with it before. Let me have it without this other torment."

"Tell me where the boy is and I will have my alchemist return you to this so-called death."

"I—I need assurances that you won't hurt my friends."

"I'll need assurances that your information is true. If we don't find them I'll strip away much more than your emotion."

Neah was unable to stop the trembling in her hands.

Chapter Thirty-four

"NUALA SENT for me," Rom said from beneath the priest's cowl. "It's urgent."

"Do I know you?" the priest asked.

"No. But Feyn does."

"Our lady," he said, correcting his familiar use of her name, "is sequestered."

"I'm asking for Nuala. Are you deaf? Send the maid to the receiving hall to meet me or answer to the lady Feyn yourself."

The priest hesitated.

"Do you really think I present a risk to a chambermaid?"

He nodded and left.

No more marveling at the architecture of the palace. The stone gardens that had once amazed him seemed nothing but a memorial to the life that no longer filled those flower beds. The Citadel was nothing to him now but the most elaborate of coffins.

They had awakened to find Neah gone. Triphon was crushed. Avra blamed herself. But all Rom could think about was the boy. The boy was all that mattered now. The boy, and getting to Feyn. He could think of no better way than through the maid Feyn had mentioned. Nuala.

She came to the receiving hall for him, approaching nervously.

"I don't know you, do I?" she said as he drew her aside. The woman's face was pinched in worry.

"No. But you know of me," he said grimly, thinking of the newspapers. "I have an urgent message for your mistress. If you care for her life, I have to see her."

She froze.

"She told me your name," he said quietly. "You have to know I wouldn't risk coming here otherwise. Please."

"Not here," she whispered. A little louder: "Come, Father." She led him down the hall and up a small flight of stairs. The chamber she took him to was not Feyn's, but a small, elegant suite. Perhaps her own.

She latched the door and turned toward him.

"Who are you?" she asked, her face a mask of anxiety. She couldn't stop twisting her hands.

"I'm Rom Sebastian—"

She gave a short cry, but he said, "Even though they're calling me an outlaw, I swear I'm a friend to your mistress. I have to see her immediately."

"I thought so. Bliss, I thought so," she said, pacing now. She wore the dark colors of the court, a simple black robe over the long skirt that just cleared her ankles when she walked.

She stopped and faced him, clasping and unclasping her hands. "I'd take you to her, but I'm telling you the truth when I say I haven't been allowed to see her for two days. Saric has another maid attending her."

"What?"

"I don't think he trusts me, not since her disappearance. I will be attending her for the ceremony, but until then—"

"That's too late!"

"Too late for what?"

He didn't know how much he could trust the maid, but Feyn had sworn by her. And he wasn't in a position to pick and choose the perfect accomplice.

"Listen to me." He glanced at the sealed door. "You must believe me when I say that Saric is up to no good. If you can't take me to Feyn, then I must speak to someone else in power, someone beyond Saric."

"I never trusted Saric," she said. "He brings out the fear in me. He's not himself these past weeks."

Because he's inflamed with the blood, Rom thought.

"Who can I trust here? Please!"

She shook her head, her eyes searching this way and that. "I can't think—"

"You have to! Saric can't have corrupted the whole government. There has to be someone you can approach."

"Rowan," she said. Her gaze locked on him.

"Who's Rowan?"

"The senate leader."

The elder statesman had the reputation of being fair.

"Take me to him."

"I'm not sure—"

"We have no choice. If you value your mistress's life, you must do this."

She paced, judging him with wrinkled eyes.

"Wait here."

"Hurry. Please."

When she'd gone, Rom moved to the window, shoved back the hood of his robe. Feyn had loved him. And he had loved her as well. Not the same as Avra, but love, nonetheless, beyond the loyalty her office demanded of him, beyond the respect her sheer intelligence required of him. He had loved the woman on the knoll. The same woman now lost, swallowed up in death and the machinations of its Order once more.

The door flew open ten minutes later. Nuala stood in the narrow frame.

"This way."

He pulled up the hood. "Where?"

"Follow me. Hurry!"

He did, down a long hall, head down, watching her heels as her robe brushed about them. They advanced through an ornate doorway into an unexpectedly simple office.

Despite the early afternoon, darkness crept along the edges of the plastered walls and flagstone floor. A stately man whom Rom assumed was Rowan stood in the center, watching their entry. With a last glance, Nuala stepped out, leaving them alone.

"I don't know what this is about except that Nuala petitioned me in our lady's name. Whatever it is, I'm busy. Please, make this quick."

Rom drew back the hood and watched Rowan's expression change.

"You?" The senate leader's face narrowed.

Rom spoke before he could throw out his accusation. "The outlaw, Rom Sebastian, yes. I'm also the last person who saw Feyn alive before she returned."

"You're turning yourself in?"

"No. I'm here to save Feyn."

"Don't be absurd. She doesn't need saving."

"Are you so sure? I may be the only advocate Feyn has right now."

"You're outside Order!"

"And I'm telling you, I may be the only one who can save the Sovereign of that Order!" Rom snapped.

Rowan's chin lifted a notch. "She's sequestered until the day of her inauguration. Saric vouches for her safety."

Saric. "Have you actually seen her yourself?"

"Yes."

"And she gave no indication that Saric might present a threat to her?"

"No! He was out of his mind with fear when she went missing. If he says she's safe——"

"Don't you see that Saric is after her office?" Rom shouted.

"Impossible. She will become sovereign tomorrow according to the laws of succession."

"And those laws of succession provide no way for Saric to take power?"

"No, not before she becomes Sovereign. The laws have been changed."

Rom stood still, rooted.

"What do you mean, changed?"

"The Sovereign has changed it."

"Vorrin changed the law?"

The head of the senate paused, as though deciding how much to say.

"Vorrin is dead. Saric is Sovereign until Feyn takes office."

Saric? *Sovereign?* It was impossible!

"How?"

"Under the former law, the office passed to the oldest child. Saric took exception to that, but the senate insisted. He agreed to serve as Sovereign on the condition that the law change. The new law reads that if a seated Sovereign dies, power reverts to the previous...Sovereign." Even as he said it, his face changed.

"So if Feyn comes to office and dies, her successor—"

"Would be...Saric." The senate leader looked ill.

"You're a pack of fools!" Rom cried.

"No. That can't be," Rowan whispered. "It's too great an offense. Murder is against Order."

"Then you don't know Saric as well as you thought," Rom said.

Fear darkened Rowan's eyes as the implications settled in. "He wanted my seat. When that didn't work... We have to stop this."

Rom decided then that the senate leader could be trusted. "There's a boy. He's the seventh who must come to power. It's too much to explain, but Feyn knows. What she doesn't know is that I've found him. He exists. He's alive. She must be told."

Rowan lifted a hand to his brow. "What boy?"

"The next seventh in line. You have access to the archive. Check the royal birth record and see if there wasn't a boy born who fits the description exactly. A cripple, born in the last eligible cycle."

"Feyn said something..." The senate leader stiffened. "The last cycle... That would make him—"

"Nine."

The senate leader turned away, grasped the edge of his desk. "Sirin, guide me. Maker, help us—"

"What is it?"

Rowan looked back. "Saric issued an order to kill the nine-year-old royals. All of them. To protect his own ascendancy."

Rom felt the heat drain from his face. For a long beat they stared at each other. Had Saric outplayed them all?

"This order stands?"

"No, I've intercepted it."

"Thank the Maker."

"But surely none of this will come to pass," Rowan said. "Feyn's alive. She'll succeed Saric."

"If she does, she won't live long, but not on any boy's account. Saric will see to it. He's possessed by a forbidden passion. But he needs her to come to power or else he loses it to a boy—or any of the other sevenths in line. Don't you understand?"

Rom faltered. Saric needed Feyn in power, if only briefly. But as for the boy... Saric must know about the vellum. Rom couldn't explain to Rowan the importance of the boy, the importance of his blood. Not yet. If, as the vellum said, the boy must come to power, then it was not Saric but Feyn who stood in the way.

Feyn.

The keeper's words whispered through his head: *All you believe. All you love. It will all be required of you.*

"There's a man in the dungeon called the Book," Rom said. "Take me to him. In the meantime, tell Feyn everything. She's safe until she becomes Sovereign, Saric will see to that. But now I need to see the prisoner called the Book. He needs to know about the boy. I have to see him now!"

The man dipped his head.

"I'll have you escorted immediately."

Rom barely registered their swift strides to the grotto, Rowan's words to the guard. And then he was running down the corridor.

Toward Saric's dungeons.

Chapter Thirty-five

THE GUARDSMAN escorted Rom to the mouth of the large, torchlit chamber. He hesitated with a visible shudder as they stepped inside.

"I know the way from here," Rom said, his priest's cowl pulled up over his head.

The man nodded, visibly relieved. "Don't get lost, Father."

Rom's mind was solely on the keeper now. He had to hear the thing that he did not want to know, to hear it from the keeper himself.

Only the keeper would be able to tell Rom how far he was to go in seeing the boy into power—if, indeed, Feyn would have to die.

What if it would fall to him to kill her?

Sweat beaded his neck.

The sounds and smells of the dungeon clawed at his senses—the whir of the recycling air, the echo of moans, the odd cocktail of laboratory sterility and musty stone. Alchemy and death.

Pools of intermittent electric light glanced off stainless-steel counters, off varied burners and glassware, off the doors of conditioned chambers that looked like ovens along the wall.

Rom kept to the shadows, which meant passing too closely to the cages along the middle. The scent of neglected human flesh choked him. Sickened him.

He made his way to the far wall and then veered into the first tunnel he came to. Rowan had warned him clearly: "Be quick, word spreads swiftly in that world down there."

He broke into a run. But this tunnel did not lead to the keeper's cell. Instead, it ended in a steel door he had not seen last time. He mentally retraced his steps. With a glance back toward the larger chamber, he wondered if he'd gone too far. Wasn't this a separate passage? The one housing the keeper must be back through the lab and farther down. Or was it through this door?

Rom unbolted the door, pulled. It swung open on soundless, heavy hinges. The antechamber inside was little more than a landing that descended in a broad staircase to another room. Dim, electric sconces were set into the wall.

Rom dragged back his hood, suddenly unable to breathe deeply enough. He closed his eyes and summoned the image of a young, dark-haired head, the small hands clasped around a sparrow, the fathomless eyes.

His breathing evened. The handle of the knife he had tucked into his waistband dug into his side. He pushed away from the wall and descended the steps, coming to a door at the bottom. He turned the handle and pushed.

The door opened into a broad room perhaps twenty paces long, filled with tables, refrigeration units, and humming computers. At the end of the room stood five tall vessels of water, each of them occupied by a male about his own age, floating in the fluid.

They were all naked. Thin tubes came out of their noses, their veins, their other orifices, connecting them to a series of machines. Now he could hear the faint whir of them, similar to the air recyclers in the larger outside chamber, and as he watched could even see the pulse of fluids through them.

He stepped inside, eerily drawn by the sight. The sound of the machines was an unnatural breath, the slow thrum of a heart at rest.

The eyes of the males were shut. Rom edged up to one of the

tanks. He reached up and touched the glass. It was warm. Thick. He tapped the glass once, lightly.

The eyes of the man inside sprang open.

Rom leaped back, pulse pounding in his ears. No other signs of life, no movement in the man's chest or nostrils—just those open eyes staring past him. Gray, glassy eyes, absent of life. This was not a man but a creature of Hades.

"Amazing, isn't it?"

Rom spun around to the soft, low voice. A tall man—pale and finely attired—stood watching him. His hair was tied back at the nape. In this light, his skin seemed as delicate as an onion's. Rom imagined that beneath the maze of dark veins, he could see the skeletal jaw, the hollow sockets of his eyes.

The man walked in, eyes on him. "So, you're the one."

Rom cleared his voice. "The one?"

"The artisan. Rom, is it?"

He felt the handle of the knife pressing against his ribs.

"Honestly, I don't see the attraction." A heavy ring glinted from the index finger of the man's left hand. The ring of a Sovereign.

Rom stood rooted to the concrete floor. "Saric," he said.

This man struck Avra.

"It's *sire*. But we're past that, I think." Saric's eyes lifted. "Do you like my warriors?"

Rom's gaze stayed on the Sovereign.

"They're in stasis, a state often spoken and written of but only recently perfected by the alchemists." He walked to one of the vessels, stroked a long, thin finger down the front of the glass. "They're like you and me, in a way. But different from us both. A new breed, so to speak, based on superior genetics. Strong. Alive. Feeling." He sighed. "True monsters."

"Monsters?"

Saric turned back. "There's nothing a man won't do when his ambition soars. When his lust is up. When he is in a rage. Give me ten men with emotion, and I'll rule a world of dead. Give me a hundred . . . and I'll crush them like so many roaches."

"The irony is that you speak this as a dead man," Rom said.

"You intend to kill me?" A slight quirk of the man's lips.

"How can I kill what is already dead?"

"You drank the blood so you think you're alive, is that it? But your blood has proved inferior."

"Inferior?"

"The keepers' blood is rife with weakness, love foremost among them. The only emotions allowed to progress into my new age are those that will bring the world under my control."

Was it even possible Feyn could be related to this man? The Zealot War of Chaos had been waged by men like him. Maybe Megas had been right all along. In the face of a man like this, Legion seemed a godsend.

If so, true life might be the worst possible curse. What if Rom had it all backward, and the keepers were but a cult to usher in Chaos once again?

"We were sold a bad bill of goods, you and I," Saric said.

"Were we?"

"We were taught that Chaos was wrong, when all along, those truly in power—Sirin, Megas, those that rule by truest fear—have used it to control us. We haven't evolved." He glanced at the man in the vessel in front of him. "We've become more mindless than they."

"I don't think creating monsters is what Sirin had in mind," Rom said.

"Perhaps. But surely he didn't mean for the world to be ruled by a boy."

Rom tried to keep his voice even. "Boy?"

"Please. We've come too far for pretense. We both know that the only way a boy can come to power is for Feyn to die before she's inaugurated. We both also know that I would never allow that."

"I don't know what you mean."

A smile nudged Saric's mouth. "She said you were clever."

"But not as wise as she," Rom said. "Feyn won't be so easily deceived."

"Feyn? Oh, I agree. But I was speaking of someone else."

Rom's eyes darted over Saric's shoulder as a woman emerged in the doorway. He hardly recognized her at first, her face was so swollen, apparently from crying.

"Neah?"

Saric lifted his hand and motioned her forward. She came closer, propelled by the guard who had ushered her in. She reached for the Sovereign's hand.

Saric kissed the backs of her fingers. "You see, I have an order of my own. The boy will die. Your whore, Avra, will also die. And your friend Triphon." His pale eyes rested on Rom. "If they aren't dead already."

Rom was moving toward the door, mind lost to Saric's words, uncaring of what happened to him now. A single thought possessed his mind.

Avra.

He took the stairs two at a time. Through the door and down the aisle of the cages, chased by cackles and screams.

Tears clouded his vision. A single sob cut through the shouts and cries. His own. The vellum, the blood, the boy—what did it matter compared with her? What was life if she was not in it?

Saric watched him go with an appreciative stillness. "Let him go. He's no longer a threat to us." He turned away from the captain who had brought Neah to him. "The warriors are gone?"

"An hour ago."

"Send another rider to follow Rom. He'll go after them. I want him as well."

"Alive or dead?"

"Dead. Like the rest."

CHAPTER THIRTY-SIX

THE ORDER forgot us. But that time is over now, isn't it?" the boy's mother said.

Avra and Triphon had found the estate and the boy, as Rom said they would. The last hour had been busy, a rush of packing saddlebags and preparing the horses. With Triphon and Jonathan in the barn, everything seemed quiet in the house.

"We have to assume that they know who he is," Avra said, "and that they know he's here. We can't have much more time. I'm so sorry. Do you want a moment to yourself in the house?"

"No." Lila sat still, looking around. "It's just strange to imagine it without him."

Avra took the woman's hands in her own. "A whole Order of Keepers has lived and fought for the sake of your boy."

Lila nodded. "I can see that you're like him in some way. That, somehow, you feel more than I do, as you say. Like Rom—it's how I knew to let him see Jonathan. But it frightens me."

The ride to the estate had been a sober one. Triphon had been uncharacteristically quiet. Neah's disappearance troubled them all, but Avra knew it had wounded Triphon most deeply.

Avra had kept to herself, unable to relax the knot in her stomach since leaving Rom. She had kissed him and watched him hurry down the cobblestone lane. The fleeting sight of him had struck a painful chord within her.

He'd said he would never leave her again, and yet there he was, running to the Citadel. Of course he had to go. Feyn had to know that Rom had found the boy. And so Avra had watched him go.

She forced her thoughts back to Jonathan. She would never forget his first words to her. "Hello, Avra. Where's Rom?" He'd asked it as if Rom and he were old friends. To think that in this boy's body lived the purest blood on earth—a living remnant from the Age of Chaos! But it was his earnestness and his sweetness that had won her. Now she understood why Rom was willing to go to any length to save this child.

"Somehow I knew that this day would come," the boy's mother was saying. "I've been gathering Jonathan's things since Rom left here."

"I'm so sorry." It was the only thing Avra could think to say.

"The canyonlands north and east of here are treacherous. Take him to the ruins on the north side. They're unknown to the Order. The nomads hold them sacred."

"The nomads? The ones who shun Order?" She hadn't been able to help the acceleration of her own heart. "So they're real?"

"Yes. Contrary to what's said, they're good people. They took Jonathan to live with them for several months after we reported his passing. I didn't know if I'd ever see him again, but they returned with him as they said they would. They've been devoted to him his whole life, ready to hide him away if we ever needed it." She looked down at her hands. "I suppose that day has come."

So not only were the nomads real, but Jonathan had lived with them!

"Find the ruins," Lila was saying, "but you have to look carefully or you'll miss them. From the side or top of the plateau, they're impossible to see. Because of that, they're virtually unknown except to the nomads themselves."

"We won't miss them with you to guide us."

"I won't be going."

"What? But you must!"

The boy's mother spoke quickly. "If the guards come looking for him and find me gone, they'll know that we've fled and are hiding something. If I'm here, I can simply deny that I have any child."

"But they'll know Jonathan lived here either way," Avra protested.

"We began to destroy all traces of him the moment Rom left us. I'll follow you when it's safe. But for now, this is my path. And his lies with you."

The thought of Lila staying filled Avra with misgiving. But Lila was right. Her flight would only confirm Jonathan's existence.

"I'll look after him as though he were my own," Avra said.

Her heart broke for this mother who could not feel true love for her son. And her heart broke for Jonathan, who had given love without receiving it in return.

"Thank you," Lila said.

Avra lifted her hand, kissed her knuckles, and hurried out of the room.

She stopped on the threshold of the barn. Inside, Triphon leveled a sword at an imaginary foe as the boy watched from his perch atop a hay bale, swinging his legs. Triphon had snatched up a sword and slashed at the air when Lila uncovered the stash of weapons. It was the first sign of his old self Avra had seen all day.

"Gifts of the nomads," Lila had said, startling Avra. These gifts were forbidden to ordinary citizens. "I found them in my husband's things after he died. I didn't know what else to do with them, so I hid them in the barn."

Triphon gestured the boy over. On one knee, he showed Jonathan how to grasp the weapon's hilt, which wasn't long and straight like those Avra had seen, but slightly curved.

"You see this? If you hold it like this, you can cut both ways by twisting your wrists." He brought both their arms down in a slashing motion. "And because it's curved, you can do it from horseback, and the sword doesn't get stuck in...ah, in anyone when you make contact. Yes?"

The boy nodded.

"Now swing it," Triphon cried. "Like this! Ha!"

The boy swung it. "Ha!" he cried.

Triphon whooped. "That's it!"

He picked up another sword and exhibited several impressive moves. Avra had never seen Triphon with an actual weapon, yet the bullish man was practically graceful with it, as though it added a missing counterbalance to his bulk.

"Try it," he said, handing the second sword to the boy.

Jonathan was small, and his leg wouldn't allow him to move as smoothly as Triphon, but he went through the motions that he'd been shown with surprising ease.

"A natural!" Triphon said.

The boy laughed and swung again, with more gusto.

"There you go! When you grow up, you'll be a warrior like me for sure."

"And you'll be with me," the boy said.

"I will?"

The boy nodded. "I saw it in my dreams."

"Really? You see your future in your dreams?"

"Only some things."

"What else have you seen?"

Jonathan suddenly noticed Avra standing in the doorway. After holding her gaze for a too-silent moment, he leaned forward to whisper something too quiet for Avra to hear.

Triphon twisted back and looked at her. His smile was gone.

Why did that expression give her chills?

She pushed away from the door and went toward them, wondering what the boy had said. "I hate to interrupt such an important lesson. I can't imagine what I've missed."

They both watched her cross the barn.

"What is it?"

Triphon nodded, the strange look still in his eye. "We're packed. Blankets, clothes, food for days, all on the horses."

She gestured at the weapons. "And those?"

"They're called swords."

"I know that. It doesn't mean I have to like them." Her first sight of the stash had actually made her shudder.

"I'll check the mounts." Triphon handed his sword to Jonathan and left them alone.

The swords hanging from Jonathan's hands were obviously too big for him. Without looking away from her, he dropped both and sat down on a hay bale.

"Does your leg bother you?" she asked.

"Sometimes. It gets tired."

"But you're a very strong boy for being only nine. I saw you swing the sword."

His cheeks flushed and he smiled. "Triphon's a great warrior."

"Yes. Yes, he is, isn't he?"

She sat down next to him.

His eyes went to her shoulder, where the weight of her cloak had pulled the neckline of her tunic askew. She had been less concerned the last few days with keeping it so diligently covered, going so far as to tell Triphon and Neah the story of the night Rom and his father had saved her.

"We're the same, aren't we?" he said. "They say we're not right."

She looked away, choking back a sudden rush of emotion, for his sake more than hers. He was so young—too young—to know the fear she had lived with all these years.

Maker, spare him, she thought.

"Only because they don't know that we have good hearts," he said. He looked down at his feet, too short to reach the ground. "I told Triphon that you have a good heart. Everyone will see that."

She knew then that she would do anything for him. A tear slipped down her cheek. She gently laid her hand on his bad leg.

"That's kind of you, Jonathan. I think that's the kindest thing anyone has ever said to me. Thank you."

He looked up at her and she saw that his eyes were riddled with emotion. "I'm afraid," he said.

"Oh, don't be!" She quickly put her arm around him and drew him against her side. "You're a very special boy and that's why we came to protect you. You saw how strong Triphon is! And Rom..."

Rom. Her heart.

"But of course, you already know Rom."

"He's my friend."

"He'll be here soon. I know all of this must be terrifying to you, but you'll see, everything will work out. Right?"

"Yes," he said in a small voice. And then. "Avra?"

"Yes, Jonathan?"

"My dreams scare me."

She could not imagine the weight borne by these thin shoulders. The keepers had protected their vision of his blood, but what about his heart? He was only a young boy!

"Then I will hold you whenever you dream bad dreams, Jonathan. I promise. We'll be like two—"

A cry from outside the barn cut her short. Triphon spun into the doorway.

"They're here! Hurry, they're here! Get to the horses."

"What's happening?"

But she already knew.

Triphon scooped up the boy and their two swords and together they ran for the side door. The horses waited, three of them. Lila was running toward them from the side of the house.

"Hurry!" She took Jonathan from Triphon and dropped to one knee, so that she was eye-to-eye with her son. "I'll meet you soon. Remember me, Jonathan! Remember your mother." She kissed him, her hands shaking so hard she could barely hold his face between them.

Jonathan clasped her neck, tears streaming down his face. "I love you, Mother."

"Don't cry. Never fear—I'm right behind you."

She lifted him onto one of the horses, picked up her skirts, and ran for the house.

Triphon mounted and grabbed hold of Jonathan's lead as Avra clambered into her saddle behind them, aided by adrenaline. Within a few steps, it became clear that the boy was no stranger to riding horseback.

They galloped up the hill behind the line of cypress trees where they pulled up and looked back. The estate looked peaceful as a small cadre of mounted guards dismounted at the gate. A bird chirped. The wind rustled through the trees. *Peace*, the world seemed to whisper.

But the world was full of deception.

"We should leave a sword for Rom," Jonathan said.

Avra spun at the sound of his name. The boy looked frightened, but there was a measure of certainty in his eyes. "Rom? Why?"

"I think he might need it."

Triphon leaned over and shoved a sword partway into the earth. It wavered, hilt up.

"Let's go!"

They wheeled their mounts and headed north at a hard gallop. Toward the canyonlands. To the ruins.

Chapter Thirty-seven

HER NAME drummed through Rom's mind as he slapped his stallion's hindquarters with his open palm, demanding speed.

Avra, Avra.

Yesterday he'd abandoned the stallion at the edge of the city and it had found its own way to the Citadel stables. He'd recognized the horse immediately upon fleeing the dungeons. It had seemed an auspicious gift from the Maker.

The horse slowed to a walk several times, and Rom let it amble forward until he could stand it no longer. Then he'd cried out and beat the beast into a run. He could not let the poor animal rest; Avra's face was ever before him.

The sun was nearly at its zenith when he thundered over the final crest to see the estate in the valley below. Quiet. Not a horse to be seen at the front gate. Had he beaten Saric's guard here?

He thundered down the hill to the gate. He slid off the saddle before the animal came to a full stop, nearly tripping over his own feet.

"Avra!"

Not a sound. The front door was open. He threw it wide.

"Avra!"

A chair at the front table lay toppled, a fresh vase of flowers dashed against the floor.

He stumbled forward, through the side hall, past the kitchen, screaming now.

"Avra!"

Into the courtyard. Then he saw the body. A woman lay at a crooked angle, sprawled facedown on the flagstones beneath a cloud of buzzing flies.

Lila. Jonathan's mother.

For a minute it was all he could do to fight the vision of his own mother, lying in her own blood in the kitchen of their house. But Lila had not been cut down so much as butchered.

He lifted his eyes and scanned the courtyard, pulling out the knife tucked into his belt. No sign of the assassins.

He hurried to Lila's side, dropped to one knee, and turned her over. Her eyes were still open. Her stomach had been ripped open, her entrails spilled out the front of her torn dress. Her hands had been cut off.

Under any other circumstance he might have retched. But his mind was on Avra, only Avra.

He laid a hand on Lila's arm. Still warm. She couldn't have died long ago. An hour at most.

The thought propelled him into a run. Swiftly, silently this time, on the balls of his feet. At the back door he found the nurse lying on the ground. Also butchered.

Birdsong punctuated the stillness of the country estate, profane in the metallic air. There was no sign of the others.

He crossed the backyard in a dozen long strides and spun into the barn. Empty. No guard, no sign of Avra or Triphon or the boy they'd been sent to save.

No horses. There had been a horse yesterday. With the two Avra and Triphon had brought, there should be at least three. He allowed himself a flash of hope.

He quickly retrieved his stallion and found the tracks in the sand out the back. They looked to be more than those a few horses would make. This was practically a road of trodden earth.

It headed north into the desert.

Rom kicked the horse into a run. Along the flat and up the rise to the north.

There he saw the sword, stuck in the ground. Left by Triphon, thinking Rom might need it? Surely not the guard. If they'd seen it, they'd left it, being fully armed already.

Had he been a horseman he might have scooped it up at a full gallop. But he was no warrior. Only Rom, Avra's lover.

He stumbled off his horse and grabbed the sword, sending a desperate plea to the heavens as he remounted. He could not be too late.

Avra knelt behind a large boulder at the mouth of the cave, a sword in the sand by her side. Jonathan huddled behind her in the shadow, fear in his eyes. The faint jingle of tack issued from the dark bell of the cave as their horses shifted. Triphon was out of sight farther down, where the passage narrowed along the canyon floor.

An image of the bloody sword in his hand filled her mind.

They were pursued by five guardsmen—elite, by the striped bands on their arms, Triphon had said. His plan was so simple she had believed it would fail.

With stronger horses bred for heavy duty, the guard were gaining. The trio couldn't outrun them, and Triphon wasn't averse to taking them on. He seemed to relish the challenge. If he could thin their number to three they stood a chance, he claimed. Though she didn't see how.

He'd selected a section of the canyon with a narrow file that allowed only one horse to pass at a time. While she and Jonathan hid, he'd backtracked and taken the last of the five from behind, with a knife to the man's neck.

The guard were now four.

She'd pointed out the obvious: Wouldn't they know that one was missing? Wouldn't they retrace to recover him?

"Not the elite," he'd said. "They feel nothing but fear for their own lives if they fail Saric. To stop would only increase the odds of failure."

He'd been right.

Now they lay in wait again. She'd brought the boy and the animals to the safety of the cave as Triphon disappeared from view.

She gripped the sword, knowing that if the situation warranted, she would swing it at anyone who tried to harm the boy. To think she'd frowned at the weapon only hours earlier!

A noise on the path. Avra glanced back at the boy. His wide-eyed gaze met hers.

She had to force herself to breathe slowly as the first of the guard passed below them, his mount a dark silhouette against the gray sky.

A bead of sweat tickled her neck.

The second guard came and passed. They were too close together for a safe ambush! Triphon would have to wait for another chance.

The horses walked with unnerving slowness. The guard's swords were out, glinting in the sunlight beyond the cave.

Thirty more seconds, and all four would be past.

Twenty.

The third man passed beyond view. She could see the fourth.

Ten.

Behind her, one of their own horses snorted. She felt the heat drain from her limbs. The fourth form halted outside in the wide swath of sand before the narrowing canyon.

Go, she willed. *Hear nothing. Go!*

The guard outside moved on. Cleared the edge of the cave. Avra dared exhale as the sound of their steps faded.

The horse snorted again. A call followed from the canyon, and Avra knew they'd been exposed.

It happened so quickly that she hardly had time to think, much less react. The last guard had sounded a warning, and now Triphon would be committed. As would she.

She heard the rush of feet and skittering stone from Triphon's location. The clash of steel.

She thrust herself forward, peered down the canyon, saw the situation in a single glance, and caught her breath. Three of the four guard were in a circle around Triphon.

Where was the fourth?

Triphon's blade connected with the warrior to his left, slicing through his midsection.

But there were two more coming at him. And a third somewhere out of sight. Too many!

Rom heard them before he saw them: the clang of blades, their metallic echo pealing from the rock, shouts raised in alarm.

He took the stallion around the last bend at a full gallop, fifty yards behind the unmistakable form of Triphon. He was fighting two guardsmen, swords slicing in full combat. A third guard lay unmoving on the canyon floor.

No sign of Avra or the boy.

He spurred the horse through the dry bed, straight for Triphon, who was now fighting with his back against a wall.

Rom slid off the saddle, sword in hand, hit the ground rolling, and came up in a run, still ten paces behind the engagement.

Triphon slipped and the taller of the two guards lunged. Triphon spun away, and the guard's blade clashed into the rock, sending sparks flying.

Rom saw the rest happen in sequence, each instant like the frame of a picture: the guard's momentary loss of balance, Triphon's twisting upward cut across the guard's exposed neck, the guard's head spinning into the air, face staring at the sky.

Triphon finished high, leaving his entire torso exposed to the second guard. Rom shouted, blade drawn back awkwardly, desperately trying to close the gap. The second soldier's sword was already arcing in from the side, full-force, two-handed.

Rom lunged and swung blindly, threw all his weight at the guard's arms, rather than his body or head. At the arms that held the blade swinging right for Triphon's stomach.

Rom didn't see so much as feel and hear the impact of blade and bone. A crack and then a clank of metal against rock as his sword twisted from his hands and fell to the ground. The guard's two hands, still clutching the sword, flew over Rom's head, leaving his bloody stumps to finish the slash alone.

Rom stumbled forward as Triphon brought his own blade down through the man's head, splitting it like two halves of a hellish fruit.

Rom staggered, stunned by the sight of so much blood, the splay of limbs and bodies. Triphon stared at him in the sudden silence, his gore-smattered mouth open wide in a macabre grin.

They were both standing. Alive.

From behind him—a piercing wail. It broke the silence in a single panicked cry.

Avra. Calling his name.

"Rom!"

Avra saw it all from the cave's entrance: Rom's thundering entrance to save Triphon's life. The way he'd rushed in, thinking nothing of his own safety to save them.

He kept his promise.

That was the man she was going to marry. The world might see a simple artisan, a man more at home with a pen than a sword, but Avra saw her hero.

And then she saw the fourth warrior and watched in stunned disbelief as he rushed in from where he'd waited behind a boulder.

Rom's sword lay on the ground. Panic struck her like a thunderclap, rattling her nerves with a new terror.

Rom was going to die.

She leaped from the cave and screamed her warning, leaving the boy behind in the shadows.

"Rom!"

Triphon's eyes went wide, fixed on something over Rom's shoulder.

Rom would relive the next few moments a thousand times in the days to come.

He spun at the sound of that familiar voice. Avra's. She was running toward him from the left, her hair a dark wing behind her, his name still on her lips.

She was alive and in seconds she would be in his arms.

In that instant, he saw it all—the way he would clasp her. Hold her. Kiss her.

And then he saw the fourth warrior.

The reason for her scream. A guard, like the others, rushing him with blade raised.

His own sword lay on the sand to his right. There was no time.

The thought came to him distinctly, as if spoken with perfect calm and deliberation, surreal in that instant before death: He was a dead man.

But at Avra's cry, the guard snapped his head in her direction. He turned to protect his flank from the new threat, sword drawn to meet her rushing form.

Pull up, Avra! Rom's mind screamed the words, but she was hurtling toward him, unstoppable.

The guard's blade met Avra in full stride and sliced up through her breast toward her neck, severing flesh and bone in one sickening blow.

Avra knew before she felt the sting of metal that she was going to die. She knew it even as she rushed for Rom. She could not pull back in time. There was no out.

Two thoughts bit into her mind with the blade. The first was that it hurt, cold metal like fire, searing as it severed.

The second thought was for Rom, who stood braced for her, eyes wide. *I will never sleep in his embrace again*, she thought.

The blade found her spine and the world went dark.

Avra fell to the ground, eyes fixed on Rom.

The fourth guard continued his swing around, his blade angling now straight for Rom's midsection. Rom couldn't seem to move to defend himself. His eyes were on Avra, who was falling to the ground, gashed and bleeding.

Triphon, already past him, buried his blade in the man's neck. The guard grunted once and dropped to the ground.

But Rom barely registered any of it. Avra was lying on her back in the sand. The chamber of her chest had been split open, exposed for him to see that her heart was no longer beating.

His breathing stalled. His world tilted. For a long moment there was only silence as he waited for Avra to push herself up from the ground.

But she did not move.

A fly buzzed by his left ear. Triphon stood still, straddling the body of the fourth guard, breathing hard.

And Avra…

Avra lay on the ground.

Rom staggered forward a step and stopped. "Avra?" Her name came out as croak.

He couldn't breathe. His legs and arms began to shake. Something was wrong with the image before him. She could not be dead. She would turn her head at any moment and look into his eyes. She would jump up, rush him, and throw her arms around him, delivered from this vision of horror.

Avra lay still, wide eyes staring at the sky as the ground darkened with her blood.

CHAPTER THIRTY-EIGHT

ROM FELL to one knee, twisted to his side, and vomited. His retch echoed through the canyon, but it sounded distant, an arcane chuckle from the darkest pit in Hades, mocking his pathetic love for the woman who'd found life because of him.

He twisted and threw himself forward, scrambling on his knees, reaching for her body with bloodied, trembling hands.

"Avra!" His cry was no more than a terrible moan that hitched and became a sob. Her eyes did not move. Her chest did not rise. A fly lit on the corner of her mouth.

"Avra..."

Her breastbone had been split by the sword, baring her lungs to the sun. He knew already that she was dead, but his mind couldn't grasp the finality of that death.

Triphon dropped to his knees in the sand beside her. "She's dead," he said.

She can't be dead! Anyone could die. Anyone but Avra. He could die. Triphon could die. Feyn, even the boy, but not Avra.

But not Avra!

"They killed her," Triphon said.

"No!" Rom felt the world spin, leaving only darkness and the stench of death where there had been sun and life. He grabbed her shirt and tugged it with both hands. "Wake up!"

"Rom…"

He screamed it now, as if his voice alone might resurrect her from the dead. "Wake up!" He slapped her face. "Wake up, wake up, wake up!"

Avra only stared at a different patch of sky now.

"Rom, please…"

"No!" He could feel rage erupting up from his belly, like a boiling sea of black tar, and he was powerless to stop it.

Triphon's hand was reaching out for him. "It will be—"

"They killed her!" he screamed, now at Triphon, as if he were the one who'd swung the sword.

He sobbed once, a half grunt of vitriolic protest. One thought only crowded his mind now. And before he could apply any reason to it, he was on his feet, lurching forward, grasping the hilt of his fallen sword.

Rom whirled from the rock wall and rushed the fallen warrior who had ended Avra's life. Screaming at the top of his lungs, he drew the sword back, still three paces from the dormant corpse, and, closing, swung down with trembling rage.

The blade struck the guard's back and cut deep into his spine.

And then he was swinging the sword like a bat, hacking into the dead body. He wasn't really aware of the shredded flesh at his feet; he only reacted with the singular and vicious intent of avenging Avra's death.

All the while grunting and roaring through uncontrolled sobs.

"Rom!" Triphon's voice cut through his carnage. A hand grabbed his shoulder. "Rom…"

Without thinking, Rom swung his sword to fend off the objection. His blade hissed through the air, missing Triphon by only an inch as the man leaped back.

His friend stared at him, stunned. "What are you doing?"

"Why did you let her die?" Rom cried. He could hardly hear himself. "You swore to keep her safe!"

"You don't know what you're saying, Rom. Please——"

"She's dead!" Spittle and snot sprayed the air with his outburst. "She's dead!"

Triphon's face was set and red. He barged forward, grabbed the blade from Rom's hand, and thrust it at the hacked-up body. "*He* is your enemy, Rom. Saric killed Avra!"

But Rom no longer cared who had killed Avra. Only that she was dead, and dead under Triphon's watch.

He threw himself at the man, who jumped out of the way. Rom instinctively spun back, blinded by rage. But before he could rush him again, Triphon leaped forward and swung the blade at the fallen corpse's bloody neck, severing his head from his body in one slashing blow.

"*He* is your enemy!" Triphon cried, and he swung again, this time taking off the man's right arm. Without a moment's pause, he leaped over to one of the other fallen corpses and buried his sword into his prone body, shrieking.

He stood back, panting. A soft sobbing sound reached into Rom's heavy world. But Rom's eyes were back on Avra's body. He'd felt the terrible curse of death once already, when he'd wept over his mother's body only hours after being awakened by the blood.

He wavered, feeling that same hammer now, crushing his nerves with even greater brutality than before. This was the great terror eradicated by Order. Nothing could compare to this mockery of love. If there was peace in death, it left only horrifying pain behind.

"Jonathan!" Triphon whispered.

Rom stepped over to Avra's body, sobbing, only vaguely aware that Triphon was running toward a rock. The boy was there, curled up in a ball, crying.

But Jonathan was alive. Avra lay dead at Rom's feet. He sank to his knees by her body and set his hand on her leg.

Dear Avra! Oh Maker, Avra, I'm so sorry.

Triphon was down on one knee beside the boy, who was weeping.

323

"I don't know what to do," Jonathan said.

But it hardly mattered now. Avra was dead.

"It's all my fault," the boy was saying. A bird cawed above them. "They killed my mother, didn't they? It's all my fault."

"We don't know that."

"But Rom does."

A pang of sorrow for the boy joined Rom's own, but then it was gone. He couldn't think straight much less feel straight. His mind was being shut down by this ruthless sorrow. It was all wrong.

"Rom?"

Triphon was calling to him, wanting to know if he knew the fate of the boy's mother.

"She's dead," he said.

The boy hesitated a moment, then pushed himself up, turned his back, and limped away from them. His gentle sobs drifted up the canyon.

It was all terribly, terribly wrong, Rom managed to think.

Then he slumped to his side beside Avra, wept into the sand, and lost himself to the pain.

"We will bury her here," Rom said, stopping his horse at the top of the hill. The sun was well past its zenith, but in Rom's mind time had ceased to exist. He'd wept over her body, arms thrown around her, head resting on her belly.

At some point he had risen, stiff-legged and numb, loaded her body on her horse, and led Triphon and the boy from the canyon without a word.

He would not bury her in that chasm of death. Not among those bloody corpses in the sand.

He dismounted. Triphon pulled up behind him. Jonathan sat on his own horse off a way, on the next rise. The boy blamed himself, and in some ways so did Rom. Avra had given herself for the boy as much as for him.

It took them twenty minutes to dig a shallow grave using their swords, Rom weeping all the while. They were in Hades.

They lay Avra's body next to the grave and Rom sank to his knees.

"We have to leave," Triphon said. He held out a knife.

"What's this?"

"The boy said something to me in the barn. I didn't understand it then, but I do now. He told me that he thought we should protect her heart."

"Protect her heart?" Rom cried. "Protect her heart? She's dead!"

Triphon swallowed and nodded. "She's the first of the living to die. Keep her heart."

Rom stared at him through a prism of tears. "You... expect me to *cut her heart out*? Have you lost your mind?"

Triphon flipped the blade on end and thrust the handle toward Rom. "Take it, Rom. Don't leave her heart behind."

The knife was as long as his forearm. Straight, simple.

"Just c—" He could barely say it.

"Cut it out."

He stared at her chest, horrified. How could such an innocent boy make such a grisly suggestion? But no—he had said only to protect it. It was Triphon who wanted to take the heart.

His hands trembled.

And yet... there was mad logic to it. However disturbing, wouldn't it honor Avra to take her heart and treasure it always?

Rom cried out, sank the blade into the open wound, cut the organ free, and lifted it from her body. It was cold; thickening blood ran from his fingers.

He wrapped her heart in a white cloth and set it in a glass food jar the boy's mother had packed in one of the saddlebags.

"Avra's heart," Triphon said quietly. "We will always remember."

But to Rom the pronouncement sounded profane. She was his to remember, not theirs.

When they'd covered Avra's body with dirt, Rom took a large stone and rolled it to the head of the grave. He etched with his knife on the rock:

Life Has Been Swallowed by Death
My Heart Is Gone
Sweet Avra

It was all he could manage.

Triphon led them north toward the ruins. The boy rode behind and to the left, slumped in his saddle, silent. Crushed.

Rom followed them, carrying Avra's heart in his saddlebag. His own heart was dying.

Perhaps it was already dead.

Triphon rode in silence, mind gone to the turn of events that had so drastically reset the playing field.

Avra…dead.

Rom…near dead, riding like a ghost fifty paces behind him. A darkness had swallowed his friend—not just sorrow, but true rage that threatened to compromise him.

He could almost understand the sorrow; the fact that Neah had abandoned them in the night still followed him like a black cloud. But if they had a leader, it was Rom. He was the one who'd driven them through every turn to this point. And with Avra gone, leaving only himself as a balance in the mix, they were as good as lost.

Did this leave *him* to take charge?

Charge of what? Saving the boy, yes, but Rom had been convinced that the boy must be brought to power. How were they supposed to accomplish such an impossible task now? Never mind that—how had they *ever* expected to bring him to power?

One thing was now certain, even if Rom was lost to them: The boy was no ordinary child. He'd known that Avra would die, hadn't he? Perhaps not how or when, but Triphon was sure that he'd intuitively known it, perhaps from those dreams of his. He'd all but said so in his mother's barn.

"One day," Jonathan had whispered, "everyone will remember her."

He looked back and saw that Jonathan was staring at him as if trying to determine whether he could be trusted. Maker knew Rom had ignored the boy in the wake of Avra's death, not that Triphon blamed him. Neah had cursed the pain the blood had brought them. Maybe she was on to something. The emotions of Chaos had been forbidden for good reason.

The boy nudged his horse and slowly pulled abreast. He looked so fragile on the massive beast. It was strange to think that this simple boy carried any hope, a vessel for the blood that might awaken a dead world. Tears had dried on his dusty face, leaving small trails down his cheeks. His eyes were wide —the poor boy was frightened. And no wonder.

"I'm sorry," Triphon said softly. "No boy should have to live through this."

Fresh tears gathered in the child's eyes.

"Don't be bothered by Rom, Jonathan. He loved Avra. He'll come around."

"We need a keeper," Jonathan said.

"A keeper?" Triphon blinked. "Your mother said to find the nomads, right?"

"But we need a keeper." Jonathan looked at him. "Do you know where the keepers are?"

Triphon scratched the back of his neck. "As far as I know there's only one keeper left alive. He's in the dungeons at the Citadel."

"Then I think you should get him."

"Get him? He's in the Citadel, I said."

"A keeper will know what to do."

It seemed to be like this with the boy: He knew some things but not most. At least he seemed to be aware of what he didn't know. So if he said they needed a keeper, maybe he was right about that.

Triphon looked ahead at the winding canyon. *Listen to me, I'm deferring to a nine-year-old boy.*

"All right," he said. "But just how are we supposed to get to the keeper?"

"Ask Rom. He'll know, won't he?"

Triphon glanced back at his friend, slumped in his saddle. They hadn't talked about what had transpired at the Citadel, but Rom had sneaked in twice now.

Triphon could get them in easily enough. Between the two of them he was sure they could find a way into the dungeons. But breaking the keeper out would be a different matter. They would need inside help.

"We're running out of time, and that's a long way back."

Once again it struck Triphon that this boy was placing his full trust in them. If the vellum was true and Jonathan was the boy it hoped for, he and Rom were now his only hope.

Unless they could get to the keeper.

"I'm sworn to protect you, Jonathan. I promised Rom I wouldn't leave you. You're sure we need a keeper?"

The boy nodded, fixated on this one task. "He'll know what to do."

Chapter Thirty-nine

"SO ALL is as it should be." Pravus stood on the top of the Citadel tower overlooking Byzantium at midnight. A rare moon shone overhead. Saric wondered if he should kill him then. Sooner or later, the man who'd brought him the power of life would have to die.

But Pravus wasn't a fool easily killed. Even now he likely had an assassin positioned to take down Saric at any sign of betrayal.

"My men failed to capture the boy or his protectors," Saric said.

The master alchemist stared out at the calm night. "You think I don't know? I don't need to remind you that your own life hangs in the balance."

"You've made that clear enough."

"They'll come tomorrow. You must be ready for them."

"Let them come," Saric said quietly. "We will be ready, and Feyn will be crowned Sovereign."

"We can take no chances. Control your wild cravings for flesh."

Did he know about Feyn? No, they were his thoughts alone.

"You underestimate me, old man."

"How can I underestimate a man who's failed to end the life of one boy?"

"Soon the world will gain its true Sovereign. And a new Age of Chaos will begin." He looked directly at the master alchemist. "And you will learn never to question me again."

* * *

Triphon's heart hammered. Returning to the Citadel and finding Rowan, following Rom's rather indifferent retelling of his own methods, had been a relatively easy task. But convincing the senate leader to listen had not. The man had paced and wrung his hands for half an hour.

Rowan was forbidden by Saric from any audience with Feyn, he kept saying. This business that Rom had opened his eyes to had haunted him with nightmares.

If Saric was the threat, then surely the keeper, Saric's greatest enemy, stood with Feyn, not against her. In fact, the keeper might be Feyn's *only* hope for surviving any conspiracy that Saric had hatched. If the evidence that both Rom and now Triphon had laid out for Rowan turned out to be true, and Saric intended on succeeding Feyn as Sovereign as the new law required, Feyn's life was indeed in terrible danger.

Triphon thought he had done a good job with that.

From Rowan he learned of the senate leader's efforts to present a motion in the senate to subvert a standing Sovereign. But it had not worked. It had been hard enough to delay the standing Sovereign's command to kill all nine-year-old boys. Saric had raged when he learned of Rowan's actions and threatened to execute him for treason. But there was hardly time for such a command before the inauguration. And so he'd accused Rowan of putting Feyn's life in grave danger, then stormed out of his office.

"He doesn't know that I am aware of all that he is doing," Rowan said. "But now I live under a death sentence."

"Then help me get the keeper out," Triphon had said. "He poses no threat to you or to Feyn, only to Saric. You might be saving your own life, man. Help me!"

Rowan had finally given him what he needed, if only out of fear for the Order and, ultimately, his own life. This was the worst, and most selfish, side of death, Triphon thought.

Rowan would not—still did not dare—attend him directly. Luckily, five centuries without threat or incident allowed Triphon to make his way into the dungeon, wearing only a simple priest's robe for disguise, without raising an alarm.

Following Rowan's instructions, he'd made his way through the back entrance, which he knew all too well, and then down into the dungeons. It had taken him only a few minutes to locate the cavern that held the keeper.

A single torch lit the barred cell. Snores emanated from behind it.

"Hello?"

The old man snorted once in his sleep, then settled back into his dreams, oblivious.

"Wake up, old man."

"Eh?" The man jerked his head up, and Triphon thought he looked like nothing so much as a giant rodent caught eating bread crumbs in the dark corner.

This was the keeper? First a frail, crippled boy to save the world, and now this ancient carcass to guide them? With Rom lost to his own anguish and Triphon himself the only one with his apparent wits about him ... They were on a fool's mission.

"You're the one they call the keeper?"

The man cleared a hitch in his throat, then spoke in a scratchy voice. "Says who?"

"Says me. Triphon, friend of Rom Sebastian and the boy that he rides with." He would see what kind of response that brought.

"The boy?"

"Yes, the boy."

The man straightened, suddenly fully awake and fully engaged. "What boy?"

"You tell me."

"You ... You've found him?"

"I don't know, have we?"

The old man grasped at the rough-hewn wall and pulled himself to his feet. He took a step forward and made a weak attempt to wipe drool from his bearded mouth with the back of a sleeve.

"Rom found the promised boy?"

"If by *promised boy* you mean Jonathan, a cripple who has dreams and—"

"I knew it!" The keeper flew at the bars and gripped them with white knuckles like a man possessed. "He's alive?"

Alive?

"Of course. Did you think we dug up a corpse?"

"I mean alive! *Alive*, man! Is he *alive*?"

So then this was certainly the keeper.

"He was crying when I left him."

The old man sucked in a breath.

"His mother is dead. So is Avra, killed by Saric's guard. Rom's lost out there with a broken heart. The boy told me that we need a keeper."

"He did?" The man blinked, eyes round with wonder. "Did he say my name?"

"No. Are there any other keepers I should fetch instead?"

He shook the bars, rushed to the latch, and rattled his cage again. "Get me out, man! Get me out of the blasted prison. I have to go to my master."

Triphon reached into his pocket, grasped the large key Rowan had given him, and stepped up to the latch. "He's not what you might think. Certainly no master that—"

"Hurry, man!"

"Keep your voice down!"

The man's hand reached through the bars and snagged Triphon's collar. "Do you know what this means? Do you have the slightest clue how history has conspired to bring us to this single moment of hope once again?"

"If you don't let go so I can spring you, you're going to pass it unconscious."

The man's frantic eyes searched his as he let go of his cloak.

"Are you one of the five? Alive?"

Hearing it like that filled Triphon with a renewed sense of purpose. "I am."

"And your name?"

"Triphon."

"Then I am your greatest friend, Triphon. Now, get me out of here and take me to the boy."

CHAPTER FORTY

DAWN SPILLED like a wound along the horizon, seeping crimson into the eastern sky.

They had failed. Avra lay dead, buried in a hilltop grave.

Rom passed the last hours of the night on the top of the cliffs, grateful for the darkness and drone of the wind, the two together like a shroud over the mind.

But the wind had faded with the darkness, and the pain had intensified with the light. He was exhausted, but sleep refused to offer him any peace.

From his vantage point he could see the embers of the fire below in the canyon. At a short distance from the camp, the shallow pool that had provided them with water reflected the russet of the rising sun.

The boy had told Triphon they needed a keeper. Evidently Rom was no longer qualified to lead them. Not that he disagreed. He was swallowed by resentment. The whole business of ushering the boy to power to bring life to the masses sat like a bitter pill in his throat. What good was life that brought such terrible pain? His thoughts were unfair, true enough, but Rom could not deny them.

He'd played his role in finding the boy, and he'd told Triphon how he might find the keeper, but he could not see past this day to the hope the boy might bring.

To his surprise, Triphon had returned with the keeper in the middle of the night.

When he'd arrived, the keeper had rushed up to the boy and fallen to his knees. Then he'd lifted his hands to the sky and cried out his approval. "My eyes have seen the hope to whom I've sworn my allegiance. Today all those who have kept this secret knowledge for generations find fulfillment in this lineage of the first keeper, as prophesied." He'd kissed the boy's feet.

The keeper looked over at Rom. "And now when Feyn sees us at the inauguration, all will be gained."

Whatever that could mean, Rom didn't know.

Jonathan had stood there, shaken by the keeper's grandiosity. Then the keeper had taken the child's hand and led him up the canyon, where they spent two hours alone. When they returned the boy's tears were gone. Wonderment was in his eyes.

He'd stepped away from the fire and walked into the darkness.

"Let him go," the keeper said.

Rom had listened to the keeper and Triphon through the wee hours, talking about the nomads.

"We knew them from the first days," the keeper explained, pacing about the fire. "It was the keepers who confirmed what the nomads suspected of the Order's deception, the keepers who taught them survival. They can go days without water and subsist off the most barren land. And their horses are bred to be as hardy as they are. They come and go like ghosts and move entire camps within an hour."

"What happens if they find us here?" Triphon asked.

"They already know we're here, boy. They're probably watching us now, especially here, near the ruins, which are sacred to them. Every time I've ever set foot on these lands, one of them has come to meet me within a day of my arrival."

"So you've been here before."

"Of course. And now I learn that the boy lived among them for a time as well. I never knew it!"

While Triphon hung on the old man's words, Rom stewed in his misery. None of it mattered. Not anymore. Soon enough, the keeper would be as much a relic as the knowledge he had sheltered all these years, and the boy would be just another orphan.

He had left them by the fire and come here to face the sunrise alone. The keeper was pacing and talking again, Triphon at his heels with questions. The boy was nowhere to be seen. The old man took a sword from Triphon's pack and went through a series of motions, wielding it with surprising dexterity. Triphon was quick on his feet with a second weapon, trying to follow the man's movements.

As though any of it mattered.

The sky to the west was still the dark azure of retreating night. But it was cloudless. The Day of Rebirth would dawn bright and clear in Byzantium. Those in the city would take the bright sky as an omen, unaware that Rebirth was merely an illusion. The priests would pray and believe the Maker had blessed them even as Feyn became Sovereign at the point of Saric's sword.

Farther down the canyon lay the old ruins, perfectly camouflaged by the land, lost within the outcrops unless one approached up the narrow canyon or looked down on it directly. Rumored to have been a church carved directly into the rock by monks at the end of the Age of Chaos, it was thought to have been destroyed more than four centuries ago. Unknown to the Order, the keepers and nomads held the place as a refuge.

Rom stood on the ledge, warding off a passing notion to throw himself over the edge to the rocks below. He scanned the canyon.

Only then did he notice Jonathan sitting atop a rocky lip across the canyon, looking at him. Rom had believed in that boy, but what had that brought him? Nothing but the bloodied heart of the woman he loved, encased in a household jar.

He shifted his gaze and stared at the horizon. The first edge of the sun was spreading noxious light into the sky. Miles away in Byzantium, bells would soon be tolling.

He glanced back across the canyon. The boy was gone.

The wind lifted and struck a hollow note through the chasm. It was the sound that would keep company with Avra's grave through the ages. She wouldn't be there to hear it. Avra, who feared assembly, who feared death more than anything, had now found it.

The ache in Rom's throat was so terrible that he could not swallow.

The keeper's mission to protect life; the vellum that promised the day of that life; the boy who would bring that life...Avra's destiny stood in mockery of it all.

"No." Rom grunted the word through a clenched jaw. He faced the wind, fists tight now. "No." Louder this time.

But what difference would any of his denial make? What attention would death pay to his pathetic voice? He was powerless without her.

His shoulders began to shake with unrelenting sobs. His tears blurred the sky. He hung his head and wept, wishing that death would swallow him as well. For the first time since the hour of Avra's passing, Rom let his tears go. He lifted his chin into the wind, spread his arms, gaped at the sky, and groaned. The groan grew to a wail, ugly and loud, fueled by his hatred of death and its mockery of life.

He had lost them all—his father, his mother—for this. But they, at least, had never tasted the true hope of life. Avra had.

Had she been brought to life for this? Had he? Had his heart been awakened to love and joy and ecstasy only to be dashed by death? He'd been a fool to embrace life. A fool!

He wheeled and strode toward his horse, snapped open the saddlebag, and yanked out the jar holding Avra's heart. Pulled it out, barely able to see. Unwrapped it from the bloody cloth.

He took the heart in his fist, cold and bloody, and strode to the edge of the cliff, jaw tight. Then he shoved his fist at the sky and screamed. Blood flowed from the heart and ran down his forearms. He gripped it tighter, shaking with rage.

I curse you.

I curse the day that I found life.

He trembled.

If this is the pain that comes with life, I curse that life. Let me join her!

Rom drew a long breath and whispered: "How dare you give me life only to take it. Make me dead. Make me dead once more!"

Only silence answered him.

He walked to his horse, withdrew the keeper's vellum, and wrapped Avra's heart in the text that had promised life once again.

It took Rom only fifteen minutes to reach the canyon floor. But it could have been an hour. He no longer cared.

He rode the horse into the camp where the keeper and Triphon were engaged in some kind of debate. The boy sat on a ledge fifty paces closer to the ruins. The keeper was coaxing Triphon toward him. Both held swords. The taller man lunged and Rom stared, sure for a moment that he was about to cleave the old man in two. But the wiry keeper spun away. Only the barest hiss of steel gave away the parry that had saved him.

Triphon saw him and stood straight. "Rom!"

They lowered their weapons as he approached.

Rom dismounted, withdrew the vellum folded around Avra's lifeless heart, and walked to the keeper. He thrust the heart at the old man.

"If this is what your promise brings, I want none of it."

The man clasped the bundle. "Come boy, you don't know what you're saying."

Rom spat onto the dry ground at the old man's feet. "Boy? My mother called me a boy. So did my father, once. They're both dead. Your promise of life has brought nothing but *death*."

The keeper returned his stare.

"You call this life?" Rom cried. "I want to die!" He threw his arms wide. "Kill me!"

"You don't mean that."

Rom wasn't finished.

"You've deluded yourself into thinking the ancient words matter, but the truth is, it's a promise of death. Better to leave them all dead than to give them life and then steal it away."

The old man handed the bundle to Triphon. "The day will come, Rom, when you will see all of this differently. When the boy returns as a warrior dressed in a robe of red. White, dipped in blood. His own. I promise you this."

It made no sense. That boy was no warrior—nor would he ever be. The only sense Rom knew was pain.

The keeper jabbed his finger at the vellum. "Let her heart be a sign of that promise. You will see, you who have life and aren't grateful; you who speak to an old man who would give his head to see a single day of the life you now have."

"Keep your words. This pain is no life."

"You only feel pain because you're alive, boy!" the keeper thundered. "This is the mystery of it. Life is lived on the ragged edge of that cliff. Fall off and you might die, but run from it and you are already dead!"

"Then I would rather be dead!"

"And Avra's death will have been in vain. The world fled the precipice of life once. It stripped us all of humanity and established its Order of death. Now you speak like those who conspired to kill every living soul."

"What do you know? Have you felt this pain?"

The keeper stalled. "No."

Rom strode past them and headed for the outcrop of rocks that hid the pool on the far side.

"We need you, Rom," the keeper said behind him. "Our mission is failed unless we go to the inauguration and Feyn looks into your eyes."

"There *is* no mission," Rom said, whirling around.

"I made my promise to her. It's worthless without you. You yourself made a promise! You have to learn to control those emotions, boy!"

Rom spat on the ground and cast a glare over his shoulder. "I didn't ask for these emotions! I've kept my promise. You have your precious vellum. The boy is alive." He turned and strode on. "And Avra is dead."

Chapter Forty-one

IN THE WORLD, there were seven primary continents. And seven houses that governed them. Seven, for the Maker; seven, the number of perfection.

Byzantium ruled them all.

Now her population of five hundred thousand had swelled to nearly one million. Among them, senators, prelates, each of the continental rulers, and nearly all of the world's twenty-five thousand royals.

Feyn had been chosen from among all known candidates not by peer or by merit, but by the hand of the Maker himself, according to the twelve-year cycles of Rebirth, which had been completed three times in Vorrin's forty-year reign. The births of those royals born closest to the tolling of the seventh hour on the seventh day of the seventh month of each new cycle had all been recorded. And she, among the others, had been born closest of all.

According to the Order, a Sovereign must be at least nine years of age to be inaugurated, and eighteen to rule. Feyn's election had been announced nine years earlier, upon the end of the last cycle, and for nine years she'd prepared to take rule, devoting herself to all matters of Order and loyalty to the truth.

For nine years, the world had awaited this day.

This was the way of Order, and that Order brought peace to the world. Feyn's rule was to begin a new age of Order, the first time that a Sovereign would be replaced by his own daughter.

The world prepared. Across the globe, the blue light of television screens illuminated the city centers of every continent, broadcasting images of the inauguration in Byzantium.

The observance of Rebirth was required to be witnessed by all, to a man, woman, and child. The passing of authority from one Sovereign to another was among the holiest of events. Across the world, they gathered in the hundreds of thousands in every city to watch and swear aloud their allegiance as Feyn Cerelia took power over the continents of Asiana and Greater Europa, of Nova Albion and Abyssinia, Sumeria, Russe, and Qin.

The most observant had camped by the Processional Way for days. The stands had been filled with spectators holding the best seats, which opened the day before yesterday. Tents and portable bathrooms and vendors had clogged the side streets of Byzantium for a mile radius since yesterday, so that the black cars of arriving royals and heads of continents had to be ushered through at a crawl.

Overhead, the sun shone bright on the city, seemingly on the entire world.

The new age was soon to begin.

Chapter Forty-two

ROM LAY facedown on the sand next to the pool. An hour passed in silence, so empty but for the pain that he wondered if the Maker had delivered on his prayer to make him dead again after all. Slowly his emptiness swallowed him and pulled him toward the next best place this side of the grave.

Sleep.

He dreamed, a dark nightmare locked on Avra's face as the blade slashed through her chest, exposing her heart. But as happens in dreams, the scene left him, replaced by another filled with the image of a young boy who stood on the sand, arms limp at his sides, face stained with tears.

This was the boy whose life had demanded Avra's death.

Rom stood still, looking at him circumspectly, unsure what the boy wanted or what he might say after all that had transpired. The canyon was silent except for the sound of his own breathing and the very faint sound of murmuring—the keeper spinning his tales for an eager audience.

"If I could bring her back, I would," he said. "But my blood isn't ready. And even if it was, I'm not sure it would work."

This was the echo of something he'd heard the keeper say around the fire.

"I'm just a boy, Rom. And I need you to protect me."

He'd made a promise to an old man in an alley about a vial unknown to him. That had been a different Rom. A dead one.

"If I share my dream, will you help me?" the boy asked.

Guilt settled over Rom with the boy's sweet voice. Jonathan had
felt the pain of death, too. He had lost a mother and wept. He was a
cripple, a threat to all that the Order stood for, a defenseless young
boy lost in a world that despised him. The world would hunt him to
his death.

And here Rom slept, smothered by self-pity.

"I'm sorry about your mother," Rom said. "But I don't know if I
can help you. My heart's broken."

"Then maybe we can help each other, because mine is, too."

For a moment the dream faded, then replayed itself as dreams
sometimes do. This time he changed his response when the boy
mentioned sharing his dream.

"What dream?" he asked.

"The dream I'm having of Avra," the boy said.

"You're dreaming of Avra? What does that mean? How do your
dreams work?"

"I just dream. But I think they're real, so maybe you'll be able to
see it, too."

Rom hesitated and then said, "Let me see her. Please. Show me
your dream."

The boy walked forward and Rom was suddenly sleeping on his
back there in the sand by the pool. The boy eased himself down and
rested his head on Rom's belly as if it were a pillow. He curled up,
put one hand on Rom's chest, and closed his eyes.

That's strange, Rom thought. *The boy who will one day rule the
world is sleeping on me.*

But then his dream changed again. He was standing in the
canyon again, fully awake. He would swear it, even though a part of
him was certain that he was sleeping.

"Rom?"

A voice whispered through the canyon, sweet and high. A voice he could never forget. His pulse quickened, and he slowly turned.

He recognized Avra at once despite the fact that her eyes, once so dark brown, were as pale as gold.

She stood ten paces away, clothed in white. Her skin seemed to both refract and invite the sun at once. Rom's breath escaped him. They'd buried her in the ground yesterday and yet there she stood...alive.

"Avra?"

She stared at him, looking as startled to be here as he was to see her. She took an uncertain step forward. Then another, and another as she closed the gap between them.

Avra threw herself into his arms, nearly knocking him from his feet. He swept her into the air and buried his face in her neck, inhaling her scent as if it were the only air that could give him life.

"Avra..." He tried to say more, but only a sob came out.

"Rom." She was crying, barely able to say his name. "Is it really you?" Tears spilled down her cheeks.

He pulled back so she could see him. "Do I look like a ghost?"

"No," she said.

She looked so beautiful, so perfect. Rom kissed her eyes, her hair. He touched her face with trembling hands, traced the line of her neck, the wide curve of her scar. He kissed the smooth skin of it, leaving tears in the wake of his lips. But surely...

He drew the neckline down in the middle, toward her sternum, where the sword had cut through it. The skin there was smooth, unmarked.

"I missed you, Rom."

He ran his lips over her hand, her fingers, then took her into his arms. "I missed you," he said. "I missed you so much."

She was warm flesh in his arms; her heart was beating against his chest.

"The boy did this?" he said.

"I don't know, but I'm alive. Maybe not in the flesh, but I'm alive."

What was she saying? Rom looked around for the boy, but he was gone. Was he still dreaming? He must be, and yet...

"I can't be with you now, Rom."

"Then I'll come to you!"

"Shh, shh." She laid a slender finger on his mouth. "The world needs you. The boy needs you. Ask the keeper, he'll know what to do next. Lead them, Rom. Remember my heart and lead them. Don't let your sorrow stand in the way any longer."

She sounded different now, wiser, older, as if in her death she'd lived another lifetime. He clung to her, suddenly afraid she might vanish.

"The human heart is a delicate thing." She drew back and put her hand on his chest. "I know that now. It's the sorrow you feel that allows you to crave love. Without that suffering, there would be no true pleasure. Without tears, no joy. Without deficiency, no longing. This is the secret of the human heart, Rom. You feel so much pain, I can see it in your eyes, but there is also love. In the end, the only thing worth living for is falling in love. Bring that love to humanity."

He covered her hand with both of his. "I will, Avra."

"Wage war on death. Live for love."

His heart felt as though it might burst, hearing these words from her.

"I will. As long as I live I will fight for love."

"You'll have to learn to control your emotions. They're new, like a child's now, bursting with passion. Never let them fade, or part of you will die. But they can also destroy you. Hold them dear, but don't let them take hold of you."

"Never." He wasn't entirely sure what she meant, but she spoke with such tenderness and authority that he didn't dare question her. It was Avra, dear frail, fearful Avra.

She was now his queen.

Avra smiled and looked deep into his eyes. "I love you, Rom." She kissed him tenderly on his lips. "I love you with all my heart. Don't let my love for you go to waste."

"I won't! I swear, I won't."

One moment Avra was in his hands, and then she wasn't. For a long moment the world swirled around him, empty but still full of her. Of Avra.

His eyes snapped wide and he stared up at the blue sky, heart pounding in his chest. A dream. Just a dream! The blood drained from his face as the heaviness of his loss settled over him. She'd been there, in his arms, and now she was gone again.

He became aware of a weight on his stomach, and he lifted his head to see Jonathan sleeping with his head resting on his belly. The boy's left arm was hooked up, lying on his chest, thin and frail.

The world stilled around him, leaving only this tender boy's sleeping form, chest slowly expanding and contracting as he breathed through his nose, eyelashes smudging his cheek.

Rom knew then that he'd more than simply dreamed. He'd shared the *boy's* dreams—those dreams that were not merely dreams but some kind of reflection of reality.

In a way that Rom could not yet begin to understand, Avra was still with him, begging him to save this very boy.

Jonathan's eyes flickered open.

They stared at each other, frozen in the moment.

"You're here," Rom said.

The boy shoved himself up to one elbow. "Did you dream?"

"How...How did you do that?"

"I'm not sure."

Rom scrambled to his feet, bumping the boy in his rush. "I saw Avra."

The boy got his good leg under his body and pushed himself up. He looked up at Rom, uncertain. "So did I."

"Was it real?"

"It must be."

"Can you share your dreams again?"

"I...I don't know."

What a beautiful child. What a beautiful soul.

Truth. Love. Beauty, Feyn had said. Truth, he had found. Love, he had also found. Beauty stood before him.

What had become of him, that he had thrown away his loyalty so easily? He dropped to one knee, took the boy by his shoulders, and spoke past the thickness in his throat.

"I'm so sorry. Forgive me."

"I forgive you," Jonathan said simply.

"You asked me to protect you. Jonathan, I promise that for as long as I live, I'll be by your side." His voice broke. He thought he should say more, but all he could manage was, "I promise."

"Thank you, Rom."

Their task suddenly blossomed in Rom's mind. He leaped to his feet, grabbed the boy's hand, and pulled him toward the camp. "Come on!"

Triphon and the keeper were still by the fire when he got to the outcrop. As one they looked their way. For a moment, none of them spoke.

Rom released Jonathan's hand as he strode toward them. "Where's the heart?"

"The heart?"

"Avra's heart, man! Where is it?"

Triphon pulled out the bundle from his pack and held it out. Rom took the vellum, peeled back the wrapping, and held up the heart nestled in the soft leather.

"This will be our battle cry. We will not let Avra's death go to waste. For Avra's heart."

Triphon glanced at the keeper and struck his chest with an open palm. "For Avra's heart!"

"Always, always for Avra's heart." Rom turned to the keeper. "How long do we have?"

The keeper quirked a grin and turned toward his horse. "Five hours. Time is short."

"Where are we going?" Triphon said.

"We're taking Jonathan to the inauguration," Rom said.

"We'll never make it."

"Then we'd better ride fast."

Chapter Forty-three

THE WORLD had become a drone outside Feyn's window, the sound reaching even here, into her locked and guarded chamber. Inside her apartment, the tables and corners of the front room were crowded with fresh greenery of every kind brought in by the servants, the gifts bearing the names of the myriad royal families who had sent them.

Feyn had thrown herself into the preparation, selecting her own gown for the occasion, pausing to read the cards on the flowers, to hear the chanting of the crowds outside.

Anything to drown out the words of the keeper, haunting her.

Nuala had dutifully made her beautiful, dressing Feyn's hair and applying her eyeliner, touching rouge to her lips. But her servant could not hide the fear in her eyes.

Then she, too, knew: Death waited beyond that podium. Saric would not let her live long.

Feyn stared at the image in the mirror before her: the icon of the world robed in new white. But her mind was far from Rebirth.

Nuala smoothed Feyn's sleeve one last time. "The world awaits you, my lady."

Feyn dismissed her with a nod.

What the keeper suggested was impossible. It flew in the face of the very Order she was destined to uphold. The truth. But that was just it, wasn't it?

What was the truth? She, the slave to truth, was suddenly no longer certain of her master.

If what the keeper said was true...Dear Maker, she begged for it not to be so.

And yet, if it was, she alone could save that truth.

She glanced into the mirror. The face she'd known as the future Sovereign's stared starkly back. Was it possible that the keeper's way was the only one?

She walked to the window. The gray stallions, wreathed in flowers, stood ready at the gate. The gates, too, were adorned in evergreen. Beyond them, the city milled as one great living entity, a sea of people awash with green, waving leafy branches and flowers purchased from vendors on the street.

If she craned against the window, she could see the assembled royals, thousands of them gathering at the entrance to the Grand Basilica beyond the Citadel gate. Theirs were the seats at the end of the Processional Way, closest to the platform erected upon the basilica steps where the ceremony would take place.

Hundreds of thousands of souls, all come to observe Rebirth.

A pounding at the door. It opened abruptly to reveal a broad-shouldered guard.

In that moment, she had settled the matter in her mind: She would take Saric into custody within the hour of her inauguration and do what was necessary to protect the Order. If Saric intended to end her life, he would pay for his terrible crime with his own.

Then again, if what the keeper had told her was true, Saric would be the least of her problems.

"My lady, it's time."

"How much time?" Rom cried over his shoulder. The sun stood nearly directly overhead.

"Less than an hour," Triphon said. "We won't make it!"

They'd come to the edge of Byzantium's hill country and found only empty streets. The whole world had gone to line the processional route or to watch the ceremonies from areas with televisions. Every spectator could count on the punctuality of Order. The new Sovereign-to-be would be received promptly at noon.

"Ride!" Rom shouted, thundering over the hill. "Ride!"

He rode with the boy, the horse straining beneath them. The keeper drew abreast, his tattered robe flapping in the wind. Rom spurred his horse faster. The keeper kept up. This man, whose kind had lived for this day, wasn't about to let thirty minutes separate him from his destiny.

The boy had been silent. Riding in front of Rom, grasping the horse by the mane, he looked like any nine-year-old trapped by uncertainty might, frightened yet trusting at once.

Invigorated by the keeper, Triphon had sworn with fiery eyes his oath to the new Order of Keepers. He was still as exuberant and clumsy as a young bull, but his new mentor had promised to teach him the finer points of becoming a warrior. Triphon had latched onto that promise, reminding the keeper of it three times already.

And the keeper—Rom swore the man looked thirty years younger. The sun seemed to soften every line and crag of his face. Purpose was in his eyes, and though he knew himself to be dead, the corner of his mouth twitched on occasion, tempting life of its own.

If the keeper had a plan, he wouldn't go into more detail, telling them only that they were all now at the mercy of truth. "Trust me, Rom!" His eyes were fired with destiny. "Trust me, the truth will find its way! Jonathan is alive!"

Yes, indeed, the boy bouncing on the stallion in front of Rom was alive, and certainly no ordinary boy, but that didn't mean the keeper was not mad.

That they weren't all mad.

Rom never would have thought that riding to one's death could put a smile on anyone's face, but there was little doubt in his mind that was exactly what they were doing.

"Ride!" he roared over his shoulder.

The world was Saric's. Before him, the leaders of the houses of the seven continents stood on either side of the basilica steps. Below them, his elite guard stretched like a human gate, twelve strong on either side. Two hundred thousand spectators filled the Processional Way beyond, standing still in reverence, eyes fixed on their Sovereign.

They had held evergreen branches high and whispered Feyn's name in awe as she dismounted. The sound of it was unnerving and astounding at once.

Her stallion was black, to stand out from the other Brahmin grays, a gift from Saric himself. There had been trumpets, and somewhere back in the narthex of the open basilica, a choir had sung as Saric and Feyn ascended the steps to the platform together, the ceremonial scepter's warm weight in his hand.

Rowan stood waiting, the lines of his face drawn taut as he gestured them toward their places on the platform.

"My lady?" he said. Saric saw that the man noted Feyn's rigid posture. She'd done surprisingly well, he thought, even with the knowledge that she would soon die. Surely she at least suspected by now.

Feyn's gaze turned toward the gold basin that would hold the blood of the sacrificial bull. She paused, until Rowan took her gently by the arm and led her to her place. Saric came to stand at her side just as a great Brahmin bull was led to the base of the basilica steps on a golden rope. A white beast rippled with sleek muscle. He was magnificent.

Saric had heard of people being fearful at the sight of the bull bleeding out at his father's inauguration. He had often wondered if he would feel his own visceral response to it here, at his own.

After all, this was *his* inauguration as much as Feyn's.

For that reason it must be perfect, but for that reason also, he was filled with strange gratitude toward his sister. Without her, his rise to power would have been impossible, not to mention far less pleasurable.

The great basin was lifted from its stand and carried down the steps between the world's seven prelates. Saric marveled at the hands of the priests laid upon the animal's wide shoulders and head as the prelate of Greater Europa raised the broad sword.

He felt Feyn's gaze on him, cool and heavy at once.

There was something unsettling in it.

The blade slashed through the flesh of the bull's neck. The priest caught the first crimson spray in the golden bowl, then replaced it with another larger basin when the ceremonial one was sufficiently full. The animal sank to its forelegs, and then to the stage completely. Onlookers turned away.

The priest with the basin ascended to the platform and stood before Feyn. Rowan carefully lifted up her left sleeve; Saric held back the right.

But Feyn seemed not to notice, her gaze fixed on the dead bull.

"The basin, my lady," Rowan said.

When she didn't move, Saric took the basin and set it in her hands. She looked down. Blood sloshed up against the basin's gold edges. Her hands and arms were trembling.

Rowan waited. The world waited. But she stared down at the bowl, saying nothing.

"The words, my lady," Rowan whispered.

She only lifted her head and stared out at the crowd.

Rowan glanced between them. Several prelates looked back with anxious gazes.

"The blood of life. Given by the Maker!" Saric cried for all to hear.

They were the words a Sovereign anticipated speaking all his life. Saric felt them like a charge along his arms, all the way up to his shoulders.

"Born once into life, we are grateful," the priests recited in response.

The voices of one billion more around the earth echoed the words as required: "We are grateful."

In a matter of minutes the world's leaders would come before Feyn to dip their fingers in the bowl and make their blood oath of loyalty. They would give her the scepter now held in trust by Rowan.

They would pledge their undying allegiance. And Saric would later demand it of them.

But for this moment, he could stand by and drink her in. Because even in fear and outside of herself, she was the most magnificent creature in the world, like the Brahmin bull, so sleek and singular before it died.

True, she would die soon. But until then, what a spectacle, what a moment! His sister, even fear-bound, was more than regal. She embodied something greater to the populace than they could conjure within themselves. Order. The hand of the Maker on earth.

He could almost believe it himself. For a moment, he almost wanted to. He gazed out past the stage toward the throng.

A movement down the Processional Way caught his eye. Riders, three abreast. One of them was a boy.

He stared, not sure he was seeing it clearly. They had actually come? The brazen stupidity of these country fools knew no bounds.

But they were too late.

He glanced at the clock and decided the matter then. In seven minutes' time, Feyn would be Sovereign. And in ten, he would take the office from her.

Chapter Forty-four

THE SEA of bodies on either side stilled as Rom turned his horse onto the middle of the Processional Way that led to the platform, half a mile distant. He stopped, dismounted, and, with a glance back at Triphon and the keeper, led his horse on foot with the boy perched atop.

Whispers rose in the air only to die again. Even the wind had fallen quiet. Around them, the world had seemed to stop.

For a boy.

Jonathan rode in silence, eyes round, flanked now on either side by Triphon and the keeper, whose plan still unnerved Rom to his core.

Rom glanced up at the keeper. "Are you sure about this?"

"About what, son of Elias?"

"About Feyn."

The keeper nodded. "We are all in agreement."

Rom fixed his eyes on the inaugural platform with its banners as tall as the basilica's great columns, the stately torches upon their stands, flames licking at the bright sky. Though he couldn't make out faces from this distance, there was a figure in a white gown in the center of it all, standing expectantly amid the others. It could only be Feyn. She was there, and alive. Perhaps less so than she'd been in the fields with him, but *alive*. He made out Saric and the senate leader flanking Feyn, standing expectantly on the platform, watching their approach.

The eyes of the world had turned on them. Above them all, cameras mounted on tall poles peered at them, sending images to the corners of the world.

The bright sun coaxed sweat from the pores on Rom's forehead. A fly lit on the neck of his stallion and took flight, chased by its quivering flesh. Their horses' shod hooves sounded upon the pavestones, steady as a heartbeat. Yet the occasional snort of the animals gave away the fear in them all.

A dog's bark pierced the stillness as they continued their approach. The rest of those gathered dared not utter a word. To a man, woman, and child they stood in perfect fear. Surely the world knew by now that something had gone terribly wrong.

Neah strained against the tower window. Her breath fogged it, and she wiped the glass clean with her sleeve. She could almost make them out, the small group coming down the Processional Way. The stage was obscured from her vantage by the basilica itself. Her heart had begun pounding the moment she recognized them.

The old man—was he the keeper she'd led Rom to see just days ago? And there, who was that on the horse led by Rom? It couldn't be. But she could see clearly that he was smaller than the others.

The boy.

She could make out Triphon's form, but it was the boy to whom her gaze returned. She had betrayed them, and there they were. She had betrayed them in the name of Order, which had represented truth to her all the years of her life.

If that boy was real...

She could not stomach the fear that gripped her. She twisted and slid down to the floor of her tower cell.

The pain of life was nothing compared with this fear. If she was wrong, and that boy was what they said, then he walked now to his death, and the world's hope would die with him.

As for her, there would be no pit of Hades deep enough.

Feyn willed her legs to hold her upright. She hadn't expected to feel so much fear at the turning of Rebirth. In the rest of the world's eyes, she was finally and fully coming into her own, presented and crowned as Sovereign. But on the stage, she was staggering under the immense weight of that sovereignty already.

And through it all the keeper's words whispered in her ear. *There is a boy, Feyn. The world is dead. I speak the truth and you are sworn to truth.*

Someone had guided her hands through the motions of taking the bowl during the bull's slaughter. When she looked down she could see the great bulk of the animal, lifeless before her. Her heart, so loud and erratic in her ears, threatened to give out. Within her damp gown, stuck to her sides with sweat, she struggled to breathe.

There is only one way he can rule, Feyn. You must trust me. You will not die.

The mass of humanity fell silent.

She looked up and saw that the crowd had turned. She looked down the Processional Way and immediately saw what they did.

Three horses rode up the Processional Way. On them, three riders. The figure leading them on foot was unmistakable even at this distance.

Rom!

But not only Rom. There! On the right, the keeper in his flowing robe and long beard. *The keeper!*

And there, sitting on the horse led by Rom...

Feyn's breath escaped her and her knees nearly buckled. The boy...

They had found him? Her mind fell silent except for a faint hum that dared her to doubt it. She had read about him in the vellum, heard the keeper speak passionately about him, sent Rom to find him, even. She had dreamed of him coming, worried what it might mean, *dreaded* what it might mean!

But she had never expected to see him.

He was so small on top of the large mount, sitting slightly hunched over. He might have been any other unremarkable child, except for what she knew about him.

He was here to claim his sovereignty.

The keeper's words again: *If he does not ascend now, Feyn, he will never have a legal right to the throne. The world needs more than his blood. It needs his rule.*

She felt Saric coil like a serpent beside her. Below them on the stairs, the elite guard poised like nocked arrows. The keeper would die before he reached the platform.

So now there was the boy, there was Saric, and there was her. They each would claim the throne. But it was *hers*! By birthright! Proclaimed by destiny. She could snap her fingers and have the boy killed. She could cry out Saric's intentions to kill her and have him thrown in chains the moment she took power. What was there to stand in her way?

None of that would do, the keeper had said. There was only one true way.

Now she could see the old man more clearly. The keeper, who entrusted her with his deepest secrets steeped in centuries of alchemy and devotion to a life-giving boy. One word from her and the guards would destroy them all!

But now she knew, didn't she? The keeper's words had been true.

And she was truth's slave, the claws of loyalty and duty having long sunk into her heart.

And Rom...Rom, who had gone to find the boy. Rom, who had once been the face of love. If she was capable of any emotion other than fear, she might weep at the sight of him. At the faint but unmistakable memory of something both greater and stronger than fear.

Rom had returned with the boy, as the keeper had promised. And by that, she was suddenly certain: Everything was about to change.

Why?

It was the one word that pounded through Rom's mind as he led them forward. Not a soul moved to stop them. No one tried to cut them off as they advanced toward the platform. No guard cried for them to halt. No elite warrior sprang from the platform to bear down upon them.

Why?

Only one answer made sense: Neither Feyn nor Saric had put the word out to stop them. Surely their march would be cut short at one gesture from either.

Rom understood Feyn's restraint. She knew what this boy represented, what he might mean to the world. But Saric made no move to stop them, which could only mean that their coming had played to his purpose. That they were indeed marching to their deaths.

Still not a word from the keeper.

The horses' hooves clacked on the pavestones. Their equine shoulders flexed with each step. Sweat leaked down Rom's back. He breathed through his nostrils, his chin held level. On either side, the throngs watched with dead eyes, lost to their own fear.

Rom could now clearly see Feyn, standing at the center, perfectly framed by the Grand Basilica's twin pillars. They'd slaughtered a white Brahmin bull at the base of the basilica's stone steps. Its body lay lifeless as a snowy mountain where it fell, drained of its lifeblood, which had been collected in a large golden bowl atop a pedestal between Saric and Feyn.

The leaders of each of the world's seven orders stood as statues on the steps, looking between them and their Sovereign for direction. But none came.

Rom could now see the faces of the elite guard. Dressed in black, like wraiths arrayed on either side of the basilica steps, awaiting the order to kill.

"Steady." The familiarity of the keeper's voice brought only a small measure of comfort. The man had lived his whole life in anticipation of this day. He belonged here, as did the boy, saved by fate and by his mother for a purpose foretold half a millennium ago. And Triphon, who rode with his sword strapped to his mount's saddle, had transformed into a warrior.

But *he* was now their leader, wasn't he? Not because he'd asked to be, but because an old man had thrust a vile of ancient blood at him in an alleyway; because the boy had asked for his help; because, as the keeper said, Feyn had tasted life and love with him. Because she would look into his eyes and know that his heart was true.

Because Avra had begged it of him.

They were a hundred paces from the steps when Rom held up his hand and stopped them.

Feyn could see their eyes. She could see the face of the keeper, and beside him the boy.

And then there was Rom, watching her with a steady gaze. She'd convinced herself that the last hint of the love she shared with him had fled as the effects of the blood wore off. But she was wrong. It tugged at her heart once again as she stared into his eyes.

She despised it and craved it at once, the forbidden made real once again.

Her gaze darted out to the crowd, the cameras, and back to Rom, whose stare had not moved. Then to the boy behind him, who mirrored her stare.

He seemed so small, sitting astride the horse by himself. Not as pale as a Brahmin. By look alone she never would have taken him for royal. In fact, he was unremarkable in every way.

Why this boy? Why, a cripple, even? And yet his very presence

361

rendered everything true, everything written in the vellum, all she'd been told by the keeper.

Feyn struggled to inhale against the band of fear that had bound her lungs all morning. She opened her mouth to speak but found no breath to do it.

Help me.

Her gaze locked on the boy. On his eyes, locked in return, on her. She felt her lungs slowly expand as breath finally filled them.

She now knew only two truths: The first was that the Sovereign of the world did not stand on this stage. The second was that she was bound by that truth.

The keeper's words whispered in her ear again. *Trust me, Feyn. You will not die.*

"My life is yours," she whispered.

"The one who would be Sovereign has come among you," Rom cried. His voice rang out in the stillness, rich and clear. A singer's voice. "He asks if Feyn, rightful Sovereign, will bow to his name?"

Saric called out: "I am Sovereign here!"

The heads of the world's leaders swiveled. A murmur ran through the crowd. For a moment, no one moved.

And then someone did.

Feyn.

Rom could see her gown trembling as she slowly sank to one knee, and then the other.

The keeper stared ahead, somber. "She is bound by truth."

With a cry and a hard slap to the beast's hindquarters, the keeper charged. He leaned over his mount's neck, holding the reins with one hand. The ragged edge of his robe streamed behind him like the wake of a storm. The movement was so unexpected that gasps rose from the stands.

Rom steadied his breath. What was he doing? But he knew it was here: the moment all humanity had unwittingly craved. The world watched, stunned, as the old man thundered toward the basilica's twelve steps at full speed.

"Kill him!"

Saric's order, screamed to the guard.

But then another cry, this one from Feyn, who threw her arms wide.

"Let him come!"

The confused guard faltered, uncertain whether to heed the order of one Sovereign, or one who would be Sovereign. Still the keeper rode, whipping his horse faster, straight toward Feyn.

A sound of madness rose above the pounding hooves. A lone wail of terror. An anguished cry that sent chills down Rom's neck. Terrible empathy lodged in his throat at the sight: Feyn, with her arms spread wide to the keeper.

The cry was hers.

Rom glanced at the boy behind him, pale and racked with trembling.

The keeper's right hand swept back when he was fewer than ten paces from the basilica steps. His blade flashed high into the sun, and his intent became clear.

It was too late for anyone to stop him.

His stallion slid to an abrupt stop at the bottom of the steps, but the keeper did not. He leaped over the mount's head, landed on the fourth step with his leading foot, and rushed forward, propelled by his own momentum. In three leaps he reached the top of the platform directly in front of Feyn, sword held high.

His blade sliced down into Feyn's body, slashed through her neck and chest, and arced up behind him, bloodied for all the world to see.

Screams and shouts of alarm.

Feyn crumpled silently at his feet, slumping like the majestic Brahmin bull. Crimson bloomed through the white of her gown and began to pool on the platform.

Before Saric could react, the keeper spun and brought his sword to the man's neck. "Her last order stands!" he cried out. "Let the new Sovereign of the world come!"

Saric had gone white.

Rom tried to breathe. His throat was dry. He could not speak.

The crowd erupted, fear spreading like fire. Wails of terror swelled like a growing maelstrom.

The keeper spun around, sword held high, and his voice cried over the entire assembly. "Feyn is dead!" He dropped his blade on the marble stones where it clattered and came to a rest.

Then he bent down, scooped up Feyn's lifeless body in his arms, leaped from the back of the platform, and was gone.

CHAPTER FORTY-FIVE

THE WAILS of terror were almost as disturbing to Rom as the horrific shock of Feyn's slaughter. Violence was not a thing witnessed in this world. Death was not a thing embraced by those given to Order. And yet the Sovereign they had all come to see welcomed her own death before their eyes. The first assassination since Sirin's. The first public act of violence in nearly five centuries.

But now Rom understood the meaning of the keeper's words: Feyn had done it only because the life she found with Rom was quickened when she saw him and the boy with the keeper. They were all complicit in her death, most of all Feyn herself. Now through Feyn's willing death, the way had been opened for the boy to step into his place as the world's new Sovereign.

On the platform, a shaken Rowan managed to gesture them forward. Rom looked at the boy perched in shock on top of his horse, staring at the platform.

"Don't be afraid, Jonathan. This is as it was meant to be."

"I have to follow the keeper! He told me we have to go back to the ruins where it's safe."

"Not before you stand before them and give Rowan the power to rule until you are of age. Can you do that?"

Jonathan looked down at him, still shaking, but nodded.

Rom led the horse to the foot of the basilica steps. Rowan stepped up to the edge of the platform and held up his hand to the crowd until a semblance of silence allowed him to be heard.

"Feyn gave her life willingly for the next seventh in line," he cried. There was no denying his words. The keeper had called his challenge for all the world to hear. Feyn had bowed to the boy for all the world to see.

"Jonathan, son of Talus, is that next seventh, as the original birth record shows. As head of the senate, I have verified it, and the senate will see that my words are true and ratify it."

Though the masses had quieted, the sobs of those unable to get control of themselves punctuated the stillness. The head of the guard looked at Saric, who caught his questioning stare and turned away. There was nothing he could do now. Even if he killed the boy, the law provided no means for Saric's ascendancy because the boy was not yet seated. Feyn had cut him off at the knees in her death using his own law.

Rom lifted the boy off the horse and set him gently on the ground. Triphon and Rom led Jonathan, who limped up the stairs as leaders of the seven orders watched in disbelief.

The boy stopped by Rowan's side, craned his neck for a view of the much taller man, then turned slowly to the crowd, seemingly at a loss. Behind him, Saric grasped the hilt of his sword. His face was still white with shock. He seemed as lost as the boy.

But Rowan was no longer lost, and he held up both hands to Saric. "Don't be a fool, Saric. Your game is now lost."

"I'm Sovereign of—"

"You're nothing but a placeholder for the rightful Sovereign, who stands before you. Make a move and you'll die as surely as Feyn died."

Saric's eyes darted frantically among the boy, Rowan, and the inaugural throng.

"Step back!" Rowan ordered.

Saric did so, but only slowly. Fear and disdain replaced the shock on his face. The boy, however, didn't even glance at him. He seemed too fixated on the crowd, who returned his stare, collectively stunned.

Rom looked at Rowan. "May I speak?"

The senate leader nodded. "Say whatever it is you mean to say, but in three minutes the world must have its Sovereign."

Rom turned toward the people and addressed the world.

"I am Rom, son of Elias, and I come to you with a message of truth. A forbidden message of hope. Of love. Of life."

Beside him, Rowan cast a nervous stare at the crowd. Perhaps Rom was going too far.

"Feyn gave her life willingly and publicly for this boy, so that there would be no question of his legitimacy. He is a boy. He is a cripple. He is our destiny." What else could he say? Nothing, not now.

Rom turned toward Jonathan and sank to his knees. Next to him, Triphon also knelt. But it wasn't until Rowan settled to his knees that the other leaders, looking around to see if it was the right thing to do, slowly followed suit.

An instant later the masses knelt by the thousands. The sound of them falling to their knees was like the sound of pouring rain. And then a downpour. Thundering around them.

Jonathan stood before them all on weak legs, favoring his good one, sweating. He glanced over at Rom with questioning eyes. Rom nodded and looked at the assembly. The leaders of the world were on their knees, as was the senate, as were the very guard whom Saric had commanded only minutes ago.

Dead, all of them, to a person. But bowing now to the world's only hope for life, though they did not yet know it.

Rowan stood, picked up the Sovereign's scepter, and approached the boy. "I, Rowan, leader of the senate, confirm the birth record of the elect. Jonathan Emmanuel, son of Talus of the house of Abyssinia, now nine years of age, is the new Sovereign of the world."

He held the Sovereign's scepter out to Jonathan, who gave one last, hesitant look Rom's way, then gingerly lifted the ancient symbol of power from Rowan's hands.

Rowan bowed and spoke under his breath so that only Rom could hear them.

"My Sovereign, I'm afraid your life's in jeopardy. There are still dark powers aligned to cut you down. I fear you won't last the night."

"He won't be here by night," Rom said.

Rowan glanced over. "Where will he be?"

"In hiding. Until then, he will appoint you regent in his place."

The senate leader swiveled his head back to Jonathan. "Is this true?"

But the boy was still in too much shock to respond.

"Tell, him, Jonathan."

"I appoint you as regent in my place," the boy said in a small voice.

"My lord, you grant too much."

"Only what's his to give," Rom said.

Rowan dipped his head, then stood and faced the crowd. "I present to you your Sovereign. Rise and receive him now!"

They came to their feet. The roar that rose from those gathered shook the very foundation of the basilica, so that Rom feared the roof might collapse. And he knew that the cries of the citizens around the globe would be enough to rattle the foundations of the earth itself.

The boy stood before them all, frail and young. Then, while the air still thundered, he tenuously dipped his head once, turned toward the back of the stage, and left them to cry his praise.

Gone to find the keeper.

Gone into hiding.

Chapter Forty-six

SARIC CERELIA, son of Vorrin of the house of Greater Europa, stood before the mirror in his darkened chamber, trembling. The image that faced him was finally unmasked, and his mind could not hold its darkness.

He lifted his fingers to his neck and raked the blackened veins that stood against pale flesh. Like roots from a forbidden tree they had worked their way deep into his mind, his flesh, his heart, infusing him with their poison until the black ink of evil itself swam through him.

His nails dug into his skin. He shrugged out of his robe and let it fall to the ground. A pathetic and seething form stared back. Vile. Inhuman.

His veins writhed beneath his skin like vipers. This serum of the alchemists wasn't an elixir from the gods but the poison of Hades itself. He was no longer a man but an animal possessed. There were indeed demons in this world. They stared out of his own eyes. They tore at his skin, ripping at the black roots of that thing beneath it.

His hatred for the boy spread through his flesh like an electrical charge. But not nearly as powerfully as his hatred for himself, for this wretched skeleton padded with flesh.

Saric's face twisted with rage. With bitterness. With a beggar's desire to die. Tears flooded his eyes and ran down his cheeks. His shoulders began to shake.

A shadow appeared over his shoulder in the mirror.

Pravus had come for him.

Saric spread his arms and wept.

CHAPTER FORTY-SEVEN

Two Weeks Later

THEY STOOD among the ruins, framed by tall columns hewn straight from the rock face.

Nine nomads had joined them, warriors all, horsemen dressed in leather, wielding weapons forbidden by Order—scimitars, knives, and bows. In a world that outlawed violence, they were rebels who'd broken away from society to follow a call of their own, hunted for defying the world's dead Order.

Neah had reportedly taken her life. Besides the boy, only Rom and Triphon were alive in all the world.

They were the keepers now, led by the Book. This was now their new Order of Mortals, born of blood and fully human.

Jonathan sat on a rock to their right, legs hanging over the edge. Rom caught his eye and winked. The boy grinned and returned the wink.

The keeper approached the boy. "We're packed, Jonathan." A smile tugged at the old man's mouth. "Or should I call you *sire?*"

The term was used by the nomads when addressing the boy. "I would think you, being my elder, would want to be called that," the boy said with a wry smile.

"Only if you insist."

Rom chuckled and looked over the loaded horses. The canyonlands with their ruins were too close to Byzantium to offer them safety for long. They would travel north, into Greater Europa, and join the nomads there in more distant, barren lands. There would be no more Order for them now. The boy's safety was their only concern.

As for the rest of the world, already there were whispered questions and mounting fears. As acting Sovereign for the next nine years, Rowan would have more than his share of challenges. He would rule as he saw fit, leaving Jonathan in the keeper's care, and had agreed to periodic updates. Rowan wasn't fully satisfied in the arrangement, nor the keeper fully trusting of his loyalties, but at least they had Jonathan—the Book wasn't about to risk any danger to the boy's life. Ascendancy was no longer the issue, but the elements working with Saric would have no love for the boy.

He must be sequestered.

Rom wondered what Avra might think of Feyn's death. To be sure, there was a certain mystery surrounding its nature. The keeper had vanished with her body that day and refused to speak of where or how he'd disposed of it.

"She can't be buried by the Order of death. She had tasted life," he had said upon returning to them. "The dead can bury the dead."

And they had, with an empty coffin, as was the custom.

Now they would leave the canyonlands where Avra was buried. But she would be with them, Rom thought, not in the Hades she had feared.

Jonathan had said no more about his dreams, only that there would be war, a statement that he'd made to Rom that first day. After the inauguration he refused to speak of his dreams anymore.

Their talk around the fire when Rom told them of the boy's mention of war still rung in his ears.

"War? Against what?" Triphon asked. "Saric's rumored dead. They have no army."

The keeper had looked into the darkness beyond the fire. "He wasn't alone. The alchemists have the serum. They'll come."

"Then they'll never find us."

"Elements within the Order won't rest while we're alive. Not even Rowan can hold them back. And they have time on their side."

"We'll slather the canyons with their corpses!" Triphon cried. "From now on I dub them *corpses*. May they rest in peace."

"Corpses, yes. But we will offer them *life*, not peace."

"And what does that make us?"

The keeper dug into his cloak and pulled out something wrapped in his ancient fingers. "The keepers have used many terms to speak of the living, but now I see there is only one that rings true. Because in life we risk death." His eyes shifted to Rom. "The heart can bleed. And it will."

He opened his hand. Nestled there in the deep crags of his palm was a rectangular pendant tied to a leather strap. It was a piece of flat stone, with a bleeding heart carved into its face and the word *Mortal* etched beneath it.

"Mortal," Triphon said.

"Take it, Rom. This is for you."

Rom picked up the pendant. Avra's heart. "Mortals," he said.

"Take off your amulets," the keeper said. "Throw them into the fire. We are officially no longer part of the Order. We are now *out of Order*."

And so they had, sending sparks to the sky.

"Out of Order, fully human," Rom muttered, and strapped the pendant around his neck.

"*Fully* human?" The keeper poked the fire with a long stick. "Yes, perhaps." His eyes flashed. "But don't think that what you've tasted is all there is to be had by the blood. You've been brought to life, primarily your emotions, but it's only the beginning. I think what awaits you—what awaits us all—will make this seem pale by comparison."

"More?" Rom asked. "What more could there be?"

The keeper's mouth had twisted with a knowing grin. "Call it a hunch, but I think Jonathan's blood will blow the mind. What you tasted was only that: a taste. There's so much more to humanity."

They all stared at him, then followed his gaze over to the boy, who was seated with legs crossed, talking to one of the nomads at the firelight's farthest reaches. So much was unknown about him. Rom could only imagine what might happen to them all when he stepped out of the shadow into the light.

"There sits the first true mortal," the keeper said.

"So then, we will call ourselves mortals," Rom said. "Let's only hope we can keep him safe from the dead until that day."

It was true, the Order had time on its side. Jonathan's blood was still at war with his own weakened body, not yet sufficient to bring any life. The keeper had drawn a portion and tested it himself. Rom knew nothing of alchemy, but the keeper's verdict was sure: The boy's blood could not bring any more to life, not yet. He'd suffered as a child and he would suffer even more as the virus fought to eradicate the pure blood in his body. But the day would come when the battle in his body would end, and he'd emerge the victor and restore life to full humanity.

Whatever that might mean.

For now, they would build a new order with the nomads and ensure the boy's safety until his day came. And then? And then, if the boy's dreams proved true, there would be war.

War, and more life than any of them yet knew.

"We're ready," Rom said, gazing about the gathering who waited for his word. He turned to the nomads who sat on their horses.

"Take us north."

Chapter Forty-eight

SARIC'S DUNGEONS were no more. Rowan, regent to the Sovereign, had cleansed them of their inhabitants and destroyed every known trace of the dark science that had so nearly delivered humanity into Saric's hands.

The cage that had housed the Book was now only a dusty cell with its gated door welded shut, sealed on Rowan's order. The steel doors leading down to the dungeons were all locked, their passages forbidden to any living soul. The High Peers of Alchemy had been purged and its members scattered. Saric, who had left a bloody trail through his apartments, was never found.

But hidden deep beneath them all in a sealed crypt, there remained one soul who defied all earthly order.

She lay in a sepulcher of stone where the keeper had placed her as agreed. Her body had been sewn by the most experienced hand. Tubes flowing with nutrients and the mere spark of chemical life fed her unmoving, breathless form. They would sustain her deep stasis for as long as was required.

On her finger, a pale moonstone ring.

Her name was Feyn.

Pravus made his way to the vast lab beneath his estate, followed dutifully by Corban. The sound of their boots echoed on the stone floor.

"They know nothing, sire, I can assure you," Corban said.

Pravus did not bother with an answer. He unlocked the gate that led into his deepest chamber and stepped into the vast laboratory that hummed and blinked with electric light.

The rows of upright glass cylinders stretched deep into the mountain, 121 at last count.

He walked to the newest addition and stood before it. The naked form inside was as familiar to him as his own child might have been.

"How long?" Corban asked.

"Nine years."

Pravus tapped his nail on the cylinder, and the eyes of the corpse suspended in the liquid snapped wide. Saric, brother to Feyn, stared unseeing, subhuman as before, flesh filled with the blackness of Hades.

"And then?"

Pravus turned from Saric's morbid form.

"And then we will crush the boy."

ABOUT THE AUTHORS

TED DEKKER is a *New York Times* bestselling author with more than five million books in print. He is known for stories that combine adrenaline-laced plots with incredible confrontations between unforgettable characters. He lives in Austin with his wife and children.

TOSCA LEE left her position working with Fortune 500 Companies as a Senior Consultant for the Gallup Organization to pursue her first love: writing. She is the critically acclaimed author of *Demon* and *Havah* and is best known for her humanizing portraits of maligned characters. She makes her home in the Midwest.